HOLD THE FOREVERS

HOLD THE FOREVERS

K.A. LINDE

To Sarah Kates
for not letting my ex object at my wedding

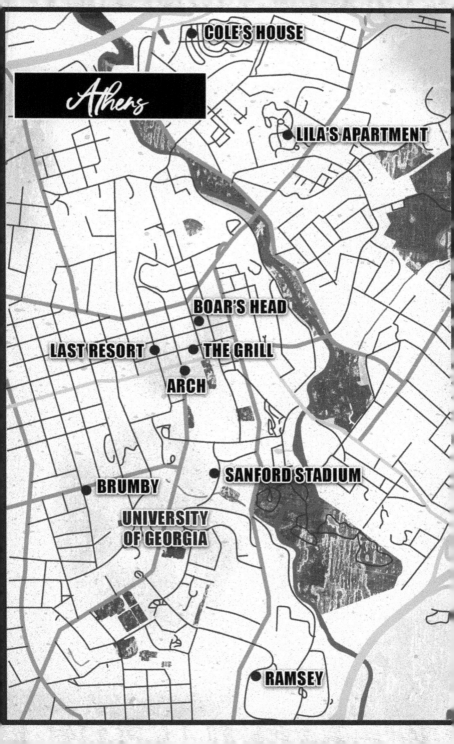

PROLOGUE

I'm in love with two men.

But I can only marry one.

It should have been simple to choose one over the other. To make my life with only one of them in it. But it isn't. And it never has been.

Not when fate spun us together. An infinite wheel that none of us could ever escape. Just kept spinning and spinning. One of us took a left turn instead of a right. We stepped off for a cycle as if that would let us leave. Let us continue on into a normal, ordinary life. Whatever normal and ordinary could possibly mean.

But then the next rotation would come around, as it always inevitably did, and then we stepped back on. The three of us. In perpetuity.

I tried my turn at the wheel. Tried to pull free from fate's death grip on my life. It was barely a moment. It was an eternity. For that time, I should have been happier. Without them. Without the drama and the heartache and the constant way my life went up in flames and reduced me to cinders.

I wasn't a phoenix; I didn't rise from the ashes.

Still, I wasn't happier.

The shattered bits of my heart sliced through me at every turn that I avoided them. That I tried to move on.

And when the wheel tugged me back into its trappings, I let it. I hung there, suspended, caught in a spiderweb, thick and viscous and unrelenting. I made my choice. Stay on the wheel. Embrace that this was where I always belonged. And slowly, the million pieces of me were put back together, one by one.

Not all of them, of course. Not without them both.

But I can only have one.

I've always known it and tried to accept it. It's still hard to believe that it's happening though.

Me and Cole and Ash.

A trio that never was.

Because I'm in love with two men.

I can only marry one.

And today is my wedding day.

WEDDING DAY

WEDDING DAY

JUNE 15, 2019

E very girl dreamed about her perfect wedding.

But I hadn't dreamed of white dresses or bouquets or *I do*s. And when it came right down to it, I'd never imagined my future husband. What he'd look like or what he'd wear or how he'd smile when he saw me that first time.

Because for so long, there hadn't been just one face in my life ... but two.

Two faces. Two outfits. Two smiles.

Two men.

Cole and Ash.

Ash and Cole.

It felt surreal that today of all days, I was going to marry one and not the other. But it was here, and there was no looking back. I'd made my decision. In the end, we'd all made this decision. With our actions and our broken promises. We'd walked right up to today and let it happen.

I wasn't the typical blushing bride. There would

always be a part of me wondering if I'd done the right thing, chosen the right guy. If all the hell that we'd gone through together to get here had been worth it.

But I didn't have cold feet. I was ready for this.

Except now, my bridesmaids were missing.

I stuck my head out of the bridal suite. My three sisters sat at a table in varying shades of red. Two in floor-length gowns and one in a red suit jacket. They were all matrons of honor for this affair, but they wouldn't be standing at the altar with me. They'd be seated in the first row.

"Have you seen Josie and Marley?" I asked my sisters about my two best friends.

We'd known each other nearly our entire lives. Been through thick and thin. It wasn't like them to disappear on my big day.

"They said they had an errand," Eve said as she poured champagne into flutes.

Elle nodded. "They'll be right back."

Steph jumped from her spot and made me twirl in a circle. "You look gorgeous. I wasn't sure on the bust, but that dress is stunning."

I beamed at my sisters.

We'd all gone dress shopping multiple times. I'd thought I'd be one of those lucky ones who picked out the very first dress I tried on. But it hadn't been the case; it might as well have been the last dress I tried on. The thousandth dress I tried on. The dress was a full tulle skirt with a lacy balconette top and thin spaghetti straps.

Josie had told me it was likely bad luck that I was that

indecisive. Marley had rolled her eyes and insisted it meant nothing. Two sides of the same coin, those two.

I drank champagne with my sisters and stared down at the massive ring on my finger as I waited for my best friends to return.

"Don't drink too much," Eve warned. "You'll want to remember tonight."

Elle burst into laughter, and Steph joined her.

"Oh, I'll remember tonight," I assured them.

I couldn't imagine forgetting my wedding night even if I had one too many glasses of champagne. I checked my phone again. Seriously, where the hell were they?

"Maybe we should go look for them."

"You can't," Elle said. "You don't want the groom to see you before it's time."

Tradition.

It was pretty ridiculous, considering how long we'd been sleeping together. But it was ceremonial, and we'd agreed. It would make tonight even more special.

I was about to send out a search party when Marley and Josie rushed back into the room, looking frazzled.

"Everything all right?"

Marley and Josie exchanged a look.

"What is it?"

"Nothing," they said together.

Josie continued, "Don't worry about it."

"Is it nothing, or should I not worry about it?"

"Both," Marley said.

I narrowed my eyes. That certainly didn't sound like nothing.

"It's this." Josie came to my side and pulled out a

black case. "I know that I've always had my differences with my mom, but she'd want you to wear these today."

My hand went to my throat as I opened the black case to reveal the white pearls that I'd always coveted. "Josie! I can't wear these."

"Something borrowed," she insisted. "You've always wanted them."

"I have," I said softly.

Josie took them out of the box and strung them around my neck. They were dainty and just brushed my collarbone. They looked perfect with the white lace of my dress and my blonde hair pulled up in an intricate updo.

"Thank you," I told her, drawing her in for a hug.

"Okay, ladies, it's time!" the wedding planner, Courtney, said as she strode into the room.

She was the best of the best. She handled everything for the day of. I didn't know how I would have survived the last six months without her expertise.

Everyone moved into place. The string quartet began to play. My sisters went in first. Marley and Josie both pulled me in for a quick hug before stepping out into the chapel and proceeding down the aisle. I was last.

I touched the pearls Josie had given me for luck. Then I took a deep breath and walked into the chapel, alone.

The crowd had risen to their feet. But I only had eyes for one person in that room—my groom.

My stomach flipped at the sight of him in a tuxedo at the other end of the aisle. His smile was magnetic, and I couldn't help but return it. My mother wiped her eyes as I passed her in the front row with my sisters. Her last baby, finally getting hitched.

And then I was there. I took the final two steps up to the altar, passed my bouquet to Marley, and faced my groom.

"I've waited for this day our entire lives," he whispered.

"Me too."

A hush fell over the church as the service began. I heard little of it. The minutes passed in a blur. All I saw was the bright blue eyes looking back at me and the smile that said I was his world.

There was a pause in the ceremony. Just a moment. Barely a breath.

And everything collapsed.

The doors at the back of the church burst open. Everyone faced the figure who stepped into the sanctuary. The wedding planner trailed him. Whatever she was saying was lost in the drone of voices.

But I knew exactly why he was here.

I'd been a fool to think that he would let me go.

"I object!" he yelled into the church. "Lila, you can't marry him!"

And there I stood, on a precipice, ready to fall back onto that wheel that had always dragged us together. I couldn't have both.

So today, I had to choose: my groom or the man objecting.

PART I

2

ATHENS
APRIL 4, 2008

The energy in the lecture hall was contagious. Pens drummed on notebooks, legs jostled under desks, the *tap, tap, tap* of computer keys was more distraction than note-taking. Professor McConnell was still droning on, but no one was listening anymore. Not with ten minutes until the end of class. Not when spring had blown in hard and fast that week, bringing with it the restless need to be out of the classroom and out on the quad.

All around me, people packed up early, stuffing papers and computers into backpacks. The noise was loud enough for Professor McConnell to finally sigh and conclude.

"All right, all right," he said with that same exasperated tone he used for everything. He was one of those 'cool' professors who wore khakis and polos instead of suits and bow ties. Youngish type with lots of girls flocking to take his classes. "We'll pick this up again on Monday, but don't forget that your term paper is due a week from today. If anyone needs help, email me or come to office hours."

Half of the class was already out of their seats before he even finished speaking.

I idled in my second-row seat, biding my time until it emptied. My term paper wasn't where I wanted it to be. I was ahead of the rest of the class, considering I'd started my paper. Intro to Kinesiology was inundated with athletes who had tutors and private study sessions and, you know, other smart people to write their term papers for them. But I was in the class for my Exercise and Sports Science degree because I actually wanted to become a physical therapist. Not the typical student.

When the room was sufficiently empty, I snapped my notebook closed and stuffed it into the leather backpack my mom had gotten me as a graduation gift a year earlier. I got to my feet and stretched just as someone walked up my desk.

I jolted. "Uh, hi."

My eyes traveled up, up, up the gorgeous body that I'd be lying if I said I hadn't noticed at the back of the room with the other football players. He always wore the same Nike gear—joggers, red-and-black T-shirt, black jacket—with the football tags hanging off of his University of Georgia backpack.

No jacket today. And the hat that normally adorned his head was absent as well. His dark brown hair was gelled perfectly, short on the sides and longer on the top. And those blue eyes. They were electric blue ... and they were staring at me. Straight at me. With a half-smile that was almost ... hesitant?

"Hey. Lila, right?"

"Delilah," I corrected. Though I had no idea how he knew my name.

"Delilah," he said with a casual nod. "I'm Cole."

"I know who you are," I said before I could stop myself.

He smirked, running a hand back through his hair. When he touched the gel, he stopped as if he'd remembered his hair wasn't its normal floppy, just-sexed mess. "Right. Yeah. Forget that sometimes."

If it wasn't obvious from his outfit, Cole Davis was a football player. He had been a highly sought-after recruit for UGA. He'd helped take us to a Sugar Bowl victory this season. Cole wasn't quite the star, but he'd sure run up a ton of points his sophomore year. Not to mention, we all noticed his face that the university liked to plaster all over the enormous end zone scoreboard.

Not to mention that his dad was *the* Hal Davis. He played ball in college and then professionally for the Eagles. Now, he was an offensive line coach for the Atlanta Falcons, my favorite team. Every time Cole did something good on the field, his dad's name and record was blasted as well. Everyone liked a good story.

"Can I help you with something?" I asked.

"You seem to be doing really well in this class."

I narrowed my eyes suspiciously. "Do you need help with your term paper?"

He laughed. "No, I have a handle on it. Man, I'm shitty at this."

"At what?"

"Asking you out."

I blinked. "If that's what you're doing, then yes, you're pretty bad at it."

He chuckled again. Shooting me the dimples that made every girl on campus swoon.

"So, okay, let's start over again," Cole said.

He dropped his backpack on the ground next to mine and held out his hand. I took it because what else was I supposed to do?

"There's a luau tonight, and I was wondering if you'd want to go with me."

"Isn't tomorrow the spring game?"

"Yeah. It's kind of a tradition," he said with a shrug.

"So, it's a football party?"

"Uh ... well, sort of."

"Thanks for inviting me, Cole," I said, hefting my backpack on my shoulder. "But no thanks."

He blinked at my response, and I left the classroom before he could say anything else. I'd email the professor instead.

I didn't know why Cole Davis had asked me out, but I knew it was a bad idea. I'd sworn off football players and dark hair and blue eyes. I'd sworn off broken hearts. I'd had one, and one was enough as far as I was concerned.

I was out of the room and into the hallway of Ramsey, the university gym, before I realized Cole was following me.

"Hey, wait up," he said. As if he needed the help to catch me. "Where are you headed?"

I stopped in the hallway. "I don't want to go to your party."

"Okay. Well, what if we don't go to the party tonight? We could hang out instead."

"Don't *you* have to go to the party?"

"Not if you don't want to go," he said with that same smile and those same blue eyes.

That wasn't the response I'd expected. I tilted my head up to get another look at him, and all I found was sincerity. Cole was gorgeous and pursuing me, and every other girl would be dying for this to happen to them.

And I wanted to say yes.

I didn't want to spend the next three years of college miserable all because one stupid boy had broken my heart.

"All right," I said tentatively, releasing the tension in my shoulders. "What do you have in mind?"

His smile lit up his entire face when I said yes. I'd thought that damn smirk he always shot the camera was his *real* smile. But no, it was nothing like that. It was megawatt, full of joy, and completely irresistible. If he'd led with that, I might have said yes to the damn party. Fuck.

"Let me take care of that." He slipped me his phone which I was jealous to see was the new iPhone. They'd been sold out in stores for months, and everyone was still raving about them after the first design had released last year. Of course, he'd have one. I entered my number into the shiny thing, still unable to believe this was happening to me. "I'll pick you up at seven?"

"Sure," I said, not able to hide my own smile. "See you then."

MY MIND WAS STILL WHIRLING when I pulled up in front of my dorm twenty minutes later. I didn't even check my phone as I climbed the hill to the all-girls dorm, Brumby. If I had, I wouldn't have been as shocked to find Josie sitting on the futon, watching a baking show.

"Josie! Oh my God!"

She jumped up from the futon and threw her arms around me. We swayed side to side with excitement. Josie —though she went by Josephine now—was one of my two best friends. She had grown up in Atlanta with her dad and spent summers in Savannah with her mom in her ridiculous mansion on the coast. We'd met at the age of six and looked forward to every summer together. Now, I was here in Athens, and she was full-time in Savannah at Savannah College of Art and Design, studying film.

"How did you get past security?" I gasped, releasing her.

She laughed, flipping her long black ponytail. "I smiled."

Of course she had. "I completely forgot that you were coming into town this weekend."

"*You* forgot?" Josie asked. "Who are you, and what have you done with Lila Greer?"

If I couldn't call her Josephine, she certainly wasn't going to start calling me Delilah.

"I just had a weird day."

"Define weird." She narrowed her hazel eyes, which were almost gold today. "Because you must have had something catastrophic happen to make you forget that I was coming up."

I winced slightly. "I ... kind of have a date tonight."

Josie shrieked, dramatically jumping up and down and twirling in place. The little drama queen. "That's such amazing news. Tell me everything."

She dragged me to the futon and muted the show.

"Well, there's this guy in my kinesiology class who asked me to a party, but it's a football party."

"Ah," Josie said, understanding without me having to say anything.

"So, I said no. And I thought that was that, but he offered to ditch the party and take me out."

"Oh my God. You said yes?"

"I mean ... I probably shouldn't have. He's ... Cole Davis."

Josie's mouth dropped. "Holy shit! He's the one we were all swooning over when I came up for a game in the fall?"

I nodded.

"Remind me why you said no the first time."

I shrugged, averting my gaze. "He ... reminds me of *him*."

Josie blew out a harsh breath. "Is this your first date since Ash?"

My body twitched involuntarily at the name. "I mean, no. I made out with a few guys at a frat party and went on a date or two. But ..."

"But?"

"I don't know. Maybe it doesn't matter. Maybe I'm being crazy."

"Crazy is good for you, Lila. Forget Ash. You're going to go out with Cole Davis tonight and have the most *amazing* time."

"What about you?"

Josie rolled her eyes. "It's *me*. I'll manage."

Understatement of the century.

"But we're still going to the spring game tomorrow."

"Oh, absolutely. I fully intend to drink a few bottles of André at the tailgate and walk into Sanford Stadium, trashed."

I snort-laughed, immediately falling back into the ease of being with Josie. We were just missing Marley, and then we'd be complete.

"You have to help me find something to wear."

Josie jumped to her feet. "My expertise is required. Come. I'll be your fairy godmother for the night."

BY THE TIME seven rolled around, Josie had done her work and I was ready to go. Cole had texted, saying that he was going to come up. Because obviously he could just walk up into the all-girls dorm.

At the knock, Josie rushed to answer first.

"Josie!" I hissed.

She swung it open. "Heyyy!"

I put my head in my hands.

"Uh, hey," Cole said from the door. "I'm here for Delilah."

"Lila, your date is here," Josie called.

I took a deep breath and stepped forward. "Yeah, I

gathered that. Thanks, Josie." My gaze caught Cole's bright blue eyes, and my stomach flipped. He had on jeans and a white button-up with the sleeves rolled to his elbows. "Hey."

"Hey, you look nice."

I bit my lip, and Josie nudged me, as if to say, *See*.

I'd wanted to go with jeans and a T-shirt, but Josie had insisted that I needed to—quote—"show off your dancer body." So, we'd compromised on a light-blue wrap dress that matched my own blue eyes and made my brilliantly highlighted blonde hair shine even lighter.

"Thanks."

"I'm Josie." She stuck her hand out.

He laughed. "Cole. Are you Delilah's roommate?"

"No, I go to SCAD. Just here for the weekend."

"Am I interrupting your weekend? Should we reschedule?"

"No!" Josie said, all but pushing me out the door. "Y'all have a good time."

She shut the door on the pair of us. I was left shaking my head.

"She seems ... friendly," Cole said.

"She's a film major," I said by way of explanation.

We left my dorm and found his white Jeep parked at the front of the lot.

"God, how did you even get this spot?" It was almost impossible to park this close to the dorm.

"Someone was pulling out right as I drove up."

"Lucky."

"It's my superpower," he told me as he opened the passenger door.

"That is a random superpower."

"I don't make the rules," he said as I hopped in. Then he jogged around to the driver's side and got in. "It's just how it happens."

"Well, the real test will be downtown."

He grinned. "I got this."

And he did. We only circled the block once before a prime spot opened up right in front of us on the most coveted corner of Clayton and College. I was so jealous of his parking luck.

"Fine, you win. You have a parking superpower." I slung my bag onto my shoulder and hopped out of his Jeep before he could jog back around to help me out.

"What's yours?"

"My superpower?"

"Yeah. Something random, like finding a good parking spot or being able to win things off the radio before nine in the morning."

He directed us down the sidewalk. "I don't know. I'm not sure I have one."

"Everyone has one."

I bit my lip, contemplating what my power was while Cole navigated us toward The Grill. It was a dive diner at the heart of downtown, known for its twenty-four-hour diner breakfast and milkshakes. It had red plastic booths and a working jukebox. Every orientation group ended up at The Grill when they came into town; it was tradition.

He pulled open the door for me. "This all right?"

"It's perfect."

The harried waitress ushered us into a booth and plopped down menus.

"I hope you like feta fries. They have the best ones in town."

I blinked. "Feta ... fries?"

"Uh, yes. They're phenomenal. We're ordering some."

"All right. I do like feta and fries. I've never considered putting them together." I shrugged as I looked back at the menu. "I think I'm getting breakfast. Don't know if feta fries go with pancakes ..."

"They're a potato. Potatoes go with everything."

I chuckled. "That is true."

Once we ordered our breakfasts and fries, complete with two milkshakes—strawberry for me, chocolate for Cole—he returned to the question at hand.

"So ... superpower?"

"Okay, okay," I said, tapping a black-painted nail on the table. "This is going to sound weird, but when I get a Coke out of a vending machine, I almost always get two."

"What?" he gasped.

"I know. It's weird. It doesn't happen every time, but it happens a frightening amount."

"Forget it. Take my parking power. I want that. We're going to have to find a vending machine and test this."

I buried my face in my hands. "No! It won't work, and you'll think I'm a fraud."

I peeked up at him, and he was grinning like he couldn't wait to try it out.

"I need to see this in action."

"Fine, but if I fold under pressure, it'll be you suppressing my powers."

"Fair."

Our feta fries showed up first, and my mouth watered at the sight of white cheese sauce drizzled all over the double-battered French fries. I dipped the fry in more sauce and then took my first bite. My eyes rolled into the back of my head.

"Oh my God," I groaned. "Why have I never had these before?"

"Exactly," he said, pointing a fry at me. "These are to die for."

And they were. I gobbled up half the tray without pause. I was almost full by the time my pancakes showed up. And though I did try to eat some of the meal, I was too focused on Cole. I'd thought that this would be awkward. First dates were always awkward. Or...the entire two first dates I'd ever been on since Ash were so unbelievably awkward that I'd really never wanted to do them again.

But hanging out with Cole, it felt like I'd known him my entire life. As if he just somehow ... fit.

"Let's take the milkshakes to go. I have an idea," he said with a gleam in those baby blues.

Once our milkshakes were properly put into giant Styrofoam cups with thick straws, Cole paid for us both, despite my protest, and we headed back out onto the Athens streets. Downtown Athens was a five-by-six block of bars, restaurants, and shopping. It was the heart of the city. And The Grill was directly across Broad Street from North Campus, where the arch stood as a proud symbol of the university.

We waited at the corner, sipping our milkshakes. The

city was busier than normal due to the spring game tomorrow. During game weekends, half of Atlanta flooded the small town, burgeoning from a hundred thousand people to three to five hundred thousand overnight.

And Cole was entirely recognizable. In the minute we waited, about a dozen girls ogled Cole as they walked past.

"Do people always act like this?" I asked.

"Like what?"

I shot him a look of disbelief. "Stare at you?"

He looked behind him, confusion clearly on his face. "Were people looking? Sorry. I know it can be weird. I don't even see it."

He was serious. He hadn't even noticed that girls were eyeing him and fans were snapping pictures. That he was a celebrity to them. But he was just a normal guy.

"You really don't?"

"Nah. I'm used to it, because of my dad. You know my dad's a Falcons coach?"

"Everyone who listens to ESPN is well aware."

He chuckled. "Yeah, probs. Well, people would approach my dad some when I was younger, and I thought it was so cool. But he always remained firmly humble. Talent doesn't make you special. It just means you have a different skill than someone else."

"That's actually a great way to look at it."

Cole shot me that megawatt smile as we crossed the street and approached the arch. He nudged me in front of one of the openings. I gasped and pushed him back.

"Stop trying to bring me bad luck!"

He chuckled. "Afraid you're not going to graduate?"

As the superstition went, if you walked through the arch before graduation, you wouldn't graduate. It was a *big* deal at graduation to get that first walk through, and people lined up for hours to get that special moment photographed. I certainly wasn't planning to ruin it.

"I have no fears of that, but gah!"

"I wouldn't actually do that to you," he said as we slipped past the arch and onto North Campus. "You seem like the smart, studious type."

"What gives you that idea?"

"You sit at the front of class."

"Lots of people do."

"And don't bring your laptop."

"So?"

"Because you're actually taking notes," he said. "And you answer half of Professor McConnell's questions."

"Only because no one else ever speaks up and I cannot handle awkward silence."

Cole chuckled, draining the last of his milkshake and tossing it in a nearby trash can. "See ... smart, studious type."

"Fine, I like school. Sue me."

"Nah, I like it." He flushed slightly, running his hand back into his gelled hair and cursing under his breath as he remembered it. "I was actually ... nervous to ask you out."

I snorted. "Why? You're Cole Davis."

"That doesn't mean anything. And anyway ... you're intimidating."

"Am I?" I asked with raised eyebrows.

"Well, not now that I know you, but yeah, you kind of are."

"I'm not sure that's a compliment."

His eyes were so bright when he looked over at me that my heart practically stopped. He reached out and took my hand in his. Our fingers threaded together. I could feel my heartbeat everywhere at once. That one easy movement changed everything. Now ... we were holding hands. And he just smiled.

"It's a compliment, Delilah."

I swallowed and looked up into his face. He tugged me toward an admin building.

"Come on."

"What are you doing? Everything is locked."

He shot me a mischievous look and opened a side entrance.

My eyes widened. "That's not supposed to happen."

He didn't respond, just drew me inside. The lights were off, but brightened his phone screen until he found what he was looking for and flipped on the lights.

"Aha!" he said.

And then I saw it—a vending machine.

I couldn't help the bubble of laughter that exploded out of me. "You dragged me into a dark corner of campus to find a vending machine?"

"Work your magic, Delilah."

"I don't have any change."

He winked at me and pulled out his Bulldog Bucks card. "Got you covered."

He passed it to me as if he never considered that there

might not be any money on his card. That it would just *be* there when he needed it.

I swallowed back my emotions on that, like I did everything, and hoped my superpower wouldn't let me down.

With a deep breath, I swiped his card on the machine and pressed the Coke button. We both waited with anticipation as the machine rattled, taking its sweet time. It was an old model, and honestly, I was surprised it had card access at all.

Then there was a sturdy clunk, followed immediately by a second clunk.

"Ohhh!" Cole cheered, throwing his arms in the air and doing a two-step, as if I'd scored a touchdown.

I burst into laughter at the display and joined him, dancing circles around him. "It worked! Superpower unlocked!"

We dug into the bottom of the machine and pulled out the two Cokes. Cole looked at it as if it were a goddamn miracle.

"This is seriously the coolest shit," he said after we shut all the lights off and headed back to his car.

"It's so random."

"That's why it's the best superpower ever."

"I accept this great achievement."

He slipped his hand back into mine and gave me another look that made me melt into a puddle. "I don't want this night to end."

I flushed again. "Me neither. I'm having a great time."

"We could go get a drink," he suggested.

"I don't have a fake."

He shrugged. "You don't need one. I can get us in."

"Are you that self-assured about everything?"

"No," he said. "I wasn't sure that you'd say yes."

"I didn't."

He leaned back against his Jeep and finished off the Coke, setting it on the hood. "Yeah. Why did you say no anyway?"

"I kind of swore off football players."

He raised an eyebrow. "You dated a football player here?"

I shook my head. "In high school."

"Well, damn, guy must have broken your heart if you swore off all of us."

"Something like that." Not that I wanted to talk about Ash *at all*.

"So, why'd you say yes then? I'm still a football player."

"Don't remind me," I said with an eye roll.

"I guess it doesn't matter. I'm glad you did. I'd been working up the courage for weeks."

"No, you haven't!"

"I'm serious," he said. "I liked that you never gave a shit who any of us were."

"So, you *do* notice that people notice you," I teased.

He held his hands up and shot me that same cocky grin he always shot the camera. "I mean ... I noticed more that you *didn't* notice." He tugged me a little closer until we were nearly sharing the same space. "I like that."

I cleared my throat, feeling everything in me set aflame from that look. "What if I said I *had* noticed?"

His eyebrows shot up. "That so?"

"Maybe," I said with a laugh.

His eyes dipped down to my lips, and for a split second, I thought he might kiss me. Right here in the center of downtown, where anyone and everyone could see us.

I realized two things simultaneously: I wanted him to kiss me, and I wasn't sure I was ready for that to happen.

This date ... this date had been perfect. Easy. Uncomplicated. I'd made out with random strangers, and it hadn't meant anything. But I knew without a doubt ... *this* would mean something.

Cole Davis meant something.

So, I took the step back that I needed to breathe in his presence.

"Why don't we get you home, Lila?"

I nodded. This time, I didn't correct him.

And I never would again.

3

ATHENS

APRIL 5, 2008

The tailgate before the spring G-Day game looked like a stampede of elephants had trampled over North Campus. Josie wove drunkenly through the crowd of people, as if she went to Georgia, easily maneuvering us from one drink to the next.

To be fair, Josie had gone to an Atlanta high school that had sixty people out of their senior class come to the university. So, it was feasible that she knew more people here than I did.

"You have to sit with us," Channing said, latching on to my arm.

"Definitely."

My buzz was tipping into dangerous territory, but how could I deny the captain of the dance team? I couldn't.

Georgia had two main dance teams. The one that marched with the band for football games and the varsity team that performed at all basketball games, volleyball games, and gymnastic meets. Channing and I were on the latter.

The lot of us pushed into Sanford Stadium, falling into place in the one hundred–student section in our array of red-black-and-white game day dresses. The good thing about being surrounded by other dancers was that we knew every cheer and doubled the volume in the stadium.

"Oh my God!" Josie screamed. "There's Cole!"

Her words were lost in the uproar as the football players jogged out onto the football field for the annual scrimmage. Half of the team was in red and half in white. They'd play each other, including any new recruits who had signed to Georgia for next season. The coveted quarterback position was typically won at this game, and we had two promising quarterbacks this year. I couldn't wait to see them both play.

Though I'd be lying if my eyes didn't follow Cole in his red uniform. I'd told him last night where I'd be sitting with the rest of the dance team. And today, he looked up at the audience and pointed straight toward me.

The crowd went wild. No one, except Josie and me, knew that the gesture was pointed and not just a thank-you to the entire crowd. My face was on fire, and Josie bounced up and down with excitement.

"He is so hot," Channing said next to me. "Not my type obviously, but I can appreciate a pretty face."

"He really is," I agreed easily.

"I heard that he's back on the market. His last relationship went down in massive flames."

I frowned. I didn't want to know more about him than what he'd told me. If I wasn't ready to discuss my relationship … maybe he wasn't either.

"Lila went on a date with him last night," Josie said gleefully.

Channing's head snapped to me. "Excuse me? And no phone call? Are we even friends?"

I laughed and shot her an apologetic look. "It was kind of last minute. We have Kinesiology together, and he asked me out."

"Holy shit! How did it go? Tell me everything."

So, as the two teams lined up for the game, I divulged to Channing what I'd already spent last night telling Josie. And by the end, Channing looked as if she were going to explode with excitement.

"So, he was pointing at *you*?" she gasped. She pulled her blonde hair up into a ponytail since the heat was out of this world today. It was like spring had come yesterday and full-blown summer hit today. Typical Georgia.

"Yes!" Josie squealed.

"Oh, I love this. Who knew our little Delilah would snag Cole Davis?"

"I mean, it was one date."

"Whatever," Channing said with a hand wave. "That was more than a first date."

And I couldn't deny that. Not one bit.

IT WAS A BRUTALLY HOT DAY. I was sticky and would have happily gone home to shower and chill in the air conditioning, but I couldn't leave my seat. The dance team continued to cheer through the fourth quarter. When the red team scored the winning touchdown, the entire stadium went wild, even with the dwindling numbers. We made up for the empty seats.

Before the clock ticked down its final few seconds, I grabbed Josie's hand and tugged her out of the bleachers. We raced down the stairs to field level. Sanford Stadium was set up with a ring of five-foot hedges surrounding the field and a path around the hedges that led to the seats. I wanted to be the first one down there to take pictures between the hedges.

Josie and I snapped pictures individually and then together when we could grab someone to take it for us. The person taking our picture gasped.

I was about to ask what was wrong when I heard the cheers of the football players behind us. Josie grabbed her phone back and swiveled to take shots of the football players in the hedges, chanting with the marching band and remaining fans.

A few players jumped the hedges and pulled themselves up into the stands in front of the marching band to dance and celebrate.

"Oh my God!" Josie cried, taking picture after picture after picture.

We were at the heart of it. I couldn't have planned it better if I'd tried.

Then I heard my name behind me.

Josie and I both whipped back around to find Cole Davis standing on the other side of the hedges. His helmet was still on, but I could see the gleam in his eyes and the wide smile on his face.

"This is crazy!" I yelled over to him.

Whatever he said next disappeared as the marching band started up another song.

"What?" I called.

He shook his head in exasperation, and then with two purposeful steps, he jumped, vaulting the hedges and sliding over to the other side. My eyes widened in shock. I'd seen other players clambering over the hedges, but he'd made it look like he'd taken a hurdle. Precise and somehow effortless.

"I said," he began, tugging his helmet off of his head and looking down at me, "I was looking for you throughout the game."

"Oh," I said. "You found me."

"I guess I did."

He took that final step forward, bridging the distance between us with ease. His hand pushed up into my hair. My head tilted up to look at him towering over me.

We hung there, suspended in space and time. Everything shifted. The world dropped away. The chanting buzzed into silence. All around us, people celebrated, and here, right now, it was just me and Cole.

Then his head dipped down, and his mouth touched mine. We melded together as if we were always meant to be. He tasted like sweat and the sweet tang of a sports drink and something inexplicably him. My fingers tangled into the front of his jersey, distorting the number eighty-eight. I reveled in the feel of his kiss. I'd been hesitant last night, but all that hesitancy had evaporated.

He hooked his other arm, still holding his helmet, around my back, crushing me against his chest. I'd never felt so small as I did against his muscular build. I stood on my tiptoes, throwing my arms around him as he deepened the kiss. His tongue sweeping in to claim mine. I groaned deep in the back of my throat.

Then to my surprise, he effortlessly lifted me off the ground. I gasped as he twirled me around and then stole another kiss.

My eyes were only for him as he gently set me back on my feet. That was when everything else rushed back in. And the cheers from the crowd had changed in volume, erupting into applause and catcalls and whistles. Which was the moment that I realized they were cheering for *us*.

My face turned beet red, and I buried it into his jersey. "Oh my God!"

He laughed. "That was quite a kiss."

"You were on the big screen!" Josie cried, snapping a picture.

"We were not!" I gasped.

Josie winked. "I got it all on my phone."

"Stop! You did not. How many pictures did you take?"

Josie shrugged. "How could I not take pictures?"

Cole chuckled softly. He put his finger under my chin and tilted it up until I was looking at him. Then he stole another kiss. "Don't listen to anyone else. This was perfect."

My eyes locked with his again. "It was."

"You're mine now," he said with all the heat of our first kiss baking in the summer sun.

Still, I shivered at the proclamation. And how right it was.

"I already was."

And that would never change.

4

ATHENS

MAY 5, 2008

F inals week wasn't the ideal time to throw a party. I definitely should have been studying for my Spanish final. Languages were not my strong suit, and I needed an A on the final to keep my B in the class. It was pathetic.

Instead, I was waiting for Marley to show up in Athens. She was the genius of us. She'd been in the Duke TIP program since middle school, which identified young talent, and had been admitted to the university with early acceptance. I missed her, as she was five long hours away. Thankfully, she didn't have any finals at Duke and was currently driving south to be here in time for my birthday party.

I texted her, requesting an ETA.

Driving down the Atlanta Highway. *insert B-52 lyrics*

She was ridiculous, but I was glad that she was finally here.

Cole had been needling me all day about coming over to his place early for birthday shenanigans. It didn't matter that we'd celebrated *his* birthday yesterday downtown. Half the football team had drunkenly shown up and gotten him so plastered that he'd blacked out the second I got him into his bed.

It was still surprising to me that our birthdays were so close. His on the fourth of May and mine on the fifth. I'd always hated having my birthday on Cinco de Mayo until college when it was apparently the coolest shit ever, and Cole had promptly declared that he was throwing a joint birthday party. Then he'd planned two anyway. Having two birthday parties after claiming we were only having one was perfectly Cole.

HERE! HERE! HERE!!!!!

I dashed out of my dorm room and down into the Brumby lobby. Marley had hiked up the hill and opened the lobby door when I got out of the elevator. We collided in the middle, laughing and practically near to tears. This was the longest either of us had ever gone without the other. I'd seen her at Christmas, and it was too long to go.

"I missed you!" Marley said.

"So much," I told her. "Let's never do this again."

"Deal." She finally released me. "So, when do I get to meet him?"

"Cole has been asking the same thing."

"Well, it's not fair that Josie was here the weekend y'all met," Marley said. She brushed strands of her curly, dark hair out of her face and adjusted the large backpack

on her back. It was likely all she'd brought with her for
the day that she was staying with me before she returned
to Savannah for the summer. If I knew my best friend at
all, the rest of stuff was neatly arranged in boxes in the
trunk of her giant SUV. Likely labeled, dated, and color-
coordinated. "I mean, she's been rubbing it in that she got
those pictures of y'all at the game."

"She sold them to a newspaper," I groaned, dragging
her deeper into the dorm.

"I know! That's so Josie."

"Isn't it?"

We hurried back upstairs, chatting animatedly about
everything and nothing.

I'd known Marley since second grade when we were
both in Mrs. Jackson's class. Marley complimented my
Lisa Frank shirt, I gushed over her scrunchie, and then
we promptly got in trouble for talking too much. We'd
been inseparable ever since.

After we both got dressed, I texted Cole to let him
know we were on our way and then took my beat-up
Hyundai north of the dorms to the light-blue house
where Cole lived with his two roommates. I knocked
twice on the front door and then let myself inside. The
party wouldn't start for another hour and wouldn't really
get going until later, but already, there were a handful of
people present, sitting around, watching TV, and
pregaming with beers.

I pulled Marley in behind me. We hurried past one of
Cole's roommates, Barry, and continued into the kitchen.
Cole turned at our presence, and a smile split his face.

"Finally," he said, scooping me up and kissing me.

"I did text you."

He patted his pockets. "I don't know where my phone is."

"You're always losing it."

He shrugged. "Doesn't matter now. You're here." He turned to my best friend. "And you must be Marley."

"I am," she said, extending her hand for him to shake.

He took it. "So good to finally meet you. Lila talks about you nonstop."

"Funny. I was going to say the same thing about you."

He grinned as his gaze shifted back to me. "You talk about me nonstop?"

"You're my new, shiny toy," I told him with a wink.

"And what does that say about me?" Marley asked.

"You're the Woody to his Buzz Lightyear."

"I don't know whether or not to be offended by that."

"You're forever, babe," I told her, slinging an arm over her shoulders. "Now, we have two birthdays to celebrate."

"Yes, what can I get you?" Cole said. "Beer, wine, margaritas?"

"Margaritas," Marley and I said in unison.

Cole blended together the drinks, and we took them into the living room to watch *SportsCenter*. I'd seen the baseball highlight plays already. Apparently, it was a casualty of spending a lot of time with Cole. More and more sports.

"So," Marley said as she sank into a chair. She tucked her legs up underneath her and looked at Cole.

"Oh no," I said into my margarita.

Cole glanced at me. "What?"

"Here it comes."

"Tell me everything about you," Marley said. "What's your major? What do you want to be when you grow up? What do your parents do?"

"Mars," I grumbled. "We talked about this."

She looked sheepish. "I know you told me to stagger my questions, but this is who I am."

Cole just chuckled. "It's fine. I don't mind the third degree from your best friend."

Cole's other roommate patted him on the back. "Good luck with that."

"Thanks, Tony," Cole said with an eye roll.

Tony leaned forward. "I've known him since high school. Trust me, he's not that interesting."

Marley and I laughed as Cole punched him in the shoulder.

"Dick," Cole grumbled. "My major is sports management and marketing. I don't ever want to grow up. And my dad is a football coach. My mom is a middle school teacher."

"Okay, okay," Marley said, holding her hands up. "I don't understand what sports management even is."

"It's someone who wants to work with sports," I told her.

"Yeah, but … what do you *do* with that?"

"Ignore her," I said. "You don't have to submit to this interrogation. She's a science person, and she wants to, like, cure cancer."

"Dementia," Marley corrected.

"Interrogation already accepted," Cole said with that same smile. His blue eyes bright as they rested on my best friend. "Sports management could be anything from professional sports to running a rec league. Personally, I'd like to be a talent scout for a professional football team, but I'm also interested in marketing and PR. Which is why I'm a double major."

"I'm surprised you have time with football."

Tony chuckled. "He thrives most when he's swamped. You should have seen him in high school. He played football, ran track, held down a job with his dad, volunteered at a nursing home, and kept a 4.0."

My eyes widened. *Thanks, Marley.* Somehow, I was learning more about my own boyfriend through this conversation. I'd known he was a double major. He'd schooled me about that on our second date. But all the rest, I wasn't aware.

"Yeah, fine," Cole said, "I like to keep busy. Nothing wrong with that."

"You were salutatorian without trying. You had to turn down an academic scholarship," Tony said, crossing his arms. "You're a monster."

"You turned down an academic scholarship?" I asked.

Cole shrugged. "I had to. I was offered a football scholarship, too, and there are all these weird NCAA rules. The academic scholarship could go to someone else."

"Whoa," I muttered.

"Oh, so you're smart!" Marley said with a smile.

"Well, I don't need help on my Intro to Kinesiology paper if that's what you mean," Cole said, winking at me.

I stuck my tongue out. "It was a fair question! Most of the jocks aren't writing their own papers. How was I to know that you'd turned down an academic scholarship?"

"It was cute."

Marley nodded as if she saw the pieces fall together. "Sports management for you and physical therapy for Lila. You'll recruit the players, and Lila will piece them back together."

"Big dreams," Cole said.

"I like your big dreams and big brain," I told him.

"Is that a euphemism?" Cole asked, rubbing his nose against mine.

"Maybe."

"You two are disgusting," Tony said. He leaned away from our very public display of affection.

I didn't mind being disgusting. I was exactly where I wanted to be.

HOURS LATER, the house was *packed*. Everyone must have invited more and more people until I was sure that the police were going to be called for noise complaints. Not that I cared too much as we cheered on Marley doing an upside-down margarita. Marley sat on a chair with her head tipped back while one person simultaneously poured a bottle of tequila and a bottle of margarita mix into her mouth.

The crowd counted for her. "One! Two! Three! Four! Five!"

She waved her hands helplessly, swallowing down the contents and grasping for a lime wedge. Everyone applauded for her as she wobbled back to her feet.

"I'm never doing that again." She clutched my arm

and pulled me away as another victim took a seat. "Why did I do that?"

"Because you're drunk, Mars."

She giggled and stumbled a step. "I am not."

"Yes, you most definitely are. Maybe that last upside-down margarita was a bad idea."

"No," she said, waving me away. "It was fine. I'm fine. It's your birthday! Plus, I rarely drink at Duke. Mostly dance rehearsals and basketball games."

"Same," I said with a smile. "I miss having you with me."

"I know. It's not the same. Though performing in Cameron has to be better than Georgia basketball."

"Not an unfair assessment." Duke basketball was unequivocally better than UGA, but I still loved watching the Georgia games.

"But," she said, her voice dipping as she leaned into me, "do you know who I saw before I left?"

My stomach dropped at the insinuation. I only knew one other person who went to Duke. "No."

"Yes, you do," she teased. "He wanted to come see you for your birthday, but I told him no."

Ice ran through my veins. "He didn't say that."

"He did!" she said, her voice rising.

"Shh," I hushed her. "Ash hasn't spoken to me in a year. He's not going to suddenly want to show up for my birthday. That's absurd."

"Fine, don't believe me. But he said he was going to text you."

My hand immediately went to my phone. I pulled it out and showed her the blank screen. "Look. Nothing."

Marley shrugged. "That's just what he said."

"What's going on over here?" Cole asked.

He appeared as if out of thin air, and I jumped nearly out of my skin. I hadn't been expecting him. My mind had been on Ash, and I definitely didn't want to be thinking about him.

"Marley's drunk," I told him.

"I'm not drunk," she countered. Making her point by trying to push off of the wall she was currently leaning on and failing spectacularly. "Oof!" She latched back on to the wall. "Maybe I am a little drunk."

"We should get you some water."

"On it," Cole said, heading back into the busy kitchen.

"He's in Athens tonight," Marley continued when he was gone.

I closed my eyes and took a breath. "Ash is *here*?"

"He offered to drive with me. Then, we wouldn't have had to drive separately."

"What were you going to do with your stuff?"

"I don't know. It's Ash. He probably had his stuff flown home." She waved her hand. "You know how he is."

"I do," I whispered.

"So anyway, yeah, I think he's downtown."

"Downtown?" Cole asked as he reappeared with a water. "I don't think that sounds like a good idea for you, Marley."

"Not me. Ash."

I closed my eyes and sighed heavily. Cole didn't know what that name meant to me. We hadn't talked about deeper topics yet in our relationship. I hadn't wanted to tell him about what had happened with me and Ash in high school ... the good or the bad. And I really didn't want to talk about it on my birthday.

"Who's Ash?" Cole asked.

Marley's eyes widened. "Um ... nobody."

Cole looked to me with raised brows.

"My ex," I told him. "He goes to Duke with Marley, and I guess he's also in town."

"The football player?"

I nodded.

Marley sipped on her water and eyed us. "Sorry. I hadn't planned to tell you."

"It's fine." I patted Marley's shoulder. "Maybe you should sit down for a bit, Mars."

After I got her into a chair to continue to drink her water and made sure she was comfortable and watched by one of my dance friends, I returned to Cole. I ran a hand down my face. "Sorry about that."

He shrugged. "Doesn't bother me. I'm still friends with my ex. Jess actually called to wish me happy birthday yesterday. It's not weird."

Right.

Not weird.

Except that he had no idea about me and Ash. Or else he probably wouldn't have said that.

"Jess is the girl you dated before me?"

The one Channing said had gone down in flames?

"Yeah. She was in love with the spotlight." He tugged me closer, dropping a kiss to my lips. "It's why I like being with you so much."

"Because I don't give a shit?"

He laughed. "Yes. One of the many reasons."

"Perhaps you could elucidate the others."

"For one, you use the word *elucidate*."

I snickered and kissed him again. Glad that our discussion of exes was coming to an end. I did *not* want to talk about Ash. So, any divergence was for the better.

"Actually, I do have something for you."

My eyes widened. "You said no birthday presents!"

"I know." He shot me a sheepish look. "But I couldn't resist getting you something small."

"Well, now, I'm a bad girlfriend because I didn't get you anything."

"You won't feel that way when you open it. And anyway, we're still going to Last Resort on Friday night for our official celebration," he said, taking my hand and pulling me up the stairs, away from the crowds.

"That was the plan. Memories over gifts," I reminded him. "Now, you're saying memories *and* gifts!"

"Lila, just open the present," he said as he forced a small box into my hand, covered in blue Christmas wrapping paper.

"A little out of season," I teased.

But I was already peeling back the wrapping paper and finding the dark green gift box underneath. I popped the lid on the thing, wondering what in the world he could have gotten me when we'd *both* agreed not to do this. When I saw what was inside, I immediately started laughing.

"You didn't!"

He grinned broadly. "Told you."

I reached inside and retrieved the small keychain of a can of Coke.

"Now, you can have your superpower with you everywhere."

"Thank you," I said, flinging my arms around him. "It's perfect."

"Phew!" He wiped his hand across his brow. "I was worried that I'd look stupid, giving my girlfriend a keychain."

"We're still going to Last Resort," I reminded him. "But it's thoughtful. I like it."

He dragged me harder against him, dropping his mouth onto mine. Promising so, so much more.

He groaned and pulled himself back. "I want to keep doing this." He adjusted his pants, proving his point. "But I also have surprise cake."

"Cake!" I gushed. "Chocolate?"

"And strawberry."

"My favorite."

He kissed me again. "I know. So, we have to go downstairs for that. Then I'm bringing you back up here and giving you your real present."

I licked my lips. "Maybe I'll give you *my* present."

"Fuck," he breathed.

"Cole!" his roommate Barry called from the other side of the door.

"Coming!" Cole yelled. He shot me a look of pure lust.

"I'm going to put this in my purse." I'd left my purse in his bedroom hours ago, and I didn't want to lose my new keychain. As small and insignificant as a keychain was for a birthday present, it made my insides squirm with excitement.

Cole went back downstairs while I attached my

keychain to my keys. Then I grabbed my phone and glanced down at the screen one last time before I joined my boyfriend for birthday cake.

I froze in place.

I had a new text message.

My stomach dropped out of my system. My heart stuttered. I could barely swallow around the knot in my throat, and my hands shook. I hadn't seen that name on my screen in nearly a year. And I hadn't believed Marley when she said that Ash would text me. It had seemed impossible.

And yet ... Ash had texted me.

Happy birthday, Lila. Missing you tonight.

5

SAVANNAH
DECEMBER 8, 2006

M y arms pumped to the time of the cheerleading chant at the Holy Cross football game my senior year of high school. I executed a little hop step, pressed my body forward, and shook my pom-poms. "Holy Cross! Holy Cross! Holy Cross!"

It was the last play of the game. The Holy Cross Academy boys had the ball, and the quarterback had just gotten into position. The crowd died down from our side as we anticipated what Ash Talmadge was about to do. I shivered in the cold. My fingers had long ago gone nearly blue in the unseasonably cold Savannah winter. But still, my eyes were glued to the number four on his jersey.

They hiked the ball. Ash stepped back, ball in hand, and searched the eligible receivers. Then with one beautifully arced ball, he threw downfield. His wide receiver caught the ball in the end zone at the last second of the clock, and the stands erupted into cheers.

We'd won!

My heart was going to burst out of my chest. I couldn't

believe it. It had come right down to the wire. And though some of the girls on the cheerleading squad for St. Catherine's Academy—the school that resided across the street from the all-boys equivalent, Holy Cross—had never cared about football a day in their life, we were all celebrating together.

"We did it," Shelly cried, throwing her arms around me.

We jumped up and down together. My face ached from smiling so hard.

And I couldn't even believe this moment.

Not that Holy Cross had won. They'd won this game the last two years that I'd attended St. Catherine's. But that I was standing on the sidelines as a cheerleader, celebrating with Shelly Thomas of all people. Though I'd been going to St. Catherine's for three years, this was my first season cheering, and I was loving it.

"Hey, stay after. I want to talk to you," Shelly said.

I nodded. "Sure."

Shelly winked at me, immediately stepping back into her position as captain. "Okay, girls, let's close out this game."

We moved back into formation, spending the next half hour cheering as the marching band played from the stands and all of the audience dwindled to nothing.

Shelly called it a wrap, letting the other girls leave to see their families who had been waiting patiently for us to finish. When it was finally just the two of us, she waved me closer.

"Delilah," she said as she slung her cheer bag over her shoulder, "I am so glad that you joined the squad."

Honestly, it had always surprised me that I'd even made the team. St. Catherine's only had three hundred and fifty high school students. Cheerleading was coveted among the girls. But there was no dance team, which was where my real passion lay. I spent most afternoons and all weekends at the dance studio with my best friend, Marley. But my mom had thought cheering would be good for my social life.

Considering I'd gone to public school until my mom got the job at St. Catherine's the summer before sophomore year, she wasn't wrong. I could use any help I could get, trying to fit in with these uber rich girls who had known each other their entire lives. I hadn't even been fortunate enough to join the school freshman year. Nope, sophomore year instead. And only because my mom got a shockingly huge tuition discount for working for the Catholic school. Which did nothing for my social standing.

I must have made some sound of assent because Shelly continued, "But I have bad news."

"Is everything all right?"

Shelly had been having some issues at home. I knew that despite her wealth, life wasn't all rainbows and sunshine. It wasn't like that for anyone even if they tried to project that.

"With me, yes. Don't worry about my parents." She flashed her teeth. "But we can't go on the ski trip."

I jerked to a stop next to her. She took another step before seeing I'd stopped. "What? Why not?"

I'd be lying if I said that I hadn't been anticipating this trip all semester. My mom had taken up another job as an overnight caregiver for the elderly to help pay for cheerleading, and I had to help pitch in at the studio to cover everything else. I'd used up a sizable amount of my savings to pay for the pants, jacket, goggles, gloves, and hat. Shelly's parents had offered to cover everyone's lift passes, which was the only way I could make it work.

She winced. "I guess some of the other girls' parents found out that my parents weren't going. That it was going to be a bunch of high school senior girls with my twenty-one-year-old brother."

"Oh," I whispered.

We'd all known this. A lot of the other girls had been excited about it, hoping that they'd get to hook up with college boys.

"Once my parents got wind of the other parents' displeasure, they canceled the whole thing. They won't even let me go visit Shane." She rolled her big brown eyes.

My mind was racing back to when I'd purchased my ski clothes. Was I still within the thirty-day window? Would I still be able to return them in time to get my money back?

"That's terrible," I told her because she clearly wanted me to say something. "I'm sorry you don't get to see your brother."

"I'm sorry that *you* don't get to go! I was looking forward to seeing you on those bunny slopes." She flipped her strawberry-blonde curls. "I still can't believe you've never been skiing."

"Right," I said with a forced laugh.

"Well, I'll see you after break. Now that I'm forced to

go with my parents to New York City," she said with a scoff. "I mean, I've been there enough times at Christmas. Couldn't we at least ski the Rockies or Alps if they're going to force me to hang out with them?"

I swallowed back the bitter taste in my mouth. It always hurt to be reminded that Shelly and I lived on different planes of existence.

Shelly waved as she jogged over to her shiny, new Lexus to head home. The rest of the cheerleading squad had already left. And the football players were trickling out of the locker rooms to head home.

I plopped down onto a bench in front of the football field and sent my mom a text to let her know we were done. I didn't have my own car. We couldn't afford it since my older sister was in college and had to have one. But if I could return the ski clothes, then I might be back on track to buy a car for graduation.

I shivered in the chill as it got later and later and colder and colder. My mom hadn't returned my text, and when I called, it went straight to voicemail. I huffed angrily. She must have forgotten to charge it again. She had said that she'd raised three other girls without cell phones and didn't understand the big deal with me. Well, right now was the big deal.

The game was outside the city. Normally, I could walk anywhere around Savannah to get to where I was going, but it was too far to walk, and everyone was gone. Crap.

"Hey," a voice said behind me.

I jumped up and found Ash standing before me.

It should have been impossible for him to be as hot as he was. Most of the guys I knew were tall and gangly and just getting used to their new almost-man body. But not Ash. He had the aristocratic air as if he always knew precisely where to belong and who he was. He towered over me as he approached with the build of someone who spent too much time in the gym. His dark hair was wet, making it appear nearly midnight black in the faint light with blue eyes so light in contrast that I could swim in them.

In short, there was a reason that every girl at St. Catherine's wanted a piece of him.

"Uh, hey."

He gestured to me. "Are you all right? Someone coming to get you?"

I glanced down at my phone and wanted to curse my mother. "My mom said she'd be here."

"You live downtown, right? I'm going that way."

I had no idea how he knew where I lived. I didn't even think that he knew my name.

"Oh, uh, that's okay. I'll wait."

He arched an eyebrow. "It's too cold, and you can't walk."

Which was exactly what I'd been thinking, but my hackles rose regardless. "I can walk."

"I see that you are capable. Well, if you don't want a ride, I can wait with you until your mom shows up."

"What? Why?"

"I don't know if you've noticed, Delilah, but we're the only ones left."

"It's Lila," I said automatically.

I'd stopped correcting Shelly, who liked to sing that Plain White T's song "Hey There Delilah" on repeat, but I still tried to get everyone to call me by my preferred name.

"Sorry, Lila," he said, switching easily. "I thought everyone called you Delilah."

"Shelly Thomas *sings* Delilah to me. It's different."

"That sounds like Shelly Thomas."

Yeah, it did. Shelly was an acquired taste.

"So, shall we wait?" he asked gallantly. "I was raised not to leave beautiful girls alone at night."

I rolled my eyes. "Beautiful girls?"

He quirked a half-smile. "What'll it be? Wait or ride?"

A shiver shot through me as he rolled the word *ride* at me. As if he were thinking of something else entirely.

"Well, I was raised to not take rides from strangers."

He laughed. "All right. That's fair." Then he stepped forward and offered me his hand. His fingers were warm —unbelievably warm—as I slid my frozen grip into his. "I'm Ash. Well, James Asheford Talmadge IV, but my dad is James, and, well, you can understand why I don't go by Asheford."

I could understand that. "Nice to meet you."

"Look, now, we're not strangers. Are you going to let me take you home?" He stared me down as if daring me to say no again.

But a twinge of worry had crept up in me, the longer I stood here. No text or call from my mom and no other way home. I really didn't *want* to walk. Fuck.

"All right. Thanks."

"Excellent."

Then he headed toward the only car still in the massive parking lot. And of course, it was a Mercedes.

Ash pulled the passenger door open for me, letting me settle in before he got into the other side and turned the heat on full blast. He even had heated seats, which normally, I'd roll my eyes at but I was thankful for it tonight.

"Thanks for this," I told him as we pulled away from the football field toward downtown.

"No problem. Seriously, I'm going that way."

I checked my phone again. Still nothing from my mom. I sighed.

"So, anything special planned for break?"

I narrowed my eyes at him, wondering if he knew about my canceled plans. But why would Shelly tell him anyway?

"No," I finally said. "I was supposed to go skiing with Shelly, but she had to cancel the whole trip. So, now, I'm not going."

Ash was unusually silent for a few moments. I'd been expecting him to say something conciliatory, but he just looked … blank.

"The trip was canceled?" he asked right as I was about to say something.

"Yeah. She told me after the game."

"Huh."

"What?"

"I don't think it's canceled."

"What do you mean?" I asked in confusion.

"I mean that Shelly's still going skiing."

"But … no, she said her parents were taking her to New York."

"I don't know what she told you, but some of the guys

in the locker room were trying to get me to go with them on Shelly's ski trip. I guess her brother is going to be out of town and gave her the entire house. She invited all the guys to drive up with them."

I blinked in horror. My stomach dropping out. "She said this tonight?"

"Fuck, sorry to be the one to tell you, but she must have pulled a Shelly."

"Pulled a Shelly?"

"She's notorious for pulling this kind of shit."

My hands were shaking. I was going to throw up. Shelly had lied to me. She'd likely never intended for me to go skiing with her. She'd invented the whole thing so that she could tear me down. It was ... unfathomable.

"Are you going?" I asked, my voice tight.

"Nah, even if I didn't have to work, I have no interest in Shelly's games."

"You work?" The surprise was evident in my voice.

"Yeah. My dad says it builds character. Plus, if I don't work, I won't have gas money."

I glanced over at Ash with new eyes. I'd seen him as a spoiled, rich kid, like so many of the students that I went to school with. As far as I knew, I was the only one at either school who worked. And while Ash and I worked for entirely different reasons, it changed my idea of him.

"I work at a dance studio on the weekends."

"That's cool. I didn't know you danced."

"Yeah. Cheering is actually a new thing. Thought I'd make friends." I rolled my eyes. "Should have known better."

"Hey, don't let Shelly Thomas get to you. She's not worth your time."

Easy for him to say.

I leaned my head against the cold window in response. A few minutes later, I directed him in front of my house downtown.

My dad had bought the house when he and my mom had first been dating. It was the only thing we still had of him after he skipped town and left the paid-off mortgage to my mom. She'd wanted to move a dozen times, and she knew that even though the free house was hush money to not come after him—which she never did—she couldn't bear to sell the place.

"Thanks for driving me home," I told him as I popped the door open and slung my cheer bag over my shoulder.

"Hey, Lila." He stopped me before I could rush up the front sidewalk.

"Yeah?"

"Do you have plans tomorrow?"

"Work," I offered.

He grinned. "After work?"

"Uh, no. Why?"

"Do you want to hang out?"

My jaw dropped slightly. I'd just thought that Ash was being nice to me. Poor little poor girl with no car and no family to come and get her.

Was he asking me out? No, there must be a mistake.

My hackles rose. "I don't need your pity."

He balked at the comment. "Who says it's pity? What if I just want to hang out with you?"

"Why?" I demanded.

He shrugged. "Do I need a reason? You seem cool. Not like the other girls at your school."

I'd never known Ash before tonight, but I'd heard plenty of other girls talk about him. I knew all about his reputation. "Hanging out" with him was likely a bad idea. He probably used that line on every girl.

And yet when I looked at him, really looked at him, he didn't appear to have any guile in the statement. He was either an incredible actor or actually sincere. The part of myself that was hurting right now from Shelly's betrayal assumed the former, but the selfish, hopeful part wanted it to be the latter. Finding out the truth would probably break me.

"All right," I said finally.

"Great," he said with a dazzling smile.

We exchanged numbers, and then I got out of the car.

I'd probably made a mistake in accepting, but I couldn't deny my pull to Ash.

6

SAVANNAH
DECEMBER 9, 2006

"Let me get this straight," Marley said the next day at the studio, "you're going on a date with the quarterback."

I scrubbed at the fingerprints on the mirror with my sponge. "It's not a date."

Marley flung soap at me. "He drove you home and then asked you to hang out." She put air quotes around *hang out*. "Then he said you were different than other girls. It's a date."

"But he didn't ask me out. Just said to hang out."

"What century are you living in, Lila?" she asked. "Hanging out is the new date language."

"Ugh! Maybe I shouldn't go."

"He's hot, you're unattached, and he asked you out. Why wouldn't you go?"

"The rumor at school is that he's a player."

"Well, if he tries anything you're not ready for, you sock him in the nuts."

I burst into laughter. I loved when Marley got vulgar.

It was such a Josie thing to say and do, and it made me miss her. I couldn't wait until she was here this summer.

"I'll take that into consideration."

We finished up at the studio, locking the building back up with the key the studio owner, Miss Alicia, had given us for this exact purpose. I followed Marley to the minivan parked at the front of the studio. Marley had been raised by her grandparents, and they prioritized safety over anything. Though Marley hated the old minivan, at least she had wheels. It was more than I could say.

"So, where are you going on this date?" Marley asked as we left the studio and headed toward my house.

Marley's grandparents lived only a few blocks over. I'd spent as many nights there as at my own house,. Since I didn't know any of my own grandparents, they'd stepped in.

"One, it's not a date. And two, I don't know. We've been texting."

Marley squeaked. "You've been texting!"

"Just like normal things, Mars. Calm down."

"His family owns, like, half of downtown. They're in real estate. You could be, like, going to Pink House."

I rolled my eyes. "No seventeen-year-old is taking a date to Pink House," I said of the fanciest and most iconic restaurant downtown.

"So, it *is* a date," Marley said with mischief in her eyes.

"Fine, Miss Inquisitive. Maybe it *is* a date."

"Eep!"

Marley dropped me off, I grabbed the mail, and entered the empty house. My mom had still been sleeping this morning when I left for work, and there was a note on the fridge when I got home, saying that she was going to be working late, with a twenty-dollar bill to order pizza. I stuffed the twenty into my purse. Should cover dinner tonight if this *wasn't* a date.

Then I darted upstairs to rummage through my mom's makeup drawer and use her curling iron. She didn't *care* about me wearing makeup or anything, but she didn't buy me the nice stuff. My lashes looked twice as long with her mascara than my crap.

A text beeped on my phone from Ash.

There in five.

My stomach flipped as I hurried back to my room and tugged on black leggings, an oversize pink thermal, and knee-high black boots. As I waited for Ash to show, I thumbed through the mail I'd picked up earlier. Ninety percent of it was bills and trash. But then my hand froze on the envelope addressed to me.

"Oh my God," I whispered.

It was from the University of Georgia. Early acceptance letters weren't supposed be sent out until next week.

I was still clutching the envelope, debating on whether or not I should open it, when there was a knock on the front door.

"Coming," I called. I stuffed the envelope into my purse, unopened, and then went to the front door.

My breath caught. I'd never seen Ash in anything but a school or football uniform. I was unsurprised to see him in the typical Savannah prep clothes, but somehow, they looked better on him than anyone else. The pressed khakis and button-up. He even had on the quintessential boat shoes. His dark brown hair was brushed off of his face and artfully arranged. Those clear blue eyes set solely on me.

"Hey, you ready?"

I nodded. "Sure. Let's go."

Nerves pricked at me as soon as I locked up and was in his car again. Maybe this was a date. It wasn't like this was my first date. Marley and I had doubled with some guys from the public school. I'd grown up with them, so it wasn't weird, but it was also *very* weird. One tried that awkward stretch at the movies to put his arm around me and subsequently punched Marley in the side of the head. It *shockingly* hadn't worked out.

"Where are we going?"

"I hope it's not too corny, but I was thinking we could ice skate."

"Not corny at all. I actually love ice skating. We just can't hurt my ankles," I told him. "I have a three-hour pointe intensive tomorrow."

His eyebrows rose. "That sounds painful."

"No, it's wonderful."

"Don't ballerinas have terrible feet from the shoes?"

"Yeah, that's true. It does hurt, but when I'm on pointe, I've never been happier."

"Must be nice to have found your passion."

"Haven't you? Or did I imagine you throwing the winning touchdown last night?"

He shrugged as he veered left down Liberty Street

toward the Civic Center, which was converted into an indoor ice skating rink every year. "I love playing football, but I'm not going to do it in college or professionally or anything."

"Well, I love dance, but I'll probably never dance professionally."

"Why not?"

"I don't know. So few people get to, and I'm not good enough. If I get to dance in college, that'll be worth it."

"Where'd you apply?" he asked as he found us a parking spot.

"All over. UGA, Georgia State, Georgia Southern, UNC–Chapel Hill, Virginia, Florida, LSU, Bama, and Kennesaw as a backup."

"And where do you want to go with that long list?"

"Well, I'd need a scholarship to even think about going anywhere out of state. Luckily, there's HOPE Scholarship for anything in state."

HOPE Scholarship was my saving grace. Anyone who graduated from a Georgia high school with a 3.0 or higher received free instate tuition as long as they maintained the 3.0 GPA at the university. It was funded by the lottery system, and I wasn't about to fuck that up.

"I'd love to go to UGA. All three of my sisters went there. Elle graduates from there in May. I don't want to be the only Greer sister to not become a Bulldog. What about you? Where'd you apply?"

He laughed derisively. "Duke."

"Fancy."

"Nah. I'm legacy," he said as he pulled into a parking spot. "There's not another option."

"There are always other options," I said as I got out of the car and came around to his side.

"Well, it's the only option if I want college to be paid for. I could use HOPE, but my dad would kill me if I didn't go to his alma mater."

"That sounds like a lot of pressure."

Ash shrugged, as if he'd come to terms with this development. "Not a big deal."

"I actually ..." I swallowed and pulled the envelope out, so he could see it. "I got this letter today."

"Whoa! Did you get in?"

I shook my head. "I don't know! I can't make myself open it."

He took the letter from me. "Do you want me to do it for you?"

I bit my lip. "Would you mind? I know my mom would want to see it, but she's not around that much right now." I realized I was babbling and shut up. "Please open it."

He made a clean tear along the envelope. He removed the papers from within. I watched him scan the papers and then look up at me gravely. My bottom lip wobbled as I braced myself for the bad news.

Then, he flipped the papers toward me, and a smile bloomed on his too-gorgeous face. "You got in!"

"I got in?" I shrieked. I snatched the papers out of his hands and jumped up and down. "Oh my God! I got in!"

Without thinking, I threw my arms around Ash's shoulders. Tears came to my eyes as all my dreams suddenly materialized before me. Everything looked possible in this moment.

He slipped his arms around my waist. "I'm so happy for you."

I pulled back slightly, suddenly embarrassed by my outburst, by throwing myself at him. We were still only inches apart. I swiped at the tears in my eyes, thankful I'd used my mom's fancy waterproof mascara.

"Sorry about that."

"Don't apologize," he said automatically. His hand brushed aside a stray strand of my natural ash-blonde hair. "It was cute."

I swallowed and took another step back to put more distance between us. "Well, I appreciate you helping me out. Celebratory ice skating?"

"I think yes."

I stuffed the papers back into my bag and jotted out a text to Marley and Josie, letting them know the good news. We walked up to the ticket booth, and as I reached for the twenty in my purse to pay for my ticket, Ash handed over cash for both of us.

"You didn't have to do that."

"Celebratory, remember?"

"Right. Well, thank you."

He handed me my pass, and then we acquired skates. I sat on a bench to lace up my ice skates, and then we stashed our belongings in a locker. Although I didn't go ice skating often, my mom had always loved roller skating. So, I adjusted quickly.

By the time I looked up again, Ash was ice skating backward in front of me.

"Show-off," I teased.

He winked at me and then held out his hands. I

placed mine in his, a tingle running all the way through my body at that first touch. His eyes lingered on my face as he pulled me along the ice.

"So ... three older sisters," he said. "How was that, growing up?"

"Amazing and trying," I told him. "I love my sisters. They're my forever people, but it's hard, being the youngest. My mom always says we're her *Little Women*. Steph is such a Meg—the oldest, already married, with a kid. Eve is definitely our Jo, headstrong and a go-getter. She lives in Chicago as a reporter. Thankfully, Elle wasn't sickly like Beth, but she's our musician. She's a music major at Georgia, playing violin."

"Which makes you Amy."

I laughed in surprise. "You've read *Little Women*?"

"Yes. Of course. It was assigned reading."

"You do the assigned reading?"

"I enjoy classic literature, thank you."

"Then, yes, I'm Amy. And my sisters would probably say, I'm the emotional, bratty younger sister," I said with an eye roll. "But I've had to live without them a lot, and that side of me only comes out when I'm with them now."

He arched a brow. "Does that make me your Laurie?"

"I don't know. Did you propose to my sister recently?"

"Should I have led with that?" he joked, tugging me off of the ice and back to our bench.

"Probably. What's your family like?"

"Only child. It's pretty quiet."

I wondered what that was like. Even when I felt alone with my mom, I was never *alone* like that.

"Do you want a drink or something?" he asked,

changing the subject again as soon as it focused on him.

"Yes, but let me get it. You got the tickets."

He opened his mouth to object, but I was already going through our locker to find some cash. Then I strode over to the vending machine.

Ash followed me. "You don't have to do that."

"It's the least I can do. This has been so much fun."

"I'm glad you're having a good time."

I fed the machine with the dollars I'd scrounged out of the bottom of my purse and pressed the button for a Coke. My Coke tumbled noisily into the bottom of the machine.

"What do you want?" I asked him.

But then there was another *clink* and another drink dropped out.

"Hey!" Ash cried. "Did you get lucky?"

"Oh my God! This happened to me last week at school. I can't believe this." I dipped my hand into the machine and pulled out two Cokes. "Two for one. Hope you like Coke."

"What kind of monster doesn't like Coke?"

I laughed and popped open my drink. The nerves I'd had earlier in the evening had disappeared. The longer I spent with Ash, the more I wanted it to be a real date. He wasn't what I'd been expecting. He didn't seem like the typical pretentious Holy Cross student. He didn't strut around like he was the star quarterback. I wasn't sure what to make of him, but I wanted to find out more.

We finished up skating and Ash took my hand as we left.

"Do you want to walk down to the riverfront?" he

asked.

"You want to walk?"

From Oglethorpe down to River Street was probably a mile in the dark. I'd walked all of those roads a million times, but I hadn't expected him to want to walk when we had his Mercedes.

"Yeah. The weather isn't as bad as last night. We could stop at Leopold's for ice cream on the way."

"Far be it from me to turn down ice cream."

I expected him to release my hand, but he laced our fingers together as we strolled under weeping willows and down the brick-lined streets of our home. Leopold's was slammed; it always was. We waited in line for scoops of ice cream and then strode down the scarily steep stairs that led to Savannah's most famous street sitting on the Savannah River.

We meandered the crowded street, finishing off our cones and darting into the confectionary stores, admiring the sugar workers handling the caramel and fudge. Alcohol was legal to drink on the streets on the riverfront, and we had to dodge one too many drunken party groups with giant slushy daquiris. We stopped right before the tunnel as a cop held up traffic on both sides to allow a couple to take wedding pictures down the middle of the street.

"Wow," I whispered. "That dress is something."

"I can't believe they're holding up traffic."

"Tell me about it."

We took the opportunity to cross the cobbled street to the river and sank onto a bench overlooking the water. Ash casually slung an arm around my shoulders. No awkwardness and no one was punched. Smooth. He drew me a little closer, and I tucked myself right into his side. Something clicked into place. Today had been pure magic. And I couldn't imagine being anywhere else in the world.

"Lila?" he whispered.

I tilted my head to look up at him from under my lashes. My heart was skittering in my chest. The rest of me frozen in place. His eyes roamed my face, lingering on my lips and then back to my wide eyes.

"Yes?"

He didn't use words. His hands slid into my hair the color of his name and drew me to him. Our lips met with all the sugary sweetness of our ice cream. That first touch sent a slow-burning fire rushing through my body. Any remaining chill dissipated in the wake of that first touch.

He withdrew to check where I was with the kiss. My eyes fluttered back open and looked up at him as I was heady with desire from the power of that one brush of his lips. Then he took my mouth for his own. His tongue swept in, caressing mine and swirling it around almost playfully. A soft groan left my lips as he dragged his teeth along my bottom lip.

I didn't know how long we kissed on that riverfront bench. I didn't remember when the world sat back on its axis. I had no recollection of the moments following that first remarkable kiss.

I knew that falling for Ash Talmadge in one kiss was foolish.

I shouldn't hand him my heart on a platter.

And yet I did it anyway.

7

SAVANNAH
DECEMBER 25, 2006

"Get bundled up, girls," my mom said. "I swear, this is the last time I'm going to say it."

My sisters Eve and Elle clambered around, trying to find their jackets, hats, and gloves. Only the oldest, Steph, was ready, and that was only because she had her own five-year-old daughter, Charity, who refused to wear any gear for our annual trip.

"Dee, please," my mom said, tossing me a scarf, "find your jacket."

Only my mom called me Dee. She had since I was a baby. Even as I grew up as Lila. It didn't matter that Steph was a Stephanie and Eve was an Evelyn and Elle was a Maryellen and I was a Delilah. We had nicknames and that was that.

"I already have it on."

"The other one. You know it's too cold for your cheer jacket."

I grumbled and went for my thicker one. I'd begrudgingly returned my ski jacket. So, I grabbed the hand-me-down that Elle had given me last Christmas. This was the only time that I was grateful for school uniforms. I shouldn't complain. There were many who were less fortunate than us. People who didn't even have winter clothes. But it was hard to keep perspective at seventeen when all my friends were on a ski trip without me.

It was probably one of the reasons for our annual Christmas tradition. Every year, Mom made us get all dressed up, and we'd dish out Christmas dinner at the soup kitchen and deliver Christmas presents to those in need. As much as we all grumbled, it was our favorite tradition. We were lucky to have a mom who cared.

The doorbell rang suddenly.

"Who is that on Christmas?" my mom asked. "Dee, can you get that?"

"Yeah, I got it."

I yanked the door open, tucking my hat into my pocket. My gasp must have been audible since the rustling in the background grew silent as I found Ash Talmadge in a suit on my doorstep.

"Ash, hey. What are you doing here?"

"Dee!" my mother said. "Invite the nice boy inside."

I breathed deeply and opened the door wider. "Why don't you come in?"

"Sure. I didn't mean to interrupt."

"It's fine," I told him quickly.

We'd hung out as much as we could since school had gotten out. I had work and dance, and he had work, so it wasn't as much as either of us wanted. Not by a long shot. But he hadn't said he was coming over on Christmas.

"Who is this, Lila?" my sister Eve asked.

"Sorry. This is Ash. Ash, this is my family." I pointed out each of my sisters, who answered excitedly at the prospect of me having a boy over. I never would have invited him in if I could have helped it.

"Pleasure to meet you all. I've heard so much about you," Ash said.

"Dee didn't mention she had a boyfriend," Steph said.

"Why don't we give them a moment of privacy?" my mom said as she saw my face turning beet red.

"We'll go to my room," I said quickly.

"Sure, honey."

Elle and Eve shared a look as I passed them. I fought the urge to punch them. I took Ash's hand and hurried him back to my room. I hadn't thought this through. Ash had never been to my house, and I definitely hadn't picked up. It was a Christmas mess. All of my presents covered my bed, and clothes were strewn on the floor.

"Sorry about this," I said, hastily hiding bras and kicking clothes out of the way.

"No, it's my fault. I shouldn't have barged in like this."

"I thought you were with your family all day."

"I am. I can't stay long. We're on our way to Christmas mass," Ash explained. "I wanted to drop off your Christmas present."

"We weren't exchanging gifts until tomorrow."

Ash's dad was going back to work right after Christmas. Something about building character again. His mom had some kind of event planning meetings, and he'd be free most of the afternoon.

"I know, but ..." He shrugged and passed me a messily wrapped gift. "I wanted to give it to you today."

"You shouldn't have. I don't have yours wrapped."

"Tomorrow is still on," he assured me.

I flushed. "All right."

"Just open it, Lila."

I tore open the Christmas wrapping paper, letting it fall to my floor. I turned the gift over in my hand. It was a copy of *Little Women*. A leather-bound copy with deckled edges and a red ribbon to mark my place.

My heart stuttered. I pressed the beautiful book to my chest. "Ash," I whispered. My gaze rose to his with a vulnerable smile on my lips. "You didn't have to do this."

"It felt fitting."

"It is. Thank you."

He pressed a kiss to my lips. I wanted to cling to him. I wanted to keep him here forever. I certainly didn't want him to go after something so thoughtful.

But then he withdrew. "As much as I'd love to stay, I have to get to mass."

"Of course. Thank you so much. I love it."

He kissed me again as if he couldn't get enough either. "Read the inscription after I'm gone."

Then, he disappeared from my bedroom. I could hear the farewells to my mom and sisters. The laughter as they tittered about his appearance. I opened the book and found Ash's clear handwriting on the inside cover.

Merry Christmas, Lila.

Always your Laurie,
   Ash

8

SAVANNAH
JANUARY 8, 2007

The whispers about the ski trip were everywhere on that first day back. Luckily, I only had my last class of the day with Shelly. So, I didn't have to face her until Spanish.

She had a smirk on her face as I stepped into the classroom. She must have known that I'd heard and was waiting for my reaction. My seat in the front row was unoccupied, but she'd taken the seat behind me. I could have chosen a different seat, but I didn't want to give her the satisfaction.

I dropped my bag and plopped down, immediately swiveling in my seat. I plastered a smile on my face. "How was break, Shelly?"

"Amazing actually." She arched an eyebrow.

"That's so good to hear. Mine ended up being incredible. Blessing in disguise that you ended up having to cancel the ski trip."

Then, I whipped back around before she could say anything else as Señora Chin began the lesson. I could practically feel her seething behind me, but I made sure not to turn around once. She had thought that she'd gotten the better of me by uninviting me to her ski trip. Well, I'd gotten something Ash out of the mix.

Once the class was over and Señora Chin handed out our first assignment of the new semester, I discreetly pulled out my phone to check for messages. Josie had sent me a series of blurry selfies with an *I miss you* attached.

"Delilah," Shelly said with a fake smile. "Walk with me."

"Sure," I said, tucking away my phone. "You have to tell me everything about break."

"Of course. Tell me about yours." She eyed me curiously. "What did you get up to?"

"I mostly worked at the dance studio, but I had a three hour pointe intensive. Plus, I worked on my tumbling. I think my back handspring is where it needs to be for competitions this semester."

"That's so good. I know you've been working on them."

We exited the broad double doors of the school. Shelly's Lexus was always parked in the first spot. She'd even chalked her name onto it at the beginning of the year, so everyone knew who it belonged to. I only lived a few blocks over. So, I always walked, even in the cold while wearing my pleated Catholic school girl uniform.

She pulled me to a stop after we stepped outside. "I don't know if you've heard, Delilah, but I ended up going skiing."

"Oh," I said, my face carefully blank.

"Yeah. Actually, like, a few football players came with us, and it kind of got out of hand. I don't think it would have been your scene. Lots of drinking and sex, and I know ... you're a virgin."

"Ah."

I tried to keep from laughing. She was going to try to claim that she had done this to me because I was a virgin and I'd have been uncomfortable. And while ... maybe I would have been uneasy with everyone naked and drunk, I still would have gone. Not that I wanted to be involved with any of that anymore. I'd been wasting my time trying to befriend Shelly and the other cheerleaders. I had Marley and Josie, and I didn't need people who would treat me like this. Didn't stop it from hurting, unfortunately.

"You understand, right?"

"Sure," I said. "I understand."

"Oh good." Her smile brightened even wider.

She thought that she'd gotten away with it and that I was just going to let her hurt me.

"I mean, if you hadn't uninvited me to your ski trip, then I never would be dating Ash now."

Shelly blinked. "What?"

"I'm dating Ash Talmadge."

"You mean you went on a date with Ash?"

"Well, yeah, like a dozen over break."

"No, you didn't."

"We spent all break together. He took me out on his parents' yacht for New Year's." I smiled daringly.

She assessed me carefully as if trying to put the pieces

together. She was silent a full beat before finally saying, "His parents don't let him date."

I shrugged. Not that I wanted to let Shelly get to me. Because I actually hadn't met Ash's parents the month that we spent together. We always met after work or over at my place or down on the riverfront. Stolen meetings and kisses and lust. But even if his parents didn't let him date or they didn't know about me ... it didn't mean we *weren't* dating.

"You didn't know that, did you?" She smirked that same look she'd given me in the classroom. "Spent all break with him, and he never mentioned that he just likes to fuck and move on because, otherwise, his parents won't let him see anyone?"

"Doesn't seem to matter."

"And he took you on the yacht," Shelly said with a laugh. "Are you still a virgin after a month spent with Ash Talmadge?"

I glared at her. "That's none of your business."

She snickered. "Maybe you should have come with me. Ash isn't exactly gentle with hearts when he decides to break them."

I was not going to have her ruin my best memory of break. New Year's on the water had been a dream come true. Ash *had* made a move, but it absolutely had not been like what Shelly was talking about. And when I told him I wasn't ready, he didn't push it. He said we could go as slow as I wanted, and he'd meant it.

"Just because he didn't care about you or how he handled your heart," I said as I headed toward the stairs, "doesn't mean he doesn't care about me."

Shelly followed me. "Delilah, I say this as someone who likes you ... you should watch out for him."

Just then, a Mercedes pulled up to the front of the school. The passenger window rolled down, and Ash Talmadge leaned toward it.

"Lila!"

I grinned with my heart full to bursting. All thoughts of Shelly Thomas fleeing my mind.

"Get in. I'll take you home."

I smiled at Shelly. Her lips were pursed at the sight. "Thanks for the advice."

Then, I dashed down the front steps of the school and into Ash's car. Shelly crossed her arms over her white button-up and navy-blue blazer and watched us with inscrutable eyes. I didn't know whether she was planning revenge or what, but I'd won this round.

Ash waved to Shelly as he pulled away. She twirled her fingers at him and raised her eyebrow before he drove out of sight.

I rocked back into the leather seat and blew out a harsh breath. "I stood my ground against Shelly Thomas."

"What happened? Was she a bitch about the ski trip?"

"Yeah. She said she did it because I was a virgin and couldn't have handled it." I rolled my eyes.

"Classic Shelly switch."

"She said something else interesting though," I said, cutting him a glance. He looked so cute in his uniform—khakis, white button-up, blue blazer, and his favorite Ray-Bans.

"Oh yeah? What's that?"

"She said that your parents didn't let you date."

He frowned. "She said that?"

"Yeah. I realized that I've never met your parents or anything."

He sighed heavily and pulled the car over to a stop in front of Forsyth Park. He jerked off his Ray-Bans and faced me. "She's not wrong."

"Then ... what have we been doing?"

"Dating," he insisted. He glanced down and then back up. "Look, my dad is ... he's an acquired taste. He's a hard-ass. He hates everything and thinks that I have to be raised the same way that he was. So, I have a job and I have to go to Duke and I can't date in high school. My mom is on too much Prozac to disagree with anything he says. We're all a mess, and I didn't want you to think that I was like them. I didn't want you to meet them and them to ruin this."

"Why didn't you tell me?" I asked, reaching across the seat and taking his hand.

"I don't have experience with this, Lila."

"Experience with what? I've heard you have experience."

"I've had sex." He traced a circle on my hand and then met my gaze. "I've never been in love."

"Ash," I whispered.

"I love you, Lila. I'm in love with you."

My throat closed, and I swallowed hard. "I love you too."

He brought my hand to his lips and kissed it. "I love hearing you say that. God, it's perfect. And I don't want anything to come between us. Especially not my dad." He kissed my hand again. "I'm going to tell them about us I promise. I just have to figure it out."

"Okay." I'd wait for it, for him. I wanted this more than anything else ever before. What was a few more weeks before he told his parents that we were together? What was the worst that could happen?

"Thank you," he said, drawing my lips to his. "I'm going to be the guy that you deserve."

"You already are," I insisted.

Then our kissing deepened until I was breathless and the windows fogged up. He unbuckled my seat belt and pulled me onto his lap. Everything felt hot and needy. I should have been heading home. I had to get to the studio tonight. But all I could think about was Ash's hands on me and his lips trailing kisses down my neck and the feel of him through his school khakis. Heat built in my core like I'd never felt before, and only the friction from his pants could make it stop.

I'd said no at New Year's. I'd said I wanted to go slow. And yet here, right now, I could go a lot further.

A tap on the window sent us both scrambling. I jerked back across the seat. Ash ran a shaky hand back through his hair as he rolled the window down.

"Afternoon, officer."

The police woman had her bike propped next to her. She looked us both over with amusement in her eyes. "You kids should probably get home."

"Yes, of course. We'll get home right away."

"This is just a warning."

"Thank you," Ash said with a radiant smile.

As soon as she was gone, Ash gunned the engine and

pulled back out on the street. I burst into laughter, and he joined me.

"Maybe we should find a better place to make out."

His eyes were still glazed with lust when he looked at me. "Maybe we should."

"Or maybe we needed the break," I said, biting my lip. "I'm not sure I'm ready for more."

He took my hand again as we parked in front of my house. "We'll go at your pace. I'm not in a rush with you, Lila."

I leaned over and kissed him again. "Thank you."

"No need," he said as he dragged a finger across my collarbone. "We can take all the time you want. This is forever."

Forever.

Ash was forever.

9

SAVANNAH
MARCH 30, 2007

Marley rolled her neck. "I pinched something in that last acro section of the dance."

"Tell me about it." I cracked my back with a sharp twist. "I really need a massage."

"Same."

We were heading out to her minivan when my phone rang in my purse. I fished it out and saw Ash's number on it. I smiled at Marley and held up a finger.

"Hey! I wasn't expecting to hear from you until later."

"Can you meet me at the park?" He sounded frantic and maybe even angry. Not at all like himself.

"Are you okay?"

"Yeah. I mean, maybe."

"Ash, are you driving? Should you pull over?"

"Please meet me at the park," he all but begged. "Near the fountain entrance?"

"Okay. Yeah, I'll see if Marley can drop me off. My mom is working tonight. She won't even notice."

He breathed a huge sigh of relief. "Thank you. I'll see you in a few minutes."

Then he hung up on me.

Marley's eyes were round. "Is everything all right?"

"I don't know," I admitted. "Do you mind dropping me off at Forsyth?"

"I can do that. It's not that far out of the way."

Marley's grandparents were stricter than my mom had ever been. If she wasn't home within a certain time frame after dance, she'd be grounded. I didn't think she'd ever date with how strict they were. They loved her, which was why they cared so much. Sometimes, I wished my mom cared a little bit more. Though at this particular moment, I didn't mind.

We pulled up to Forsyth Park, the same park Ash and I had gotten interrupted by the cop a couple months earlier. We'd spent an inordinate amount of time together in here since then, meandering the thirty acres, lounging by the fountain, and sitting lazily under the Spanish moss. Tonight, the park was dark. It was open twenty-four hours, but no one ventured in this late at night.

Marley let me out next to the passenger side of Ash's Mercedes.

He waved at her. "Thanks, Marley."

"Hope everything is okay," she said to him.

He nodded unconvincingly.

She drove away, and I sank into the passenger side. "Hey, what's going on?"

His hands still clenched the steering wheel, his knuckles gone white. "Can we drive for a bit?"

"Should you be driving?"

"Yeah. I'm better because you're here."

"Okay." I bit my lip in worry.

He put the car in drive and pulled away from the park. We drove in silence for a few minutes before he finally spoke, "I told my parents."

I straightened at that statement, my eyes going wide.

We'd been in a sort of argument about his parents for months. He'd promised back in January that he was going to tell them about me. That he wasn't hiding me. Then, every day that went by where he didn't tell his parents felt more and more like he actually *was* hiding me.

We'd been making plans to go to prom. We hadn't been going to any of the Holy Cross or St. Catherine's parties. So prom was a big day in our relationship. It was the next step. The biggest step for me. But I'd been cautious about the whole thing. Not with Ash exactly, but with the possibility that he never would tell his parents.

"They didn't take it well?" I guessed.

Because of course, they hadn't. The fantasy in my head was, they discovered their son was dating someone, and they were magically excited. They'd want to meet me and get to know me, and I'd be the daughter they never had.

But no. Of course not.

"You could say that."

"How bad was it?" My voice was even, strong. None of the meekness or general sense of impending disaster that I felt to my core.

He shot me a bleak look.

"God," I whispered.

We lapsed into silence again. I didn't even know what to say. Ash had told me time and time again that telling his parents was a bad idea. That it was better to just be us, the way that we were. Even if that meant sneaking around and meeting in the park and having adventures that no one else could ever know about.

Except I wanted more than that. I wanted Sunday brunch after mass with his parents. I wanted weekends on the yacht. I wanted lazy afternoons in his entertainment center. I wanted everything with him, and I was only getting half.

Ash after dark.

That was what I called our relationship. I got the part of him that no one else ever saw. But I didn't get the part of him that everyone else had.

He'd tossed his phone into the drink holder, and it lit up brightly every couple minutes.

"Is that them?" I asked.

"Yeah. I kind of just … left."

"Fuck. They're going to be worried."

"Let them be," he said vengefully.

"I don't want them to blame me for this."

He reached across the console and took my hand. "They won't."

But he didn't know that.

Ash drove into the empty parking lot for the Savannah Yacht Center. His parents' yacht was docked here. We'd taken it out on New Year's when they were too busy with their own party. We'd snuck back out here a couple times since then. But nothing was as magical as being on the water when the fireworks burst overhead.

He killed the engine, and I followed him down the row of docks before stopping in front of his parents'. He helped me climb on board, and we ventured below deck.

Ash found a bottle of champagne in the wet bar. "Shall we?"

"You have to drive home," I reminded him.

He drew me back into the bedroom. "What if we didn't go back home?"

"My mom would freak out."

"Your mom doesn't get home until, like, six when she's working over night. We could be back before then."

I put my hand on the bottle. "Just talk to me."

He set it down and took a seat on the edge of the bed. "They told me I wasn't allowed to date."

"Which you already knew."

"Yeah. I told them it was bullshit and that I was going to take you to prom." He ran a hand back through his hair. "That's when it got rough."

I took a seat next to him. "You can tell me."

"You don't want to hear it."

"It's okay, Ash."

"They said that this was a phase and I'd get over it. That I was too good for you and someone like you only liked me for my money."

I laughed in a self-deprecating manner. "Well, at least they got that out of their system."

"It was terrible. I defended you. I told them you weren't like that."

"You don't even have any money yet," I said with a grin, nudging his shoulder.

He chuckled. "Thanks for that."

"Look, it's not anything I haven't heard before. You don't think the girls at school haven't said every horrible thing imaginable to me? That I'm a poor scholarship student with no fashion. That I only caught you by opening my legs. That I must be some whore to keep you."

"Who is saying that?" he demanded.

I put my hand on him again. "Honestly, it doesn't matter. It hurts, but they don't say it because of me. They say it because they're projecting. I get messed up about it when it happens, but afterward, I know they only do it because they're insecure. And your parents are only saying it because they think they're protecting you. They think that keeping you from dating and keeping you from 'someone like me' will help you get further in life. They likely don't want you to make the same mistakes they made."

"That *is* very levelheaded, Lila," he said calmly.

"I've had three years of this at school. My mom handles it with a calm demeanor." I straightened and imitated my mom's gentle but firm speech. "*Girls in high school hurt people when they're hurting. Give them grace.*"

Ash relaxed a little more. "You sound just like her."

"I have a dozen of them. But she always says the same thing. *I can only be who and what I am, and I don't want to be anyone else. And I don't want to stoop to their level.*"

"That's all fine and well for the bitchy girls at school, but what the fuck am I supposed to do about my parents?"

I sighed and flopped back on the bed. "I don't know, Ash. What do you want to do?"

"Move in with your mom?"

I giggled. "She'd adopt you in a heartbeat."

"Might get awkward."

"I wouldn't mind having you right down the hall."

"Yeah?" he asked as if suddenly realizing that I was lying back on a *bed*. His hands slid up my bare legs to the skintight acro shorts and up the torso of my leotard. "You have me here, right now."

"I do. But you haven't figured out what you're going to do about your parents."

He moved his body next to mine, pressing kisses across my collarbone and down across my ribs. "We're still going to prom, Lila. Whether they want me to go or not."

"You're sure?"

"Positive."

His finger hooked the leotard strap, dragging it down my arm and exposing my breast. I shivered despite the warm, humid air in the cabin. He cupped my breast in his hand, rubbing the nipple between his fingers. I arched against him, my breathing uneven at the contact. Then, his mouth replaced his fingers, and I moaned into the empty space.

"Ash," I murmured.

He pulled down the other side of my leotard, dragging the material to my waist and baring me completely before him.

"I love your body, Lila," he said as he settled his mouth on the other nipple. "I love making you feel good."

He sucked the nipple into his mouth, grazing it with his teeth until I squirmed under him.

"I love you."

"I love you too," I gasped.

His free hand moved to my legs, spreading them slightly. I shifted self-consciously, but he didn't seem to notice. He drew his hand up, up, up my inner thigh, dragging his large, rough hand along my smooth, creamy skin until he reached the apex of my thighs. I trembled at the first touch as he pressed his palm against my core.

That friction alone made my entire body shudder. We'd gotten here before. We'd done a lot more than this. But we never had a bed and uninterrupted time on our hands. There was always a rush and sense of urgency. I never felt ready to take the next step. Which was why we'd both thought prom would be our moment. Finally our moment.

But now that I was lying back on the bed with him massaging me through the thin layer of my shorts, I knew that we'd waited long enough. He'd told his parents. He was serious about us. We both wanted it. Why wait any longer?

"Ash," I said breathlessly.

He trailed a finger down my center. "Yes?"

"I think ... I think I'm ready."

His eyes snapped up to mine. Blue meeting blue. Desire roaring through both of us.

"Are you sure? You wanted to wait until prom."

"I'm sure. I don't want to wait."

He nodded. Clearly, he wasn't going to ask me twice. He'd done this before, and I hadn't. He already wanted this, and I was filled with anticipation. Nerves built in me, but Ash was just Ash. This felt like the right time.

I wiggled out of my shorts and leotard, leaving me naked in the dim lighting. Ash shucked off his polo and khakis. I sat up to my elbow and then reached for his boxers. He stood still, letting me take the lead, letting me test the limits.

I pulled his boxers down, letting them drop to the ground, and then I took him in my hand. Not that I had any frame of reference, but he was huge. Like I had no idea how he was going to fit inside of me. I stroked him a few times, and his head dipped back. A growl escaped his throat, and I thought about doing more, but he gently pushed me backward on the bed.

He retrieved a condom out of a side drawer, and I tried not to think about what they were doing there as he tore the foil. I watched, slightly embarrassed as he pushed the condom down all the way around himself and then crawled on top of me. At the first touch of the tip of him against my opening, I jumped in shock.

"Ash," I said, suddenly wide-eyed with worry.

"Hey." He brushed my hair back and pressed a kiss to my lips. "It's okay. We can stop if you're not ready."

I swallowed hard. "I'm ready."

"I'll go slow," he assured me.

It felt good. So fucking good. Just him against me, the inch he pushed inside. I gasped in shock. I'd never experienced anything like this. Nothing compared.

He moved in and out slowly, just as he'd promised, warming me up and opening me to fit him. I was wrong about him not fitting because, he eased all the way in. The pressure was tight and almost uncomfortable. But nothing like Josie had said it would be. She deeply regretted her first time, and I couldn't imagine regretting this with Ash.

"Are you okay?" he asked once he was fully seated inside of me.

"Yes," I whispered.

He dropped a kiss onto my lips as he pulled out again, nearly as slow. A breath escaped me.

"Oh my God."

"Yes," he groaned as he pushed back in. "You ... fuck, Lila. You feel so fucking good. I've wanted this for so long."

I brought my legs up to his hips as he picked up a rhythm, pulling out and pushing back into me. My legs were trembling. My body rigid with unceasing pleasure. I didn't know what I was feeling or where it was building. Just Ash on top of me and everything coalescing into this one moment.

"I'm ... close," he said, dropping his head into my shoulder.

Then, he moved faster. A lot faster. I gasped as the pleasure shifted closer to pain. A good pain but still ... pain. Still too fast and too much. And I couldn't slow him down, but part of me didn't want to.

My fingers dug into his biceps. "Ash, too ... fast. Too fast."

"I know," he growled into my neck. "I know. I'm so close, Lila."

"Please," I whispered.

And that sent him over the edge. He shouted his pleasure into the bedroom, tipping his head back and shuddering as he finished inside of me.

I still hovered at the edge. Close to the brink but not there yet. But I was too young, too embarrassed to ask for it.

Ash finally stopped. He pulled out of me, and I winced.

"Oh, Lila, are you okay?" he asked, suddenly worried.

"Just a little sore."

"I think that's normal."

I nodded as he removed the condom and tossed it in a trash can. I got up to use the bathroom. There was a little bit of blood but nothing like what Josie had said for her first time. That was good at least. I cleaned up and then came out to find him lounging back on the bed. He patted the space next to him.

I climbed into his arms, resting my head against his shoulder. "I love you."

"I love you too." He ran his hand up and down my arm. "Was it good? Everything you expected?"

"Everything and more." I looked up into his bright blue eyes. "I'm glad we didn't wait."

"Me too."

10

DUKE
SEPTEMBER 12, 2008

"One more time through, and then that's a wrap. Here we go. Five, six, seven, eight," I called out.

The dancers moved into formation just as the music came through the speakers inside the studio. Marley was on the Duke dance team and had gotten me to come in for a weekend to teach a sideline routine for the semester. I loved the energy in choreographing. Plus, it was this amazing opportunity to work with new dancers and to see my best friend for the weekend.

"Yes!" I cried as they executed the lift perfectly for the first time all rehearsal.

I jumped in for the end, hitting the calypso at the crest and spinning out of it before moving straight into the final turn section. We all ended in a panting mess. A victory if I'd ever heard of one.

"Thanks, Lila," Hilary said as we all packed up our bags. "We were so glad when Marley suggested bringing you in. This is going to kill on the field this year."

"I can't wait to see videos!"

Marley guzzled from her water bottle as we headed out of Wilson Recreational Center and out into the fall North Carolina weather. The trees were turning colors, and the walk on campus was stunning. Georgia was all 1700s red brick everywhere you looked, but Duke was more like a gray-slate castle. Especially with the enormous chapel at the heart of it. Made me think more of being home in Savannah.

"You killed it," Marley said.

"It was so much fun, choreographing. I get some of that at Georgia but not like this."

This was pretty much the best way I could think of kicking off our sophomore year of college. I'd moved into an apartment with Channing, and then promptly driven up to Durham to see my best friend for a dance weekend. Just like old times.

I fished out my phone and saw a text from Cole.

We made a mistake. I should have come with you this weekend.

I laughed and typed back.

You have an away game. They need you on the field. #godawgs

Still.

It's three days.

You were gone all summer.

You visited four times in three months, and I came to Atlanta twice!

And?

And I'll be back in three days.

Don't have too much fun without me.

Win a football game for me today.

"Earth to Lila," Marley said. She waved a hand in front of my face.

"Sorry. Cole was texting me."

"Obviously. But ... I actually have some exciting news. I meant to tell you last night when you drove in, and, well ..."

"Spit it out, Mars."

"I have a boyfriend!"

"Oh my God!" I jumped up and down for her. "Who is he? How did you meet? Give me all the info."

"Well, his name is Samar. We met in Chemistry, and he asked me out last week. He's so cute and sweet and ugh! I'm so happy."

"Excuse me." I jerked her to a stop before the chapel. "You have been dating for a week, and I never got a phone call?"

"I knew you were coming up, and I wasn't sure if it was anything, but he's coming to the party tonight. I thought I could introduce you there. I didn't get to meet Cole for a whole month!"

"Fine, fine." I waved her away. "I'm glad you're happy, and I can't wait to meet him."

Marley prattled on about the inimitable Samar, who I truly was dying to meet. Mars had never been a big dater in high school. She had been too smart for all the high school boys. It was good to see her finding someone of her intellectual equal here at Duke.

To my utter shock, Marley had rushed a sorority. They were different at Duke than at Georgia, but still, she was the last person I'd expected to do that. So, we headed back to her sorority house to grab dinner and then go to a house party. After we changed, one of Marley's sorority sisters dropped us off outside of a house just off of campus. It was already *slammed* with people.

"You said most people lived on campus."

"They do. Mostly just fourth years live off campus," Marley said as she took my hand and pulled me inside.

We went straight for the keg on the back patio and procured beers. We dipped back into the living room, and I danced to the music blasting from speakers. Marley went in search of Samar. I nodded at her, waving her away. I could handle myself at a party. I finished off my beer quickly, wanting to hit my buzz. After another ten minutes when Mars hadn't returned, I gave up and went to get another drink.

I barely took a step when a figure materialized out of my past.

I froze. He froze.

"Lila?" Ash said over the music.

I opened my mouth and then closed it. I hadn't seen Ash Talmadge since high school graduation more than a year earlier. Part of me wished that I could say he had no effect on me. That I shrugged him off and went back to the party. But that would be a lie.

Ash Talmadge was my first love. My first everything. My heart stuttered at the sight of him. Dressed all preppy with that look of shock on his too-gorgeous face. The brown hair that he'd shorn shorter than normal and the chiseled jaw with a hint of stubble growing in. He was my Ash. And yet ... he wasn't ... couldn't be anymore.

I stepped backward.

"What are you doing here?" he asked.

I'd known he'd be here. At Duke, of course. It was his only option. I'd thought about the fact that he would be here when I visited Marley, but she'd assured me it was a big campus. The likelihood of running into him was low. But there were no coincidences between me and Ash.

"I'm here for Marley."

He held his hand to his ear and shrugged to show he couldn't hear me. Then he nodded his head toward outside. I wasn't going to go. I definitely, absolutely wasn't going to go, but my feet followed him anyway.

We stepped out into the relative quiet of the backyard after the cacophony of the party. My ears were ringing.

"Hey," I said, crossing my arms over my chest.

"Lila Greer at Duke. Who would have guessed?"

"I'm visiting Marley."

"That makes sense."

"I choreographed a sideline routine for the dance team."

I didn't know why I was still talking. There was no reason to still be talking.

"So talented."

I gritted my teeth and looked away. "I didn't think I'd run into you."

"I can tell that." He stepped back into my line of sight. "I tried to see you this summer when we were both home."

"I got your messages."

"And you're still mad at me?"

"Should I not be mad at you?"

He frowned. "No, that's fair."

"Marley is probably looking for me."

"I saw you were dating someone," Ash said before I could traipse off.

"So?" I challenged.

"Y'all were down at the riverfront this summer."

I startled at his words. "Were you spying on me?"

He laughed, and something warm settled in my stomach at the sound. I'd always loved his laugh. The way it vibrated through me.

"Savannah is a small place; you know that. I was running an errand for my dad. You didn't see me."

"Still working for daddy, I see."

He clenched his jaw. "I don't want to argue with you, Lila."

"Too late," I said, turning to stride back inside, but he grabbed my elbow to stop me.

"Hey, I don't want things to be like this with us. I know that I fucked up, okay? But you're the only person who ever knew me. Please, Dee," he said softly, "I don't want to lose you forever."

"You don't get to call me Dee. Only my mom does."

"I know," he said carefully. "Because of course, I know that. I know everything about you."

I yanked my arm out of his grasp. "Not everything."

"Can't we still be friends?"

I didn't have an answer to that. My heart was inextricably linked to Ash. I didn't know how to disentangle how I felt about him from the friendship he claimed to want. We'd never just been friends. We'd *never* just be friends.

But a part of me wanted it. I wanted to let go of this hate. I wanted things to be normal again. It took effort to hate him when I'd once loved him so much.

"Please," he added desperately.

"Maybe." I sighed. "Maybe we can be friends."

He smiled so bright that it was blinding. And as much as I wanted normal with him, I wasn't sure it would ever happen.

"There you are!"

I expected to find Marley, but instead, it was a tall redhead with a spattering of freckles across her pale skin.

"Babe!" she said, drawing out the name. "I didn't know where you went."

Then this gorgeous girl in a skintight green dress walked straight up to Ash Talmadge and kissed him on the lips.

I retreated a step in horror. We might have agreed to be friends, but I didn't know how to handle this.

He smiled down at her and slipped an arm around her waist. As if he hadn't just been pursuing me. Or maybe I'd been wrong. And his pursuit had really been in the name of friendship. Since, clearly, he was dating someone else.

"Charlie, this is my friend Lila," he told the woman. "Lila, my girlfriend, Charlie."

"Charlotte," she said as she extended her hand. "But all my friends call me Charlie."

"Delilah, but my friends call me Lila."

"I love it! What's your major here? I've never seen you around."

"Oh no, I don't go to Duke."

"Lila is here from out of town," Ash said. "She goes to UGA and studies exercise and sports science. She wants to be a PT."

I tried not to glare at him for spouting out all my dreams to this person. Or maybe it was just that he remembered all of my dreams so easily.

"Georgia!" Charlie cried. "That's so cool. What are you doing here?"

"Visiting a friend and choreographing for the dance team."

"Wow! Smart and talented. How do you and Ash know each other?"

Ash and I looked at each other. For a split second, we were back in high school, and I remembered the way he'd held me as if the world would stop turning for us and we'd be forever. Then it shattered.

"Lila and I went to high school together."

"Small world," Charlie said. She smacked Ash on the chest. "Wait, why didn't you tell me you had another friend at Georgia? We've been looking for hotels all month to go to the Georgia–Alabama game."

"Really?" I whispered.

"Yes! You don't happen to have a couch we could crash on, do you?" Charlie touched my shoulder like we were suddenly besties.

"Uh …"

Ash's face was blank. Completely blank.

What the fuck was I supposed to say to that?

"I'm from Birmingham, and I'd die to go to this game. I know we just met and all, but you seem really cool," Charlie continued. "We'll be quiet as a mouse. You won't even know we're there."

I highly doubted that.

"Sure," I said finally. I caught Ash's surprised gaze. "I'll probably be spending the night with my boyfriend anyway."

His eyes hardened. "That's nice of you, Lila."

"You are my new best friend!" Charlie said enthusiastically. "Allow me to make this huge favor up to you by showing you where the hidden liquor is at this place."

Charlie linked our elbows together and directed me back toward the house. I only looked back once to catch Ash's eye. I might be standing with his new girlfriend, but one thing was perfectly clear: he wasn't over me.

11

ATHENS
SEPTEMBER 15, 2008

"Are you sure this is a good idea?" Marley asked me over the phone. It had to have been at least the twentieth time since she'd found out about Ash. Her face at the party when she'd seen us together should be painted and hung in museums.

"No, I'm not sure."

"And you're going to tell Cole?"

"Yes, I'm planning to run it by him today actually." I put her on speaker as I tugged a dress on over my head and slid on a pair of wedges. "He's picking me up any minute."

"He's not going to like this."

"He doesn't know anything about Ash."

Marley made a small sound of protest. "For one, Lila, he should know about what happened with Ash. And for two—"

"It's going to be fine," I insisted. I picked the phone back up and took it off speaker. "I swear, I'm only doing this for Charlie."

"Not to get back at Ash?"

"Of course not."

Marley sighed. "Fine. But I was there, remember? I don't want to see you like that again."

"I remember. I love you."

"Make good choices."

"Thanks, Mom," I joked and then hung up.

I finished off my hair and makeup and went downstairs to the first floor of my new apartment. "Hey!"

Cole stood at the front door. We'd exchanged keys at the start of the semester, which felt like a big step. One that I reveled in. He was dressed to impress, changing out of his everyday athletic attire into khakis, a blue button-up, and dress shoes. He carried a bouquet of bright yellow perennial sunflowers in his hands. The head of the flower was so much smaller than what most people usually thought of when a sunflower popped into their head. They were almost more daisy-like. And also my favorite flower.

"Oh my God! These are my fav. How did you even know?"

He grinned. "I might have had help."

"Well, stop it! It's too much."

I took the bouquet and drew in the sweet scent. I loved that these flowers bloomed for literal weeks. My mom had planted them in our garden when I was a kid, and I'd gotten to watch them grow year after year.

"They're perfect. Let me put them in water."

He followed me into the kitchen as I pulled down a vase. I filled it with water as I braced myself for the next conversation. Once I put the flowers in the water, I faced him. "So, I need to talk to you."

He arched his eyebrows. "That sounds ominous."

"It's not!" I assured him quickly. "Promise. It's just, this weekend when I was at Duke with Mars, I ran into my ex-boyfriend, Ash."

"Okay?" Cole stilled, his face contemplative and cautious.

"His girlfriend wanted to come up to Georgia for the game this weekend and asked if she could crash at my apartment. I guess everything is already booked."

"It's Bama. That makes sense."

"Yeah. So, I told her it was fine if they crashed here. Is that fine with you?"

Cole wrapped his arms around my waist and tugged me close. "I don't know. Should I be concerned?"

"Definitely not." I stood tall on my tiptoes and kissed his lips.

"Well, good. If there's nothing going on between you and your ex and he's showing up with his new girlfriend, then it's not a big deal. It's not like you're still into him."

I chewed my lip. Right. I wasn't still into him. "I wanted to run it by you first."

"I trust you," he told me, lacing our fingers together. Music to my ears and also terrible nerves erupted in my stomach to be given the trust so easily, knowing how complicated things were with Ash. "Now, let's go. My friend is only going to wait so long."

I released a breath. I needed to let it all go. This wasn't the same as before. I'd been worrying all weekend about Cole's reaction, but it had been fine. It was fine.

"Okay. Remind me again what we're doing," I said once we were in his Jeep, heading out of town.

"A friend of mine is a photographer. She needed some models to take pictures for this idea she had. I kind of volunteered us."

"All right. Not a problem. Do you know what the aesthetic is?"

He grinned like he was keeping a secret. Something I'd realized was that he *desperately* loved to surprise me. The flowers were one in a long litany of surprises that he'd planned and executed.

"You'll see," was his only response.

And I did see.

I nearly shrieked with delight when he parked his Jeep next to his friend's Ford truck. The aesthetic his friend was going for was *sunflowers*. The perennial sunflowers he'd given me earlier was actually my *clue*. God, I loved him.

I jumped out of the Jeep and stared in wide-eyed wonder. The field before us was completely covered in the yellow blooms. Bright and bursting with life, like I could run for miles through the field of my favorite flowers.

"I see you approve," Cole said, slipping his hands into his pockets with a self-satisfied grin.

"You volunteered us because of this." My hand swept out to the field.

He nodded. "I knew they were your favorite."

"I never told you though."

"I pay attention. You freaked out about them in your

mom's garden on one of my visits to Savannah this summer."

"Oh yeah."

"Your mom told me they were your favorite."

"Of course she did."

"She totally winked at me, too."

I practically cackled. "That is so my mom."

"Hey!" a chirpy voice said as she hopped out of her truck. She was a curvy girl with waist-length curls, smooth brown skin, and makeup I'd kill to be able to put on. "I'm Annabelle Rodriguez. You must be Lila."

"I am," I said, shaking her hand.

"It's such a pleasure to meet you. You two look *perfect* for this shoot. Gah, I can't wait to get started." She grinned up at Cole. "Thank God we took that photography class together a year ago."

Cole ducked his head as if he hadn't wanted Annabelle to admit that.

"You took photography?" I asked.

"What? He didn't tell you? He was the best in our class."

"Ah, don't exaggerate," he said.

"He has an eye for it," she explained as we started out into the field. "If he didn't sports balls all the time, he'd probably be even better."

"Sports balls," I said with a giggle.

"I'll leave it up to the professionals," he said.

"Aye, aye," Annabelle said with an eye roll. "Now, go frolic."

I caught Cole's eye, and then together, we frolicked through the field of sunflowers. He twirled me in place, dipping me until my head was almost on the ground. I couldn't stop smiling or laughing through the whole thing. At one point, he lifted me into his arms, one of my legs bent as he kissed me.

At the end, we flopped back into the flowers, our limbs tangled.

He pulled me closer and brushed a heated kiss against my lips. "I want it to always be like this."

"Running around in a field of sunflowers?"

"That's what it's like to be with you, Lila."

My heart thudded at the words.

"I always thought that *rainbows and sunshine* shit was fake. Just some Valentine's Day–esque marketing objective to get people to watch shows and buy candy. I didn't quite realize the truth until you."

"Like you're giddy and you can hardly breathe and everything feels right in the world?"

He plucked a sunflower and placed it behind my ear. "Like I'm finally living."

THE PICTURES CAME BACK a few days later.

Cole framed his favorite, us lying down and him tucking that sunflower behind my ear. He brought it over with another bouquet of flowers and a note.

Here's to really living, sunflower.
—Cole

12

ATHENS

SEPTEMBER 26, 2008

"Cole?" I asked as I slipped into his house.

"He's out back, on the phone," his roommate Tony told me.

"Thanks."

I dropped my overnight bag at the bottom of the stairs and went to find my boyfriend. Cole was leaning against the back deck railing with his iPhone pressed to his ear. He smiled when he saw me. He pressed a kiss into my hair, and then held up one finger to say he'd be just a minute.

"Yeah, yeah. I don't think that should be a problem." He chuckled softly. "I know, and I do appreciate that. Sure, yeah, I'll see you later. Bye."

Cole hung up and then tugged me into him. "There you are!" He dropped his mouth onto mine. "I thought you were coming over right after class."

"I would have come over earlier, but I had to pack first."

"For what?"

"I'm staying the weekend, remember?"

But he clearly did not remember. His face was blank.

"I knew that you'd have people in town, but we didn't discusse you staying here."

I stayed here all the time. Most weekdays, I was here, locked away in his bed after classes, dance rehearsals, and football practices were over. I didn't know why he was being so weird about it.

"Well, yeah. I figure the apartment is going to be packed. I'd rather stay with you."

He ran a hand up the back of his neck. "Actually, Jess is coming back into town for the game, and I told her she could stay here."

My eyes widened. "Jess ... your ex-girlfriend?"

"Yeah."

"And she's coming by herself?"

"Well, yeah."

"Is she still single?"

"It's not like that. You know that we're just friends."

I did not know or believe that. Jess had graduated at the end of last year, but this wasn't the first time that they'd hung out. I strongly suspected that Jess would do anything in her power to get her clutches back into my boyfriend.

"So, I'll stay with you in your bed, and she can crash on the couch," I said with a shrug.

He managed to look even more uncomfortable. "It's actually her bed."

"Excuse me?" My voice was low and grating, full of incomprehension.

"Well, when we were dating, she bought a new mattress. She left it with me. It belongs to her."

I blinked at him. "Your ex bought you a bed while you were dating and is now *claiming* that the bed still belongs to her? Is that what you're saying?"

"It does belong to her."

Wasps had invaded my stomach. "Let me get this straight … Jess is going to be sleeping *in* your bed?"

"In *her* bed."

"And where are *you* going to be sleeping?" I asked, crossing my arms over my chest.

"On the couch, of course, Lila. It's not like that at all."

"Right. Sure. Not like that at all. Which, of course, you have to say out loud because it's so damn obvious that she wants to fuck you this weekend."

"That is not what is happening. And I don't even know why you're upset about this. How is this any different than your ex staying at your house?"

"My ex is staying on the couch with his *girlfriend*. Your ex is staying in your bed, and she's single. There's only one reason she's doing this."

"I don't see the difference."

I clenched my hands into fists. "If you were upset about Ash coming into town, then you should have said something two weeks ago. I double-checked with you to make sure it was okay. I would have told them not to come, but his girlfriend had begged me to let them stay."

"I'm not upset."

I almost rolled my eyes at the sheer gall of that statement. He *was* upset. I could see that now. He'd been so cool about it all, but it was a facade. And now he was bringing Jess in. Ugh, the whole thing was frustrating. Why couldn't he have just told me?

"This is a bad idea."

Cole shook his head. "It's not a bad idea. You have nothing to worry about. I already told her she could stay."

"Then, tell her to stay somewhere else. She went to Georgia. Surely, she has other friends."

"Most of her friends have graduated, and it's last minute."

He was resolute on this. I could see him stiffen up, as if he wouldn't even listen to reason. But apparently, I wasn't changing his mind.

"Fine," I spat.

Barry had joined Tony on the couch to play video games when I stormed through.

"Lila," Barry said, raising his hand.

I waved as I snatched up my bag off of the ground and stomped for the front door.

"Everything all right?" Tony asked.

"Ask Cole."

Then, I slammed the door in my wake, and Cole didn't follow me out. He let me walk away with this absurd problem between us. One I didn't know how to fix.

CHANNING WAS in the kitchen when I stormed into the apartment like a thundercloud. I threw my bag onto the couch and went straight for the fridge, pulling out a water and guzzling it.

"Uh, everything all right, Lila?" Channing asked.

"Cole is an asshole."

Channing laughed. "Uh, well, yeah, but I thought he was a sweetheart with you."

"He's being a fucking idiot," I growled.

"I'm making stir-fry. Why don't you sit at the table and eat something and talk to me?"

I slammed my water down on the table and plopped into a seat. Even though all I wanted to do was pace angrily. Cole was infuriating. Yes, Ash was coming over tonight, but he wasn't staying in my *bed*. I wasn't even planning to see him. I'd been *planning* to be at Cole's the entire time.

Channing dished out stir-fry for both of us and then sank down. "So, what happened?"

"Jess is staying at Cole's this weekend. In his bed."

"What the fuck?"

"Right."

"And you're just going to let this happen?" she asked, seething. "Who lets their ex stay in their bed? Is *he* staying in the bed with her?"

"Supposedly, he's taking the couch."

"They're going to fuck."

"Don't you think I know that?" I snarled. "I'm not stupid. Jess is clearly out to get him."

"And he just doesn't care?"

"I don't know. He said they're just friends and I have nothing to worry about."

Channing rolled her eyes. "He's naive if he thinks that Jess isn't going to put the moves on him."

"He wants me to trust him."

"You do. You don't trust *her*."

I dipped my head back in frustration. "I don't even know why they broke up."

Channing's eyes rounded, and she looked down at her stir-fry, moving it around on her plate. "Well, I might know that."

"You said their relationship went down in flames, but I never pressed for information. You or him."

"Maybe you should ask him about it."

"Maybe I should," I said, still staring at her.

"What I heard might not be true."

"What exactly did you hear, Channing?" I was getting nervous.

"Well, I heard that they'd been dating for almost a year, and then video footage leaked of some guys ... running a train on her."

"What?" I gasped.

"And it was sent to Cole."

My jaw hit the floor. "Holy shit!"

"I heard that Cole got into a fight he couldn't win, and the rest of the team jumped in. The coach had to break them up, and he almost suspended Cole and the other guys from playing because of the fight. I don't know how they worked it out."

My mind was whirling. "Why the hell would he let someone like that stay at his house? Why would he still be friends with her?"

Channing shrugged. "I don't know, Lila. But a girl like that isn't going to be afraid to go after what she wants."

I dropped my forehead onto the table, my stir-fry forgotten. I felt sick. Truly nauseated. "Fuck."

Channing ran a hand down my back. "Just talk to him. It'll be fine."

"Thanks, Chan."

"Anytime. Mary Elizabeth's sister is coming into town, and I'm supposed to meet her at her place in fifteen. Are you going to be okay?"

I sat up straighter and wiped a hand down my face. "Yeah. I'll be fine. Go see your girlfriend."

"Call me if you need anything."

"I will."

Channing left to go see her girlfriend, leaving me very much alone in my apartment. I should have called Josie or Marley and talked my way through this, but it was too fresh. I couldn't believe what Jess had done. Maybe it was just a rumor? Why else would he still talk to her after she cheated on him with a bunch of other guys and filmed it?

I cringed. The whole day was a disaster. It couldn't get any worse.

Then, there was a knock at the door.

I closed my eyes. I'd spoken too soon. I peeled myself off of the chair and opened the front door.

Ash Talmadge stood on the front step in all his glory.

"Hey," I said, holding the door open.

He entered, carrying a duffel bag and messenger bag. I looked past him in confusion.

"Where's Charlie?"

Ash waited for me to look at him before responding, "We broke up."

"On the way here?"

"Yesterday."

He was so calm. But today was *not* the day. I was

furious about Cole and Jess and everything I'd learned. I couldn't deal with Ash too.

"And you're here, why?"

Ash shot me that confident smile that normally worked quite well on me. But right now, it made me see red.

"What? I can't stay?"

"No," I snapped. "No, you can't stay. The only reason I even let you come up is because you had a girlfriend."

"Is there a reason I can't stay now that I'm single?"

I glared at him. "Don't. Just fucking don't. I was being generous because I liked Charlie. I don't like you."

He didn't even look offended. He didn't believe me. "Come on, Lila. I thought we were past that. Friends."

"We're *not* friends. You know we're not. Go stay with one of your other friends."

"Their places are full. That's why I needed to stay here."

"Why *Charlie* needed to stay here! This has nothing to do with you."

"Well, there's nowhere else for me to stay."

"Then, go home!"

That must have gotten through to him. Because that delicious smile slipped off of his mouth, and I saw the other side of Ash that I'd always known was lurking underneath. The one who dealt with his hard, traditional father and drugged-out mom. The one who knew exactly where to push to get the reaction he wanted.

"Why should it matter if I'm here? I thought you were staying with your boyfriend."

I clenched my hands into fists. "Change of plans."

I had no intention of telling him about Jess, but I didn't want him here either. Even if Cole fucking deserved it for his bullshit.

"Trouble in paradise, love?"

"Go fuck yourself," I snapped at him before turning on my heel and heading toward the stairs that led to my second-story room.

"Wait, wait," Ash said, softening.

He grasped my hand, and sparks shot through my body. I hated that he could still draw that reaction from me. That the year apart hadn't dampened anything between us. I yanked my arm back.

"I already had a ticket to the game. I didn't think it would be a big deal since you'd be with Cole. If it's a big deal, then I can try to find somewhere else to stay."

"I'd appreciate that. If *nothing* comes up, you can crash. But it's just the couch. There's nothing ... you know."

His eyes smoldered at the insinuation. "I do know."

Nothing would be happening with us. The whole thing would be easier if he wasn't here. Because as much as I didn't trust Jess with Cole, I didn't trust myself alone with Ash either.

SEPTEMBER 27, 2008

"This game is terrible," Channing said. She leaned drunkenly on her girlfriend. "Mary Elizabeth, make it better."

I laughed hysterically. Channing and I had gotten way too hammered, pregaming all day for the Georgia–Alabama blackout game. We'd gotten up at the ass crack of dawn to get on *College GameDay* and progressively gotten more intoxicated all day, waiting for the night game to start. And now, we were losing.

More than ninety thousand people in the stadium, the first official use of Georgia's black uniforms, everyone screaming our heads off, and none of it mattered. Alabama was still running over us. It was embarrassing. If I didn't love my team so much, I might have left after it started to look bleak. Worse than that, Cole looked terrible. Completely off his game. I'd been to every game this season and sat through hours of footage of him playing. But damn, today, he arguably looked like shit.

I wondered how much of that was due to our argument. If him dropping that last pass when he normally had sticky fingers was my fault. And if the whole damn game had gone to pieces over one stupid argument. I wanted to win. I didn't want to be fighting with my boyfriend. But that was where we were. And frankly, there was nothing to do but sit by and watch the train wreck.

By the time they called the game, everyone was as beaten down as the team. We streamed out of the stands and headed downtown to drink away our despair.

"The rest of the girls said to meet them at Boar's Head," Channing said.

Channing tugged us farther down Jackson Street toward Boar's Head—an enormous bar with a two-story outdoor patio packed to the gills and an underground bar, complete with pool tables, shuffleboard, and beer pong. We took the stairs to the basement bar. Half of the dance team was in attendance, shaking their asses to the rap music. We joined them on the floor while Mary Elizabeth went for shots with her sister. They returned a few minutes later, holding out shots to us.

"Here we are!" Mary Elizabeth cried.

I held it up to toast as Channing shouted, "To still being better than Alabama."

The entire bar went up in a round of shouts and applause at her proclamation.

"Hell yes!" I called and then tipped the drink back. It burned all the way down. I blinked back the tears in my eyes. "What the hell, Mary Elizabeth?"

She grinned. "Four Horsemen."

"Jesus, no wonder I saw black."

I stumbled away from my friends to grab a drink that wouldn't ruin my liver quite as fast. Who had let them choose the drink anyway?

I leaned over the bar, waving at the bartender to get his attention. He tipped his head at me, and I called out for a vodka cranberry. Meanwhile, I held tight to the bar to get the spinning under control.

"Holy shit! Look, y'all, it's 'Hey There Delilah'," a guy said as he approached me.

My face soured. Only one group of people had ever called me that. And go figure, I'd managed to end up at the same bar as Ash and his asshole high school friends. I didn't blame Ash for not wanting to crash with Chuck Henderson. His lackeys, Greg and Joseph, weren't too bad, but Chuck was as much of a ringleader as Shelly Thomas.

"Chuck," I all but growled.

"Delilah, I must say, you have cleaned up nicely," he said, his eyes roaming my body. "No wonder you were fucking her in high school, Ash." He smacked Ash in the chest.

Ash's fist clenched, and he shouldered Chuck out of the way. "Why don't you shut the fuck up?"

"That would be excellent advice."

Chuck held his hands up. "Hey, I was joking."

"No, you weren't."

"No, he wasn't," Ash agreed.

Our eyes met, and that mutual understanding passed between us. I'd been lucky the last year to not run into anyone at UGA who had gone to my small high school or the all-boys equivalent. Now, Ash had brought them right to me. Great.

"Of all the bars in Athens, you had to choose this one."

He shrugged. "Chuck's choice."

"Here you go," the bartender said, sliding a drink to me.

"I got it," Ash said. He withdrew his credit card and passed it to the bartender. "Can I get a Jack and Coke and five shots of tequila as well?"

"Sure, buddy."

"You didn't have to get my drink," I told him as I sipped on the drink that tasted mildly like swill.

"For the trouble," Ash said with a dazzling smile.

I shrugged but wasn't going to turn down a free drink.

The bartender passed Ash his drink and then laid out five oversize shot glasses, filling them nearly to the brim. Salt and limes were dropped onto a napkin next to the drinks. Ash nudged one toward me.

"Oh no, I already had a Four Horsemen."

"Damn, Delilah," Chuck said. "Who knew you could hold that kind of liquor?"

I couldn't. But the challenge in Chuck's voice made me pick up the tequila shot. Mind you, it was definitely more like two or two and a half shots. And the last thing I wanted to do was drink it, but fuck Chuck Henderson.

"To high school," Chuck declared.

"Ew," I said under my breath as I clinked glasses with Ash.

Then, I downed the contents of the drink, latching on

to the bar to keep from spinning. I scrambled for a lime to try to douse the fire in my gut.

I was not going to be sick. I was not going to be sick. I was not going to be sick.

Maybe if I said it on repeat, it might be true.

"Lila, there you are!" Channing said. "You've been gone so long. We had to send out the search party."

Chuck took one look at Channing and stepped forward, as if he were king of this place. "Hey there, baby."

Channing wrinkled her nose. "Not interested."

"Come on," Chuck continued over her objection.

"She said no," Ash said.

"Not that I need a reason," Channing snarled, "but I'm here with my girlfriend."

"Oh, I'd watch that."

I stepped between Channing and Chuck before Channing could deck him, which he rightfully deserved. "Go fuck yourself, Chuck. You weren't cool in high school, and now, you're a fucking prick."

Ash shook his head. "What the fuck, man?"

Chuck laughed, as if the entire thing were a joke. "I was just kidding. Christ, everyone is so sensitive."

Ash ignored him and followed me and Channing away from the guys he'd gone to high school with. "Hey, I'm sorry about him."

Channing rolled her eyes. "As if that's the first time I've heard that."

"Still shitty."

"It is," I agreed. "Channing, this is Ash."

"Ash," Channing said with raised eyebrows. "*The*

Ash?"

He shrugged, all nonchalant. "Sure."

"The one who showed up without a girlfriend this trip?"

"Didn't work out."

Channing grinned devilishly at him. "Oh, I like you. Dance with us."

I giggled at Channing's easy acceptance of Ash. Just like that. Despite all the frustration she'd had with him earlier, he'd stood up for her, which made him cool as far as she was concerned. Plus, she was still mad at Cole. As was I.

It was another hour of drinking and dancing before I realized that I might have started the night off a little too strong.

"Lila, are you all right?" Ash asked.

He steadied me against him, and I giggled all over again.

"I'm fine," I said, my speech slurred. I was also seeing two of him, which made me laugh louder. I reached my hand out to touch the second part of him. "Oh my God, what a trick. There's two of you."

His eyebrows rose. "Jesus, you're trashed."

"Shh," I said, putting my hand on his mouth. I missed the first time but managed it the second. "I'm fine, Ash. Fine."

He took my hand off of his lips and held up his fingers. "How many fingers am I holding up?"

"Three." I counted them with my hand, missing one and starting over again. "Maybe four."

"Okay, I should get you home."

"Nooo," I cried. "Party pooper."

Ash ignored me and turned to Channing. "Hey, I'm going to get Lila home. She's plastered. Do you and Mary Elizabeth need a ride?"

"No, we're good. I don't think we had as much as her. We're going to stay until bar close."

"Cool," Ash said. Then he slid an arm around my waist and directed me toward the stairs.

"I don't want to leave."

"I know," he said as he maneuvered me up the short flight of stairs. After two unsuccessful attempts, he slipped an arm under my legs and hoisted me into his arms. He carried me up the steps and then set me back down.

"That was gentlemanly."

"Not the first time I've had to carry your drunk ass."

"Hey!"

Ash chuckled, and we shared a moment of easy reminiscence. "I suppose that time was my fault."

"You stole a bottle of bourbon from your dad's wet bar, and we played strip Truth or Dare until I threw up in the bushes."

He laughed again. "Yeah, okay, but it was totally worth it."

"Ass."

He was still grinning about the memory as he called us a cab. Shockingly one showed up quickly. Must have been because we were leaving before bar close. I gave the guy my address, and we pulled away.

I tipped my head back against the seat. "You didn't have to come with me."

"Yes, I did."

I touched his hand. "Thanks."

"Anytime, Lila."

A few minutes later, the cab pulled over in front of my apartment. After I nearly fell out of the car, Ash got an arm around me and steadied me for the walk up a flight of stairs to my door. I rummaged through my small purse for my keys and failed twice to insert it. The keys fell out of my hand and I cursed violently.

"God, you're a mess."

He picked up the keys I'd dropped on the ground and got the door unlocked, pushing it open so I could stumble inside first. I didn't think anything about the lights being on. I must have left them on this morning when Channing and I hurried out for *College GameDay*.

"Lila," Ash said softly. He nodded his head into the apartment.

I whirled around, nearly falling again. I reached out for the stair banister to keep me upright. And then I saw what Ash had been gesturing at.

Cole was here.

MY STOMACH HIT MY FEET, and I sobered up in the same split second. I righted myself against the banister. The moment stretched into infinity. Me and Cole and Ash. All in the same place. All together.

"What exactly is going on here?" Cole asked. His voice was tight and controlled. Anger. Very barely suppressed anger.

I knew immediately how this looked. I'd told him that Ash was staying here with his girlfriend. And now, we were here sans girlfriend and I was drunk to boot. It wasn't how it appeared, but it sure looked bad.

My face flushed red. "Uh, Cole, this is Ash." I gestured behind me. "Ash, Cole."

Neither moved. I didn't know why I'd ever envisioned them coming to a place where they could look at the other as an equal. There was no truce here. No stepping forward and accepting the other's presence.

"Where's his girlfriend?"

I bit the inside of my cheek. This was going to hurt.

"We broke up," Ash said levelly. He arched an eyebrow in challenge and shut the door behind him. Bold. And pathological.

"He's not staying," I assured Cole. "And he didn't stay last night either. He was just making sure I got home okay."

"I'm sure he was." He looked like he wanted to put a fist through the wall. Or maybe through Ash's face.

I needed to wrestle back control of this situation. "What are you doing here?"

A muscle in Cole's jaw flexed. Apparently, that was the wrong question to ask.

"I thought you were with Jess."

Ash shifted behind me. I glared at him for a minute, but he just smirked. I hadn't mentioned what was happening with Cole and his ex-girlfriend. But he'd assumed something was up, and he'd been right.

"I came to apologize," Cole said. "Maybe we should talk somewhere more ... private."

"Yeah. Sure. Of course." I turned toward Ash. "We'll be right back. I don't know if you want to …"

"I'll wait," Ash said.

Fuck, the look he shot Cole. He wanted to goad a fight out of him. He'd always been that way, but it was *not* helping right now.

"Fine." I nodded my head toward the stairs. "Come on."

I didn't wait to see if Cole followed. I stomped up the stairs. This whole week was a huge pass. I wanted it to be over and never think about it again.

Cole did follow me, closing the bedroom door behind him. "Lila …"

"Nothing was happening with Ash," I told him before he could say anything else. "I don't want you to think that you and I were in a fight and so I'd do anything stupid. He was at the same bar as me, and I was hammered, so he was making sure I got home okay. That's all."

"Okay," he said, his arms crossed over his chest. "I believe you."

"Do you? Because you look skeptical."

He gritted his teeth. I could see him trying to control the anger burying through him. "Yeah, it sucked to watch you walk in that door with him. And it's fucking suspicious that he showed up here without his girlfriend. Not to mention he just *happened* to be in the same bar as you."

"I know how it looks."

"Bad," Cole said.

"Yeah, well, I was pissed at him for not telling me about Charlie, and I kicked him out. This isn't what it looks like."

Cole dropped his arms and sighed. "I want to believe that, but I saw the way he looked at you."

"Then you can understand how I felt about Jess staying with you."

"I can," he said. His hands rested on my shoulders, and he dropped his forehead onto mine. "We didn't need privacy because I was mad about Ash or came to talk about Jess." His hands moved into my hair, tipping my head up to meet his big blue eyes. "We needed privacy because I need to apologize."

His lips crashed down on mine. All the notes of his apology in that one fervent moment of desire. My response mirrored his. I was still drunk enough to be on fire with need for him. Not to forget our argument, but to use it as fuel. To fan the flames.

"Cole ..."

His hands slipped down to my thighs, hoisting my legs up around his waist and walking me back to the bed. We slammed down on it, breaking apart with a short laugh at the squeaking from my bed.

"Should we talk first?"

But Cole was already sliding down my front and hiking up my short black game day dress. His fingers hooked under my thong, yanked it down to my ankles, and then tossed it to the floor.

"Talk later," he said.

Then, he dived between my legs. I gasped at the first touch of his lips on my body. The gentle nips along my inner thighs before he reached what he was after. He flicked his tongue along my clit, and I bucked beneath him.

He used his arms as leverage to hold me open before him on the bed. He was so much stronger than me. I couldn't move even if I wanted to, and as he ravaged my pussy with his tongue, I couldn't imagine ever moving from this spot.

"Fuck, you taste good," Cole said.

I squirmed under him, hot with need from the comment. "Oh God."

"I could eat this pussy every day."

My face and back flushed at the filthy words. I clutched the mattress as he released one of my legs to bring his fingers up to my opening. He dragged two fingers through my wetness before delving inside of me.

I bucked off the mattress. I was so close. Unbelievably close.

"Come for me, baby," Cole said, pumping his fingers in and out and then trailing his tongue in tight circles around my clit.

Between the alcohol coursing through my veins and his tongue on me and his fingers inside me and those words urging me, something snapped. I cried out shamelessly. My body went taut as a bow. Everything tightened as the orgasm ripped through me.

Then it released, and I lay, spent on the bed. My eyes slowly opened and stared at him in a drunk, just-sexed stupor.

He withdrew and removed the remainder of his clothes. His dick sprang free of his boxers, and I could see what my orgasm had done to him.

He leaned his muscular body over mine. The tip of him sliding across my wetness. "I want you to come at least one more time. I'd keep you coming all night if I could."

His lips pressed to mine, and I tasted myself on him. My body was shaking with anticipation. I wasn't ready for more, and also, I was so fucking ready for more and more and more.

"Tease," I groaned, lifting my hips to try to get him inside of me.

"Oh, did you want something?" He pressed a kiss to my nose and then sat up, angling my hips up to meet him. Then with exaggerated slowness, he slid into me.

"Oh fuck," I murmured.

"Fuck, fuck, fuck," he said when he bottomed out. "You're so tight."

"Cole." I wiggled my hips to try to get him moving. But it was a sight to see him on his knees with his dick buried in me. His head tipped back and eyes closed as he enjoyed the feel of me. "Please."

He leaned down on one elbow, brushed a kiss to my lips, and began to move. Slow and steady at first to bring me back to the brink, but then neither of us could hold out any longer. I dragged my red acrylic nails across his back, leaving my own marks. His fingers dug into my hips, using them as an anchor as he plunged into me over and over again on the creaky bed.

"Close," I told him. "So fucking close."

He lifted me up into his arms so that we were both sitting up and I was on top of him. I leveraged myself against his hips, slamming back on him. Wanting the sweet release that was within reach.

He took over the rhythm and used my body, bouncing

it up and down on him until I cried out as my orgasm hit at the same time as his. He grunted, shooting up into me one last time. I threw my arms around him as everything went hazy and I saw stars.

I flopped backward on the bed, my hands over my head, and I smiled up at him.

"Wow," I whispered.

"Yeah. Fuck, Lila."

"That was some apology."

He fell onto the bed next to me, kissing my forehead. I padded out of bed to clean up, and then he followed. When we both got back in bed, he wrapped an arm around my shoulders and tucked me in tight.

"One day, we're going to have to not use sex to solve our problems."

He kissed me again. "You're right."

We lay in silence. Both of us knew that we needed to have a real conversation, but neither of us wanted to go there yet while still trapped in the afterglow of our sex.

Then the downstairs door slammed shut, loud enough to practically rattle the hinges.

I winced at the sound. Ash must have left. He'd probably heard everything. Fuck.

"I'm sorry about Jess," Cole said in the bubble of silence that fell after Ash departed.

"I'm sorry about Ash."

"Yeah."

"I don't understand how you could still be friends with her after what she did to you."

Cole sat up on an elbow. "We've never talked about this before. What did you hear that she did to me?"

I flushed again, unable to say the words.

He nodded his head. "You heard about the train."

"Uh, yeah …"

"I'd hoped you'd never hear about that. I hate that it's still circulating. It's a vicious rumor." He tipped his head back in frustration.

"Well, what really happened?"

"Look, I didn't tell you what happened with Jess because it isn't my story to tell."

"Your breakup isn't your story to tell?" I asked skeptically.

"Jess was raped."

I sat up in horror. "Oh my God."

"Yeah." He ran a hand back through his hair. "She was at a party, and a guy slipped something in her drink. Then, he took her out back and …" He gestured to off to indicate what had happened. "One of her friends found it happening and swore she was going to call the cops, but she brought her to me first. By the morning, Jess didn't want anyone to know. She was humiliated and ashamed, and … she still can't talk about it. She wouldn't go to the police. She said they wouldn't do anything."

I squeezed my eyes shut. "I hate that she's right."

"Well, her friend told me who did it. I found the guy, and a few other players and I beat the shit out of him. Decided it was as much justice as he deserved. He tried to get us kicked off the football team." Cole shrugged. "Didn't work."

"Wow," I breathed.

"Yeah. And well, it didn't work out with us after that. She broke it off and asked to remain friends. That it wasn't me, just that she couldn't be with anyone right now. She's in therapy in Atlanta and doing a lot better. But it will never be that way with us again."

"God, Cole, I'm so sorry. That's ... that's terrible. I can't believe that happened ... and yet ..."

"Yeah, and yet I can. It's so utterly fucked." Cole shook his head, the anger of the incident still with him. "And Jess said it was okay for me to tell you. I wanted you to know the truth."

I put my hand on his. "Thank you for trusting me."

"Lila, I love you."

My throat closed in shock. We'd been together almost six months. I was sure that I was in love with him, but I hadn't wanted to say it since he'd never said it. "I love you too."

He swiped my hair out of my face. "I've wanted to tell you for so long. I just ... I was jaded. So cynical about relationships. You were everything I wanted, and I don't know ... I kept waiting for the other shoe to drop. But I don't want to feel that way anymore. I want us to be together."

"I want that too."

"Tell me everything," he said, pulling me close again. "Tell me everything about you. All the barriers, all the walls, all the cynicism. And I'll tell you everything too. I'll do anything to make this work."

I nodded, letting the words finally out. "It started with my dad. He left when I was a baby. He stayed around for my sisters, but it was like I was one too many kids."

"Fuck."

"I never met him. He left my mom the house so that

she wouldn't come after him." I shrugged. "It's hard to trust anyone after that. To not take it personal."

"I understand," he said, looking off into the distance. "I feel like I'll always be in my dad's shadow. How much of my talent is because my dad had talent? How much of it is his connections in football? How many more times do I have to hear that I'm the son of the great Hal Davis before that's all I am?"

"I never thought about how upsetting that would be. I always envied your relationship with your dad."

"I love him," Cole said at once. "He's a great dad, but I want to be great on my own. Without always following in my dad's wake."

"We're both a little fucked up."

He laced our fingers together. "I guess we are."

"Maybe we can try to heal each other ... be something besides what our dads made us."

"I'd like that," he said softly.

I could feel the fight leaving him. He'd played a four-hour game today. I was sure he was tired, and after our declarations and the shift in our relationship, he was ready to sleep.

And I could have let him.

I could have held back. I could have kept my secrets. But we'd agreed to heal. How could I heal without confessing everything? Giving him it all?

"Before you sleep, there's more," I whispered.

He patted my hand. "I'm awake. Tell me."

So, I did.

I told him everything about me and Ash.

And how we'd burned to ashes.

14

SAVANNAH

MAY 5, 2007

Prom on my birthday couldn't have been more perfect. My mom had taken the day off from work, both jobs, to make sure she was here for the big moment. We'd gone shopping earlier in the month to find me *the* dress. Then Josie had come into town, and with Marley, the lot of us got mani-pedis. We spent the rest of the afternoon doing my hair and makeup.

Now, I stood in my bedroom with Marley and Josie impatiently waiting for Ash to show.

"I can't believe your dad let you drive down here all by yourself," I told Josie.

She grinned, leaning back in her midriff-baring shirt and tiny skirt. Clothes Marley and I could never get away with. "Yeah, he said if I wanted to be there for your birthday, then I should be. You only turn eighteen once!"

"Nothing about your mom?"

She shook her head. "He didn't say that I had to stay with her. And thank God, right? That would suck. I'm crashing with Mars. We're going to do the whole slumber-party thing."

I rolled my eyes. "Do try not to corrupt our lovely Marley."

Marley swatted at me. "You two need to cut it out. It's not like I'm unaware of what happens in high school—parties and alcohol and boys and stuff."

Josie shot her a wicked grin. "We're going to find a party and get in trouble."

"Your grandparents are never going to let you go."

"They think we're with you," Josie said. "It'll be fine."

Marley shrugged. "It's going to be a disaster."

I laughed. "I wish I were going with."

"We wish we could spend this night with you too!" Josie said.

"Your eighteenth birthday!"

"What do you think Ash is going to get you?"

I shrugged. "I have no idea."

But my eyes drifted to my bookshelf, where four different copies of *Little Women* rested in a place of prominence. One for every month we'd been dating. And this was month five and my birthday. I was hoping for another book. I wanted to fill a library with them.

The doorbell ringing sent all of us shrieking with excitement. I stuffed my phone into my dainty little purse and exited out of the bedroom after Marley and Josie. My mom was already at the door, pulling it open.

"Hello, Ash," she said.

"Mrs. Greer," he said with a nod. He'd never gotten used to calling my mom Deb, like she'd asked.

"Why don't you come inside?"

"Thank you." He entered, carrying a corsage box in his hand.

It felt like something straight out of a movie. My friends parted, allowing me to step forward so he could get his first real look at me. My dress was a full-bodied Cinderella number in a silver blue that made my blonde hair shine. The top was strapless and corseted with a sweetheart bodice.

It was the first dress I'd tried on and the most expensive. I'd tried on everything else in the whole damn store to try to convince myself I didn't love it. But in the end, my mom had conceded that I was only going to prom once and it was worth it. I'd never loved her more.

"Wow," Ash breathed. His eyes were wide as they dragged up and down my body. "You look incredible."

"Thanks. You look great too."

He was the kind of guy who already owned a tuxedo, but he'd personally gone to get a bow tie and vest in the same ice blue of my dress. It was practically the same color as his eyes. As I stepped up to greet him with a hug, I'd never felt like we were more of a matched set.

My mom hurried to the fridge to retrieve the bouton-niere that we'd purchased. After a few awkward moments and a pricked finger, I managed to attach it to his tuxedo. Then, he slid the bracelet corsage onto my wrist. It matched my dress with ivory and dark blue roses mixed with baby's breath.

My friends oohed and aahed at the arrangement. My mom took pictures. Then we were herded outside, where we posed together for picture after picture. It felt kind of ridiculous, but it was Ash, so I couldn't even be uncomfortable. He kept a smile on his face and didn't complain once about the number of pictures my mom wanted of us.

What felt like an hour later, we were ushered into Ash's Mercedes and driving away for our dinner reservations at Garibaldi's, an upscale Italian seafood restaurant that I couldn't even imagine stepping foot in, let alone eating in.

"So ... how'd it go with your parents?" I asked him now that we were alone.

He'd only told him parents about me five weeks ago. Their blowup had been like dropping an A-bomb in his living room. His relationship with his dad had always been tenuous at best, but now, it was outright hostile.

"It's fine," he said.

"You didn't tell them," I accused. Even though I knew that his parents were the worst and they would have stopped him from going, I still deflated.

"I told my mom," he said with a sigh. "She kept my dad distracted." He glanced over at me with a grimace and took my hand. "I know it's not what we wanted, but at least I didn't have to sneak out. Let's forget about it."

I nodded. It definitely wasn't what we'd thought it would be. I still hadn't really ever been at his house. He had a trellis that I used to climb into his second-story bedroom, but they had a full-time cleaning staff, and he didn't want to risk one of them finding out and telling his dad. Nor had I ever met his parents, obviously. Ash after dark remained in full effect.

Despite that fact, I tried to let it all fall off my back. We couldn't change any of it, and I might as well enjoy our night. Garibaldi's was even more delicious than I'd imagined.

"You ready for the dance?" Ash asked.

He took my hand as we headed back to his car parked several blocks away. We hadn't been able to find a spot downtown for fifteen minutes and had almost been late to our reservation.

"I am very ready," I said with more bravado than I felt.

In fact, I was nervous. This was actually the first time Ash and I would be out together. We hadn't gone to any parties or been seen together, except with my friends and family. We skipped Holy Cross parties. We avoided the St. Catherine's bonfires on Tybee Island. Instead, we spent all of our time together. Where we didn't have to deal with the rest of the high school having an opinion about our relationship. And where I'd also come to realize ... no one could go back to his parents about us. Strategic, if a little heartbreaking.

But Ash had insisted on prom.

We were doing this.

His dad would find out, but it was one night. And we'd get to have this night. On my birthday of all days.

Ash parked in the Westin parking lot on Hutchinson Island across the river from the riverfront. We entered through the lobby to the first-floor ballroom. The two high schools had joined together for prom, as was tradition. Otherwise, prom would have been too small for both. The ballroom was decorated in some vague Hollywood theme. But the best part of the space was the outdoors grassy area, complete with a dozen chic couches and chairs in front of firepits. The view across the river into downtown Savannah was spectacular, and more than a few people were already posing for pictures with their dates outside.

"This is even better than I imagined," I gushed.

"Me too. I thought it'd be cheesy."

I laughed. "Same. Or like that time Meg went out into society and everyone called her Daisy."

"Laurie saved her then," he reminded me as he pulled me out onto the nearly empty dance floor.

"Laurie was an ass!"

He grinned devilishly. "Yes. He generally was. But they danced all night after he apologized."

"True."

"As we shall."

I gasped as he spun me around in a quick circle. "And who taught you how to dance?"

"I, unfortunately, was part of a cotillion last year. I had to be an escort and dance and everything."

"Oh my God." I chuckled, picturing him being so uncomfortable, doing just that. "Who did you escort?"

He frowned slightly. "Shelly."

"Oh," I said.

"Yeah. Ancient history."

I chose not to think about that fact and went back to dancing. I knew everyone at my school. It was impossible not to with only three hundred and fifty in four grades, but I wasn't *friends* with pretty much anyone. Not after how Shelly had treated me about the ski trip. Even the other girls I'd grown close to distanced themselves.

"Y'all!" someone called, rushing into the ballroom. "Shelly just showed up in a Hummer stretch limo!"

A group of girls hastened outside to see the vehicle. I rolled my eyes and kept dancing. But I was anticipating the moment when she showed up. It was hard not to with that kind of entrance.

Shelly Thomas made quite an appearance with Chuck Henderson on her arm and her group of lackeys following in her wake. She had on a bright red dress that clung to her skin and rippled in the lighting. She'd bragged over the last weeks about how she'd had it custom-made by a designer in Paris. Her dad had flown the designer in for adjustments.

I'd rolled my eyes then, but it was truly stunning. Definitely nothing off the rack for her.

I chose to ignore her, and while Shelly and her entourage were outside, taking pictures, I spent the next hour enjoying the freedom to be with Ash exactly how I'd always wanted. It wasn't like we were hiding our relationship, but we weren't *not* hiding. So, this felt like a whole new world with him.

We danced and ate dry cake and watched one of the Holy Cross guys spike the punch. "Hey There Delilah" came on the set list, and we both groaned. But then I said *fuck it*, and we were out there, singing and dancing louder and bigger than anyone else. The night was like a dream that I never wanted to end.

Until Shelly appeared out on the dance floor.

I tried to pretend that she wasn't there, but she tapped me on the shoulder.

I took a deep breath and whirled around. "Hey, Shelly! Love the dress!"

"Thanks, Delilah. Yours is … nice too."

A few people snickered behind her.

"Thank you," I said, pretending that she wasn't trying to insult me. "Have a nice night."

Shelly sighed heavily, and I could feel her eyes on us. "I can't believe it's come to this."

"Come to what?" I asked.

Ash looked steely. "Let it go, Shelly."

"I mean ... you two really *are* dating."

"We've been dating for months."

"Yeah. It was one thing for you to say that and another thing for him to bring you here." She looked over at Ash. "It was funny at first, but now, it's just sad, Ash."

"Stop it," he ground out.

My stomach fluttered. "What's funny?"

"I don't know how long this joke can go on, Ash."

My voice was very small. "What joke?"

"I mean, obviously, he went out with you as a joke because I asked him to," Shelly said, as if it were obvious.

"What?" I asked. "That doesn't even make sense. Why would you do that?"

"It was a joke. Just one date and I'd tell everyone that it was fake." She shrugged.

"But no ... it's not fake."

Shelly pulled out her phone and scrolled through her texts. "Here. See for yourself."

I numbly took the phone out of her grasp and read the text messages. My eyes rounded as I read and the last two jumped off the screen at me.

So, you'll do it? You'll go out with her?

Yeah, I'll ask her out. It'll be funny. She'll think I'm actually interested.

I shoved the phone away from me. My hands shaking. I didn't want to believe this. I didn't want to believe any of this. This was Shelly Thomas. She wanted to hurt me. And Ash...Ash and I had something special. We did, didn't we? It wasn't just a joke concocted for Shelly's benefit.

My eyes found Ash, but he had his closed, as if he couldn't believe this was happening. Then, those ice-blue eyes opened, and I saw the truth in that look. A gunshot went off in my gut.

I staggered back a step. "Ash?"

"Lila ..."

"No, no, no ..." I said over and over again.

"It's not like that."

"I mean, I know that you wanted to humiliate her. But you took this to another level, Ash," Shelly said with teeth. "I keep waiting for the punch line. Were you waiting for sex?"

I stumbled back another step. There was buzzing in my ears. Everyone was looking at us. Shelly's lackeys were laughing. Chuck Henderson stepped up to congratulate Ash. Ash shoved him out of the way. He must have said something because Chuck gave him a look like he was insane. It all happened in a millisecond.

Then, it crashed back down around me.

"Lila, please," Ash said, reaching for me.

And I couldn't handle it.

I couldn't stand here and see Shelly's triumphant

smirk and Chuck's bewildered face and the laughs from the cheerleaders and the entire fucking world crumble into pieces. And Ash ... Ash standing there, pleading.

Before I could second-guess myself, I fled the ballroom. More students laughed as I ran. A few teachers and adults looked on in concern, but no one stopped me.

I ran like Cinderella escaping the ball. I'd been living a fairy tale the last couple months, and now, I was finally about to turn back into a pumpkin. No glass slipper could fix this.

Once I was outside, I pulled out my phone and dialed Marley.

"Lila!" she gushed.

"How drunk are you?"

"I refused alcohol. Josie, however, is drunk."

"Can you pick me up?"

Marley was silent a second. "From prom?"

"Yes. Ash ..." I choked on the word. "It was a joke, cooked up by Shelly Thomas. He was to date me and then humiliate me."

"Fuck," Marley said, completely out of character. "I'll be right there."

"Thanks," I said with a sniffle.

I stuffed the phone back in my purse and trekked away from the hotel. I couldn't stay here another minute. I'd meet Marley somewhere along the main road.

"Lila!" a voice called from the entrance to the Westin.

I ignored Ash and kept walking.

"Lila, please, stop walking."

I heard him jogging in his fancy shoes to catch up to me.

I cursed myself for wearing high heels and nearly took them off to fling at him.

He reached for my elbow, and I swatted at him. "Leave me alone."

"Would you stop walking, so we can talk?"

"No," I bit out.

"It's not like Shelly said. That's not what happened."

"Leave. Me. Alone."

"I swear, that's not the truth."

I glared at him. "I saw the texts Ash. I read them for truth."

"Lila ..."

"Stop!" I shrieked. "Go back to the party, Ash. Enjoy your victory."

"It wasn't a victory," he told me. "I swear ..."

"Your word means nothing."

"I've never lied to you about how I feel."

I stopped dead in my tracks. He'd been marching next to me, and he nearly stumbled as he came to a stop.

"Then, tell me it's all a lie. Tell me *none* of it happened."

I'd seen his face when Shelly blurted out the truth.

"Gah," he groaned, running his hand back through his hair. "I did go out with you at first because Shelly had told me to, but—"

I put my hand out. "That's all I need to know."

"But the rest—"

"Stop! You lied to me! You told me that you *loved* me," I screamed at him. Tears were now hot in my eyes, and I tried to blink them away, but I couldn't. They ran down my cheeks. "You told me you loved me, and all this time, it was based on a lie! How could I ever believe another fucking word out of your mouth?"

He was silent, his jaw clenched and body rigid.

"I *do* love you."

"You don't know what love is, Ash, because *this* isn't it."

I saw Marley's minivan speeding down toward me, and I flagged her down. Ash was still trying to stammer out some words to absolve himself when Josie practically jumped out of the still-moving minivan and vaulted between us.

"Leave her alone!" Josie said, glaring at him. "Lila, get in the van."

"Don't leave," Ash cried.

"If you don't back up, I'll deck you," Josie threatened.

"Please, this isn't what you think."

I hopped into the van and took a seat with Josie following me. I didn't glance over at Ash, didn't say another word as Josie closed the door and Marley sped away.

It wasn't until we were home that the tears finally came. And my heart completely shattered.

15

ATHENS
APRIL 27, 2010

C ole shoved his way through the crowd of people lining up along the sidewalk in downtown Athens. I waved at him, jumping a little so that he could see where I was standing. I'd staked out the perfect spot to watch the annual cycling competition, Twilight. It was optimal primarily because it was on a corner to watch the inevitable crashes, which was what people really came downtown for.

Oh, and beer.

Cole passed me a drink and squeezed in tight to me. Barry and Tony, much to the crowd's dismay, shuffled around us.

"Thanks for holding our place," Cole said. He bent down and captured a kiss.

"We should have probably left Tweedledee and Tweedledum," I said, gesturing to his friends. "They take up more space."

"Hey!" Barry said.

"We take offense to that," Tony added.

"No, you don't."

"No, we don't," Barry agreed. "But it's fun to appear upset."

I shook my head at the pair of them. I couldn't believe in ten short days, all three of them would be graduating. Two years since Cole had asked me out that afternoon in Intro to Kinesiology. I was in all major classes and working at a physical therapy place in town. Tony and Barry were both moving to Atlanta after graduation with jobs in sales. But Cole …

"So, have you heard anything else?" Barry asked Cole as the first round of cyclists rode past.

"No," Cole said tightly.

Cole didn't have a job. Not for lack of talent, but he was much more specific in his interests. He wanted to work in marketing and development or scouting for a professional football team. As anyone could imagine, these were sought-after positions. And not many people were getting those jobs right out of college without experience in marketing or scouting elsewhere.

"Are you sure you won't ask your dad?" Tony asked.

"I'm not going to do that," Cole said. "You know that I don't want to ask him for anything."

That was the other problem. Cole could have had any entry-level job that he wanted if he dropped his dad's name or asked for his help. But he was resolute that he was going to do this on his own. He didn't need anyone's help or a leg up. It was admirable, but again, he didn't have a job.

I'd learned not to bring it up. Tony and Barry could get away with nagging him about it. I knew the depth of his despair, the longer he didn't get a position. As job after job came back filled. He wanted to prove that he could do it on his own, and ... he was finding out that he couldn't. I could see the existential crisis building.

"Don't badger him," I said. "We're supposed to have a night off."

"We're just messing around," Tony said.

Cole put his arm around my shoulders and pulled our bodies closer. "Thanks, babe."

The guys changed the subject from there as we watched the cyclists. People left around us, and the spaces were filled back up with more eager watchers. Channing and her new girlfriend, Kandice, showed up for a half hour before retreating to a nearby bar.

"I'll be right back," Cole said against my ear. "I have a phone call."

I waved him off. It was almost too loud to hear him right next to me. I definitely wouldn't have been able to hear a phone call. Right as Cole left the vicinity, another round of cyclists came barreling down the street. I leaned in with Tony and Barry as they veered in our direction. And one cyclist cut the turn too sharp. He skidded sideways, taking out three other cyclists. All of them hitting the bales of hay on the corner at alarming speeds.

The crowd all around them cheered as if they'd won the whole thing. It was what we'd all been waiting for. And of course, Cole had missed it.

"I can't believe he walked away, and it happened," I said to the guys.

"If that was all it took, we should have sent him away a long time ago," Barry said.

We all laughed, making jokes about when the next one would happen and waiting for Cole to return.

"He's been gone awhile. Maybe I should check on him," I said.

"We'll save your spot," Barry said.

I nodded at them and then bullied my way back through the crowd. I inhaled deeply once I was past the crowd and back on the slightly less busy sidewalk. Cole wasn't immediately visible. I stood on my tiptoes to find him. At least he was taller than the average guy. So, even if no one could usually find me, I could always find him.

Sure enough, as soon as I stepped around the corner, I found him leaning up against the brick wall on Jackson Street. His phone was pressed to his ear, and his finger was in the other to block out the street noise. He hadn't seen me yet, and I watched his adorably serious face as he talked on the phone.

I got close enough to hear him end the call.

"Yes, thank you so much." He chuckled. "I look forward to meeting you. Thanks again."

He hung up and then stared forward, as if lost in a daze. Then he blinked out of it and saw me approaching.

"Hey, you were gone forever. Everything all right?"

He scooped me up into his arms and swung me around right there on the sidewalk. I held him tight. People grumbled as they passed us. A few girls *aww*'d at the scene.

"What happened?" I gasped as he set me on my feet. "Tell me everything."

"I got a job offer."

"Oh my God!" I shrieked. "Doing what? Which one?"

"Marketing. It's an intro position, but it's something. And I got it all on my own, Lila."

"I knew you would."

He cupped my jaw with his hand and kissed me long and hard. I was half-ready to drag him back to his house to celebrate. Forget the rest of Twilight. This was what we'd been waiting for.

"What team?"

He paused infinitesimally. That should have been my warning, but I wasn't prepared. "The 49ers."

I managed to hide how crestfallen I was at the news. I kept my smile on wide. "That's amazing. San Francisco."

"I know it's far away, but there are direct flights out of Atlanta every day. We can still see each other. We can make this work."

I nodded. "Of course we can. We've been together two years. What's a little long distance?"

Inside, my stomach was all twisted up as I wondered if it really *was* possible. I'd only heard nightmares about long-distance relationships. But I loved Cole so fucking much. I didn't know how I was going to get to San Francisco or what the future held, but there was nothing that we couldn't get through.

16

FRAT BEACH

OCTOBER 29, 2010

Georgia–Florida weekend was called the world's largest outdoor cocktail party for a reason. Every Halloween weekend, the two rival teams traveled to a neutral playing field in Jacksonville, Florida. The masses descended on the town and the surrounding beaches. The Landing, which was typically a desolate tourist trap, transformed into the biggest Jacksonville party scene. A mere hour north, St. Simons Island, dubbed Frat Beach, was one long stretch of beach parties, crazier than any spring break trip.

And I loved every minute of it.

My only regret was that Cole was in San Francisco and not here for the annual meet up.

Even though I wasn't in a sorority, many of my friends on the dance team were, and we were filling up a bunch of beachside hotel rooms for the weekend. I'd agreed to share the room with Channing; her girlfriend, Kandice; and our other dance team friend, Denise.

As soon as we arrived Friday afternoon, we changed

into bikinis and cutoff jean shorts and headed straight for the beach with a few bottles of cheap champagne and a case of beer. The dance team had erected a tent for all our belongings right next to a music platform. Everyone was drinking and dancing. The beaches were descended on like locusts.

Denise had been crowing the entire drive about her "friend" from Brunswick coming here for the weekend. We were all wondering if this mysterious Tanner actually existed by this point.

"I swear, he's coming. He texted me and said he's trying to find us." She latched onto my arm. "Come up to the hotel with me to see if we can find him."

Channing shot me a look, and I just laughed. I was pleasantly buzzed. Why not?

"Sure."

We left the team and hiked through the crowd and back up to our hotel. She had left the navigating to me as she typed fiercely on her phone.

"Do you see him?" I asked.

Denise looked around and then pointed. "Tanner!"

She shrieked and then ran right to him.

He picked her up and drunkenly swung her around in a circle. "Denise, there you are."

I stopped in my tracks when I saw who was standing *next* to the mysterious Tanner.

I blinked.

"Ash?" I breathed.

He was shirtless, in nothing but board shorts the color of his sea-blue eyes.

"Lila!"

I hadn't seen Ash since the beginning of last summer. We'd had it out after he visited for the Bama game sophomore year. Though I hadn't exactly wanted him to hear what happened with Cole, it hadn't made me any less angry with him for what he'd done in high school. We'd run into each other in Savannah some the next two summers, but I'd kept the encounters brief. It was easier to have him out of sight, out of mind.

Cole didn't say anything about Ash. He didn't have to. I knew the fire of hatred that had been there from seeing me drunkenly walk in with him. The what-ifs running through his mind. There was a reason he'd pulled me upstairs and fucked me when Ash could still hear us. And Cole wasn't going to like me running into Ash now.

Ash stepped forward and pulled me into him. "It's so fucking good to see you."

I tried to ignore my pulse racing from his presence. "Yeah. What are you doing here?"

"Wait, you know each other?" Denise asked.

"Oh, sorry, Denise, this is Ash Talmadge."

Ash nodded at her. "We've met. She's friends with Tanner." He gestured to the mysterious Tanner. "Tanner's my roommate."

I really must not have been paying attention to Denise. I had no recollection that her Tanner from Brunswick was also at Duke.

"And how do you two know each other?" Tanner asked.

I glanced at Ash and shrugged. "We went to high school together."

"I thought you went to an all-girls Catholic school." Denise waggled her eyebrows at me.

"I went to the adjoining all-boys school," Ash explained.

"All-boys school," Tanner said with a shudder. "Can't believe they still have those."

"It's not all bad."

"What a coincidence that you ran into each other," Denise slurred.

Ash looked straight at me when he said, "I don't believe in coincidences."

I had to look away to hide my blush.

Denise, however, didn't seem to notice. "You should come party with us!"

She didn't wait for a response, just took Tanner's hand and dragged him through the crowd. I glanced at Ash. My stomach was suddenly in my throat. This wasn't a good idea.

"It's good to see you, Lila."

"You too," I admitted. It was strange how much I could be furious with him for how everything had gone down in the past and also miss him. Because I did miss him.

"When did you get here?" he asked me, falling into step with me.

"This afternoon. No classes on Friday. Everyone wanted to drive up Thursday after classes, but I had to work. So, my car waited to come in today."

"Same. Well, we have classes. We're skipping."

"Scandalous," I said with a laugh.

His eyes lit up as if he'd forgotten what I sounded like.

Then we were lost to the crowd, meandering through the people to get back to our tent. I handed Ash a beer and was immediately attacked by Channing.

"Wait," she gasped, drunk and sloppy, "it's *the* Ash?"

Ash arched an eyebrow. "That'd be me."

"Oh my God, what are you doing here?"

"Just in town with a friend."

"We didn't get to chat last time we met," she said drunkenly. "So, like, is it all that shit true? Like what happened at prom?"

"Channing," I groaned. "Can we not? Go find Kandice."

"Ugh. You ruin all my fun, Deedee," she said, pinching my cheeks before disappearing again.

"Deedee?" he asked.

"Don't even get me started on drunk Channing."

He glanced down at the lukewarm can of Natural Light. "So, you talk about me?"

"Um …"

"And she knows about prom?"

"She's been my roommate for more than two years. I would think that she knows most things about me."

"Hmm," he said.

I could sense an argument coming on, and I didn't have the energy for it. We'd had the same argument over and over again since prom. I didn't want to have to disagree with him here when I was with my friends.

"Why don't we forget about it today?" I suggested. "Just have a good time and not worry about anything?"

He met my gaze, as if trying to find the catch but finding none. "I'm game."

Then he punctured the center of his beer can and shotgunned it. I gasped, and everyone else around us cheered him on as he guzzled the entire contents of the can in one go. I couldn't stop laughing to see my refined Catholic school boy, who wore bow ties and boat shoes, shotgunning a beer.

"Had to catch up," he told me with a grin.

Thankfully, after that point, it was so easy to be around Ash. It always had been. It was half the reason I'd avoided him this long. Not because I wanted to kill him—though sometimes, I considered it—but because if I let my guard down, it was almost too easy to go back to how things had been.

We got drunk and danced and made fools of ourselves. Frat Beach was the perfect balm for our blistered relationship.

NIGHT HAD LONG FALLEN when I remembered to check my phone. I patted down my jean shorts, extracted it from the back pocket, and flopped down on our already-sandy blanket. I blinked a few times to adjust to the unnatural brightness. Then I frowned when I saw the screen.

Cole had called a bunch. That was weird. He knew I was here this weekend and that I wouldn't be by my phone. I should probably call him back.

I hauled myself off of the ground and hiked back up to the hotel where it was quieter. Though my mind was still spinning from too much alcohol. Probably not the best time to call, but I wanted to make sure he was okay.

He answered immediately, "Hey."

"Cole!" I gushed. "There you are. Is everything okay? You kept calling."

"Not really," he said, his voice rough.

"What happened?"

"Are you with Ash?"

I glanced around. "Uh, no."

He ground his teeth. "I know that you've been with him, Lila."

"Oh, he's here with his friend Tanner, who is, like, hooking up with one of my dance friends."

"So, he's with you."

"Not right now."

Cole made a frustrated noise. "There are pictures of you with him all over Facebook."

I stopped smiling at that. There were pictures of us on Facebook? Of course, my friends had taken hundreds of pictures since we'd gotten out here. And I was with Ash. But I hadn't considered that pictures of us together would end up on the internet.

"Oh."

"Yeah, oh. He's all over you. What is going on over there?"

"Nothing!" I gasped. "Why would you think something was going on?"

"What is he doing there with you?"

"I already told you," I snapped back. "He's here with Tanner."

"And you just let him hang all over you?"

"No! I didn't."

"You know that he wants to get with you."

I did know that. There was no point in disagreeing.

"That's not going to happen."

"I don't fucking know that!" he roared. "I'm thousands of miles away, in a shoebox apartment, and you're out on a beach with your fucking ex! I don't know what's going to happen."

"It's not my fault that you're in San Francisco. And you shouldn't blame me for something that isn't even going to happen."

"I know I chose this. I know. But I don't want you near him."

"God, don't you trust me?" I asked.

"Of course I do."

"Then trust me!"

"I don't trust *him*," he yelled. "And I haven't trusted him since that night you came back with him."

"Ugh," I groaned. "Nothing happened then and nothing is going to happen now."

"I don't know that."

"Then you're a fucking liar," I snarled. "And you *don't* trust me."

"I can't do this, Lila," he said, his own voice filled with a boiling anger.

We'd spent six months apart. I'd flown into San Francisco twice over the summer, and he'd come to Georgia once in August, but we hadn't seen each other in months. The distance was taking a toll on the both of us. I missed him. He missed me. But missing each other didn't seem to be enough when I was here on a beach with Ash and he didn't trust me.

"What are you saying?" My voice was so small.

"I can't sit here while you're off, partying with him. I can't do it."

I swallowed hard as tears pricked my eyes. "Cole?"

"It's not fair to either of us."

"Stop," I whispered.

"I didn't think long distance would be easy, but it's not working."

"So what? You're breaking up with me?" I cracked on the last line.

"Yeah, I guess I am."

I didn't even know what to say to that. A bomb had gone off in my chest. Like he'd scooped out my heart and left me empty.

"Don't do this," I whispered.

"It's already done."

I stared at the silent phone after we hung up. Then I sank to the ground and buried my face in my hands. It felt too unbelievable to cry. As if I'd walked into someone else's nightmare. My boyfriend couldn't have done that. We'd been through so much. More than two years, and now, gone ... in a phone call.

"Lila?"

I lifted my head and found Ash hovering above me. "What?"

"You disappeared. Channing was freaking out."

"Right. Tell her I'm fine. I had to take a phone call."

Ash's eyes slid over me, and he frowned. "Some phone call."

"You have no idea."

He sank onto the ground next to me. "Want to tell me about it?"

"Not really."

He nodded, and we fell into silence. All around us, people were partying like the night would never end. If the world ended, this would be the place to be for it.

"I've seen that look on your face before," he said softly after a few minutes.

I glanced at him hollowly, wondering if tears would ever breach the shock. "When?"

"Prom," he said the word harshly. "I'll never forget the way you looked at me that night."

"You deserved worse."

"Who deserves it tonight?"

Something broke in me at the question.

"Cole." I choked on the word.

Ash wrapped an arm around my shoulders and drew me into him. I leaned my head against him, and we sat there for a few minutes until I was sure that the tears weren't going to come after all.

Once I had to talk about it, that was when it would all hit me.

Ash finally straightened and pulled me to my feet. "I can't be Marley and Josie for this. There's no one to threaten to deck."

I laughed a harsh, painful thing.

"But maybe we could dive back into the party, get wasted, and forget about tonight entirely?"

"I should probably just go upstairs."

"Why? So you can obsess about it all night?" I opened my mouth to object. "Don't tell me that you won't. I know you will."

"Fine. You think getting drunk will be better?"

"At least you'll be numb."

I took a deep, fortifying breath. "All right. This is stupid, but maybe I need to be stupid for a night."

"That's my girl," he said with a broad smile.

Everything tightened in a tangled mess in my gut, and I had to look away from him. At the reason Cole had called in the first place.

But I let Ash drag me back to the party. And I drank enough that I didn't remember the rest of the night ... or the next morning.

17

FRAT BEACH

OCTOBER 30, 2010

I woke up on a cloud. The bed was so comfortable and the comforter so lush that I was sure I'd never slept on anything this soft. Definitely not at the crappy hotel we'd gotten for the weekend.

Maybe it was way better than I remembered. Though I couldn't remember much from yesterday. It was a big blur.

I blinked against the light streaming in through the enormous glass windows in the bedroom. Then I froze. That definitely was *not* the right kind of windows from my hotel. And the room was shaped wrong, bigger, but missing a queen bed. And I was in a king.

Oh fuck.

My mind played catch-up with the rest of what my body was realizing. I rolled over and nearly jumped when I saw a body in bed next to me. A very naked body.

"Ash," I gasped.

I nearly tumbled out of bed, taking the sheet with me

and covering my own naked body. I hovered on the edge as his eyes fluttered open, bright blue.

He blinked a few times, as if he, too, needed a minute to recover. Then he smiled. "Lila."

It was such an erotic sound that I actually did step off of the bed this time. "What am I doing here?"

He glanced around his hotel room with a yawn. Our clothes were strewn all over the floor, as if they'd been haphazardly thrown into positions across the room. When he looked back at me, it was with bedroom eyes.

"We both know the answer to that."

I shook my head. "No. This couldn't have happened."

"It definitely happened. Don't say you don't remember."

I squeezed my eyes shut, and it all rushed back. His mouth on mine and that tongue doing unspeakable things. His hands on my body and him inside of me.

I shuddered and took another step back. "Oh God."

He scooted closer to me and held his hand out, as if I'd get back into bed with him. "Come on. It's not like it was bad."

"I have a boyfriend!" I yelled.

"Had."

"What?"

He arched his eyebrows. "You *had* a boyfriend."

And then that memory hit me too. The phone call. I nearly wept, but I was too horrified with what had happened to do anything at all.

"I can't believe we did this."

He dropped his hand back to his side. "Don't regret this, Lila."

"Too late."

"It was too serendipitous for us to not end up right here. I had no idea you were here, and then you're newly single in the same instant. Can't you see that we're meant to be?"

"All I can see is that I was drunk and hurting, and you took advantage of that."

"Advantage?" he said in disgust. "I didn't take advantage of you. I comforted you when that asshole had the fucking nerve to break up with you over the phone."

"Don't try to get on your high horse," I snarled. "As if you have no sins at your feet."

"I have plenty. But I'm not going to keep hiding behind them, Lila. I want you. I've always wanted you. And I won't apologize for having you when you needed me."

"I was drunk and hurting. You should have put me to bed and let me sleep it off. That's what I needed! I needed you to say no!"

"I'll never say no to you."

And he said it with so much force that I immediately knew it to be true. Ash would never say no to me. Not in any situation. Definitely not this one.

Still, it frustrated me. That he couldn't see what I'd needed and had taken what I'd offered instead. I was responsible too, of course. It hadn't happened by itself, and I'd regret it happening forever. But it didn't absolve him either.

I huffed and looked away from him. I couldn't stay here. I couldn't be here any longer.

I dropped the sheet. It was pointless anyway; Ash had

seen me completely naked more times than I could count. Then I went in search of the rest of my clothes.

"What are you doing?" he asked, grabbing his boxers and tugging them on.

"Leaving," I said as I pulled my clothes on.

"Don't storm out of here. I can drive you back to your hotel."

"I'd rather walk."

"Lila—"

"Don't," I snarled at him as he came closer. "Just … don't."

Ash must have heard the desperation in my voice because he stopped moving. He watched me gather my things and leave. All the while, I avoided his gaze, so I wouldn't have to see what he was thinking. I couldn't stomach it right now.

THE WALK back to my hotel was farther than I remembered. But the fresh air, even for a walk of shame, helped to clear my head. I still felt like shit. I wasn't sure if it was from all the alcohol yesterday or the breakup or what I'd woken up to. Either way, it was terrible. Every last part of it, and not even the sea breeze could put it all back together.

Channing and Kandice were still sleeping when I crept back into the hotel room. Denise was nowhere to be found. I breathed a small sigh of relief. At least I wouldn't have to explain myself to anyone.

I went straight into the bathroom and turned on the

shower as hot as the water would go. The tiny bathroom steamed up within minutes. Then I peeled off the remnants of my dirty little secret and stepped inside. The blistering heat hit me full-on, but I didn't back away from it. I pushed myself under the water and let it pour over my face and hair and down my body.

I grabbed the bar of soap and scrubbed and scrubbed and scrubbed. Every inch of my body was lathered and washed three times until I couldn't wash anymore. There was nothing left to remove, no traces of what I'd done.

My knees hit the bathtub as the first sob racked my body.

I had to live with what had happened. And right now, I couldn't live with it. I couldn't live with myself. Tears ran down my cheeks, hitting the bathtub and melding the salt with the shower water. My chest heaved as sobs that I'd somehow managed to hold in yesterday finally came hard and fast.

I couldn't breathe. I couldn't think. My eyes burned. Everything felt so small and distant and yet so close and oppressive. As if time itself were stopping to inspect the moment.

Cole had broken up with me.

I wrapped my arms around my chest and bent over, touching my forehead to the bottom of the shower. He'd broken up with me. We'd been together two and a half years, and the whole thing had gone up in flames over some Facebook pictures and a drunken weekend with my friends. I couldn't fathom it.

He'd been mad, sure. But I hadn't thought that he'd be *that* mad.

But I should have seen it. I should have seen his anger for what it was. He was so chill, but he had a slow burn temper that exploded when it was activated. And he *hated* Ash. It was his trigger. It was why he'd gotten so mad that night after the Bama game. I could see it, but I hadn't been expecting it. I hadn't seen it burn this hot in so long.

I'd only been three weeks away from seeing him. I was going to skip out on Thanksgiving with my family to fly to San Francisco for a week. And now, that was canceled. Everything was canceled. Like the end of a TV show in the middle of a season.

And then I'd gone and proven him right.

Did the exact thing that he'd worried would happen.

Cole had been right. Ash was our Achilles' heel. He was the boy I had never completely left behind despite all the horrors of our past. And I didn't know how to let him go or turn him away. I didn't know how to say no to him any more than he did to me.

Even though I wanted Cole, I knew now that it couldn't happen. That it wouldn't happen. Not after last night.

When the water ran cold, I shut the thing off and stumbled wearily out of the shower. I dried off and wrapped my long blonde hair into a second towel. I'd stopped crying somewhere during my inner tirade, but now, I felt wrung out. I couldn't imagine going to the game today and pretending like everything was okay. I couldn't imagine doing anything.

Somehow, my roommates were *still* asleep, even after my long-ass shower. I put on fresh clothes and left them a note that I'd gone to the beach.

I set my toes into the sand, looking on in dismay at the state of the beach from all the trash left behind from the parties, when my phone rang. Besides a few texts from Marley and Josie about the pictures online last night, I hadn't heard from anyone, and I wasn't in the mood to respond.

But when I checked the screen, Cole's name appeared.

I took a deep breath and slowly released it before putting the phone to my ear. "Hey."

"Hey," he said, his voice as thick and raw as mine.

Silence stretched between us like it never had before. The weight of his betrayal ... and mine heavy like molasses.

"Cole—"

"No, let me go first," he said quickly.

"Okay," I whispered.

"I don't know what happened last night." I could practically see him running a hand through his hair, trying to get himself together. "I said all the wrong things. I saw you with Ash and freaked out. I lost my mind. And I'm so sorry."

"Cole, stop."

"Lila, please, I shouldn't have lost my cool like that. It's not fair to you when you weren't doing anything wrong. I might hate Ash, but I should have trusted that nothing would happen."

I squeezed my eyes shut. But something had happened. It *had* happened. But I couldn't say the words.

"I know that I can't say that I'm sorry enough. I don't know how else to apologize for how I acted."

"Stop," I repeated. "Just stop."

"I can't. You know I love you. I love you so much, and I just ... I miss you."

"You were right," I blurted out.

"What?"

"You were right," I repeated. "This long distance isn't working."

Cole sucked in a sharp breath.

"It's not. You wouldn't have said it last night if you didn't think so. You're in San Francisco, working your ass off to get ahead. I'm still ... here." My voice cracked on the last word. "I'm still here."

"Wait, Lila, please."

"You know it's true," I insisted. "It's tearing us apart."

He huffed. "It's hard," he admitted softly. "It's really fucking hard. I miss you every fucking day."

"Me too," I said, tears coming to my eyes again. I couldn't even believe I still had some left. "So much. But when does it end?"

"I don't know."

"Me neither. I graduate in May. There's PT school, and I'm working on getting certified in athletic training." I shook my head. "I don't know how it would work. I'll still be here, and you'll still be there. When are we ever going to be in the same place again?"

"I don't know."

Neither of us did. He'd gone off to follow his dreams, and I was planning to follow mine as well. Our dreams just didn't cross.

"So, you were right."

"Yeah," he said. "I hate this."

"I know."

"This doesn't work ... not right now."

"But someday?" I offered.

"Someday, Lila."

I clutched the phone to my chest as I said good-bye to my college love. Free of both Ash and Cole for the first time in my life, I had no idea where I was headed. Right now, I wasn't ready to find out. But one day ... someday.

18

ATHENS

MAY 10, 2011

E veryone I knew and loved was in Athens for my graduation ... except the two people I was missing the most.

Cole and Ash.

It felt ridiculous to miss them, but I couldn't seem to help it

My friends had said that it would pass. That I'd stop thinking about them when I met some hot stranger who flipped my world. But seven months later, I hadn't met anyone who made me want to flip anything.

Maybe it would all change next week when I moved to Atlanta with Josie.

"I'm not nervous," Josie insisted.

Marley shot her an incredulous look. "You're bouncing around like a fucking bunny."

"Whatever." Josie stopped moving and gnawed on her nails.

I slapped her hand as we waited in line at the arch for pictures. "Stop it. It's all going to work out."

She dropped her hand and wrinkled her nose at me. "We have no way of knowing that. The likelihood that the pilot will be picked up is zilch. And I was just a fluke anyway."

Marley and I looked at each other. A look that said everything. This was completely normal neurotic behavior from our best friend. And she had every reason to be freaking out right now.

While I'd been making poor life choices on Halloween weekend, Josie had been premiering her first independent film at the film festival. The film didn't go over well, but afterward, she bummed a cigarette off of some strangers in an alley, who happened to be a director and producer. Everything happened for her in that moment. They offered her an audition for a new CW-esque drama they were working on. They needed a lead for a pilot to pitch to the studio. She thought it was a joke.

All through the audition, when she got the leading role, even when she filmed the pilot in Atlanta, traveling back and forth from Savannah so she could still graduate since this was far from a sure thing, one big joke. Except it hadn't been a joke, and now, we were here. The pilot was being assessed by the studio *today*. She'd finally have her answer if this whole thing was anything at all.

"Honey, stop worrying about it," my mom said as we reached the front of the line. "It'll happen, or it won't. Worrying won't fix it."

"Thanks, Deb," Josie said, beaming.

"Your turn!" Steph cried.

I darted up to the arch on North Campus. It was the symbol of the university and the first official time that I'd be allowed to walk through it. My sisters had all graduated from UGA and cheered for me as I made the first walk through. We stood around for pictures, taking one with each of them, and then foisting the camera off to a stranger to get one of all us girls.

"Thanks!" I said, taking the camera back and scanning through the photos. "This is perfect."

"My baby all grown up," my mom said.

"I can't believe it's graduation," I said.

"You're going to do amazing things."

I smiled at my mom as we all fell into step on our way to Sanford Stadium for spring graduation. I was already in my gown, holding my cap under my arm and following the stream of people.

"So proud of you, honey," my mom said. She kissed my cheek as we made it inside. "I'll text you where we're seated so that you can find us."

"You'll be hard to miss."

She laughed. "We're going to cheer like crazy for you!"

I believed her. "Keep an eye on Josie."

"She's in good hands."

Marley squeezed my shoulder. "I'm so excited for you."

Unlike Josie and me, Marley was heading to Harvard after graduation for her PhD. I'd always known she was a genius, but she was still just Marley to me. I'd gone to her graduation the weekend before at Duke. My nerves were shot the entire time as I anticipated running into Ash. He had also graduated that weekend, but somehow, I'd never seen him. I wasn't sure if I was relieved or not.

"Love you, Mars."

She hugged me tight, and then I left my family and walked down to the field, where thousands of seats had been set up for spring commencement. Channing and I had agreed to meet at one corner so that we could sit together. She was moving to Austin, so she'd dumped Kandice two weeks ago. If anything, I was the reason she'd decided long distance wasn't going to work. Either way, I was going to miss her so much.

"Let's find some seats!" she said, clutching my hand and dragging me down the long aisle toward the front.

UGA graduation was an enormous affair. Each college had their name called, and then as a whole everyone stood to be recognized before sitting back down. The individual college graduations were more important for a lot of the smaller majors, like mine. I'd graduated from the College of Education with my bachelors in Exercise and Sports Science yesterday afternoon, but something about being back in Sanford made it feel official.

Channing and I found empty seats and plopped our hats on our heads.

"So, are you ready for the big Atlanta move?" she asked.

We'd packed up our apartment together all week. I couldn't possibly believe that she was going to be in Austin, and I wouldn't come home to her cooking for me every afternoon or that we wouldn't have late-night shenanigans downtown or Thursday night movie nights after basketball games.

"Define ready," I said.

"Girl, you need some more pep in your step. You're a Falcons cheerleader! It's kind of a requirement."

A shiver shot through me. Channing had convinced me to audition for Falcons cheer, but I had never in a million years thought that I'd make it. But four years on the dance team had prepared me for the opportunity, and now, I'd be on the sidelines every home game all season. I was more excited about that than my full-time job in a physical therapist's clinic or my part-time job as an athletic trainer at a local gym.

Neither were exactly where I wanted to be, but I'd decided to take a year off of school before jumping into physical therapy school. I wanted to make sure that it was definitely what I wanted to do before dedicating the next three years of my life to it.

I shook off my disappointment. It wasn't like I had to decide what to do with the rest of my life at twenty-two. I was just getting started after all. Even though all my other friends knew exactly where to turn didn't mean that I was an outlier. Maybe they were.

I'd always thought PT was my dream, and now, I was floundering a bit. I hoped that the next year in a physical therapy clinic would bring back the certainty that I'd had when I chose my major.

My mom texted me to look up into the stands. Channing and I found them and waved like crazy. Then graduation started. We sat through the speeches and stood when our colleges were called. All my sisters, Josie, Marley, and my mom stood up and screamed as loud as they could when I got off of my chair. I couldn't stop laughing at their antics. I was both moved and embarrassed. God, I loved them.

Hats were thrown.

Hugs were exchanged.

Graduation was over.

Channing and I agreed to meet downtown tonight, and then I left her to find my family. I approached them in the stands. My heart constricted. I loved each and every one of them, but God, I wished the men in my life had stayed too. Ash and Cole were gone. I wasn't sure I'd completely accepted that until this moment. Because otherwise, they'd have done anything to be here. They'd always been like that.

The hardest part of it all was that another graduation had gone by, and my dad still wasn't here. I hadn't expected him to be here, but still, I'd hoped.

My thoughts were intercepted by Eve all but tackling me. Elle and Steph followed.

"You did it!" Eve shrieked.

"We're so proud!" Elle added.

Four sisters, all Georgia grads.

My mom pulled me into a hug next. And then Josie shrieked loud enough that the rest of the people in the stands looked at us.

There were tears in her eyes as she found me. "The network picked it up," she said, her voice barely a whisper.

"Josie!" I gasped.

"Oh my God!" Marley said.

"I start shooting the rest of the season next week!"

We all jumped up and down for another brilliant reason. I'd never felt luckier to be surrounded by such an incredible group of women. I might not have any of the men in my life, but I had *this*. And this was good enough for right now.

PART II

19

ATLANTA

MAY 29, 2015

"Hey, new girl." A woman snapped her fingers at me. I blinked at her, trying to remember her name. Kristen, Kirsten, Krista? I wasn't sure, but I forced down my snarky response. I *was* the new girl after all. I'd done my time, completed physical therapy school, and I was only one week into my new job as an Atlanta Falcons physical therapist and athletic trainer.

"Yes? How can I help?"

"Ferguson wants a coffee. Here's his order." She passed me a piece of paper with the coffee order for the head athletic trainer.

And when the boss said he needed something, it was better to jump than ask questions.

So, I jumped, heading back out of the training room and into the main break room with its fancy espresso machine. Three years in physical therapy school, and I was back to making coffee runs.

It was hard to complain when I finally had my dream job. Sure, I'd had that momentary existential crisis, where

I worried this wasn't what I wanted to do, but I'd come around quickly after graduation. I'd worked my ass to get here. Eventually, someone else in the training room would acknowledge that. I'd have to prove myself and work my way up like anyone else.

The break room was relatively empty. I headed straight to the espresso machine and stared down at it. Someone had shown me how it worked a few days ago, and I eventually made it how Ferguson liked it before returning to the training room. I wordlessly handed him the coffee. He didn't thank me. Then, I went back to my work, which was currently cleaning out a whirlpool. The grunt work wasn't beneath me, but man, I wanted to do more.

By the end of the day, I was beat and ready to have a good, long soak with a much-needed glass of wine.

"Hey, new girl!" the same woman said.

I faced her. "It's Lila. Lila Greer."

"Right, Lila. Thanks. I'm shit with names." She was beaming. "I'm Kristen Ng."

We shook hands. "Nice to officially meet you."

"Yeah, I know you've had a rough time since you started. Ferguson is in a real mood. Training camp is still six weeks away, but he's pissed about everything."

I chuckled. "Seems to be his MO."

"Yeah, I've been here three years, and he's never exactly been warm and fuzzy."

She slid out of her jacket as we walked out of the overly air-conditioned building and into the Atlanta summer sun. Post–Memorial Day weekend until almost Halloween was Georgia's blistering summer. It stretched humid and oppressive for months and months. I'd always loved it, but a part of me missed the Savannah breeze off of the Atlantic.

"A few of us are meeting up at The Ivy later. No Ferg in sight. You interested?"

"Definitely," I said eagerly.

I'd been desperate for friends. I'd lived in Atlanta for a year after graduation, but gone to PT school out of the city. Only two weeks back in Atlanta, I'd realized that my friends from my Falcons cheer days were long gone. Josie was in LA right now. Marley had defended her dissertation and would be starting as faculty at Emory this fall. But she wasn't here yet, and I missed people.

"Cool. We're meeting up at eight."

We exchanged numbers, and I agreed to meet her there. I left work with more pep in my step than I'd had in a while.

THE IVY BUCKHEAD was practically an institution in Atlanta at this point. It was *the* place to be for young professionals. After college, I'd spent many nights in the converted mansion with my fellow cheerleaders. It felt like homecoming, returning to spend time with my colleagues.

I'd grabbed a quick shower before blowing out my long hair, which had long outgrown the bleached highlights from college and was back to its natural ash-blonde. I'd paired a teal sundress with strappy brown sandals, and I entered The Ivy.

I scanned the first floor, bypassing the bar to see if I could locate Kristen. I found her in a red-and-white patterned strapless jumpsuit at a booth in the back. She jumped up onto her platform heels and gestured for me to follow her.

"Lila, you made it!" she gushed. She looked like a different person out of her training room attire. We both probably did. Her black hair was parted down the middle and stick straight to her shoulders and her lips a ruby red.

"I made it."

"Let me introduce you to the guys. You probably met Matthew in the training room," she said, gesturing to one guy. "Damien, Jared, and Casey are in other departments. We're just missing one more. He went to the bar. But we have a pitcher if you want a cup. It's Blue Moon."

"That'd be great," I said as Matthew poured.

I nestled into a seat next to Kristen and took a sip of the beer. The guys dived back into the conversation they had been having before I got here. I tried to keep up with what they were discussing, but it was clearly a long-running conversation.

"Oh, there he is!" Kristen said.

I looked at who was approaching and nearly spat out my drink. "Cole!"

"Lila?" His eyes were wide and disbelieving.

I jumped out of my seat, abandoning my drink, and took the few steps to meet him.

Cole Davis was here. He was in Atlanta. In this very bar.

And he looked ... amazing. His height and bulk,

which had served him so well in college athletics, had only broadened into appreciable ways in the intervening years. He was dressed to impress in a navy-blue suit and light-blue tie. His own bright blue eyes were enhanced by the color combo.

"What are you doing here?" we asked at the same time.

I gestured back to the table. "Kristen invited me."

His eyes were still glued to mine, as if he were seeing a mirage. As if *I* were the one who couldn't possibly be here. When he was the one who had been living in San Francisco the last five years.

"How do you know Kristen?"

"We work together."

"You work ... for the Falcons?" he asked.

"Yeah. In the training room. I finished my physical therapy degree and got the job."

"Lila, that's incredible."

"Thanks," I said, beaming. "But what are *you* doing here? I thought you were still in San Francisco."

"I just moved here. I've been in Atlanta about a month."

My jaw dropped. We'd seen each other a few times in the five years since we'd broken up, but this was different.

"And you're working for the Falcons too?"

"Yeah. Marketing."

I couldn't believe it. My brain must have been misfiring. Cole Davis was here, in Atlanta. My throat constricted as I looked up at him. This felt too good to be true. Serendipitous. But if I'd learned anything about the two men in my life, nothing was ever left up to chance. The world managed to always bring us back together.

"I didn't think you'd ever come back to Georgia."

"It wasn't in the plan. Remember when I told you about the marketing business I was working on?"

"Yes." I bit my lip. My heart panged at the thought of that night last year when I'd seen him, when he'd told me all about this.

He glanced away briefly before proceeding, "Falcons are subcontracting the whole thing."

"Wow! Congratulations! Just what you always wanted."

"And I got it all on my own merit."

"I'm so proud of you."

And it was true. This was what Cole had always wanted—recognition in his own right.

"Ahem," Kristen cleared her throat behind us. "You two know each other?"

I'd completely forgotten that we had an audience. A common occurrence when I was with Cole. He captured all of my attention and held it. He always had.

"Yeah, we do," Cole said as he took the last steps to the table and set down his drink.

Meanwhile, I suddenly needed something to do with my hands.

"Lila's only been here a week. How did you meet?" Matthew asked.

Cole and I exchanged a look. History lay in his eyes. Whether or not to divulge how far back we went. I knew that feeling well.

"Lila and I went to college together," Cole offered.

Kristen picked up on the tension in the room. "Uh-huh. It sure looks like more than that."

"We dated in college," I told her.

"Ohhh," Jared said.

"That's so cute," Kristen said.

"Tell us all the sordid details," Matthew said, making room for us both to sit again.

"Nothing to tell," Cole said. "We dated for two years, and then I got a job in San Francisco."

Which was the understatement of the century. Not that I was about to dispute it.

Kristen drummed her fingers together. I barely knew her and could already see the cogs moving as she worked out how to play matchmaker with us. I was grateful when Jared changed the subject, and we could all let the moment pass. The last thing I wanted was to discuss my past relationship with people I'd just met.

Cole and I had a past.

But maybe we could have a present too.

Two hours and several drinks later, the rest of the group was drunk enough that they staggered into cabs.

I'd stopped after one. Getting drunk around Cole was asking to fall into his bed. As appealing as that sounded, I couldn't go there again. I wanted to be coherent around him. It seemed safer in this new territory, where we worked at the same place and had the same group of friends.

He'd barely had anything to drink too. Nothing in the last hour.

I headed out of The Ivy with him, searching out his white Jeep on instinct.

"I upgraded," he said, as if reading my mind.

And then we were next to his shiny, new Jeep in a bright Georgia red.

"Go Dawgs."

He chuckled. "Sic 'em."

"I'm over there," I said, pointing out my black Hyundai. It wasn't much, but my last car had died spectacularly a few months ago, and I'd needed something.

Still, I didn't go toward my car.

"I didn't think this would happen again," I said

"Me neither." He ran a hand back through his hair. "You and me in the same place."

"I know."

"I'm surprised that you stayed when you saw that I was here," he said, leaning back against the Jeep.

I winced at the words. "It's fine."

"Is it?"

"Yes. This is fine."

"It's okay that we go out for drinks?" He tilted his head, the expression so familiar that my chest tightened at the sight.

God, I'd missed him so much.

I nodded.

"Lila," he whispered. His eyes implored me to get what he was asking. To get past the bullshit and straight to the point.

Oh. I knew what he was afraid of. Not if it was okay

for me to go out for drinks with him, but if it was okay for me to see *him*. He was asking if there was someone *else* still in my life. If I was still with Ash. But I didn't even want to think of him right now when I was looking up into Cole's face.

"Ash and I broke up."

"I'm sorry."

I arched an eyebrow. "No, you're not."

He grinned then. The first perfect smile that I'd missed so completely. "No, I'm not. Good riddance."

I laughed then. It was so Cole.

In that moment, I wanted to kiss him so desperately.

But I held back.

Butterflies beat through my stomach. Everything felt warm and hazy and completely possible. I'd never thought that we'd make it back to this place. Had given up on that idea, but I wasn't going to ignore it now that the opportunity had presented itself.

Cole and I had said that someday, if we were in the same place again, this could work. And I wanted to believe that the universe had finally made that happen.

20

LAKE LANIER
AUGUST 1, 2015

Summer training camp was in full swing. The football players had reported to their camp in Northeast Georgia near Lake Lanier, three weeks earlier. My job was pretty much nonstop during the days, but Kristen and I had coordinated it so that we got our days off together. The team had put us up in a hotel near the facility, but she had insisted on renting a lake house, so we could actually enjoy ourselves.

Anyone else was welcome to crash at the place, which made it a rotating party house full of staff sunbathing in the August rays. Kristen knew everyone. Though some of the people were there for the training facility, many of them had driven up from Atlanta to partake.

I was in a tiny black bikini, my hair in a messy bun, with a beer in my hand as I pet my puppy, Sunny. She was a silky brown miniature dachshund, who I was mildly obsessed with. I was so focused on Sunny that I didn't notice until the puppy abandoned me that Cole was on the deck in nothing but green board shorts. My heart leapt as he scooped up my pup. We'd been circling each other for two months. Both of us on the cusp of starting something over again and then backing off. We hadn't discussed it, but we didn't have to. I knew what he was thinking. That he didn't want to get his heart ripped out again. That neither of us could survive that hurt again.

But damn, did I want it.

"Hello there," he said, scratching Sunny's head. "Yes, aren't you so cute?"

I came to my feet. "She loves everyone."

"But me most, right?" he asked the dog.

Sunny licked his face.

"What's her name?"

I flushed. "Sunny."

Cole's eyes swept to mine. Heat seared between us. "Sunny, huh?"

I swallowed and nodded.

"Well, Sunny, you're perfect." He set her down on the ground, and she ran around in a circle before settling on my abandoned towel. He sank into a chair. "It's so damn hot here."

"You went off to San Francisco and got soft," I teased.

He narrowed his eyes. "You don't have to rub it in that I had perfect California weather for five years, and now, I'm back to drinking the air."

"Poor baby."

"Can't beat the cost of living at least."

"That's for sure. You had a literal shoebox in San Francisco."

"It got a little better, the longer I was there," he said. "But not by much."

"You could have a mansion here for what you paid for that shoebox too."

"Hey, I'm glad that I'm back."

I waited a heartbeat before responding, "Me too."

His eyes swept up my body before landing on my eyes. The sincerity in them. The ache at him leaving for San Francisco, at us not working out, at the circling we'd been doing all this time.

"Hey, y'all!" Kristen yelled. Sunny barked at her. "We're heading to the store to get more booze. You'll have the house to yourselves. Be back. Bye!"

Then she was shepherding the other people who had come up early that Friday out of the house. The place would be packed with people tomorrow, but today, it was relatively empty.

"She's not subtle, is she?" Cole asked.

"Not at all."

Kristen had gotten it into her head that she was going to play matchmaker. When I'd given her some more of the details about what had happened with Cole, she'd made it her life mission to get us back together. This was our *someday*.

"I like her determination."

"Yeah. She thinks if she gives us the house alone, we'll fall into each other's arms."

"Is that so?"

I bit my lip and nodded. "She thinks that this is our break."

"And what do you think?"

I took a deep breath. Was this a trap, or did he really want to know? I'd always thought Cole was such an open book, but lately, he'd been so guarded. I wasn't sure if he was ready for the truth from me.

"I don't know," I lied.

"What do you want, Lila?"

The question caught me off guard. The earnestness in his voice that said he was ready for me to admit it.

"You," I whispered.

"You want me?"

"I always have."

"And the last two months?"

I huffed. "Surely, you know I've wanted you the last two months, but the ball was in your court."

"And here I thought, this was your call."

He beamed that bright Cole Davis smile and held his hand out. I tentatively stepped forward and put my hand in his. He tugged me toward him, and I climbed into his lap. He wrapped an arm around my waist.

I belonged here. That much was for certain. I fitted against him so effortlessly as if no time had passed at all. I decided to revel in that and not think about anything that had kept us from this moment.

"You know I've always wanted you, Lila. You're the only person I've ever wanted."

My heart constricted. "Really?"

"I know we've waited these two months, but I thought you wanted the time. It's been a long time since we were here."

"We've seen each other since the breakup."

"That's different. This isn't like that time I saw you when you were cheering for the Falcons or ... in New

Orleans." I swallowed at those words, but he continued. "You know it isn't the same."

"It is, but I wasn't sure if you wanted to try again."

"I never wanted to end things."

"Me neither."

That day on the beach when he'd ended things on the phone felt like a lifetime ago. The heartbreak was no longer fresh. The betrayal no longer so keen. We both deserved a fresh start.

"So, what do you say, Sunflower?" He pressed our foreheads together. Our lips mere inches apart. I could feel his breath hot against me. "Can we try again?"

My heart was in my throat. "I'd like that."

His hand snaked up into my hair and pulled my mouth down to his. I'd spent hours kissing Cole. I'd memorized the feel of his lips and the brush of his tongue. The surety with which he used his mouth and hands and body. But I'd never been kissed like this before.

Not that first time in a stadium full of people with our faces on the jumbo screen. Not the last time before the breakup when I'd held on in San Francisco so long that I'd nearly missed my flight. Not even when we'd run into each other in the interim and everything had changed and nothing had.

No, this was a new first kiss.

A fresh start.

A promise.

Unlike the other times we'd tried this, this was going to take.

21

ATLANTA
NOVEMBER, 27, 2011

"That's a break, ladies!" the Falcons cheer captain called from the sidelines.

The Falcons were up big against the Vikings at the end of the first half, and we'd earned our break. I dropped my poms and took a good, long drink from my water bottle. Dancing for four hours straight always left me both energized and exhausted. It was a strange yet potent combination.

I retrieved my poms once more and faced the half-time performance. The players had already run back into the locker room, leaving only a few staff and photographers behind.

"Hey, you went to Georgia too, right?" one of my fellow cheerleaders, Monique, asked.

"Yeah," I said. "Why?"

"Jasmine and I have a bet going. Help us settle it?"

"It's not a bet," Jasmine said with an eye roll.

Monique looked victorious. She pointed toward the sidelines. "That guy, is he Cole Davis?"

My heart stuttered as I followed her finger. "Holy shit."

"I knew it!" Monique said. "It's him, isn't it?"

"It is," I whispered.

She held her hand out to Jasmine. "Pay up."

"I'll be right back," I said and then left formation.

I'd nearly crossed the line into the Falcons sidelines when Cole turned around, as if he'd been waiting for me all along. He fumbled with the DSLR camera he was holding when he caught sight of me.

"Lila?"

"Oh my God, Cole."

I ignored everything else around me and threw myself into his arms. He picked me up as if I weighed nothing. Neither of us cared that people were watching us. What else was new?

"What are you doing here?" I demanded. "I thought you were in San Francisco."

"49ers played on Thanksgiving Day," he said, placing me back on my feet. He threw the strap of his camera around his neck. "I booked a flight for after the game and spent the weekend with my family. Dad got me a guest pass for the game."

"That's amazing. I wish I'd known. Are you back into photography?"

He ducked his chin. "Sort of. I'm not any good, but I carry the thing with me anyway." He brushed back his hair, which had grown longer than a year ago. It curled at the edges around his Falcons hat. "I had no idea you were a cheerleader."

"Yeah, I made the team this spring. It's been quite an experience."

"Are you in PT school here?"

"No, I took a year off."

"What? Why?" His eyes were round with surprise. "That's all you've ever wanted."

I didn't want to admit the truth. That I'd been lost after he dumped me. That our breakup had shattered me into pieces I didn't know how to come back from. I was still stitching them back together.

But I said the half-truth instead, "I decided to take a year off school and work in a PT clinic first. Make sure it's what I really want to do. What about you?" I quickly changed the subject. "How's marketing going in San Francisco?"

"Boring," he admitted. "I've started a side project with a friend. We'll see if it goes anywhere. I'd rather spend all my time on that, but I have to afford San Francisco."

"I get that. I'm living with Josie, not that I ever see her."

Cole shook his head. "Isn't she on that new show? What's it called?"

"*Academy*," I said. "She never thought it would go anywhere, and now, it's one of the most-watched shows on television in its first season. Who knew she'd ever become the face of a supernatural school?"

"Probably everyone who met her knew she'd make it big. She has that thing." He snapped his fingers. "You know what I mean?"

"Yeah. Charisma."

"The *it* factor."

"Gah," I said, glancing back at the sidelines. My friends motioned for me to return. "Look, I'd love to chat more, but I have to get back to the team. Do you have plans after?"

"No plans."

"Can we play catch-up then?"

He nodded.

"Okay, I'll text you."

He snagged my elbow and pulled me in for another hug. "I've missed you, Sunflower."

I shivered at the nickname. I'd missed him so fucking much that I felt tears spring to my eyes. Just his arms wrapped around me felt right. So damn right.

"I've missed you too."

He reluctantly released me, and I headed back to my fellow cheerleaders.

Monique arched an eyebrow. "Damn, girl. That is how it's done."

Jasmine fluffed her Afro. "Get it."

I laughed at them both. I wondered what our interaction had looked like from the outside. For people who didn't know our history.

"Tell me you got his number," Monique said.

I winked at her, and both girls crowed with excitement for me. As if I'd just snagged myself a man. Instead of found a way to get back together with the one I'd always wanted.

～

WHEN ALL THE fans had left the Georgia Dome, celebrating the Falcons victory, the cheerleaders finally left too. I stepped out into the brisk November weather, pulling my jacket tight around me. And standing outside, waiting for me, was Cole Davis.

"Hey." My stomach fluttered at the sight of him. Everything should have hurt to even see him, but instead, all I saw was possibility.

"What a game," he said.

"Yeah. Falcons victory always makes for a good day."

"Dad thinks so too."

"I bet," I said. Considering Hal Davis was the offensive line coach, I would think that he'd been pleased. "Where are you parked?"

"I drove in with my dad. Can I catch a ride with you?"

"Definitely."

Cole fell into step with me, his elbow brushing against mine as we walked. We cleared the parking lot and came up to my little Hyundai. I tossed the keys to Cole to get the car warmed up, and then as he did that, I dropped my bags in the trunk.

"Where to?" I asked, sliding into the driver's side.

"Wherever you want."

"Are you hungry? I don't have much at my place, but we could order delivery."

"Sounds good."

I drove us away from downtown to my empty apartment. Cole flipped through the back of his camera.

"I got some pictures of you."

I blinked over at him. "What?"

"I took some cheerleading pictures in the second half. Since I knew where you were."

I glanced over at his camera, and my eyes were wide. "Cole, that's amazing."

"It's nothing. Just for fun. I thought you'd want some."

"I do. And they're so good." I looked at the next one. "Jesus, you're so talented."

"Nah, just a hobby."

"Well, people can be excellent at their hobbies, Cole."

He laughed. "I suppose you're right."

"You should do more of this."

"It's easy to remember to breathe when I'm with you."

I bit my lip, a flush suffusing my skin. Somehow, he'd managed to take the words right out of my mouth. That was exactly how it had always felt to be with him. Like I could finally breathe again. As if this was just meant to be.

I pulled into the parking lot of my apartment complex. Cole lugged my cheer bags into the building and pressed the button for the elevator.

"It's been broken for months," I said. "We called maintenance, but no one has come out to fix it."

"Stairs it is."

We climbed up to the fifth floor.

"Seriously," I huffed when we made it to my door, "this is the only reason I don't have a dog."

"You want a dog?"

"So bad," I told him. "A little wiener dog."

He chuckled. "That suits you."

"Yeah, but there's no fucking way I'm trekking up and

down four flights of stairs in the middle of the night to take them outside to do their business."

"Fair. What would you name her?"

I pushed inside, and Cole dumped my bag on the table. "How do you know it would be a her?"

"Because I know you."

I met his searing look. "I'm not sure. I haven't decided."

"Sunflower."

"That's *my* nickname."

"You could call her Sunny."

"Sunny?" I tilted my head as I looked up at him. He'd come closer. So close. We were only inches away. I could feel the heat off of him. "I like that."

There was something between us. Something that had never disappeared. That time and distance couldn't possibly eradicate. And I pulled on that thread, not caring if we unraveled or were knit into a new pattern.

"Lila," he said like a prayer.

Then his hands tangled in my hair and our bodies pressed tightly together and his mouth was hot against mine. All thoughts of getting dinner evaporated. Had it ever existed? Or was it an excuse to get us alone? Because I could think of nothing else when he was here now.

"I missed you," I gasped as I tossed his baseball cap to the floor. I ran my fingers through the longer strands, the gentle curls on the ends that called to me.

"So much," he growled.

I jerked at his shirt, tearing it over his head and revealing the toned six-pack underneath. I dragged my nails down his chest. He made some faint sound of approval before he lifted me in the air and dropped me down onto the couch. His body ground into mine. My leggings no match for the length of him against me.

Everything slowed down and sped up at the same time. As if time didn't have meaning here. Just the feel of him rubbing against me. The taste of his lips against mine. The sweep of his tongue in my mouth. And the desperate, unmistakable need rushing through my body.

"Cole, please."

In the years we'd been together, he'd spent hours savoring my body. If he tried that right now, I might combust. I needed him, all of him. And I didn't want to wait another minute.

We stripped out of our clothes, leaving them in a pile on the floor of my apartment. Then, he was there, hovering over me. No hesitancy. No questions. Just a look I knew all too well. It said I was his, and I couldn't deny that fact one bit.

He slipped a hand under my hips, tilting me up to meet him. I groaned at the first feel of him. My eyes fluttered closed.

"Look at me, Lila."

I bit my lip and met his cool blue gaze. Then he thrust forward, and I could feel every inch of him inside of me. I gasped at the perfect fit, the feel of finally being full again.

Fuck, I wanted this. I wanted this and more. I never wanted it to end.

He withdrew slowly, and I thought I was going to collapse. But then he drove forward. I clutched at his shoulders, bringing him down for a kiss.

"More," I begged.

And he obliged.

I wrapped my legs around his hips, using the leverage to meet his every thrust. A thin layer of sweat coated our bodies as we ramped up. But I couldn't even care; I was so close. Ready to tip over the edge.

"Please," I said.

"Fuck."

Then he bottomed out inside of me. I gasped and hit the ceiling. Everything felt fuzzy and distant as my body pulsed all around him at the same time that he came hard and fast.

I collapsed backward on the couch. My brain was slow on the uptake. I felt foggy and disoriented. As if I were in a euphoria cloud.

Cole leaned his forehead against my shoulder. His chest was still rising and falling heavily with the exertion. "God, you're amazing."

I kissed his shoulder. "You're pretty amazing yourself."

"Was this your idea all along?" he asked, trailing kisses across my collarbone.

"Yes, I'm so sneaky."

He chuckled, pulling back to kiss my swollen lips. "You cast a spell on me."

"Someone else must have done the casting because I'm equally under your thrall."

"A love spell," he agreed.

"Or maybe," I said gently, "you can't resist me."

"That is a fact." He rubbed his nose against mine once. "You've always been addicting."

"That doesn't sound good."

"I keep needing a bigger hit. I never want to let you go. And when I'm without you, I go through withdrawals."

"When you put it that way, it doesn't sound so bad."

He sighed and finally pulled back. "Except that I'm still in San Francisco and you're still here."

"When do you go back?" I hated the question as soon as it left my mouth.

"Tomorrow."

I flinched.

It was the obvious answer. Of course he had to go home tomorrow. He had a job and a life in San Francisco. And I had a job and a life here.

Cole headed to the bathroom. I used Josie's to clean up and change into sweats. Then I put in an order for Thai. I already knew Cole's order. We used to order Thai every Friday night for almost a year while we'd dated in college. The memory panged the way it always did when I thought about him and the impossibility of us.

Cole appeared a few minutes later, back in his clothes. He dropped onto the couch next to me, slinging an arm around my shoulders and bringing me in close.

"I have an idea," I said. "What if you didn't go back?"

He chuckled softly and kissed my hair. "I have to."

"I know," I said with a resigned sigh. Then, another thought hit me. "Okay, what about ... what about if I went to PT school there?"

Cole pulled back to look at me. His face a mask of skepticism. "You'd do that?"

I bit my lip and nodded. "I mean, I could apply. I'm

applying right now to all the Georgia schools. My number one has been Emory, but UC-San Francisco has a good PT program."

His face was completely blank. I had no idea what he was thinking.

"Say something," I begged.

"You'd move to San Francisco for me?"

"I don't know," I said, suddenly unsure if I'd overstepped. "I just … I don't have to go to PT school here."

"That would be amazing," he finally said.

I broke into a smile. "Yeah?"

"Yes. Absolutely. I want nothing more than for you to come to San Francisco."

I swallowed back the rise of emotions. This was what I wanted too. So bad.

"Well, I still have to get in."

"I have every faith in you."

He kissed the top of my head and let the subject drop as our food arrived. It wasn't a guarantee that we'd work out, but it was a kernel of hope. A kernel that I hadn't had in a long time. I held on to it for dear life, and the next day, I set to work on the PT applications I'd been ignoring since graduation.

22

SAVANNAH

APRIL 8, 2012

My mom liked for all of us girls to come home for Easter Sunday. Even though none of us had been raised Catholic and I was the only one who had gone to a Catholic private school, she insisted on mass.

So, I'd driven down to Savannah for the weekend. I sat with Mom as we went through the pile of PT school acceptance letters. I'd gotten in everywhere, except my two biggest reach schools. I could go to Emory and stay in Atlanta. I'd still get to cheer for the Falcons on the weekends and only be four hours from my mom. Or go to the University of California, San Francisco and try something new. Move a thousand miles away to a place I'd never even been, let alone lived. All for the hope that things with Cole would work out again. Maybe I could even audition for 49ers cheer. Anything was possible right now. I hadn't felt this light in ages.

My mom was excited that I'd gotten my spark back. I'd been floundering for too long, and I felt more like me again. I had to make my final decision.

"You remember that girl that you went to school with, Amanda Rochester?" my mom asked as mass finally finished and we rose to our feet to stretch.

"Uh, no?"

"She was the blonde. I think she was in your Chemistry class junior year."

"Hmm ... maybe?"

"Well, she married Destin Holloway. Do you remember him? Such a nice young man."

"Nope."

"Anyway, they had their second baby. She's such a cutie."

My mom did this. She liked to regale us all with people that we might have casually known as an adolescent and then talk about them as if we were all still friends. If Amanda had been in my Chemistry class, I had no real recollection of who she was now. But my mom had been working at St. Catherine's since I was a sophomore and now actually knew everyone. I was glad that she was full-time at the school and didn't need a second job anymore.

We filtered out in the aisle, and I scanned the cathedral seating. It was packed for Easter. I hoped that the sheer size of the place gave us some anonymity. Because though I never knew the people my mom was talking about, I did know people here in Savannah. Especially a certain someone who would likely be here for Easter mass with his parents.

Running into Ash Talmadge was low on my priority list. Really low.

I hadn't seen him since we'd slept together that night

on Frat Beach. I'd been furious with Ash and not returned a single message since. Not that it stopped him from sending them. I still occasionally received messages from him that I should have deleted but hadn't.

We'd almost made it out of the church and onto safer ground. I could see the exit in front of me like a beacon. Then my mom was stopped by an elderly couple a few feet from the welcoming double doors, and my sisters broke off into clusters to talk to friends.

"Mom, I'm going to step outside," I told her.

"Of course, honey."

She'd be at this for a while.

I took two steps outside and breathed in the air of safety when I heard a voice behind me. My eyes closed, and I sighed. Should have known better.

Ash stood in front of the church. He looked so ... Ash. A crisp black suit, pressed white button-up, blue seersucker bow tie. He'd definitely tied the thing himself. His blue eyes swept my body, taking in my toned legs, the flirty skirt of my pink sundress, and then the intensity of my eyes. My body wanted to take a step toward him. I wanted it. I always had. But I remained rooted in place.

"Hi," I said.

"You're in Savannah."

"Obviously."

"Just for the holiday?"

I nodded. "My mom is helping me decide on where to go for PT school."

"That's incredible, Lila. I know you've always wanted that."

"I have to go."

Being around him hurt. Here we were, in the same city we'd been five years ago when he shattered my heart. And it could have been so easy with him. It could have been my whole world. Some days, I thought that I was over all the pain we'd caused each other, that maybe we could even be friends. Actual friends. Then, I would get one glimpse of those blue eyes, and I knew the truth.

"Wait," he said, grasping my elbow.

"Ash."

"You never responded to any of my messages."

"Shouldn't that be a hint?"

"I don't want you to hate me forever."

I bit my pale pink lip. "I don't hate you."

He scoffed.

"I don't," I insisted. "Hate is too one-dimensional. We're complicated."

"We don't have to be."

It was my turn to laugh. "Okay, Ash. I'm going to go."

"It was good seeing you."

And despite fucking *everything*, it was good to see him.

I whipped around, prepared to ask him why he always fucking did this to me, but then a petite brunette traipsed out of the cathedral and ran right up to him. My eyes widened to saucers as she threw her arms around him and pressed a kiss to his lips.

"There you are!"

Ash drew her in close. He smiled down at her. A real smile. An Ash smile. Something panged in my chest. I'd never seen him look at someone else like that. Even when he'd been dating that girl in college—whatever her name was—it had seemed like temporary bliss. Something about this girl was different. The perfect cookie-cutter Easter Sunday dress. The fact that she was even *here* with him. Which meant ... she was here with his parents too.

I took another step back. I should have run. No need to make this more difficult for either of us.

"Who's your friend?" she asked.

Ash's gaze shifted back to mine. "This is Lila."

"Oh!" the girl said. Her eyes skittered back to Ash in question.

So, this girl knew who I was. Peachy.

God, it was so like Ash to do this. To pursue me here like this when he had his girlfriend inside. He couldn't ever just be alone.

"This is Heather," Ash said to me.

I nodded. "Cool. Nice meeting you."

"Um ... nice to meet you too," Heather said uncertainly.

It was so uncomfortable that there wasn't another real answer.

"Have a nice Easter," I told her, and then without looking at Ash, I strode down the steps and rushed to my mom's car. I waited for her there without looking up. Just played some stupid game on my phone.

A text came in while I was still waiting.

Sorry that was awkward. I'd planned to tell you about Heather.

I hadn't responded in over a year. It was a record.

I was about to break it.

Go back to your girlfriend.

It's not like that.

What the hell did that mean? Why was he so maddeningly cryptic?

Like I said, we're complicated.

At least you're responding again.

I growled and almost flung my phone. The man was infuriating.

My mom returned then, and I stuffed the phone in my bag without responding. We went back to our house, but my sisters had to go home. They promised to be back for dinner with their families. Our house couldn't accommodate everyone anymore, but my mom still hosted.

"Dee," my mom said once we were back inside.

I checked my phone once more and saw three more texts from Ash. He had been right. The mistake had been in responding.

"Yeah?"

"Can I talk to you for a minute?"

"What's up?"

I settled into the lumpy chair that was my favorite in the house and yawned.

"Well, I have some news."

My mom looked nervous. My mom never looked nervous.

"What kind of news?" I straightened in my chair.

"I don't know how to tell you this. So, I'm just going to say it. My kidney is rejecting."

My jaw dropped, and my vision went blurry. "What?"

"We knew this day would come," she said with all her practiced calm. "I had the kidney transplant right after you were born. Most transplanted kidneys only last twelve to twenty years from a live donor."

And I was twenty-two. She'd gotten more use out of it than they'd expected. But I still hadn't thought about it. Of course my mom took anti-rejection medication every day and would for the rest of her life. We'd all hoped the medicine would do its job forever. That wasn't realistic.

"Yeah, we knew that, but I didn't know it would be now."

"Me neither."

"What does this mean, going forward?"

I suddenly saw the weight my mom had been holding since I got here. She hadn't told me until now, right before I was going to leave. Everyone else must already know.

"It means that I'm back on the donor list."

My vision went black. "But ... you might never find a match! How long do you have?"

"I have enough time to be on the list."

"Well, I'll go get tested."

My mom reached out and took my hand. "No, I could never ask you to do that."

"You're not asking. I'm telling you."

She shook her head. "A parent should never have to take something like that from their child. You have a long life ahead of you."

"You're only in your fifties," I argued. "*You* still have a full life ahead of you. Don't talk like that."

"That's what the list is for, Dee."

"But isn't it likely that one of us is a donor? Have Steph and Eve and Elle gotten tested?"

"I told them not to."

I jumped to my feet. "And since when have they ever listened?"

"Dee, please, it's a lot to take in right now. I know it's upsetting, but we can get through this together."

"And you?" I asked, my voice catching. Tears coming to my eyes. "What's it going to be like for you while you wait?"

My mom's jaw set. "I can live a normal life. It's going to depend on how long the transplant takes. I'll have more appointments, dialysis."

"Oh God," I whispered. I pressed the heels of my hands into my eyes. "Mom ..."

"I know, honey. But it's going to be okay."

And she sounded so calm.

Like it really was all going to be okay.

The news was too fresh for me. She must have found out weeks ago to already be on the transplant list. She had waited to tell me in person. And now, it all hurt too much.

I pulled her into a hug. "I love you, Mom."

"I love you too."

"I just ... I need to process this."

"I understand. Your sisters needed time too." She stroked a hand down my hair. "I'm going to start making

Easter dinner. Maybe you should call your sisters and talk to them about this. It'll help you."

I nodded. "Yeah. Maybe."

I watched her walk away with a sick feeling in the pit of my stomach. I wanted to be there for my mom. I couldn't let her deal with this alone. But she seemed determined to appear as if everything were fine. I knew it couldn't possibly be.

I snatched my purse and keys off of the front table and headed out to my car. I skipped a text and called Ash before I could stop myself.

"Hey. This is a surprise," he said easily.

"Can you meet me at the park?"

"Uh ..."

"Please, Ash," I said, my voice breaking.

He was silent before answering, "Yeah, give me a few minutes."

"Thank you."

I hung up and drove straight to Forsyth Park. It was busy for Easter Sunday, but I found a parking spot nearby. I hadn't changed out of my heels and was regretting it as I crossed the cobbled streets and into the park. I walked the Spanish moss–lined walkway to the fountain and took a seat at the base while I waited.

It was another twenty minutes before Ash Talmadge walked to the fountain. His gaze was set on mine, and his stride quickened. "Hey, is everything okay?"

"No," I said. "I didn't know if you'd be able to get away."

"Well, no one was happy about it, least of all Heather, but you sounded upset."

"You told her you were coming to see me?"

He nodded. "I told her it was an emergency."

"I bet she didn't like that. I'm sorry."

He took a seat next to me by the fountain. "What happened?"

"So, you know how my mom had a kidney transplant after I was born?"

"Yeah?"

"Well, it's rejecting, and she's back on the transplant list."

"Fuck," he whispered.

"I know."

"Lila, I'm so sorry. That's terrible."

"She's okay for now," I told him. "But it's going to get worse, and she doesn't want any of us girls to get tested to see if we're a match. She said she can't take an organ from a kid or whatever."

"That sounds like your mom."

"I know," I said, and then I couldn't hold it in any longer. I burst into tears. I didn't want my mom to die. I didn't want her to wait forever on a transplant list with no hope. I couldn't be away from her while she was going through this.

Ash didn't say anything at all; he just pulled me into his arms and held me there. Let me cry on his expensive suit without a word. He ran a hand through my hair as I let it all out.

I sniffled and swiped a hand under my eyes. "I know this sounds so selfish, but now, I have no idea what to do about PT school."

"That doesn't sound selfish, Lila."

"But why am I even thinking about myself right now?"

"Because you love your mom, and now, you're reconsidering your life."

"Yeah," I whispered. I debated telling him the truth. I could have held it back and not let him know, but he was telling Heather everything. Actually, he was *dating* Heather. So, why should he care about what I was going to say? "I was going to move to San Francisco."

Ash stiffened. "For PT school?"

I nodded.

"Why?"

Our eyes met.

"You know why."

"Ah," he said, his jaw tightening. "I didn't realize you two were still talking."

"We aren't really," I admitted. "But it felt like maybe we would if I moved there."

"That's a big move for a maybe."

He wasn't wrong. I'd thought about it so much over the last six months of applications. But a part of me knew that if I went there, it would work out. The only reason Cole and I had ever had real problems was distance and the man sitting right next to me.

"What are you going to do?"

I choked. "I don't know."

"Okay. Think about it like this: if something happened with your mom and you were a thousand miles away, how would you feel?"

"I can hardly stomach the idea of being four *hours* away."

"Then that's your answer."

Fuck. I hated when he was right. And I knew he was. There was only one answer. It had nothing to do with Cole and everything to do with my mom. I'd never forgive myself if I wasn't here when she needed me.

"Thanks, Ash."

He released my shoulder now that I didn't look like I was going to fall apart. "Always, Lila."

Our eyes met, and something passed between us. A current of energy. The same feeling I'd always had with Ash. Even through my anger.

I coughed and shuffled a little further away. He was dating someone. I had been prepared to move across the country for Cole. Ash might be acting like my friend right now, but I hadn't been wrong when I said we were complicated.

"You should get back to Heather," I said carefully.

He nodded and stood. "I probably should."

"I should talk to Cole."

His gaze was dark as he said, "Tell him I said hi."

I glared at him. "Don't be an ass."

He smirked. "Can't help myself. I kind of hate that guy."

"I'm sure the feeling is mutual."

"I'm sure it is," he said as he bent down and kissed my cheek. "Call me if you need me."

Then he strode away, leaving me alone to call Cole and ruin any chance we'd had at getting back together. He practically had a skip in his step. Bastard.

23

SAVANNAH

AUGUST 3, 2012

I stepped out of the hospital room. My stomach felt wobbly as I returned to the lobby.

"You're all set," the man at reception said to me.

"Thanks," I said, taking another sip of the juice box the nurse had given me when I'd had my blood drawn.

Ash waited for me in the lobby with his head buried in his phone. He'd told me on the way over that he was reading the recently released thriller, *Gone Girl*. His head popped up when I walked out, and his frown deepened.

"Are you okay?"

I shrugged. "Apparently, my blood pressure was low. I did too much research before we got here and freaked myself out. Plus, blood."

"That sounds like you."

"They said I should hear in a few days if I'm a match, and then if I am, I can come back in for more tests."

"To check your kidney's health?"

I nodded.

We'd discussed all of this ahead of time. Ash listened

as I spiraled into the medical side of the internet. I went way overboard, but I couldn't seem to stop researching. The only reason I'd put off getting tested this long was because my mom had insisted that she didn't want me to get tested.

I'd decided that I couldn't wait any longer. Ash agreed to take me to my appointment since I was squeamish. I hadn't told my mom. The average person was on the transplant list for three to five years, but I'd rather know if I was a match than wait until it was too late.

"Maybe we should get you some lunch," he said as we left the hospital behind.

We walked over to his brand-new dark blue Mercedes, and he helped me into the passenger seat.

"I have a better idea," I said once he was seated. "I know I start PT school in, like, two weeks, but I want to get a puppy. I didn't pull the trigger when I lived in Atlanta because I didn't want to deal with one while living in an apartment."

"But now, you have a house."

I nodded. I'd rented a small two-bedroom downtown after I decided to attend PT school here in Savannah to be closer to Mom. I was renting with Marley's twin brother, Maddox, who was like a brother to me and had always not-so-secretly crushed on Josie. He had a floppy shih tzu mix that mostly lounged on the couch all day. We'd agreed, no cats.

"Yes, a puppy will make me feel better."

Ash shook his head. "I shouldn't have worn a suit."

"You always wear a suit."

"It's kind of my job."

"Whatever. Don't try to act all fancy on me."

"That never appealed to you anyway."

True. It never had.

FIFTEEN MINUTES LATER, we arrived at the Savannah Humane Society.

"Hi, can I help you?" a woman asked from behind the desk as we stepped inside.

"I've come to adopt a dog," I said.

"Oh, wonderful. Have you been here before?"

"No. Kind of spur of the moment."

"Well, great! I'm sure one of our dogs would love to go home with y'all."

Of course it looked like Ash and I were about to pick out a dog together. I opened my mouth to object, but Ash put a hand on my lower back. Our eyes met in the small space. It wasn't an absurd suggestion and probably more awkward to say something than to let it stand.

"Yes, I can't wait," I said instead.

The woman went through all the adoption information with me, and then finally, I got to find a puppy. My heart ached to walk the building. So many puppies without homes. I wanted to adopt them all.

I turned the final corner and found the most adorable little dachshund jumping at the bars. She had the silkiest dark brown fur with a long nose and big puppy eyes. It was love at first sight.

"Oh my God, look at you," I gushed.

She was teeny. Clearly not exactly a puppy anymore,

but so very little. I stuck my hand out, and she nuzzled into it and then licked my fingers.

"Yes, you are the cutest thing, aren't you?"

"She suits you," Ash said behind me.

"Do you love her too?" I asked, looking up at him.

His eyes shifted from the puppy to me. "Yes, I do love her."

My cheeks flushed at the words and the way he looked at me. I hastily returned my gaze to the dog.

Ash and I had been spending time together and texting, but he had Heather. That was safer and better for him. We were too complicated, and I'd spent so long not trusting him that it felt all new and different to be here as friends. To actually feel like I was starting to trust him again.

"I want her."

The woman from the desk came out and put a leash on the dog. We walked her around the premises and played with her, off leash, in a pen. I was smitten. There was no doubt about it; this was the dog for me.

"I'm so glad that you found a dog for you!" the woman said after I finished filling out paperwork and paying the fee. "What are you going to name her?"

I looked at the puppy, and my stomach flipped. I knew exactly what I was going to name her. The name had been picked out for me almost a year earlier. There was no way she could be anything else.

"Sunny."

❧

WE WENT to a local pet store and purchased everything I thought Sunny would need and more—carrier, crate, beds, toys, food, treats. The list felt endless, and I winced at the final number. Ash scooted me out of the way and paid for the whole thing against my protests.

"I can afford it!" I insisted angrily.

"I know you can, but I want to help you take care of her."

"Ash ..."

"It's done, Lila. Just say *thank you*."

I sighed. "Thank you, but you shouldn't have done it."

He shrugged. "I wanted to. She's too perfect, and she needs all the things."

There was no arguing with him. Unless I returned it all and then rebought it, there wasn't much else I could do. And I decided to be grateful.

"Plus, I got her a bed and food and treats for my place too."

"You think I'm going to let her out of my sight?"

He shot me a look. "I guess you'll have to come over more."

"I'm sure Heather will love that."

"She knows we're just friends."

He said the words, but they rang false. How could Ash and I ever just be friends?

We got all of Sunny's new things into the trunk. I set her on my lap, plying her with love and treats as we drove across town. I barely looked up until we reached Ash's place. My Hyundai was parked on the street, where I'd left it before we went for my appointment. The ghost of it had left me behind with my puppy's enthusiasm.

I got her on a leash and let her do her business in the bushes by his place before following him inside.

"Okay, Sunny, try not to pee on anything," I said with a laugh at Ash's stricken face. Then I took her off the leash, and she sprinted into the house.

"Oh!" a voice gasped from the kitchen. "Who are you?"

Ash and I looked at each other. Fuck. Heather was here.

"Yes, hello, aren't you so sweet?" Heather appeared in the living room, holding my dog, who was indiscriminately licking her.

"Oh," she said again as she looked between us. Ash holding all of Sunny's new equipment while I still held her leash. "What's going on?"

"Hey, Heather," I said, trying for normal and calm. "That's Sunny. I got her from the Humane Society."

"She's *your* dog?" she asked.

"Uh, yeah."

"What is she doing here?"

"I went with Lila to pick her out."

Heather squinted at him, carefully putting Sunny back on the ground. She crossed her arms. "You went with your ex-girlfriend to get a dog?"

That was my cue to leave. I sank to the floor. "Come here, Sunny."

"Well, I told you that I was helping her go to the doctor."

"Right. Which I thought was strange to begin with."

"Sunny," I said, patting my knees.

The dog didn't seem to care or know its name yet. It was circling Heather and sniffing her.

"And then after that, y'all went to get a dog together?"

"It's Lila's dog," he told her. But he was using the placating voice. I knew what that one meant. Every girl did.

"So, why do you have a bunch of stuff for it? Is the dog staying here? Is Lila staying here?"

"No," Ash said. "But look at her. She's adorable. I'm kind of attached."

Heather's face darkened at those words. "Are you talking about the dog or Lila, Ash?"

I grimaced, giving up on Sunny listening to me. I scooped her up into my arms and reattached the leash. "I'm going to just go home."

"Oh no," Heather said, seething. "No reason to leave on *my* account." She grabbed her purse off of the coffee table. "I should have seen this coming."

"Heather, come on," Ash said. "This isn't what it looks like."

"What does it look like?"

"Nothing," I said quickly, backing toward the door. "It's nothing."

"I think it is something. When Ash told me your whole sordid story, I thought he was moving past it. That we could work despite his past with a girl who clearly didn't appreciate him. I've bitten my tongue at the *just friends* bit for long enough."

"Heather—"

"But I was wrong. You're not over her. You're fucking *obsessed* with her."

I winced at her words. The surety as she spat them at him.

"The one who got away and who your parents didn't like and who you had to fight for. And I'm tired of trying to compete with that."

Heather shouldered past us both and burst out of Ash's house. He stood there for a full second, as if in shock that she'd walked out on him.

He looked at me in distress.

"Go after her!" I cried, pushing his shoulder.

Ash dashed out of the house, running after his girl-friend. I picked up the rest of my stuff while Sunny jumped up on the couch and made herself comfortable.

"Well, that makes one of us," I grumbled at her.

I wanted to leave, but I didn't want to be outside while Heather was yelling at him either. It had been awkward enough, being here as she'd gone off. And I hardly blamed her. I probably should have stayed away from Ash. Let him have his relationship just the way it was. Healthy and happy. But staying away had been impossible. It always had been.

Ash came back inside ten minutes later. He looked like he'd been beaten up. His hair a wreck. His suit disheveled. His eyes wide and lost.

"Fuck," was all that came out when he sank into the couch next to Sunny.

She settled into his lap, curling into a tiny ball. He stroked her back.

"So, that ... was a disaster."

"Yeah. Fuck."

"Is she going to give you another chance?"

He shook his head. "I don't know what the fuck she's going to do."

"Sorry."

Finally, he looked up at me. Those blue eyes so set on me. "Well, she wasn't wrong."

I flushed. "Ash ..."

"You have to know that I'm still in love with you."

My body broke out into goose bumps at the words. Of course I knew. I wasn't immune to him any more than he was to me. But I also wasn't ready for that. Ready for anything from him. Especially not minutes after his breakup.

"We can't do this, Ash."

"Why not?"

"Heather just dumped you."

"I know," he said with a sigh. "I know that."

"I can't be a rebound or hidden or anything. That's not fair to me or to her. We need to trust each other, to actually be friends before this could ever happen."

"So, there's hope," he said with a sad smile.

"Be alone, Ash. Just ... be alone for once." I picked Sunny up off of his lap. "Then, maybe ..."

"That's a lot for a maybe," he said, repeating what he'd said to me about Cole months earlier.

"Maybe it is. But only you can figure out if it's worth it."

Then I walked my puppy out of his place.

24

SAVANNAH
DECEMBER 31, 2012

Marley popped open another bottle of champagne. The good stuff—yellow-label Veuve. It was pretty much the only champagne that Ash would drink, which was why he'd stocked the yacht with it for his blowout New Year's Eve party.

"Are you sure this is a good idea?" Marley asked as she poured flutes for me, Maddox, and Maddox's girlfriend, Teena.

"This being?"

"Look, I like that we can use his yacht and drink his fancy champagne and shit," Marley said. "But should you be dating him?"

"Shut it, Mars," Maddox growled. "We get these benefits too."

Teena laughed. "It's pretty amazing."

"I'm just being practical," Marley argued.

"Josie asked the same thing," I said.

Marley snorted. "Josie did not ask that. Josie blew a

fucking fuse when she found out that you and Ash were —quote—'casually seeing each other again.' "

"Well, Josie holds grudges."

"She *sure* does," Maddox said. "You definitely shouldn't listen to what Josie says."

"Shut up, Maddox," Marley snapped. "Just because you and Josie are at each other's throats has nothing on this situation."

He shrugged. "Josie's just Josie."

"She is," I agreed. I'd watched Josie and Maddox step around each other since we were teenagers. He'd been smitten in high school and then something had happened when she'd been at SCAD that neither of them talked about. Since then Maddox had been so weird about Josie, and Josie shrugged it off.

"Anyway," Marley said with an eye roll. "I'm just saying ... maybe you should learn to hold grudges too."

"They take so much energy. And anyway, Josie isn't one to talk. She went and eloped with her costar on Christmas. Didn't even invite us!"

"Sounds right," Maddox said under his breath.

"She's a whole other topic. My best friends are so much work."

"You love us."

"I do. But I'm still worried about you."

"Look, what happened with Ash was so long ago. We were kids, and I don't even know how much of what happened was what Shelly even said."

"Okay, let's choose to ignore that statement. Because that's a lot to unpack, considering we've spent the last five years deriding him for every little problem." Marley took a sip of the champagne.

"I know we did. I was there. I remember how much it hurt."

"Can I interject?" Maddox asked.

"No!" Marley said.

"Ash seems like a nice guy. He loves Lila and Sunny."

Marley waved her hands at her twin brother. "That's enough from you. You weren't there after prom and you didn't hear about what happened at Frat Beach."

I blew out heavily. "I get it, Mars. But we've spent the last couple months *not* dating. Just being friends. And it feels different this time. I'm not walking into this blind. I want to be with Ash."

Marley shrugged. "Okay, I said my piece. If you're happy, I'm happy."

"Are you happy? I haven't heard about a new boy anytime recently."

Marley crinkled her nose, and Maddox laughed.

"Oh, here we go," Maddox said.

"Hey, if you have deets, you could tell your roommate," I said, smacking his chest.

He laughed harder. "She hasn't told you about the grad school guy who showed up at her apartment to serenade her?"

My eyes widened. "Excuse me?"

"It wasn't like that," Marley insisted. "It was a guy I'd dated for three seconds at Harvard last semester. I guess he was still into me."

"He played a guitar outside of your apartment and sang a song he'd written about you."

Marley rolled her eyes at Maddox. "So fucking cheesy."

"It sounds nice," Teena said.

"That is so not Marley though."

"It reeks of desperation," Marley said.

"One day, you are going to find someone who sweeps you off of your feet so completely that all that desperation will look like love."

She shot me a quintessential Marley look. "I'm not you."

"True."

I drained my glass and then let her refill it before I went in search of the person who had swept me off of my feet.

"There you are," Ash said when I found him across the deck. He pressed a kiss to my cherry-red lips. "I'm glad Marley agreed to come to the party tonight."

"Me too."

"Is she still mad at me?"

I made a face. "She wants me to be happy."

"And Josie?"

"You'll have a harder time with her. Grudge-holder and all."

"Why don't we plan a trip to LA to see her?"

"I'd love that," I gushed. "Maybe spring break."

"I'll get us tickets."

I bit my lip. "Thank you."

"Just because I've won back over the love of my life doesn't mean I'm going to stop trying to win over her friends. I know how important they are to you."

"They are," I said. I leaned into him and looked across the Savannah waterfront. "I miss Sunny."

"Me too," he said, pressing a kiss into my head. "Maybe we should have brought her with us."

"She hates fireworks. She'd have been a wreck. It's better that she's at the vet."

"Probably."

I reached up on my tiptoes and kissed him again. "This is right where I want to be."

"Good."

His hand slipped down the back of my silky red dress until he grasped my ass. I tilted my head up to look at him. He smiled that same Ash smile that I'd always fallen for. One that was all mine.

We'd only been dating a few weeks ago. I'd still been hesitant that this would work despite the last few months of friendship while I was in PT school. It was a grueling semester, and it was good to have Ash there when things got hard with school and Mom. Then he'd come over with an early Christmas present—a new copy of *Little Women* for my shelf—and I'd realized I had no reason to hold back.

Though we were together, we hadn't quite moved to the next level. I hadn't exactly thrown caution to the wind, like I'd let Marley believe. I wanted this, but I wanted it the right way. And now, I was here, staring up at his perfect lips, with his hand dragging me closer against him, and I had no idea why we were waiting.

I released a breath. "Maybe we should ..." I tipped my head toward the stairs to go below deck.

This was where we'd shared our first New Year's.

Where we'd had our first time. It felt symbolic that this was where it would all start again.

"Maybe we should," he agreed, walking me away from the rest of the party.

We headed downstairs to the small bedroom. It'd been renovated since we'd used it five years earlier, but it still felt the same.

The party roared overhead. Way more people than should probably be on the deck, anticipating the annual fireworks display. But here in this space, we were cocooned against the noise.

Before we even made it fully through the door, Ash's hands were on me, pulling me against him. He kissed me hard, his tongue brushing against mine.

All the restraint had evaporated.

We'd pulled the pin on the grenade.

I'd wanted this to be a perfect moment for us to be back together, but now that I was here, all I wanted was him. I couldn't seem to slow down and revel in what was happening. There would have to be time for that later. We'd inched toward the precipice and not fallen over it. Now, there was nothing between us, nothing to stop us.

His hands fumbled my skirt up to my hips, wrenching at the string of my thong and snapping it as if it were made of tissue paper. I gasped in an almost protest, but then his lips were against mine. I fumbled for his belt, yanking his shirt loose from his pants and pushing them off of his narrow hips.

"Fuck, Lila."

He walked me backward until my knees hit the bed. Then, he lifted my ass up, dropping me on the comforter, never breaking our lip-lock. I stroked him up and down once before he pressed me flat.

"God, I've missed you," he said, wrapping my legs around his waist and positioning himself at my opening.

"I've missed you too."

We were in a position to rewrite our relationship. We could have a fresh start and finally put the past behind us.

"Come here," I said, reaching for him.

He leaned forward and pressed his lips to mine. His hand slid up my arm before pinning it over my head. He did it with the other one as well, so I was practically immobile before him.

"You're mine."

"Yes," I whispered.

I squirmed, wanting him to move forward, to claim me in every way.

Then he plunged forward, and we were fitted together again. I was completely full of him. My shout smothered by his kisses. My body there for his taking. My heart raced ahead of us both.

"Ash," I gasped.

"Yes. Lila, God, you feel so fucking good. So fucking good."

He stole my breath again, holding both of my hands down with one of his and using his free hand to grip my hip as he pushed in and out. Gradually picking up speed as he worked me into a frenzy. I was already so hot for him that I thought I would combust, but he kept me from the edge as he used every trick he'd learned about my body over the years to take me there.

His fingers slipped down between my legs, and the first brush of his thumb against my clit sent me jumping.

"Oh!"

But he didn't stop. He circled my clit as he drove into me over and over again. I saw stars as everything built up and up and up. Until I could hold out no longer and I shouted my orgasm into the bedroom. He kept pumping in and out as I contracted around him.

"Fuck," he growled before jerking to a halt and finishing inside of me. He pressed his forehead to my chest once he was done. He mumbled a chorus of, "Fuck, fuck, fuck …"

He released my hands, and I slowly dropped them down into his hair. I didn't care that I was messing up the perfectly gelled strands. All I cared about was how incredible I felt and that I was here right now with my Ash.

"Hey," I whispered.

He looked up at me with sex eyes.

"Give me a kiss."

"Anything for you."

His mouth met mine one last time, a slow, generous kiss. One that sent my core tightening all over again with him still inside of me. We stayed like that longer than we probably should have, considering we were hosting this party. But it was worth it.

By the time we'd righted our clothes and returned to the party, we were in the beginning of the midnight countdown. Marley shot me a suspicious look, but I just smiled at her. Who cared what anyone else thought? I knew that this thing with Ash was right. It had never felt more right than with his arms around me as we counted down to a whole new year.

"Lila," he murmured into my ear.

"Hmm?"

"I want everything with you."

I laughed softly. "You have everything with me."

"No, I want ... more ... all of it."

I looked up at his very serious expression. "What do you mean?"

"Now that I have you, I never want to lose you." His mouth brushed the shell of my ear. "I want the whole lot: you in my house, you with my name, you with my kids."

I froze at the words. At the future that he'd painted for us. I could see it so clearly. And somehow, I'd never thought that far ahead. Never let myself consider where I was going or when wedding bells would ring.

"Why don't we take it one day at a time?"

But Ash knew me too well not to understand my hesitancy.

"It's too soon," he said automatically. "I know it is. But with you, Lila, I always seem to get ahead of myself. First step: move in with me."

My jaw dropped at the quick proposal. "I have ... the house with Maddox."

"We could make it work."

And so I gave him the truth. "I'm not ready."

There was hurt in his blue eyes. He was ready. Ready for everything with me. Ready to marry me on the spot if he could. I could see it all in his eyes. But I wasn't there yet. I'd been the one who was hurt, and while I could argue with Marley all day long, she had been right. I needed to be careful. I needed to be *sure*.

Then the countdown rang down to zero, fireworks exploded in the sky overhead, and Ash pulled me in for a lasting kiss. A new year, a new promise, a new life.

25

ATLANTA

MAY 14, 2016

My fingers slid along the spines of my books artfully arranged on Cole's bookshelf. Three years ago, I'd been too afraid to move in with Ash when he'd asked. I refused to make the same mistake again with Cole now that we had our chance. So, when he'd asked, I'd responded with a resounding yes. And then promptly commandeered his bookshelf for my own. He'd rolled his eyes as I'd emptied my boxes of books onto the beautiful mahogany hardwood shelves.

I heard a camera flash behind me and whipped around to find Cole pointing his DSLR at me.

"What are you taking pictures of?"

"I want to remember this day forever."

"Oh?" I asked, arching an eyebrow.

He grinned. "The day we moved into our first house together."

I reached onto my tiptoes and kissed him. "Can I see?"

"Let me take some more first."

"Fine." Then I went back to organizing.

"Are you still obsessing about the bookshelves?" Cole asked.

"Define obsessing."

He laughed and then snapped another picture of me. And another. And another.

"How many are you going to take?" I asked.

But he'd let the camera drop from the strap around his neck and lifted me up over his shoulder. I squealed as he carried me away from the bookshelves and effortlessly tossed me down on our couch. *Our* couch. I still wasn't used to that.

Sunny popped her head up from her bed in the corner and then hopped over to squeeze her way in between us. I petted her, and Cole dropped a kiss on her head.

"Good puppy," he cooed. "You, however," he said, tugging my hair loose from its messy bun and brushing his fingers through it. "You need to take a break. Be more like Sunny."

"I can't be that lazy."

"True, but people will be here soon. It doesn't have to be perfect."

"I know."

"You know, but it does need to be perfect?"

"No! I just don't want there to be visible boxes for our first official housewarming party."

"Literally no one is going to care but you."

"So?"

He kissed all over my face. "I love when you're irrational and stubborn. It's my favorite combo."

"Hey!"

"I'm serious. It's the best. Can I help move some boxes, so no one can see them?"

"Yes, please."

He lifted me back to my feet, putting his camera on the bar, and then let me direct him to clean up in the last half hour before all of our friends burst into our new house. Well, Cole's house. He'd put down the down payment, and it was in his name. It was hard to believe that we'd been dating for over a year already. Moving in together was a big step for me. I'd never lived with anyone I was dating.

We tucked away the last remaining box right before the doorbell rang. I dashed to answer it, and Marley entered with Josie on her heels.

"The party has arrived," Josie said, dumping a giant box into Cole's arms and drawing me into a hug. "I've missed you so much."

"I've missed you too."

We squeezed even tighter, moving back and forth like it'd been a decade since we'd seen each other instead of a few months. We used to go the whole year without each other, but then we used to get the entire summer together too. And now, I never got enough Josie time. She was too busy, being famous.

Sunny ran around barking at us until Josie picked her up and loved on her.

"Mars," I said in welcome.

She handed me a square present. "I hope Cole likes it."

I laughed. "Oh boy."

She grinned wickedly. "Anyway, who else is coming to this thing?"

"Mostly work friends."

"Boring," she joked.

I was so fucking glad that Marley had gotten a job as a professor at Emory. She had her own genetics research lab and was generally saving the world. But I was mostly glad we were both in Atlanta. As much as I liked my work friends, no one else was Marley.

More people trickled in. Kristen brought a present to rival Josie's, and the rest of the guys brought cards and nodded at us.

"So, wait," Kristen said once she had a drink in hand, "you're Josephine Reynolds?"

Josie nodded and held her hand out. "You can call me Josie."

"Holy shit!" She smacked me. "Why didn't you tell me you were friends with Josephine Reynolds?"

"Uh ... I didn't know that you were an *Academy* fan?"

"Who isn't an *Academy* fan?" Kristen asked.

Matthew, who was also in the training room with us, raised his hands. "No offense."

"None taken," Josie said. "It's not for everyone."

"You're winning, like, fucking Emmys," Kristen gushed.

Josie was the best with fans though. She'd always been that way, even before she became a famous TV star. People had trailed her for who she was long before then. "Thanks, babe. Should we selfie?"

"Fuck yes, we should."

Marley rolled her eyes at the display. "You'd think this was unusual."

"Nope. Just Josie."

Cole slung an arm around my shoulders. "Can confirm that Josie was like this before television."

Josie snapped the picture with her best angles and then grinned at Cole. "Obviously. I was the one who took those incredible pictures of you at the football game."

"It's still unfair that Josie was there and I wasn't," Marley added as we all settled into the living room. Sunny curled up into Marley's lap and looked like she was never planning to leave.

"Wait ... I've heard this story," Kristen butted in. "There are pictures?"

Josie held up one finger. "Hold, please."

"Oh, here we go," I said with an eye roll.

Josie passed her phone to Kristen. "There. I took those when they first met."

"Why are those still on your phone?" I asked, my cheeks going red.

"I never delete pictures."

"Dear God," I groaned.

"I can't believe you two started dating your freshman year," Kristen said, handing the phone back. "That's so romantic."

Minus the years in between when he had been in San Francisco and everything had crumbled to pieces.

"We got lucky," Cole said as he pressed a kiss to my hair. "Found our person early."

"If I were still with the guy I'd met in college, I'd be

divorced, or one of us would have been murdered," Kristen said.

Marley nodded. "Same."

Josie shrugged. "I didn't date anyone in college."

Marley and I snorted at the same time.

"What? I didn't!"

"Define date," I said with an arched eyebrow.

"Whatever!"

"SCAD was a breeding ground for cute, charismatic, artsy types," Marley said. "You were the queen of that breeding ground."

Josie huffed. "You two are the worst."

Kristen grinned. "I love this."

"Anyway," Josie said with a pointed look at the two of us.

"Aren't you engaged?" Kristen asked.

"God, you do stalk her," I joked.

Kristen shot me a look with a half-shoulder shrug that said she really did. "Sorry."

"I am engaged!" Josie exclaimed.

"At least we can go to *this* fucking wedding," I grumbled.

"It's not my fault that I eloped."

Marley laughed. "Isn't it kind of your fault?"

"Okay, yes, but it was the right decision at the time," Josie said. "And now, a full wedding where you all can be there and be bridesmaids makes more sense this time around."

"What about the next wedding?" Marley deadpanned.

Josie swatted at her. "You're lucky you're my best friend."

"When is it happening?" Cole asked. "I'm about wedding'd out. We had three this spring and have three more this summer."

"Sorry, man," Michael said. He'd gotten married in the spring.

"I swear, everyone we know is getting married."

"Is one of those Elle's wedding?" Marley asked.

I nodded. "Yes, I'm a bridesmaid for that one!"

"I'll be there. I just got the invite. It'll be good to be home and see Maddox."

"Yes, Savannah weddings are all beautiful," Cole said. "But, Josie, seriously, wait a year at least."

She rolled her eyes. "Sorry to disappoint. I was thinking fall ... but maybe next summer."

He sighed. "That will be wedding number *seven* this year."

"I think that's sweet," Kristen said. "Soon, you'll be planning your own nuptials."

I froze at those words and the abrupt change in conversation. A wedding. We'd hadn't even been together a year. Of course, we'd been together for over two years before, but that had been in college. That was different. Now, I was twenty-seven, and that was kind of the next step in life.

Not that it was the first time I'd ever thought about it. I'd thought about it with two people. And we were here again, discussing something I actually wanted with Cole. I just didn't know how to not think of Ash too.

"Let's not scare her," Marley said.

"I was joking," Kristen said. "The patriarchy dictates when people get married or if they even do. People can live a perfectly happy life together without some legal piece of paper."

"Hear, hear," Josie said, holding her glass aloft.

Cole squeezed me tighter, letting the conversation change.

The rest of the evening was wonderful. And by the time the last person left, we were tired and somehow also buoyant. Cole ordered in Thai for a late dinner, and we sank down into the couch with the pile of presents in front of us. Sunny had overexerted herself with all the attention and was passed out in her bed like the lazy pup she was.

"Marley said this was for you."

"Should I be scared?" he asked, shaking the package.

"Probably."

He tore the paper and then looked skeptical. "Why did Marley get me a rice cooker?"

I covered my face and burst into laughter. "I might have told her about that time you burned the rice."

"Lila!"

"It was too funny."

He poked me in the ribs until I giggled.

"I surrender!" I gasped.

He released me and then drew me in for a kiss. "Tonight was special."

"It was."

"I want nights like this all the time."

I nodded and leaned against him. "Me too."

"Were you spooked about the wedding talk?" he asked after a second.

"No ..."

He tilted my chin up until I was looking at him. "Yes, you were."

"Okay, maybe a little. But not because I don't want that."

"I'm not proposing today," he said with a grin.

"Yeah, but people said that all spring at all of those weddings we went to. They kept pointing at us and being like, '*You're next!*'"

"That's what people do at weddings."

"I think it's weird."

"I know you do, Sunflower."

"Even if we are next," I whispered.

"Technically, Josie is next."

I rolled my eyes. "Fine, Josie is next. Again. But I meant that ... that future looks possible."

"I like to hear you say that," he said as his lips covered mine. They were hot and needy, as if my words had triggered something in him. As if the thought of marrying me turned him on.

We made out for a few minutes, his hands roaming my body and both of us getting flushed with the heat. Then, the doorbell rang. I groaned and flopped backward as he went to get dinner.

He returned with the food and made a space for it on the already-cluttered coffee table. "Before we eat, I did get you a housewarming gift."

"What? But it's *your* house."

"Yeah. So?"

"You're ridiculous."

He dashed back into our bedroom and came back a minute later with a carefully wrapped package. I took it out of his hands and pretended to shake it to figure out what it was. Just like he had.

Then I tore back the wrapping paper, ripping the entire front away. I stilled at the title on the book—*Little Women*. My hand touched the cover. A special-edition leather-bound hardcover that I'd never seen before. It looked old. Really old. The binding was red. The font a small gold embossing. The pages were gold sprayed and stunning.

I picked the book up, letting the paper drop to the floor.

"Do you like it?"

Truthfully, I was speechless. It was the most beautiful copy of *Little Women* I'd ever seen. A very thoughtful and likely expensive gift. And every other part of me squirmed to be holding a copy from *Cole*.

I opened to the first page, half-expecting to find the inscription *Always your Laurie* written into it, as it was with the nearly dozen copies Ash had given me over the years. But of course, this was from Cole. He'd seen my love of the book. He'd wanted to get me something special. He had no clue that the reason I had so many copies was because Ash always bought them for me. Fuck.

I read the inscription.

5.14.16
Our first house.

"I know you have a bunch of copies," Cole said. "But I wanted this one to be ours."

Ours.

"It's beautiful. I love it. Thank you," I breathed. I met his blue gaze. "This one is *ours.*"

26

SAVANNAH

JULY 9, 2016

When Steph had gotten married, I'd still been in high school. She'd worn an empire Cinderella gown, and we'd all hated our yellow floor-length dresses. Eve had worn a smart white power suit when she married her wife in Chicago. She'd foregone bridesmaids and told us all to wear casual attire. But Elle was maybe the most stunning of all in a bohemian dress, complete with a flower crown.

I loved her dress even if the flowing dresses she'd picked for the rest of us looked ridiculous. Not to mention the decision to get married outside in Savannah in *July*.

"I'm going to sweat through this before the ceremony," Steph grumbled.

Eve crossed her arms. "She should be fucking glad I wore the goddamn dress."

"At least she didn't try to do your hair."

Eve looked at me in outrage. "Oh, we already fought

about that." She ran a hand back through her short, slicked-back, bleach-blonde hair.

"The rest of us have these flowers," I said, pointing at the thing in my hair.

"Well, I'm not a pushover."

Steph snorted. "Or you're too stubborn for someone else's wedding."

"Let's not fight today."

Elle appeared then like a vision. She looked like something out of one of those flashy wedding magazines.

"I think we're ready," she said.

We all shuffled into position. No wedding planner here. Elle had done everything herself, down to the floral arrangements and composing six original pieces for the orchestra she performed with. They'd play for the wedding and then join us for the reception.

I picked up my eucalyptus bouquet and got into line with Eve and Steph behind me. The groomsmen were waiting at the front of the outdoor pavilion with Elle's soon-to-be husband, Gary. The orchestra picked up the opening chords, and I began my procession down the aisle. The wedding easily had three hundred people in attendance, plus the orchestra.

The faces all blurred together as I stepped carefully along the grass path in my heels. My mom was standing at the front with tears in her eyes. Cole was a row behind her, and his smile was brilliant.

But then I looked across the aisle, and I nearly faltered.

In the sea of people, Ash Talmadge managed to stand out.

Cole on one side and Ash on the other.

The story of my life.

I looked straight ahead, anxious to get to my place at the front. Despite all of the eyes on me, I could feel them both specifically looking at me. Like fire creeping over my body.

The two men who had always been in my life.

And the divide between them felt fragile. As if a nail dragged along the film would rip it in half.

I RUSHED STRAIGHT to Cole as soon as the wedding was over and I was cleared from pictures. Thankfully, the wedding party did not have to walk into the outdoor tent to music. The bride and groom were about to be announced, and everyone was mingling, waiting for that moment.

"Hey! Sorry you've been alone all day," I said as I threw myself into his arms.

He dipped his lips down to meet mine. "It was a beautiful wedding."

"Elle was like out of a fairy tale."

"She and Gary look so happy."

I nodded. "So happy." Then I bit my lip and looked down. "Sorry about ... that other thing too. I didn't know he'd be here."

"Ah, yeah. That was unexpected."

"Completely. I didn't think he even knew Elle."

Cole shrugged. "He was on the groom's side. Must know Gary."

"Oh fuck," I said, smacking my forehead. "He does know Gary. They used to work together. I totally forgot."

He arched an eyebrow. "It's fine. Let's talk about something other than your ex-boyfriend."

"That seems fair."

Just then the band announced the bride and groom, Mr. and Mrs. O'Malley. Everyone cheered, and we all settled down to eat. Toasts were given by their maid of honor and best man, and then they stepped right into their first dance. We all oohed and aahed over them before joining them in dancing and drinking.

I thought we'd make it the entire evening without stumbling into Ash's path when he walked right up to us as we were getting drinks at the bar.

"Lila," he said calmly. There was fire in his eyes when he looked at Cole, but he held his hand out. "Cole."

I swallowed, sure that this was going to end in a fist-fight, but Cole shook his hand as if it were an everyday occurrence. As if they both didn't hate each other for how it had all gone down.

"Ash," Cole said stiffly.

"I didn't know you'd be here," I said.

"Gary and I used to work together," Ash said, supplying the details that I'd already remembered.

"Right."

"You were a beautiful bridesmaid," he said, all casual. As if the words didn't make Cole bristle.

Cole wrapped an arm around my shoulders. "She was, wasn't she?"

Ash clenched his jaw, and then it loosened. As if he'd told himself he wouldn't throw the first punch, but he'd try his hardest to get Cole to do it. "Well, I wanted to come over and say hi. I guess I'll probably be seeing more of y'all soon."

Cole's hand tightened on my shoulder.

"You will?" I blurted out. My stomach sank at the prospect. This couldn't be good.

"Oh, didn't your mom tell you?" Ash asked. "I got into the MBA professional program at UGA at the Atlanta campus. I'll be moving there in August."

August.

In one month's time, our sanctuary would be shattered. It didn't matter how big Atlanta was. Distance had never mattered. We always found each other. And once he was there, I knew we'd never be alone again. I didn't know how to feel about that. Terrified? Relieved? Anxious?

"She didn't tell me," I muttered.

"Ah, well, now, you know." He tipped his head at Cole and winked at me. "Have a nice wedding."

Then he walked away, leaving tension in his wake.

"I hate that guy," Cole said once he was gone.

"I'm so sorry about that," I said with a sigh. "I didn't expect him to be here at all. I know Savannah can feel small, but I don't know ... I definitely didn't think that he'd come talk to us."

"I don't know why he'd even want to talk to us."

"Oh, really?" I asked, turning to look at him. "As if you'd never do that."

He gave me a conspiratorial grin. "I didn't do that on purpose. He did this on purpose."

"Uh-huh."

Cole pressed another kiss to my lips. "Well, it was worth it to see his face when I showed up in Savannah."

"I'm sure he feels the same way right now."

Cole shrugged and handed me a drink before taking my other hand and pulling me out onto the dance floor. "He can do whatever he wants. You're mine now. Now and forever."

I nodded and leaned against him as we danced. But over his shoulder, I saw Ash waiting in the wings. He arched an eyebrow at me and smirked. Then he lifted his glass to me as if in cheers. And I wasn't so sure what was going to happen when he came to Atlanta.

27

SAVANNAH

JUNE 15, 2013

"I s there anything else that you need me to pick up for the party tonight?" Ash asked through the phone.

"No, just the list I gave you and your cute self."

I was sitting on my mom's couch, blowing up balloons with the helium tank and looking in dismay at everything else I had to do before the party. I'd been in PT school in Savannah for a year, dating Ash for six months, and despite the sheer amount of work I had to do, I was relieved. It certainly helped that my mother had gotten a donor match and was recovering wonderfully. Hence the call for a celebration!

"I will be there. Bow tie and all."

"Good." I bit my lip before asking, "Have you heard from your parents about today?"

Ash was silent for a second before sighing softly. "I don't think they're coming."

Of course not. Why would they do that?

"Sure. Okay. No problem."

"It's not that they don't like you," Ash insisted. A

mantra he'd been continuing with for the last six months but that I wasn't entirely sure was true. "They're busy. And they're ... you know ..."

"Stuffy?" I volunteered.

He chuckled. "Yes. They'd ruin the party anyway."

Probably.

"All right," I said with a sigh. It was easier to let him think that they weren't coming because they were stuffy rather than because they didn't like me and never had.

"Don't worry about it. The party is going to be great."

"It will be."

"I got to the party store. I'll text you if I can't find anything."

"Sounds good."

"Love you."

"Love you too," I said and then hung up.

My mom strode out of the kitchen. "Was that Ash?"

I nodded. "He's picking up the last-minute supplies."

"I didn't know we needed more supplies, but you're in charge."

I pointed my finger at the chair. "You should be resting. The transplant was only a few weeks ago."

"I'm fine. Don't nag," my mom said, but she sat gratefully in the chair I'd indicated.

My mom had gotten lucky. A donor came forward after just over a year on the transplant list. I'd matched with Mom, but she'd outright refused to even listen to me. I'd been kind of pushy about it. We'd fought, but the whole thing ended up being unnecessary. But I would have given her my kidney if nothing had come through. Watching her suffer had been horrible.

The doorbell rang, and I glared at it. Just when I was in the middle of balloons.

"The party isn't until six. Who did you invite early?" I asked my mom.

"No one. It could be Elle or Steph. Eve isn't in from Chicago yet. She's going to be cutting it close."

I huffed and abandoned my balloon. I dusted off my short-shorts and pulled down my tank before reaching for the door. I swung it open, and then my jaw hit the floor.

"Cole?" I asked in a strangled voice.

"Hey, Lila," he said. His charming smile in place. Those blue eyes as wide and bright as the summer sky. "Surprise!"

"Um ... wow. What are you doing in Savannah?"

"I was in Atlanta, visiting my family."

"Atlanta is four *hours* away."

"Hence the surprise." He grinned. "I thought I'd have to wrangle where you live now out of your mom, but you're here?"

"No, I'm not living at home. I'm just helping my mom today."

"Dee, who's at the door?" my mom called.

"No one."

"Hello, Mrs. Greer."

"Is that Cole?" my mom asked, rising from her seat. "Oh my goodness, it has been too long. Why don't you come in?"

"Mom," I hissed.

"Oh, let the poor boy in."

I breathed out heavily and then held the door all the

way open. "Come on in."

Cole stepped over the threshold with a smile and went to embrace my mom. My eyes darted behind him, wondering how long I had to get him out of here before Ash showed up. I shut the door and retreated back into the living room. This was going to be a disaster. Fuck me.

"Dee didn't tell me that you were going to be here for the party," my mom said.

"He's not here for the party, Mom."

"What party?" Cole asked.

"Oh, she didn't tell you?"

"She got her kidney transplant," I told him. Not that I would have had an opportunity to tell him because, again ... we weren't talking, and I'd had no idea he'd be here.

"Congratulations!" he gushed. "I'm so happy for you. I know Lila was so worried about your health."

My mom actually rolled her eyes. "She worries too much. She wanted to give me her kidney."

Cole's eyes swept to mine. A look of pain crossed his face. I flushed and looked away. It was one thing to try to convince my mom to let me save her life. It was another thing altogether for her to casually drop it to my ex-boyfriend when he knew how much it meant to me.

"That sounds just like Lila."

"Always so giving," my mom said. "But she needs to take care of herself first. Like moving here for PT school ..."

"Not this again," I groaned.

"You had your *pick* of schools. You could have gone anywhere."

"I know, Mom."

"You don't want to get stuck in your hometown when you have everything going for you."

"I'm not stuck here."

Cole smothered his laughter. "She made the right choice. She needed to be near you."

My throat closed at the words. I turned away from him, so he wouldn't see the tears prick at my eyes. It had simultaneously been the hardest and easiest decision of my life. I'd second-guessed myself about it until I was blue in the face. But it helped, knowing he thought I'd made the right choice too.

"Well, you have to stay for the party now that you're here."

I cringed.

"I'd love to," Cole said.

"Dee, put him to work. You still have balloons to blow up."

Then my mom disappeared to give us privacy, heading into the kitchen, where she could safely eavesdrop on us.

I plopped back down onto the couch. "Are you really staying?"

"Your mom invited me. I feel like it'd be rude to decline."

"Cole," I muttered.

"You don't look happy to see me."

That wasn't accurate. I was in fact very happy to see him. It had been over a year since I'd last seen him at the Falcons game. We'd gradually stopped talking after I decided to stay in Savannah. It wasn't purposeful. It was just hard when he was still in San Francisco.

"I am," I said. "I really am, but ..."

"But?"

"Well, I'm seeing someone."

"Ah."

"Ash," I whispered.

"Fuck ... seriously?" Cole asked, his temper flaring.

"Don't."

"Lila ..."

"Cole," I snapped. "You don't get to show up here, unannounced, and then judge my choices."

He clenched his jaw. "Fine. But for the record, I think it's a bad choice."

"I figured you might." I blew up three balloons before responding again. "Are you staying for the party?"

"I'm not driving four hours back tonight. Might as well stay."

I sighed. "Cole, you should probably go."

"Why? Is he going to be that upset?"

I arched an eyebrow. "Excuse me? Do you remember how *you* reacted when you knew that I was with him?"

"That was different."

"No, it wasn't!"

"Dee," my mom called from the kitchen, "if you are threatening our guest, I'm going to be unhappy."

I gritted my teeth and pulled out my phone. "I need to warn him. If he walks in and sees you sitting here ..." I trailed off. I didn't know what he'd do. But I knew that it would be messy.

Cole sighed. Then he put his hand on my phone. "I'll go."

My eyes shot up to his. The space between us had

shrunk, and his hand was still on mine. I felt warm all over at his touch. This was Cole. My Cole. And God, I'd missed him. I wanted to demand he stay. Demand to know why he'd always insisted on being so far out of reach. But I couldn't do any of those things.

I could only stare into his earnest blue eyes and see the boy I'd loved so fiercely for so long. The boy I'd wanted forever with before we wrecked it.

"Why did you really come?"

"I wanted to see you," he said simply.

"You could have called or texted."

"I know. Would you have seen me if I had?"

Yes.

He must have seen the thought flash through my mind because he smiled softly.

"No," I lied.

"Then I guess it's good I didn't. Since you're ... otherwise occupied."

"I guess it was," I whispered.

I loved Ash. I didn't want to hurt him. But what I felt for Cole was just as real. I didn't know when it had happened, but I couldn't deny it. Couldn't ignore it.

I loved two men.

But I could only have one.

I'd made my choice.

Right?

I pulled back, breaking contact with Cole. "I'll walk you out."

He nodded and followed me to the front door. There was nothing left to say. Nothing that he hadn't seen in my eyes. We were living in two different worlds. I'd thought it would work if we were ever back in the same place, but it didn't seem likely that would ever happen. He was in San Francisco. I was here. Our paths had crossed and then diverged. There was nothing I could do about that.

I took two steps outside when I saw Ash's Mercedes pull up to the curb. I froze, a rabbit caught in a snare. I was too late.

"Fuck, fuck, fuck," I said under my breath.

"That's him?" Cole asked behind me.

"Yep."

"This should be fun."

Fun wasn't the word I would have gone with.

Ash threw open his door and stepped out. His eyes were narrowed and his body tense. I bounded down the rest of the walkway to his car.

"Hey, baby," I said, forcing false enthusiasm.

"What's he doing here?" His voice was tight and laced with anger, hot enough to burn.

"*He* was just leaving."

"Lila," he growled.

Cole strode down the walkway with his hands in his pockets and a smug-ass look on his face. He stopped before the car, eyeing it appreciatively. "Nice car."

"Thanks," Ash said reflexively.

"Cole was just leaving," I repeated.

"I am," Cole said.

Cole and Ash stared at each other from either side of his Mercedes. The body of the car forcing distance between them. My heart pumped furiously at the show-down, the goddamn posturing. I'd thought I would have enough time to get him away before Ash made it here.

"Well, have a safe drive," Ash said. Which sounded more like, *Good riddance*. Then he broke eye contact, dismissing Cole completely. "I got everything that you wanted at the store. Do you need help with anything else?"

"Um, decorations," I said. "I have some balloons to blow up and hang."

"I'll carry this in for you, and we can get started," he said, going for the backseat.

"I'll, uh, meet you there."

Ash froze. "Lila ..."

"I will be right behind you."

His eyes darted to Cole, who still hadn't moved, just stood there and waited for me. Then Ash snaked an arm around my waist and kissed me. It was brief but said everything he needed to say. *Mine*.

"Don't be long," he said.

I nodded, dazed by the force of the kiss. "It'll just be a minute."

Ash took the decorations inside. I was sure that he was counting down the minutes before he could burst back out here. The hate was a mutual thing. Living, breathing death in their presence.

"I thought he might hit me," Cole said.

"You sound disappointed."

Cole shrugged and gestured down the street, where I saw his Jeep was parked.

"If he'd hit me, then I could have caved in his face."

"Cole!"

He laughed, and it was so achingly familiar that it hurt me.

"I wouldn't have hit first."

"Yeah, well, you're both acting like jealous, possessive assholes."

"With good reason." Cole stopped in front of his Jeep. "We're both clearly in love with you."

I bit my lip and dropped my gaze. "Cole, don't."

"Why are you dating him, Lila?"

"Please don't do this."

"You don't love him," he roared, unable to hold on to his calm. "You don't love him because I know what you're like when you're in love. You're a hundred and ten percent. You're a sunflower in bloom. You aren't scared of a damn thing. And you wouldn't have hesitated to kick me out of your house."

"I didn't hesitate!"

"Yes, you did," he growled.

"This isn't fair. What did you expect to happen when you showed up?"

"I don't know," he said, running a hand back through his hair. "Not ... this."

"You're in San Francisco. I'm here."

"What if I moved here?"

"What would you do *here*?"

"I don't know," he grumbled. "I don't know, Lila. I just know that it's always been you. Always. And I can't stand here and watch you be with him when I know you should be with me."

"Is this about us, or is this about Ash?"

"Us," he said automatically. "But ... him too."

"You should go," I said, taking a step backward.

"Tell me the truth, Lila. Tell me you choose him. Tell

me this is what you want." Cole's gaze was level with mine. "Tell me, and I'll walk away."

My tongue stuck to the roof of my mouth like it had peanut butter on it. I'd said I'd made my choice. And I had. I was here in Savannah. I was with Ash. But was that a choice or just circumstances?

"I'm happy," I whispered.

"Are you?" he pressed.

I nodded because I couldn't get the words out. I was happy. But I was split in two. Half of my heart was here in Savannah, and half of my heart would always belong with Cole.

He stepped forward, clearing the distance in one long stride. "I want you to be happy, Lila."

And before I could do a damn thing, his lips were on mine with all the force of a hurricane. I clutched on to him as he ravaged my mouth. As if I were hanging on for dear life in a gale with rain lashing down all around me. Like if I held on long enough, I'd weather the storm and come out on the other side.

There was no weathering the love of two men. There was only standing in the heart of the storm and praying for more rain.

When he released me, it felt like coming out from under water. And I stood in the road as he got into his car and drove away. I stood until I couldn't see his taillights. Then I stayed a little bit longer.

Ash was waiting.

My lips were still on fire.

And my heart was in two pieces. One for each of them.

28

NEW ORLEANS

OCTOBER 10, 2014

"Come *on*, Lila," Trish said, a fellow student in my physical therapy program. "I know you don't go out with us on the weekend at home, but we're in New Orleans!"

"I have an eight a.m. panel," I reminded her.

"So do I! Come down to the hotel bar with me. We can do Bourbon tomorrow."

"Blah. I don't know. I need to go over my presentation again."

It was my first physical therapy conference, and I was set to present my research at a panel in the morning. I was both overly confident and nervous as hell. I knew that drinking wouldn't help anything. I should look over my slides and call it a night.

"One drink," Trish begged. "Your boyfriend can't be mad about one drink."

I laughed. "Ash doesn't care if I drink."

"Really?" She flopped down on the bed next to me. "I

thought he was, like, super possessive, and that's why you never go out with us."

"I've gone out with you," I said. At least once or twice. "I'm just busy. Between school and working as a tech and athletic training, I'm wiped."

"Well, you don't have those excuses today. Text your boy-toy that we're going out and not to wait up."

I shook my head at Trish's enthusiasm. I hadn't realized how much of a hermit I'd become in school. I was constantly juggling too much at once and retreated into myself. I needed to be better about that.

"Fine, I'll go. One drink at the bar."

"Bourbon tomorrow?"

"If you're lucky."

Trish cackled and headed to her room as I rummaged through my suitcase for something to wear. I settled on black skinny jeans and a black square-cut top that I'd planned to wear on Bourbon because it made my boobs look amazing. I paired the outfit with red high heels, touched up my hair and makeup, and then went next door to find Trish.

"Girl!" she gushed. "So fucking hot."

"Thanks. You look great too."

She looked like she was single and ready to mingle in the tiniest little black dress I'd ever seen. But somehow, it worked on her.

We went downstairs with three other girls from our school and settled into a booth in the back of the bar. I'd texted Ash when I was heading out the door, and I got his response as we were ordering drinks.

Have a good time. Call when you're back in your room?

Will do. It's only going to be one drink.

"Vodka tonic," I said, stashing my phone.

"No! We're in New Orleans. We need something fun," Trish insisted.

"You order for us then," Mazie said.

"Don't mind if I do."

An enormous red drink was planted in front of me. My eyes widened. "What the hell is this?"

"Hurricane," Trish said. "I got them for everyone."

"When I said one drink, I didn't exactly mean this."

Trish shrugged. "Should have been more specific then."

She held her drink aloft, and we all cheers'd to the weekend. I decided to kick it back. It wasn't like my presentation was going to make or break my career. It was important, but I was here in New Orleans. It was the first time I'd been here since I'd road-tripped with Channing for the Georgia–LSU game sophomore year. We'd gotten shit-faced all weekend, and I'd snuck into Cole's football hotel to have sex with him after we won the game. Different time.

When I finished my drink, I was super buzzed. "What the hell is in this?"

"Rum."

I blinked at Trish. "How much?"

She shrugged. "A lot."

"Fuck. I need to get a water to survive."

She patted my back. Mazie let me scoot out of the

booth. On wobbly legs, I traipsed across the room to the U-shaped bar, regretting my heel choice and the choice of alcohol. The Hurricane hadn't even tasted like it had alcohol in it. I'd sipped it down like it was Kool-Aid. What a dangerous beverage.

I leaned against the bar and requested a water from the cute bartender. He slid it across to me. I took a careful sip, trying to clear my head, and stared hard at the guy seated across the bar from me. I blinked. No way. It looked like Cole's college roommate Tony.

Well, I had to see for myself. I walked around the bar and tapped him on the shoulder.

"Lila? Holy shit!" Tony said. "What the fuck are you doing here, babe?"

We hugged tight. It had been four years since I'd seen him. I'd thought he was in Atlanta.

"What are you doing in New Orleans?" he asked.

"I'm at the PT conference at this hotel. I thought you were in Atlanta."

"I was, but I moved here with my fiancée last year."

"Oh my God, congratulations!"

"Thanks," he said with a megawatt smile. "It's pretty amazing. She works for a distillery here, and I'm in computer tech now."

"That sounds awesome. So very you. It's crazy to see you here. What are you doing at the hotel?"

He opened his mouth to answer and then laughed, tipping his head behind him. I whipped around, and there was my answer.

"Cole," I whispered.

He stood a few feet away, staring at me as if he'd seen a ghost.

Tony broke the tension. He pushed out of his seat and hugged Cole. "Good to see you, man."

"Yeah, it's great to see you."

"Can you fucking believe that I just ran into Lila?"

Cole met my gaze. "I honestly can't."

"Well, say hi and then sit down, asshole. I'm buying. Do you still drink cheap swill?"

"Get me the expensive stuff," he said with a shake of his head.

"Lila?"

"I'm good," I said, holding up my water.

"Shut the fuck up. I haven't seen you in four years. I'm buying you a drink."

I held a hand up in surrender. "I was drinking a Hurricane."

Then Tony sat at the bar to order, turning his back on the pair of us. I took a sip of my water just to have some-thing to do with my hands. It had been over a year since I'd seen Cole. Since he'd kissed me with everything that he had outside of my mom's house. I didn't know how to be with him right now. How I should even feel?

Besides exactly the same.

"Hi," I said. "Surprised to find you here. Visiting Tony?"

"No, I'm staying at the hotel. My business partner and I are pitching my new marketing company to the Saints."

My eyes widened. "Wow, Cole! That's incredible! What an opportunity."

"Yeah. It's sort of taken off in the last six months or so.

I've been hopping all over the country. Saints are our last pitch."

"New Orleans would be a big move."

He nodded. "It wouldn't be that bad though. My girl-friend's from here."

My stomach hit the floor. My throat felt like a boa constrictor had tightened around it. Everything was suddenly hazy and shaky. Maybe I'd had more to drink than I'd thought.

"Your girlfriend?" I stuttered out.

"Yeah. Harper."

I nodded, and then I realized I hadn't stopped nodding and glanced away. "That's ... great, Cole."

"And you?"

"What about me?"

"Why are you in New Orleans?"

"Oh. Right. I'm also at this hotel for a PT conference."

"Still with Ash?" he asked, his voice low.

I swallowed and nodded.

"I see."

"Here we are!" Tony said. He passed us each a drink. "Lila, you're going to have to stay and reminisce on the good ole days with us."

"Oh, I can't. My girlfriends are over there." I pointed across the room. "I should probably get back, but it was great to see you."

"Come on! It's been years."

I glanced at Cole, waiting for his objection.

"One drink won't hurt you," he said.

A shadow passed across his vision, and then tension

lifted off of his shoulders. I didn't know how to interpret that.

"Okay. One drink."

I seemed to be saying that a lot lately. I jogged over to Trish and said that I'd run into friends and to not wait for me. Then I went back and took a seat next to Tony, keeping him between me and Cole.

"Y'all will have to come to the wedding. We're saving up for it, so it might not be for another two years. I want to give Gina the best wedding I can," Tony explained. "I actually wanted to see if you'd be best man."

Cole beamed. "Hell yes, I will."

"Gah, that sounds amazing," I said.

Though I doubted that I'd ever end up at that wedding. Even if I wanted to be there. Cole and I would have to be in a completely different place than where we were now for that to happen and that seemed impossible.

Cole regaled us with his new marketing project, and I told them all about PT school and the insufferable job market. How much I wanted to work in the Falcons training room and how unlikely that was to happen. Tony gushed about Gina like a man besotted. He kept telling us how much he wished that we could meet her.

One drink turned into two and then three. I was definitely drunk by then. I knew that I should have stopped after one. Guzzled some water and then disappeared for the night. It was nearing midnight, and I hadn't gone over my presentation once. Even worse, I was definitely going to have a hangover in the morning. Whoops.

"Gah, is it really this late?" Tony asked, rubbing a hand down his face. "Gina is going to kill me. I hate to cut it short, folks, but I'm outta here. It was so good, seeing you both."

He hugged Cole and then me before dropping some cash on the bar. "Text me tomorrow, and maybe Gina can come out with us."

"I will," Cole agreed.

"You too, Lila!"

I laughed. "I might just do that."

He nodded at us both and then ambled out of the bar. Leaving us all alone.

"How does this keep happening to us?" I asked, leaning an elbow against the bar and looking at him.

He shrugged one shoulder and tossed back the rest of his bourbon. "I've given up on coincidences."

"Same. Third time in three years," I muttered. "Crazy since you live on the other side of the country."

"Almost like we keep getting pulled back together."

"Almost." I sighed and reached for the water in front of me. "How'd you meet Harper?"

"Mutual friends. My business partner's wife's best friend."

"Must make for great parties."

"Yeah. Well, they tried for a year to get me to go on a date with her, but I wasn't interested."

"What changed your mind?"

He shot me a look.

I already knew the answer.

I'd let him walk away that day. There was nothing to hold him back.

"And you're still happy?" he asked instead of answering.

I nodded. "And you? You're happy?"

"Yeah. Harper is ..." He waved the bartender down for a refill. "I don't know. You want anything else?"

"No, I have a panel at eight in the morning. I'm already going to be fucked up for it."

"You'll do fine. You're brilliant."

"Thanks for the confidence," I said as the bartender set his drink down in front of him.

Cole picked the drink up and then took Tony's unoccupied seat to fill the space between us. I held my breath as I caught the scent of him. My stomach fluttered, and I wet my lips, glancing away.

"I should probably go."

He put his hand on my arm. "Stay for my drink."

"It's late."

"I'll walk you up."

I swallowed. That sounded like a bad idea. But I remained where I was sitting.

"Is it serious?" I asked.

"With Harper?"

"Yeah."

He shrugged. "It's been six months. You? It's been, what, two years?"

"Almost. Two years on New Year's Eve."

"Are you living with him?"

"No."

I didn't know why he'd asked. I didn't know why I had answered. Why were we hurting each other like this? Why did I have to torture myself with answers?

"Why not?"

"Are you living with Harper?"

"God, no. We've only been dating six months."

"Living with Maddox as a roommate is really easy."

He arched an eyebrow. "You live with a guy, and Ash hasn't fucked him up?"

"He's only like that with you," I muttered.

"Yeah, well, I'm the competition."

"He and Maddox get along fine. Why are we even talking about this?"

"Because it's the elephant in the room."

He was right. Maybe if I knew all about his girlfriend and whether he was in love, then I wouldn't feel like a bowling ball was sitting in my stomach. I'd be able to see it for what it was and then just finally ... move on.

"Probably not long before he proposes," Cole mused.

The bowling ball slipped. "What?"

"Two years together. You've known him since you were in high school. Next steps and all."

"We haven't talked about it."

Cole smirked. "Yes, you have."

I turned away from him. Ash talked about it. He'd been talking about it since our first date. He wanted forever with me. And it wasn't even that I didn't want that. I *did*. But there was only one problem, and he was seated next to me. I'd never felt more split in half about anything.

If only I could have both without them killing each other.

I stood from my seat. "I should go to bed. I hope that you're deliriously happy. You deserve it."

"Lila," he said on a huff.

I swallowed. "It's too hard to sit here and talk about this with you."

"I know."

"No, you don't. You don't even seem fazed. As if none of it matters."

"Are you out of your mind? Of course it matters. Of course it fucking hurts to hear. But ... this is reality." He gestured to me. "People between us. Space between us. Everything is between us."

"I know," I whispered. "I know."

We stood there in the busy bar with history crowding in. Suffocating us. And there was nothing to do about it. We'd each chosen a different path. It didn't lead here. No matter how many times fate had brought us back together.

"Good night, Cole."

He gently touched my hand. "Good night, Sunflower."

I walked back to my room on leaden feet, remembering at the last minute to let Ash know I'd made it back to my room. I didn't have the stomach to see his response. I curled into a ball and wondered why my heart ached for two men. And if I'd ever be whole.

29

NEW ORLEANS
OCTOBER 11, 2014

My panel had been shit.

I'd barely slept, and I had been even more hungover than I'd thought I'd be. It hadn't helped that I had a half-dozen texts from Ash about last night that I didn't know how to answer or have the bandwidth for.

When the girls begged me to go out on Bourbon Street, I was ready to put the whole day behind me and dive straight into a Hand Grenade. We slutted up our outfits for the night—teeny miniskirts, plunging necklines, impractical heels, and beads. So many beads.

Trish led us down Bourbon. People called down to us from wrought iron balcony railings. Religious zealots patrolled the streets, demanding we turn away from sin. Everyone drank from long plastic tubes filled with sugary concoctions so potent that one could knock you on your ass. Outside of a bar, we were hassled by a woman with a tray of shots in test tubes that you were supposed to drink out of her boobs. Trish shrieked with delight and bought us all one. I declined the boob method and downed the terrible, sugar-packed shot. Trish tipped back the boob shot.

Trish held her hands aloft. "Hell yes!"

The crowd went wild. I liked Trish, but she was something else. It made me miss Marley and Josie.

"Oh! Karaoke!" Trish gushed.

"Oh God. *Not* karaoke," I said, stepping backward.

Mazie and Trish clutched my arm and dragged me inside Cat's Meow. The place had two tiers with a small stage at the front. A man played a piano on the stage, and someone sang an atrocious chorus of Bon Jovi's "Livin' on a Prayer."

"I'm going to sign us up," Trish said and then headed for the stage.

"I'm not singing."

Mazie laughed. "Me neither. We'll just send Trish."

"Deal."

"But drinks?"

"Definitely."

We ordered a round of something to wash down the terrible test-tube shot.

Trish appeared a few minutes later. "We're slot number ten. They said thirty or forty-five minutes."

"Sounds good."

We stood around with the other girls, singing every song that you could possibly imagine someone would want to karaoke. Between Journey's "Don't Stop Believin'," a truly uncomfortable rendition of Whitney's "I Wanna Dance with Somebody," and a Freddie Mercury lookalike who strolled in and sang a flawless "Bohemian Rhapsody," I realized I was actually having a good time.

No one could hear that I couldn't sing when we were all shouting the lyrics into the abyss. And by the time Trish got on the stage to sing "... Baby One More Time," I was drunk enough to agree to get onstage with Mazie as Trish's backup dancers.

Luckily, due to one too many dance team rehearsals in high school, I knew the original music video dance. I hadn't ever performed it drunk and in heels, but being onstage felt right, and soon, people were coming in off the streets to hear Trish's amazing vocals, coupled with my dancing. We finished to an unprecedented volume of cheers. People on the streets were screaming for us to give an encore. And then in the sea of faces, I saw two that I recognized. Cole and Tony were standing in the street. Tony's jaw was nearly on the floor despite the number of basketball games he'd seen me perform at. Cole had his arms crossed. I couldn't read his face from this distance.

I hastily took a bow and hurried offstage. The MC gave me a high five as I passed.

"Killed it, Britney!"

I flush of embarrassment hit my cheeks. Not from being onstage, but post-dance mortification.

Trish was jumping up and down. "That was amazing! Where did you learn to move like that?"

"Uh ... actually, I was on the dance team at Georgia and a Falcons cheerleader."

Trish's eyes bugged. "What the fuck, Lila? Why didn't I know this? I mean, I knew you wanted to work at the Falcons, but I didn't know you were a dancer."

I shrugged. "Ancient history." I gestured toward the door. "I think I saw my friends from last night outside."

"Oh! Introduce us," Trish said.

And before I could say anything, Trish dashed toward the door. Mazie and I jogged to keep up with her as we stumbled back out onto the humid New Orleans street. The crowd had dispersed some after our performance, and people had gone back to drunkenly wandering the street.

But Cole still stood outside with Tony along with a short, freckled woman with curly red hair—presumably Tony's fiancé, Gina—and another tall Black guy that I didn't know.

"Is that them?" Trish asked.

I nodded. "That's them."

"Hey!" Trish said, walking right up to them.

"Britney Spears!" Tony said with a laugh.

Trish grinned and held out her hand. "That's right. I'm Lila's friend, Trish."

Tony shook her hand, and Gina stepped a little closer to him. A reasonable assessment based on Trish's outgoing behavior. You'd never know she had a super-steady boyfriend at home. She just liked people.

"You looked like you were back out on the field," Cole said to me.

"Felt good to be back ... except drunk and in these heels."

Cole frowned. "Are you not dancing?"

"There's not a place to dance in Savannah as an adult. I taught a master class at my old studio, but it wasn't the same." I shrugged. "Hard to feel inspired to teach high school students after dancing professionally."

"Well, are you going to introduce me to the infamous Lila?" his friend asked.

I gritted my teeth at that word. *Infamous*. Oh boy.

"Sure. Curtis, this is Lila. Lila, this is my business partner."

Business partner. The one whose wife had set Cole up with her best friend, Harper. Great.

"Nice to meet you."

We shook hands.

"I've heard a lot about you," Curtis said.

I had no idea what to say to that. Curtis was likely his closest friend back in San Francisco and that Cole had bitched a lot to him about everything that had happened. I couldn't imagine that it was a positive image.

Cole butted in before I could say a word, "Where are you headed next?"

"Oh, Pat O's for real Hurricanes and dueling pianos," Trish answered for me.

"Pat O's it is!" Tony agreed victoriously.

Trish shuffled forward with Tony and Gina. Curtis struck up a conversation with Mazie, and Cole and I took the back.

"Is this okay?" I asked.

"Us together like this?"

"Well, yeah. I mean, clearly, Curtis doesn't like me. He's probably going to tell Harper that we were together here."

"Nah, he wouldn't do that."

"Are you going to tell her?" I stared up at him, and my heart skipped a beat.

He was so fucking handsome. Even in jeans and a

polo. Even with his hair slightly mussed. And those blue eyes staring back at me.

"Lila, can't we just enjoy the night? Do we have to make this a big thing?" He grinned down at me, and my entire body melted. "I've missed you. Let's just hang out tonight."

And I wanted nothing more than that. Our friends all crowded around a table in front of the dueling pianos, sipping Hurricanes and singing at the tops of our lungs. We requested the Georgia fight song, and I got up to do the cheers that would be ingrained in my brain until the day that I died.

It was early in the morning after bar close when we all stumbled out of the bar, prepared for the trek back to the hotel. Tony and Gina went one way. Curtis held up Trish and Mazie as they nearly fell every other step. Cole and I hung back. Drunk but still not ready to leave.

"Beignets?" I asked. "Café du Monde is open twenty-four hours."

"I'm down. Let me see if Curtis wants to come."

Cole jogged up to his friend and told him our plan. What ensued was so heated a fight that ended with Curtis storming off with the two girls back to the hotel.

I lifted my eyebrows. "What was that about?"

"He doesn't think it's a good idea for us to go off alone."

"But you asked if he wanted to go."

"He didn't want to go. We have an early flight."

"Oh," I whispered. "Do you still want to go?"

"Definitely. It'll be fine."

Famous last words.

Café du Monde was finally empty at three in the morning. We ordered a plate of beignets and two café au laits. The doughnuts came out piping hot, covered in a literal *mound* of powdered sugar.

Cole took out his phone and snapped pictures of the food. Then he turned it to me, and I posed with the mountain of powdered sugar, laughing as half of it landed in my lap.

"Do you miss your camera?"

"Always, but the new iPhone is nearly as good. Less manual manipulation but handier," he said, shoving the thing back in his pocket. "Do you miss dance?"

I nodded. "Always."

"What are you going to do after you finish PT school?"

"Job market and pray," I said, taking a sip of my coffee.

"Still want to work for the Falcons?"

"Always."

"Still have your superpower?" he joked.

I pointed at him. "I'll have you know that last week, I snagged two Cokes out of the vending machine at school. Trish thought I was a goddess."

"You are," he said softly.

I flushed. "You still have your superpower?"

"With the rental, I got the first spot in the lot at the hotel."

"Magic."

He drained his coffee. "God, it's so easy to be here with you."

"It really is."

We finished off the plate of doughnuts. My fingers were all sticky from the powdered sugar. When the napkins did nothing, I licked them clean. I was glad that the carbs and coffee had helped sober me up some. I didn't feel quite so out of it as I had when we were in Pat O'Briens.

"Should we head back?" I asked reluctantly.

He tipped his chair back onto two legs. "Or we could walk."

"Where?"

"Anywhere, Lila."

I squirmed at the affection in the way he'd said my name. "Okay."

He dropped cash onto the messy table, and then I followed him out to the street. We crossed Decatur to Jackson Square. Most of the artists and performers had already packed up for the night. We wandered the empty square, pausing in front St. Louis Cathedral to admire the soaring heights of the eighteenth-century church before continuing through the French Quarter.

I lost track of time.

Or maybe when I was with Cole, time stood still.

After an eternity of walking, we ended back at our hotel. I dawdled in the unoccupied lobby. I wasn't ready to let the night end. I didn't know if I'd ever see Cole again. And though we'd been in love for a long time and we'd been friends just as long, we couldn't be either when I went home.

"I can walk you up," he offered.

And this time, I nodded as we headed for the elevators. Silence stretched between us on the ride up to my floor. After this, he was going to go back to his room, catch an early flight, and disappear from my life forever.

Should I want that? Because I didn't.

We stepped out onto the padded hallway carpet and I finally gave in, kicking off my heels and carrying them to the door.

"You made it all this way, and you couldn't wait until you were inside?"

"You try walking around on four-inch spikes for hours."

"Nah, I'd never survive."

"Men are the weaker sex."

Cole chuckled, stopping when I did before my door.

"This is me."

He leaned against the doorframe and stared down at me, as reluctant to leave as I was.

"What are we doing?" I asked.

"Standing outside of your hotel room."

I pushed his shoulder. "So literal."

He caught my wrist and dragged me a pace closer. "What do you want me to say, Lila? You know what we're doing."

"Being reckless," I offered.

"I'd rather live one reckless night with you than a life-time of caution."

My chest ached at the words. I shouldn't feel the same, but I did.

"Cole ..."

"I don't know how to let you go. I'm with someone else, and I still can't do it." He brought my hand up to his shoulder. His arms circling my waist, he dropped his forehead down to mine. "It's too hard, being away from you."

"I know," I whispered. "I never wanted this. You were the one who left."

"I'm here now."

I shook my head. "It's not the same. Tomorrow, you'll go back to San Francisco again. Just like every other time."

"What if I didn't?"

I lurched back. "Don't. It's not fair."

His own anger bubbled up. "Fair? When has this ever been fair? How I feel about you isn't fair, Lila."

I balled my hands into fists. I didn't want to be wrecked by this boy again. "What does that even mean?" I demanded. "How do you feel?"

He took my hand, gently uncoiling my fist, and placed it over his heart. "Like you've owned this every day since I met you."

"Please," I whispered. I wasn't sure if I was asking for more or begging him to stop.

"If you don't feel the same, then tell me to go. Tell me it's over. Put me out of my misery. But if you do feel the same ..." He let the words hang between us.

I could have walked then. Let him think that I didn't feel exactly how he felt, but it was hard to conflate a lie with the right thing.

"Lila?"

"I do."

He stepped forward, a question in his eyes, waiting for the moment where I told him no, where I stopped him, but we were beyond that now. We'd been beyond that for a while. We shouldn't have gone for beignets or walked around the city or taken the elevator ride. No to it all. But I hadn't. I couldn't.

His hands pushed up into my hair, tilting my face up to look at him. Those big blue eyes and perfect lips and the five o'clock shadow. This was my Cole. The one I'd loved since college, since the day he'd been nervous to ask me out and then kissed me in front of the entire university. I hung, suspended in his grasp, the decision for where we went after this squarely in his hands.

Nothing could stop this train as it barreled down the tracks. We were a runaway, just waiting for the crash.

And then we crashed.

His lips on mine. His tongue pushed into my mouth. Our bodies pressed tight.

I fumbled with the key card against the door and toed it open. Cole followed me inside, filling the space as if he belonged here. As if he always had.

We stumbled backward, slamming the door in our wake. And we were now alone in my darkened hotel room. I had never been more glad that I'd decided not to share with Trish. That I'd wanted the privacy to work on my presentation.

We landed on the bed in a tangle of limbs. I had no idea where I stopped and Cole started. We were just one. Finally complete.

My skirt rode up to my hips as I wrapped my legs around his waist. I wanted to feel him pressed against me, feel every inch of his solid body.

I knew it was wrong. We shouldn't be doing this. Not when we had other people back at home. But it didn't *feel* wrong. It was the rightest thing I'd done in a long time, and I didn't know what that said about me.

The only thing that was clear was that I wasn't over Cole Davis. Not even close. And I didn't know if I ever would be.

"Lila," he gasped, running his hands up my bare legs. "Fuck, I want this, but ..."

He didn't have to finish. I met his gaze. This was a tipping point. And we hadn't crossed it. Not yet. Not entirely. But we were about to unless I told him no. Unless I told him to stop.

I didn't.

"You want this," he said as a statement, not a question.

"Yes."

His mouth was on mine again, desperate for heat and friction. The culmination of trying to deny for hours, days, years that we would reach this moment.

I ripped at his belt, freeing him from the constraints of his jeans, and he slipped me out of my thong. His lips came to mine. His body flush against mine.

"Lila," he groaned as he slid inside of me.

"Yes," I moaned. "Yes, Cole."

"God, I love to hear you say my name. So fucking sexy."

"Oh God."

He wasn't slow or controlled. As if he was as frantic for me as I was for him. Our bodies remembered this song and dance. It had been a few years, but it was as if no time had passed at all. We were more than in sync; we were one.

I dragged control from him, and he let me flip him

onto his back, so I was riding him. I drew my dress over my head and flung it on the ground. My breasts bounced as I moved up and down on his cock. His fingers dug into my hips, slamming me down on him hard. I was going to have bruises on my thighs. Completely unexplainable bruises.

"Close," he bit out.

"Yes."

I was *so* close. Any second, I was going to explode.

He stared up at me with sex eyes filled with love, and it pushed me right over. I came shouting into the night, heedless of the neighbors. Let them complain.

Cole released with me, coming hard and fast until he was spent and sated under me. I collapsed forward against his chest. My breath coming out in uneven pants as he put his arms around me.

"I love you," he whispered.

"I love you too."

And even though I knew I'd made a big mistake, I couldn't bring myself to think about it. Nothing with Cole felt like a mistake. Maybe I'd feel differently in the morning, but right now, I was exactly where I needed to be.

30

NEW ORLEANS
OCTOBER 12, 2014

"Oh!" I gasped as I slowly dragged myself back to consciousness.

I jerked up the covers to find Cole spreading my legs wider and brushing his tongue along my clit. I fell backward into the pillow as he slipped a finger inside of me.

"Oh God," I groaned.

My hips bucked against his face, but he held me down easily with an arm across my hips. I squirmed and squirmed, but there was nowhere to go; I could only let the pressure build.

I came, gasping as pleasure rippled through my body. I was barely awake, and he'd just pushed me over the edge in a matter of minutes.

He grinned devilishly as he slid up my body. "Good morning."

I blinked sleepily. "Morning."

"Going to come for me a second time, Sunflower?" he asked.

"I ..."

And then there were no words as he settled head at my wet entrance. There was just holding on to him for dear life as he plunged forward, taking me with abandon until I fucking *did* come a second time.

"What a morning wake-up," I said when we were finished.

We both were sprawled, naked on the sheets. His arm was under my neck. I was tilted into him, as if I couldn't escape the pull of his gravity.

"You're welcome," he teased.

"Can we stay here forever? I don't want to catch my flight."

He kissed my forehead and then trailed his fingers through my hair. "I wish we could, but we have to leave."

"No, I don't want to go back to reality."

"I know. What are you going to do when you get home?"

I curved in even tighter against him. "Don't make me think about it."

"I'm going to break up with Harper," he said so calmly.

"You are?" I peeked up at him.

"She's not you."

I flushed at the words. I'd wanted to hear them. Selfishly. But did it change anything for us? He was still across the country from me, and I was still in school for the rest of the year.

"Lila?"

"Hmm?"

"You *are* going to tell him, right?"

I squeezed my eyes shut. I didn't want to think about

this. I had no idea what it would be like when I got back to Savannah. Would I confess to Ash? Would he hate me forever for it? Could I survive his hate?

"Lila," Cole said more urgently. He forced me to look at him. "You're going to tell him."

"I …"

Cole retreated like I'd hit him in my hesitancy. "Fuck," he hissed. "Fuck, fuck, fuck." He shook his head.

"I am. I'm going to tell him," I said quickly, watching him slip away from me.

"You're not."

My throat closed. "I am. It's just … different than with Harper."

"It's not fucking different," he insisted. "Except that you've known him longer and his sole mission in life is to ruin us."

"Technically, you're ruining him right now."

"Fuck. Him."

I flinched at the words. It was wrong to want them both. So wrong. And I couldn't fucking change a thing. I couldn't disentangle them. The last thing I wanted to do was go home and tell Ash what had happened. I couldn't stomach his reaction. I vibrated with fear and uncertainty. I didn't regret this, but I was afraid of what would come. How I would hurt Ash.

"I don't know why I thought this would be different," he said. Not mad, just resigned. He flipped off the bed and threw his clothes back on.

"Cole, wait … please. It is different."

"Are we going to be together?"

"You're in San Francisco!" I said, raising my voice. "I still have a year of school."

"So, we're back to waiting to be in the same place again?"

"You're the one who left!"

"And now, things are different."

"How? You taught me that long distance was impossible."

"When we were twenty-two!" he roared. "I don't know how we could spend all night together, wake up like that," he said, gesturing to the bed, "and still think that nothing is different."

"I do. I do think things are different. They're *more* complicated. Before, we had distance between us, and now, we have relationships and years," I said, trying to keep the tears from coming. "I want us, Cole. I want *this*. But tell me how it works right now because I don't see it."

"If you don't see it, then it doesn't work."

He pulled away from me and stormed toward the door.

"Wait," I said, the tears coming anyway. No matter how I'd tried to stop them. I rushed toward him, catching him at the door. "I don't want you to leave like this."

"I don't want to leave at all, Sunflower." He brushed the tears off of my cheeks. "You're even beautiful when you cry."

"Please," I whispered.

"Maybe someday, right?" He brushed his lips against mine. "But that decision is yours. I can't wait for you my entire life. I can't sit around and hope that you'll tell him that you choose me. And I won't be second."

"You're not second."

He met my gaze. Must have seen the sincerity. "Then, I won't share first place. There are no ties here."

"I know."

"I love you, but love isn't enough." Then Cole yanked open the door and walked out.

And I let him walk away this time because what else could I do?

It was a tie. And no one could suffer a tie.

THE FLIGHT HOME was long and exhausting. I picked up my car at the airport and drove home in a daze. Maddox wasn't home when I got back. I hadn't told Ash that I was home yet. Though he had my flight schedule, so he must have known. I wasn't ready to talk.

I showered instead. A long, steamy shower to wash off the events of last night. Even though I'd already showered at the hotel after Cole left. It didn't matter. I could still feel him all over me.

When I got out of the shower, I had a dozen missed calls from Ash and frantic messages about whether or not I was dead.

I closed my eyes in pain and then sent him a text back, letting him know I had made it and was on the way to his house. I would rather have an escape plan if I needed it. Having him here would only mean that there was nowhere to go if this went south. Ash was too stubborn to ever leave before we fully had it out. And I didn't particularly want to run to my mom. How the hell would I even explain this to her?

I threw on jeans and a T-shirt and then headed over to Ash's. I pulled up in front of the two-story white Colonial. The house he wanted me to live with him in, to have a life together. I'd never been certain. I'd been handy with excuses. Just not the real ones. Today would change that.

Sunny rushed my legs as soon as I opened the door. She attacked me with her unconditional love. I gave her all the pets and hugs and kisses, putting off the inevitable. Then, I went to find Ash.

He was in his office when I arrived. He was still in a suit from church with his parents. We'd started going to make them hate me less. Though Ash had denied that was the reason.

Sunny sank into a bed in his office and promptly passed out. Lucky dog.

"Hey, baby." He jumped up from his chair and pressed his mouth against mine. "I missed you. How was the conference?"

"It was fine. Trish got me drunk, so I was hungover most of the time."

He laughed. "Well, at least you had fun, I assume? You were out late."

"I ... yes, I had fun."

And I could have left it at that.

His eyes were wide with excitement. He really had missed me. I could feel it in his enthusiasm at seeing me. This was the longest we'd been apart in two years. He'd wanted to come to the conference, but work had kept him in Savannah. Oh, how different things would have been if he'd been able to get off work.

"Have you eaten? We could order in, or I could make something," he offered, heading toward the kitchen.

But I stopped him with a hand at his elbow. "Wait."

He really looked at me. Not clouded with his own excitement. The real me. And all the anxiety and fear coating my body.

"What's wrong?" he asked. He looked wary.

"When I was there, I ran into Cole."

Ash went as still as a marble statue. Only his eyes narrowed. "How did that happen?"

I swallowed. *Here we go.* "He started a marketing company and has been going to football teams to pitch his services. He was in NOLA, talking to the Saints."

"And you ran into him?"

"His college roommate lives there now, and they were meeting for drinks. They just happened to be at my hotel."

"What a coincidence that he'd picked *your* hotel."

"He was staying there."

"He was *staying* at your hotel?"

I nodded.

He clenched his hands and then released them. "So, you had drinks with him?"

I nodded again.

Ash searched my face, waiting for me to say more but I had no idea where to even begin. There was so much I needed to say. I needed to decide what the hell to do, and I hadn't figured it out on the flight or in the shower or on the drive over here. And now, I was tongue-tied in front of my boyfriend, who loved me very much.

"It's fine," he said finally.

"What?" I blurted out.

He put his hand on my shoulder. "I can tell you're freaking out because you saw him, but it's fine, Lila. You can't control if you randomly run into him in a bar in New Orleans. All that matters is that, at the end of the day, you came home to me."

"I thought you'd be mad."

"I'm not happy. I don't want you around him, but I'm *not* him," he insisted. "I remember how he freaked out just when we saw each other. As if my presence alone meant that he couldn't trust you. I don't want you to feel that way with me. What we have isn't flimsy. It's not breakable. It's not going to crumble because you saw your ex."

His words were meant to be reassuring. Make me hate myself less for running into Cole. And maybe it would have worked if Cole and I had never gone out on Bourbon, never agreed to Café du Monde, never walked around the city and ended up in my bed. It might have made me feel better then, but it didn't now.

I took a step backward. I needed the distance to think and breathe. But he didn't like that. He didn't like that he'd shown how oh-so generous he was and my response was to back away from him.

And he knew me too well not to know what that meant.

"Unless there's more?"

I squeezed my eyes shut. I couldn't say the words.

"What did you do?" His voice was low and menacing.

"I'm sorry," I choked out. "I'm so sorry."

"For what?"

I couldn't keep the tears back this time. I saw his pained face, lined with anger, and knew that this was going to shatter everything.

"I didn't mean to do it."

"You didn't *mean* to do it?" he said in disdain. "Did you *fuck* him?"

I strode away, pressing my hands to my eyes. "It wasn't like that."

Ash stared at me. I could feel his eyes boring into me. As he waited for me to say something that made sense to him.

"Tell me what happened."

"I can't," I gasped out. "I can't say it."

Ash grasped my shoulders, digging his fingers into my skin. Not hard enough to hurt, but enough to make me stop and look at him. "I need you to tell me."

"Why?" I demanded.

"Just fucking tell me, Lila."

"Fine. Yes, we slept together."

Ash's grip tightened. His hands shook my body with his own fury.

"Stop," I pleaded. "Let me go."

He released me with more force than I'd expected, and I was pushed off-balance, stumbling into his desk. I caught myself hard against the hip. Another inexplicable bruise.

"Tell me everything. Tell me how it happened."

"You don't want to know."

He glared at me. "Tell me," he commanded with all the deathly calm of a man used to being in charge. It was the voice I'd heard his dad use. It made me freeze.

"It will just hurt you."

"I can't possibly hurt any more than I do right now."

"I'm sorry."

"Sorry isn't good enough!" he yelled. "I need to know. I need to know everything. I have to understand why you'd do this. Did he force you? Did you ask for it? Did you come? How many times?"

"Stop, stop, stop," I cried. Tears streaked my cheeks. I couldn't stomach this. I couldn't do it.

"Just tell me why!" he cried.

"I don't know," I gasped out. "I don't know. I don't know."

"You know. You won't tell me. You're still protecting yourself."

"Please, I don't know."

Ash shook his head, disgusted. "Tell me the truth, Lila. I deserve that much."

I swiped at the tears on my cheeks and tried to control my body trembling. But it was impossible.

"I don't know," I shouted, at the end of my rope. "I couldn't say no to him."

Ash staggered back a step. As if that were the worst possible thing I could have said. It was the exact answer he'd given me when we slept together after Cole dumped me in college. He'd said that he would never say no to me. And now, the words were a slap in the face.

"You couldn't say no," he said, all lethal calm.

"I'm still in love with him."

Ash's jaw set. He looked like I'd punched him. "You still love him?"

"I love you too."

"You *can't* love us both."

"I know! I know I'm not supposed to, but I do. And I don't know how to stop."

Every word landed like a blow. I kept expecting him to throw me out. To tell me to get the fuck out of his house and he never wanted to see me again. That I'd done the unforgivable. That I should be alone and miserable.

But he didn't say any of those things.

He stared at me, as if I'd reached my hand through his chest and wrenched out his heart.

"You're never going to see him again," he said finally.

"I know."

"No, Lila, you're *never* going to see him again."

"I didn't plan to see him this time."

Ash glanced around his office, looking at everything but me. Until finally, his cool blue gaze found mine. "You love me?"

I nodded. "Yes. So much."

"Then you'll never see him again. We'll cut him out of our lives, like severing an appendage where only the ghost of the pain remains." Ash stepped forward and pulled me against him. I went in willingly but in shock. I'd never thought he'd touch me again. "And then you'll be mine, just mine."

"Ash," I whispered.

I was so confused. How could he want me at all after this? How could he be saying these words?

"I love you, Lila. You're the only one I've ever wanted. I'm not going to let him take you from me."

"What are you saying?" I asked, looking up at him through my tears. "I thought you'd hate me."

"I'm furious. I want to kill him. But I don't want to lose you either."

"You can't possibly forgive me."

"No," he agreed. "No, I don't, but we can get through this."

My heart panged at the words. I wanted to believe them. I wanted to believe that we could move on. That what had happened could be put behind us. That we'd have a rough few months, and then we'd move on and be happy. That I could love Ash forever and never see or think about Cole again.

But that thought left me breathless and nauseated. It was impossible. Impossible to think that I would move on from Cole. It had been *years*, and my heart still beat for him. It still knew him as mine.

And worse, I knew that Ash forgiving and forgetting was just as impossible. It would be torture. An earned torture but one nonetheless. One that neither of us should have to endure. We shouldn't have to feel this pain and see each other every day as we went through it. It would never heal. It would be a scab that we kept picking at, festering with the anger and betrayal.

"No," I whispered.

Ash frowned. "No?"

"I can't do this."

"Lila?"

I stepped away from him. "I can't stay here. I hurt you.

I betrayed you. It'd be so easy to try to pretend that it hadn't happened and forget about Cole. But we can't pretend, Ash. The pain will spread like an infection, and we can't treat it by staying together and hoping for the best."

"I know that I'm mad now, Lila, but we'll work this out," he said. Fear crept into his voice, as if he was realizing for the first time that this might really be the end.

"I'm sorry. I'm sorry for all of it."

Tears were coming again, and this time, I didn't wait to let him convince me otherwise. Because I knew he could do it. I knew that he could ply me with *I love you*s and I'd eventually cave. I loved him so much, and I didn't want to leave. I wanted to stay with him here forever and find happiness again. But it wouldn't happen. And I couldn't pretend like it would.

I scooped up Sunny and headed for the door.

Ash chased me all the way to my car.

"Don't do this," he begged. "I love you."

"I know. I'm doing this *because* I love you."

"That makes no sense. I don't care about what happened. We can get past it."

"You don't care? You *should* care. I can't do this, Ash. I'm sorry."

I extracted myself from his grip, slowly, one finger at a time. I pressed one more careful kiss to his lips. A goodbye that I hated saying. Then I climbed into my car and drove away from my forever.

31

ATLANTA

AUGUST 16, 2016

K risten yawned. "I hate days when we have to stay late."

"Away games," I said with a shrug. "What can you do?"

"Nothing, I suppose."

We went out into the empty parking lot. Most people had gone home over an hour ago. But the training room had still been full up to a few minutes ago. The preseason had started last week with a win against Washington. The team was flying out tomorrow for their match against Cleveland, and I wasn't looking forward to being gone on a Thursday. But it was football season, and that was how it went.

I'd been working for the Falcons for a year and had come to accept that this was how things went.

"See you tomorrow," Kristen said, waving good-bye. "Say hi to that hunk of a man you're going home to for me, will you?"

"Yes, I'll let Cole know that you said hello."

"And after the season is over, we're going to get trashed."

"The season just started," I reminded her.

She winked. "I know. I'm already looking forward to the postseason festivities."

"You're ridiculous."

Once I was in my car, I texted Cole to let him know I was heading home. He responded immediately. My phone dinging noisily in the car.

I'm making dinner, and we're out of pasta. Think you could run to the store on your way home?

I responded in the affirmative and then drove to the grocery store. I should have picked the one nearest to home, but my favorite coffee shop was next to a grocery store that was a little bit farther away. The benefits of coffee outweighed the added distance.

I jogged into Kroger and picked up spaghetti and penne since he hadn't been specific, and then I walked next door to the hole-in-the-wall coffee shop. When I'd been on Falcons cheer a few years ago, I'd driven out of my way all the time to get their iced lattes. No regrets.

For a Tuesday afternoon, the coffee shop was packed. It wasn't far from a few campuses, and college students covered every inch with their laptops open as they laughed with their friends. Ah, easier days.

The line was at least short, and I ordered an iced latte and a flat white to take home for Cole. Then I stood off to the side, dicking around on my phone as I waited for my name to be called.

"Lila!" the barista said, dropping my iced latte down in front of me.

"Thanks."

"The flat white will take a minute."

"No problem."

I took a sip of my drink when I heard my name being called again. I glanced up at the barista, confused because she'd just said it would be a minute. But it wasn't the barista. Seated at a table in the back corner of the coffee shop was none other than Ash Talmadge.

I hadn't forgotten that he was going to be moving to Atlanta, but I hadn't thought that I'd actually run into him. Atlanta was huge. This was something different.

I should have pretended not to hear him, grabbed my coffee, and left. Instead, I walked across the room to a smile I knew all too well and a man that I didn't want to love anymore. Not that my heart gave a shit.

"James Asheford Talmadge IV," I said when I reached his table. "What a coincidence."

"Is it?" he asked.

His laptop was open and off to the left, a book out in front of him, his meticulous handwriting covering a legal pad.

"Suppose nothing is a coincidence anymore. You're here studying?"

"Yeah. I remembered that you said you loved this place. I thought I'd give it a shot."

"In case I showed up?"

"That's a bonus."

Two years ago, I'd broken our love, destroyed his

trust, and walked away, empty-handed. How could he look at me the same way he always had?

"How's school going?"

He shrugged. "It's challenging and a lot of work, especially with a full-time job."

"I know nothing about an MBA. You're still working?"

I'd been able to work in a clinic and do some athletic training while in PT school, but it wasn't anything close to full-time.

"You have to," he explained. "It's a *nights and weekends* kind of gig. Made for people who are already running their own business and trying to level up."

"I see. So, how are you working here when the company is in Savannah?"

"We're diversifying," he said with that cocky grin he always got when he talked about his family's real estate business. Sometimes, I forgot that his family owned half of Savannah, and sometimes, it was painfully obvious that we had come from different social classes. "I'm running the Atlanta office of Talmadge Properties."

"That must be nice. Not being in daddy's shadow here."

His face clouded, as he remembered that I knew him better than anyone. That I knew what this MBA was really about—a way to shine without the persistent presence of his father's disapproval.

"You know me too well, Lila," he finally said.

I swallowed at the words. At the easy way he'd said them. The intimacy as he'd leaned forward and rolled my name across his tongue.

I couldn't deny how terribly we'd ended. How many

regrets I had about how that conversation had gone down. Least of all that I'd lied and most of all how bad I'd hurt him, demolished nearly a decade of a relationship.

We couldn't start over. There was nothing here that I could have when I was with Cole. That was obvious. Even telling him that I'd seen Ash would probably send him into a panic. But it was so hard when Ash was sitting right in front of me and all the old, familiar feelings washed over me.

I took a step back.

That wasn't who I was.

I could love two men, but I could only have one.

And I wouldn't do to Cole what I'd done to Ash.

Never again.

"It was good seeing you," I said, swallowing hard.

His smile faded as if he'd read my thoughts. "You too, Lila."

"I'm going to ... go get my coffee."

"You have your coffee." He gestured to my ignored iced latte.

"Right. Cole's coffee."

His eyes hardened at the word. As if even saying his name was taboo. And it probably was. But I was with Cole now, and that was how it was.

"Bye," I muttered.

He didn't respond, but I backed up and hurried to the counter just as my name was called. I grabbed Cole's drink and booked it out of there.

∾

I CARRIED THE PASTA, coffee, and a heavy heart into the house. I could smell Cole's mom's famous spaghetti sauce recipe, waiting for the noodles I'd brought home. Sunny rushed over to greet me.

"Yes, I know, cutie. Let me set this stuff down," I told her as I entered the kitchen. "I have pasta." I held the grocery bag up. "And coffee."

"I knew I loved you for a reason." He took the grocery bag from me, set the coffee down on the counter, and then pulled me in for a kiss. "Missed you. I hate when you work late."

"Going to hate that I'm heading for the away game even more."

"Mostly that I can't go with you."

"Next time."

"Absolutely." He kissed me again and then dumped the penne into the already-boiling water. "How was work otherwise?"

"Fine. Just a lot going on." I scooped up Sunny and gave her a bunch of kisses as he stirred the pasta.

I debated on telling him about the chance meeting at the coffee shop. But the thought of the subsequent argument left me exhausted. I wasn't going to see Ash again. I'd learned my lesson the hard way.

"Do I have time for a shower before this? I need to wash the training room off of me."

"Go ahead."

"Thanks."

I released Sunny and then went for a quick shower. I towel-dried my hair afterward, pulling it up into a messy bun on the top of my head. The hot water had relaxed all my tense muscles, and I felt more like myself again.

But when I stepped back out of the bedroom, I found Cole in the dining room, holding my phone.

"What?" I asked when I saw his stricken face.

"Your phone was going off. I went to grab it to put it on silent. I know you always forget."

"Yeah. Sorry about that."

I kept it on loud at work because Ferguson would send messages while I was in the training room. It always dinged when I left, and I'd get mad and have to put it back on silent. So frustrating.

"That's what you're sorry about?"

I stared at him. He didn't look confused; he looked mad.

"Uh, what am I missing?"

"What the fuck is this, Lila?"

He thrust the phone out at me, and I took it from him, not knowing what he was getting at. But there on the screen was a series of messages from Ash. My face fell.

You ran out so fast that I didn't even get to say good-bye.

But it was really good to see you.

Just to talk to you like normal even.

Didn't realize how much I'd missed you.

My stomach knotted at the words. At the fact that they were from Ash. That he'd ever say these things to me. And also that he'd be stupid enough to put them in a text. Fuck.

"Lila?" Cole ground out.

"Ugh! Look, I saw him at the coffee shop. He was there, studying. Completely random."

"And you stayed and talked to him?"

"It was five minutes. I was waiting for your coffee."

"Why didn't you tell me? Why did I have to find out from him sending you love messages?"

"It wasn't a big deal."

"It's *always* a big deal!" he shouted.

I took a step back. "I wasn't trying to hide it from you. I had no idea he was going to text me. Don't you think if I was going for subterfuge, I would have at least turned my phone down?"

"That's not a good argument." He crossed his arms over his chest. "You would have been sneakier if you'd wanted to hide it, isn't a good answer. I don't fucking trust him. He's doing this on *purpose*."

"God," I said with a shake of my head. "This is why I didn't tell you! You're blowing the whole thing out of proportion."

"No, I'm not," he insisted. "I remember when I ran into you when you were dating him."

I took a step back. "Are you seriously doing this right now? Are you trying to say that I'm going to cheat on you? Are you equating a five-minute conversation at a coffee shop with New Orleans? Because this isn't that, and I can't even believe you'd say that."

"I didn't mean it like that."

"Maybe say what you do mean."

Cole stomped back to the pasta to keep it from boiling over ... just like him. He took a minute before facing me again. "I don't fucking trust him, Lila."

"You don't have to trust him. Just trust me."

"He was in that coffee shop on purpose!"

I sighed and dropped my head back. "How would he know that I'd be there? I didn't even know that I was going to be there."

"I don't know. But fuck, Lila ..." Cole abandoned the pasta and stepped back to me. The fire had died in his eyes. His easily riled anger replaced by fear. He put his hands on my jaw and tilted my head up to meet him. "I'd feel better if you blocked his number."

I swallowed and nodded. "All right. But nothing happened, and it's not going to."

"I know," he said, dipping down to kiss my lips. "I'd still feel better if he couldn't reach out to you."

I bit my lip as he served up the pasta. I stared down at the messages on my phone. I flipped it to silent. And another message came in.

Maybe we could meet up again.

I sighed heavily and stepped away from Cole. He was right. Ash knew I liked that coffee shop. Even if he hadn't planned to be there when I was, he'd gone there because he knew I frequented it. I should cut him out of my life. But I felt as sick about it as the time Ash had commanded me to never see Cole again.

I sent back a quick response to let him know I was going dark.

We can't meet up. You shouldn't send me any more messages.

He responded almost instantly.

Why not? Get in trouble?

Stop it.

I miss you, Lila. I don't care about our past. I don't care about any of it. I love you. You can't say that you don't feel the same. No matter who you're with now.

This is why we're not talking.

That wasn't a denial.

Good-bye, Ash.

I deleted all the messages. My finger hovered over the Block button, but I couldn't do it. I couldn't bring myself to push the button.

Never good-bye. Only until next time.

I deleted that message, too, and told myself that was good enough. Not responding anymore was enough. It was.

32

ATLANTA
NOVEMBER 19, 2016

Marley arrived early to pick me up for her awards ceremony. Thankfully, I'd known Marley nearly my entire life. So, I'd anticipated her telling me to be ready by six when, in actuality, she'd show up at five forty-five.

"I'll get it," Cole said.

He disappeared to answer the front door as I put on my favorite pair of black high heels. I stuffed my phone in a tiny purse, double-checked my cherry-red lipstick, and then went to meet my best friend.

"No, don't do that," Marley said to Cole. "I don't need any congratulations. The whole thing is embarrassing."

"It's embarrassing to win an award for your achievements?" Cole asked.

"Yes!"

"Don't try to talk sense into her," I told Cole. "That's why I'm going to be there. So she actually gets onstage to accept the damn thing."

"It's a lot of pomp for something that isn't that important."

I rolled my eyes. "Agree to disagree, Mars. You're a genius, and you should allow people to lavish you with praise."

Marley crossed her arms over her black party dress. "Maybe we don't have to go."

Cole went for the door. "No way. You're going, and you're going to tell me all about it when you get back."

Marley sighed heavily. "Fine. Come on, Lila. Let's get this thing over with."

I kissed Cole good-bye. "Have fun at Michael's bachelor party tonight but not too much fun."

He snagged another kiss. "I'll miss you the whole time."

"I love you."

"Love you too. Have fun with Mars."

"Will do," I said as I followed Marley out.

We drove my car into town, and she was nervous and fidgety the entire ride to the Hyatt Regency in Midtown. There was nothing I could do or say that would get her to relax. When we arrived, I insisted on a valet over her protests so that we could just walk inside for the event. The last thing I wanted to do was park and have Marley second-guess herself again.

Marley touched my arm. "Thanks for agreeing to go with me."

"I *insisted* on attending with you."

"Well, I'm grateful."

"Here." I dragged her across the room for alcohol. "This will help."

Marley nervously downed the entire glass of champagne, and I passed her another one.

"Just don't get drunk."

She sipped the second glass more slowly. "Yeah. I'd hate to forget my speech."

I took a sip of my own champagne. The event was beautiful. The room was completely decked out, and all the attendees were in formalwear. It was a big deal to have a huge association presenting Marley with an award for her achievements in neurological disorders before she was thirty. Whether Marley wanted to acknowledge that or not.

We wandered around the room together. Marley loosened up from the alcohol enough to say hi to her friends and colleagues. I only half-listened to the incomprehensible conversations and was glad when Marley disappeared backstage to prepare for her award.

I took a pose as a wallflower at the back of the room just as everyone quieted for the speaker to announce Marley. She stepped onstage to a huge round of applause. She'd practiced her speech on me last weekend and had been so nervous. No one would have guessed that based on how much of a pro she was tonight.

I was so engrossed in her acceptance speech that I barely felt my phone buzzing against my hip. I pulled it out to silence the vibrations. But when I looked down at the screen, I froze.

Ash was calling.

Why was Ash calling?

We hadn't spoken in three months. Other than the five-minute conversation at the coffee shop and the unfortunate moment at Elle's wedding, we hadn't talked in almost two years. Texts, yes. He sent them with semi-frequency when he was thinking about me. Calling was something else.

I chewed on my bottom lip and then declined the call. I couldn't answer that. Answering was a bad idea. He could tell me why he was calling in a voice mail that I could delete and never think about again.

Except he didn't leave a voice mail.

He called back immediately.

I couldn't think of a single reason that he would call me twice in the same minute. He didn't even like to talk on the phone. He'd always been a text kind of person. What the hell?

I cursed and then backed out of the room just as Marley finished her speech.

"Hello?"

"Lila, thank God you picked up."

Ash sounded ... frantic. I furrowed my brows.

"What's going on? Why are you calling?"

"I got into a car accident."

"What? Are you okay?" I gasped.

"Yeah. I was T-boned by a truck."

"Jesus."

"My car is totaled. Air bags deployed. They're taking me to the hospital."

"Oh my God, Ash, are you okay?"

"I'm beaten up," he said, his voice wavering, "but they mostly want to check to make sure everything is okay internally."

"Fuck."

"I just …" He paused on the line long enough that I got worried. "You're the first person I thought of to call. My family is in Savannah. I have friends here, but …" He coughed into the phone and then cursed at the pain. "I freaked out and called you."

"It's okay. Do you need me to come to the hospital?"

This was Ash. No matter what the fuck had come between us, I couldn't leave him to suffer.

"I don't know. They'll probably do some tests and send me home."

"How are you getting home?"

He paused. "I haven't thought about that."

"Okay. Text me the hospital information, and I'll meet you."

He sighed in relief. As if he'd been holding his breath, calling me, expecting me to tell him to go fuck himself. But this wasn't him asking us to get back together or trying to ruin my relationship with Cole. This was a real crisis. I didn't know what I'd tell Cole, but I couldn't leave Ash stranded.

"Thanks, Lila. I'll text you."

We hung up, and I got his message that he was going to Emory. Adrenaline ripped through me, and I rushed back inside to find Marley.

Her eyes darted over my face. "What's wrong?"

"Ash called. He got in a car accident, and they're taking him to Emory."

"What?" Marley asked, wide-eyed.

"He was T-boned. His car is totaled." Tears came to my eyes, and my hands were shaking. "He said he thinks he's fine, but I don't know. I need to go to him. I can't sit by and not know."

"Right. Of course," Marley said at once. "I'll go with you."

"It's your big night," I protested.

"Ash has been in my life as long as he's been in yours. I want to make sure he's okay too. But also, if you go alone, Cole is going to freak out."

I closed my eyes and nodded. "He's going to freak out either way."

She nodded. "Yep."

"I hate this. I don't want to take you away from this."

"Honestly, take me away from this," she said with a short laugh. "Let me tell someone I have a family emergency." She squeezed my hand and then darted away.

I bounced uncomfortably from one foot to the other while she made her excuses. My phone was a weight in my hand. I needed to tell Cole, but what the fuck would I even say?

I took a breath and texted him.

Ash got in a car accident. Marley and I are heading to the hospital. Please don't be mad.

"Okay. We're good. Let's blow this Popsicle stand," Marley said.

"I love you."

"I know," she said with a wink. "I'm your one true love."

"So accurate," I agreed as we made our way back to the valet. "I texted Cole. I haven't heard back yet. He's at a bachelor party, so he might not even look at it."

"You look green."

"I feel like I'm going to throw up. I had a five-minute conversation with Ash, and Cole threw a huge fit. I don't want more of that."

Marley touched my shoulder. "It's okay. He's going to understand that these are extenuating circumstances. It's not the same."

"I know that," I said as I slipped into the driver's seat. "But Cole isn't rational when it comes to Ash."

"He has reason," Marley said.

I swallowed back bile. "I know."

We almost made it to Emory when Cole's call came in. I cringed and put him on the Bluetooth in my car.

"Hey," I said.

"Lila, what the hell are you doing?"

Marley and I cringed at the same time. He sounded a little drunk and a lot furious.

"I'm here with Marley. Marley, say hi."

"Hi, Cole," she muttered.

"Mars," he said curtly. "Y'all are going to the hospital to see Ash?"

"Yeah," she said.

"Lila," he groaned.

"It's not at all what you think. I'm going because when someone calls you, freaking out because they were in a car accident, you go. So, I'm going." I paused. "You can meet us there if you want."

"Oh, yes, good idea," Marley said at once.

"Yes, because on the night of my friend's bachelor party, what I really want to do is see Ash fucking Talmadge."

I bit my lip. "I just mean, it's so not a big deal that you could be there."

Cole blew out an exasperated breath. "How did he even call you? I thought you'd blocked his number."

I winced and glanced at Marley, who looked like she would rather be anywhere else in the world than in the middle of this argument.

"Uh, I didn't block his number."

Cole's silence was worse than his words.

"We haven't been talking or anything," I said quickly.

"I just ... fuck," Cole said. "Fine, go see him in the hospital. It's not like I can stop you. Even if it's idiotic."

And then he hung up the phone.

Marley grimaced. "That went ... poorly."

"Yeah," I whispered. "As bad as I'd expected."

"Or worse."

I nodded mutely. What else could I say? We'd been together almost a year and a half. If he couldn't trust me when someone was hurting and there was no ulterior motive, would he ever trust me?

WE PARKED in lot in front of the emergency room and then hustled inside, still dressed to impress in ballgowns and heels. A nurse informed us that Ash was getting tests done right now and to wait. We paced anxiously for another forty-five minutes before they allowed us back to see him.

I burst into the room and found him sitting in a

hospital bed with a wrap around his middle and some bruising on his face and shoulders.

"Lila," he said in relief. His smile lit up when he saw me. As if he'd won a prize out of one of those impossible claw machines.

"They wouldn't let us back for almost an hour."

"I'm glad you're here."

Marley stepped in. "Wow, you look like shit."

Ash laughed and then touched his ribs. "Fuck, don't make me laugh like that."

"Sorry," Marley said.

"It's fine. I'm fine. Some broken ribs, I guess. They finally gave me some pain meds. Now, I'm waiting on the last tests, prescriptions, and shit. It's impossibly slow here." He eyed our attire. "You didn't have to get all dressed up for me."

I chuckled. "Marley won an award. We were at her ceremony."

"Shit. Sorry, Mars. I didn't mean to take you away from that."

Marley wrinkled her nose and sank into a chair across the room. "Trust me, you were doing me a favor."

"Then, as ever, I'm at your service."

"So, what happened?" Marley asked.

Ash shrugged and then winced again. "I don't even know. I was going through a green light, and some old lady wasn't paying attention. She drove straight through the red and hit me on the driver's side."

"Damn," Marley said.

I sank into the chair next to his bed. We hadn't talked in

so long, but sitting here right now, I knew that nothing had changed. That I felt exactly the same as I always had for Ash, and that I wanted to comfort him as I always had. He was still *my* Ash. Even if he could never be my Ash again. I'd broken that between us. I was the one who had walked away and said we couldn't fix what was broken. And I was the one who had to suffer the consequences of that.

Ash glanced over at me. Blue meeting blue in the small space between us. My heart skipped a beat.

"I'm glad that you're here."

"You know what?" Marley said, jumping up. "I'm going to go find the vending machine. I can't get us two Cokes like Lila, but maybe I can get us some snacks since you'll be here for a little while longer."

"Sure. Thanks," he said with a big smile for Marley, who promptly disappeared, leaving us alone.

Ash took my hand in his as soon as she was gone.

"Don't scare me like that again."

Time was supposed to dull feelings. It was supposed to let you move on. But if anything, one look at him, and everything was Technicolor.

"I'm sorry," he said, squeezing my hand. "I didn't mean to scare you." He brought my hand to his mouth and pressed a kiss against my skin. "I feel better, having you here."

I gently extricated my hand from his grip. I didn't even know what to say.

"You look sick."

"I was upset," I said. "And I told Cole."

He clenched his jaw. "That you were coming here?"

I nodded. "He said coming here was idiotic and hung up on me."

Ash shrugged and then winced again. "Fuck that guy."

I laughed, self-deprecating. "Not looking forward to the argument when I get home."

Ash's eyes hardened. "I don't understand him. He has everything I could ever want, and still, he fucks it up?"

"Stop," I whispered. "That's not why I'm here."

"Why are you here?"

"You know why."

He arched an eyebrow, wanting me to say it, but I couldn't.

"You needed someone, and you were there for me through the stuff with Mom."

He was silent for a stretch. I could tell that the drugs were starting to kick in. He leaned back heavier against the pillows, his breathing evening out. "I am sorry though. As much as I'd love for you to dump Cole, I'm not trying to ruin your relationship … like he did ours."

I winced at the words.

Marley knocked on the door and peeked her head in. "Uh, I got some Coke and a bag of Cheetos and a Butterfinger. That's about as good as I could do."

"Sounds perfect," Ash said.

With Marley back in the room, conversation resumed its normal course. We sat around, eating junk food while we waited for the doctor to show up. She eventually cleared him to leave with a request to come back in to check on those ribs. Everything else had thankfully come back okay.

We exited the hospital together. Marley and I got Ash into the backseat of my car and then drove him to his apartment.

"Thanks for the ride," he said as he got out of the car.

"Feel better," Marley said as I got out of the car.

"Are you going to be able to make it inside okay?"

He nodded. "Sure. I'm just a little woozy."

"Ash ..."

"I'll be fine."

Marley was purposefully occupied with her phone as Ash tugged me into a hug. I wrapped my arms around him, careful of his broken ribs.

"I want to see you again," he whispered into my hair.

"We can't."

He pressed a kiss into my hair. "I love you."

I pulled back, refusing to say the words back. "Take better care of yourself."

Ash sighed. "I wish things were different."

"I know."

Then I got back into my car and watched as he ambled back into the apartment. I swallowed heavily as I backed out of the parking spot.

"So ... you still love Ash?"

I swallowed. "Yeah."

"And Cole?"

I nodded.

"Fuck."

"Tell me about it."

~

THE HOUSE WAS dark when I got home. I opened Sunny's crate and let her out in the backyard to do her business. I changed out of my ballgown and into sweats. I texted Cole to let him know that I was home but heard nothing. I knew he'd be out late with the guys. They were probably at a strip club.

Sunny came back inside, and we snuggled together on the couch, watching a Disney movie I'd seen a hundred times. I could barely focus on it as the minutes ticked by with no word from Cole.

Just as I was dozing off, the front door opened. I jerked up at the same time as Sunny, who barreled toward Cole.

"Hey," I said, rubbing my eyes and coming to my feet.

"I thought you'd be asleep."

"I couldn't sleep. I texted and never heard back from you."

"Phone died," he said, tossing the dead thing on the dining room table.

"Oh."

"How was seeing Ash?" he bit out.

"Uneventful. He has a few broken ribs and some bruising." I shrugged. "Marley and I sat around most of the night."

"Ah," he said, finally looking up at me. "Was it worth it?"

"Worth what?"

"This argument?"

I clenched my jaw. "I don't know why we even need to have an argument."

"You still cared enough to go to him," he growled.

"And you told me you'd blocked his number, and you didn't."

"I've known him since I was seventeen. I can't stop caring that someone is hurt. This isn't the same as going to see him because I miss him."

"Do you?" he demanded.

I squeezed my eyes shut. "I hate this, Cole. I hate that you have to ask me these questions. That you get so mad every time anything happens. That you clearly don't even trust me."

I'd had such an emotional night that I couldn't hold the tears back. Everything about today was too much.

"Hey," Cole said, coming to stand before me. "I'm sorry. Don't cry. I don't want to be the reason you cry."

"What are we supposed to do? How do we go on if you don't trust me?"

"I do," he insisted with a sigh. "I just want him out of our lives."

"I know. But I don't want to keep being punished when this happens. I can't help it, but I do know that I come home every night to you. That I'm here, in Atlanta, with you. I moved in with you. I love you. I thought we were happy."

"We are happy." He tipped my chin up. "I'm sorry. I'm sorry for hanging up and for yelling at you. He just makes me irrationally angry."

"You need to figure it out because I can't keep doing this," I told him honestly. "By the time you apologize, the damage is already done."

33

SAVANNAH
DECEMBER 25, 2016

After the Christmas adrenaline wore off, exhaustion set in, and I couldn't show it to my mom. Not when I'd promised her a normal Christmas. Whatever normal was after working for twelve hours straight at the Falcons–Carolina game in Charlotte and then driving four hours to Savannah. At least Cole had been at the game and driven down with me, but we were both tired and had to drive back into Atlanta tomorrow for more work.

Still, we pushed it aside to open gifts and do our annual family trip to the food pantry. It was important to me even if I wanted to nap. I snagged a full twenty minutes, crashed out in my old bedroom, when my mom announced we were all going to the night service.

"It's asking too much," I grumbled to Cole.

"She skipped midnight mass on Christmas Eve for us. I think it's fair."

"I mean, yes, of course, when we're being all reasonable and shit."

My mom had become devout in the years working for the church. I didn't blame her for wanting to attend church on Christmas, especially if she missed mass, but that didn't mean I wanted to go with her.

"It'll be fine. It's one hour. Should we stop and get you a coffee before the service?"

My eyes lit up. "Could we?"

"It's a necessity at this point."

"My mom doesn't drink coffee. It's so weird to have that much energy without additional sustenance."

Cole kissed the top of my head. "Hurry up and get dressed, so we can stop on the way."

That got me moving.

We grabbed a coffee on the way there, much to my mom's disapproval, and made it to the service right before it started. I hurried into a seat between my mom and Cole. Luckily, since we were almost late, we didn't have to sit in the front, where my mom preferred, and had to make do in the back of the church.

Service was slow and methodical, but at least the coffee was waking me up enough to make it through the whole thing.

"I'm going to talk to the priest," my mom said as soon as the service ended. "It won't be more than a few minutes."

"Oh boy," I muttered under my breath. "We'll be here for another half hour."

Cole grinned. "My mom called while we were in the service. I'm going to give her a call back."

"Okay. I'll try not to fall asleep in the pew."

"You're ridiculous."

He headed out of the sanctuary, and my sisters and their kids followed. I sat back down on the bench, letting everyone else file past me. I was in no rush to get out of there. I pulled out my phone and scrolled absentmindedly, trying unsuccessfully to suppress my yawns.

"Was the service that bad?" a voice asked next to me.

I nearly jumped out of my skin. Because of course, I knew that voice. I glanced up and saw Ash Talmadge hovering before me. His parents shot him a side-eye and then continued out of the sanctuary.

"I thought you would have been at midnight mass."

He shrugged. "My dad had a business meeting."

Ah. Same old, same old.

"I didn't think you'd make it. Weren't you in Charlotte for the game?"

"Yeah. We drove in after, so I could spend Christmas with my family."

"That's nice."

"It is nice, except that I'm exhausted."

He grinned and sank into Cole's unoccupied seat. I scooted over to put more space between us. "I can't thank you enough for coming to see me in the hospital. I'm sure Cole hated it, but it was good to have you there."

I flushed at the intensity in his words and cleared my throat. "How are your injuries?"

"Pretty much healed. There's still some lingering ache in my ribs, but otherwise, I'm back to normal."

"That's good." I hadn't messaged him to find out how he was doing, and it was nice to get confirmation. "I should probably ..." I gestured away from him. We both came to our feet at the same time. The distance interminable. "It was good, seeing you."

"Is it always going to be like this?"

I bit my lip. "I don't know, Ash."

He sighed, dropping his gaze to his boots and then meeting my eyes again. "It shouldn't have to be this way with us. We've known each other too long."

"Which is precisely why it is this way."

"I wish we could go back to the days when you were my Amy and I was your Laurie."

I laughed. I couldn't help it. "As if the days were that easy then."

"The feelings were always real."

"The feelings weren't the problem." I took a step back. "I should go."

But before I could step away, Cole had returned, and he looked pissed.

"What's this?"

Ash dropped his remorse like flipping a switch. He glared at Cole. "Just the person I didn't want to see."

"Don't. We're in the church," I reminded them.

Not that either of them heard me.

Cole took a step toward Ash. "I know what you're trying to do, and it's not going to work."

"Cole, stop it." I put my hand in his and tugged him backward. "I'm tired. We drove all night to get here. It's Christmas. Please."

Cole and Ash stared at each other for another second before Cole looked down at me.

He nodded once. "He's not worth my fucking time."

Cole let me drag him out of the church and onto the

steps of the cathedral. We still had to wait for my mom, but I wasn't going to wait inside any longer. The tension between them was the pin on a grenade. The longer they spent in each other's presence, the more likely it was going to be pulled.

I smacked Cole. "Why did you have to do that?"

"Why were you even talking to him?"

"It was *nothing*. I'm not getting back together with Ash. You need to get this through your head. All you see is red when he's around, and *that's what he wants*."

"That's all good and well, Lila, but he's trying to come between us. I won't let him do it."

"He's *not*," I insisted. "Can't you hear a word I'm saying? It is my choice, and I'm standing right *here*."

But Cole didn't hear what I'd said because Ash hadn't stayed in the church and let us walk out, like I'd wanted. He followed behind us, and Cole was beyond rational. He was a lit fuse.

I'd seen that anger directed at me in the past. I knew the intensity of it. That his temper was his downfall. It was why he'd gotten so mad that night of the Bama game, and the day we'd broken up on Frat Beach, and every *single* time since when Ash came up. It burned so slowly until he erupted, and then Cole couldn't come back from the anger until it burned itself out.

"Please, don't," I gasped, tugging on his arm. "Let it go."

"It ends today."

Ash stopped in front of us with a sneer on his face. Ash had no temper. Not like Cole. But he loved me, was obsessed with me, and he always had been. He knew what set Cole off. He would happily antagonize him into this showdown that was a long time coming.

Fuck.

"Stay the fuck away from her," Cole spat.

"Or what?" Ash demanded. "What are you going to do if I don't stay away?"

"Please don't do this." I closed my eyes and prayed for it all to stop.

This wasn't fair. This wasn't how it was supposed to happen. I'd caused this whole mess, but I didn't *want* it to happen like this. I couldn't help that I loved them both and that I always had. It would be easier if they didn't *hate* each other so much.

"What if she *wants* to see me?" Ash taunted.

Cole's anger bubbled fully to the surface. He left my side and got up in Ash's face. "You're completely deluded if you think that she'd ever want you again. You're an annoyance, holding on to something that isn't yours anymore. You're a fly, a gnat. You're just in the way. Always in my fucking way."

"If you didn't think that I was a threat, you wouldn't be standing here right now," Ash said with a smirk.

Cole clenched his fists. "You're just jealous we're together. That she chose me over you," he snarled. And I saw the second before he went in for the kill. "Still mad that I fucked her in New Orleans."

I froze at the words. The look on Ash's face. He'd never gotten over that. How could he? I'd thought that the last two years had fixed it, but the split second of devastation on his face told me everything I needed to know.

Then it was carefully replaced with a forced laugh. Almost a cackle. "You can have New Orleans. Just like we had Frat Beach."

Cole froze at the words. Processing what Ash had said. Then it hit him, and his gaze shifted to me.

"Fuck," I whispered.

"Oh, she didn't tell you about that?" Ash asked.

But my *fuck* was confirmation. We hadn't hooked up when I was with Cole, but he didn't know that. It had happened, and that was enough to pull the pin on the grenade.

Cole launched himself forward, slamming his fist into Ash's jaw. Ash's head whipped to the side, and for a second, I thought it would end there. He was still recovering from broken ribs after all. But no ...

Ash had been waiting for this fight his entire life. He wasn't as big as Cole, but he came at him with years of fury. And no amount of yelling on my part could tear the two apart. I had to watch as they fought on the steps of the cathedral.

My hands shook, and I thought I was going to be sick. Something had been broken here. Something that had long been rotting and ignored. Cole's temper had ignited, and Ash's antagonism had won. And they were both so wrong. It wasn't like on television when a person was being fought over. This was terrible. It wasn't even completely about me. It was about ego and pride and male territorialism.

This was about winning.

And in the end, no one won. Except for my clarity that I couldn't keep doing this.

I couldn't be with Ash.

I couldn't be with Cole.

Not with our history always hovering around us. Not when I loved them both. Not when they hated each other. This would never get easier. It would never go away. Time kept pulling us back together, always together, and it didn't care who got hurt. Inevitably, it was always me.

Every time they hurt each other, I held the brunt of it, and I had for years and years. Love wasn't enough here. Not with hate so close to the surface.

An apology wouldn't fix anything this time.

A group of Holy Cross football players dived into the fray to tear Cole and Ash apart. They were both bleeding, chests heaving, fighting to get back to it. To take out their anger in an animalistic way. As if it would solve anything.

"It's over," I said so soft that they almost didn't hear me.

"What?" Cole asked.

"It's over," I repeated. "This is over. Both of you."

"Lila," Cole said.

"Wait," Ash began.

I shook my head. "No, I'm done."

"You can't be done," Cole said.

But I was. "I'm tired of having to choose and getting hurt in the process. I can't do it anymore."

"Lila," Ash said.

I stared between them, utterly empty and spent. I was too tired, too broken to go through this. I'd hurt when it all sank in, but right now, I felt resolute.

"Please ..." Cole said.

There wasn't a way. I knew that. And we couldn't keep

doing this. If only they didn't hate each other. So, I threw out the only caveat that I knew they'd never accept.

"It's either all of us or none of us," I said clearly.

Both guys balked at my words. The words they had surely never expected to hear. I'd only thought them in abstract, knowing it was impossible. But there was nothing holding us back from the precipice now.

"We're a trio, or we're not. That's the only offer I have."

"That's crazy," Cole said.

"That would never work," Ash insisted.

I glanced between them. Blue eyes and brown hair and red, red blood. I'd known they'd say no. How could they say anything else? But they must not have realized what the alternative meant.

"Then it's nothing."

They argued and fought and tried to get me to hear what they were saying, but they'd made their position clear while they rolled around on the church steps. It was over.

I'd spent my entire life fighting between these two men. I'd had casual dates with other people, but part of me had known I'd always end back up with one of them. It was only now that I knew that I had to try something else. There had to be something ... someone else out there. Without the history and the baggage and the pain.

My mom kept the boys back and herded me into the car. She didn't say anything as we drove home.

"How much did you see?" I asked once we were inside.

"Enough."

I nodded and sank onto the couch. My eyes were dry, but I knew it was only a matter of time. "What have I done?"

"The only thing you could with that ridiculous behavior on the church steps." She sat next to me and pulled my head into her lap. She ran her fingers back through my hair as I tried to cry but felt nothing.

"Yeah," I whispered. "I thought he was forever."

"Cole?"

I stared up at her blankly.

She patted my arm reassuringly. "Both of them."

"It was never going to happen though, was it?"

My mom sighed. "I don't know, honey, but you don't need a man to be happy."

"Like you? Do you miss Dad?" I asked the question that I'd always held back.

My mom didn't talk about my dad. It was bad enough that he'd abandoned her with four daughters right after my birth. It was worse that she still obviously loved him.

"Some days," she said. "But just because he was my one doesn't mean I'm not better without him. I got to raise four beautiful girls. I've had the best life for me, and you'll find the best life for you."

I sure hoped she was right.

34

SANTA MONICA

JUNE 23, 2017

"Keep the mimosas coming," Josie said.

She waved her fresh manicure at the waiter and rolled over on the cushioned chair to look at me and Marley. We were in the swank Santa Monica Hotel Casa del Mar for Josie's wedding. She'd booked us suites for the weekend, and we were currently lounging poolside in skimpy bikinis, drinking Dom Pérignon, and soaking up the California sun.

"I can't believe you're getting married tomorrow," Marley said from the pool.

"Again," I said.

Josie stuck her tongue out at me. "It's going to be amazing. Like, just imagine the Santa Monica beach decked out for our wedding. I'm thinking we all run to the pier afterward and jump on the Ferris wheel."

I laughed. Marley turned green.

"You know how I feel about heights."

"Just one turn!" Josie insisted.

"I'll keep you safe," I told Mars.

"I'm going to need to be drunk. A drunk bridesmaid."

"Whatever. It's LA. It's fine."

"When does Craig get back from Vegas?" Marley asked.

"Tomorrow morning."

Josie's groom, Craig, had been gone the last three days on some Vegas bachelor party extravaganza. His best man had planned and decided to tell Josie that it was going to be à la *The Hangover*. They'd even gotten the penthouse at Caesars. Josie had opted for something more low-key. We'd spent all morning at the spa, and after our mimosa pool day, we were doing a decadent dinner out in Malibu and going to some swank nightclub.

Josie had planned her own bachelorette party. To no one's surprise.

I flopped back on the cushion. "I can't believe this is your life."

"I know," she gushed. "I mean ... I still can't believe that *Academy* is going into its seventh season."

"Hottest show on television." I waggled my eyes up and down. "Literally."

"When they dropped the PG rating, it increased viewership," she agreed. "I mean, look at HBO shows. We can compete with that."

Marley wrinkled her nose. "You were supposed to be family fun."

"And it was for four straight high school seasons. We know college isn't that way."

"Even in supernatural college," I said, barely suppressing a laugh.

"Precisely," Josie said.

"So, do you think season eight will be your last season?" Marley asked. *Academy* had already been green lighted for another season, but none of us knew if it would go beyond that. "Since you'll finish the college years?"

Josie shrugged. "A girl can get a PhD."

Marley snorted. "PhDs aren't glamorous."

"I love this for you. All your dreams coming true."

"And what about you?" Josie asked, turning the tables. "Are all your dreams coming true?"

"Lila has the best dating stories," Marley said.

"Ugh!" I covered my eyes. "I don't want to talk about it."

"Tell me!" Josie insisted. "It's my wedding. I want to hear the wonderful life of Lila dating."

"Just imagine every bad thing that could happen in dating, and that's been my life."

"It can't be that bad," Josie said.

"Oh, it can," Marley said. "Probably worse."

Josie's eyes widened. "Do tell. It can't be worse than your boyfriends duking it out on the church steps on Christmas Day."

I narrowed my eyes at her. "I wasn't dating *both* of them."

"Semantics."

"You're a bitch."

"I love you too." Josie blew me air kisses. "You were devastated after that. Dating can't possibly make you think that it wasn't that bad."

"I mean, it was terrible, but in a different way," I said. "Dating is like slowly having the air sucked out of your lungs and some guy mansplaining to you about how to breathe."

"Now, I must know!" Josie said. "Actually, I'm offended that you haven't already told me."

"You've been filming and wedding planning. When would I have told you?"

"Oh shush, give me the deets."

"Fine. I joined Tinder and then Bumble because everyone said Bumble was better. They both didn't work for me. The first guy I talked to catfished me. He'd claimed to be this guy, and then we met up two weeks later, and he was, like, a fifty-year-old man. Super fun. There was a promising guy. We talked for almost a month before I felt comfortable with meeting him. I'd been catfished before, and he swore he was into me. We went on three dates and then hooked up, and then I never heard from him again."

"Eesh," Josie said.

"Yeah, I mean, if he was looking for a hook-up, why spend a month talking to me about a relationship?" I shook my head. "I've had a few hook-ups, and those were better than the relationship bit. At least we were all honest about what we were looking for."

"Oh, tell her about the guy in Macon."

I sighed. "I met him in Atlanta, but he worked in Macon full-time. We went on a few dates when he was there on business."

"Oh no," Josie whispered. "I see where this is going."

"I drove an hour out of town to see him in Macon, only to find out he had a wife and two kids."

"Fuck."

"So, that was super fun."

"You had that one nice guy," Marley said.

"Ah, yes, blow-job guy."

"What?" Josie asked.

"Real-nice guy. Took me out for a fancy steak dinner. Second date, he tried to force me to give him head in a hot tub. I politely declined and never talked to him again."

"How does this happen to you? All of these guys in such a short period of time?"

"The tip of the iceberg," I told her, defeated. "I mean, it doesn't include the numerous unsolicited dick pics or the random strangers who, after two texts back and forth, insist they're going to suck my ass all night."

Josie burst into laughter. "Stop. It's too much! They did not."

"Oh, let me pull up Tinder. I bet there's some juicy ones in here."

"They cannot all be duds."

"They might not be," I told her as I passed her the messenger feature of Tinder to scroll through. "But I haven't found a good one."

Josie scrolled through my phone. "Oh my God, is that his real dick?"

"Probably not."

"Fuck. This guy wants to eat pussy. Oh, and then two texts later, he calls you a bitch ... and a cunt."

"I'm called a bitch or a cunt every week."

"Jesus Christ." Josie passed the phone back. "Plan B: move to LA. I can hook you up with all my hot film friends."

"Oh God, no. One, I'm not leaving my job at the Falcons. I *love* my job. And two, I can't handle the Hollywood personas."

"Just give it time," Marley said. "It doesn't have to be either terrible Tinder dates or nothing. Someone is going to come around and knock your socks off."

"I hope so," I told them. "Right now, it feels hopeless."

"Okay, you know how I feel about those boys who hurt you," Josie said diplomatically. "But you're in a low place. What happens if you see one of them again?"

I swallowed. "I really don't know."

"You need to be alone longer."

"I know," I whispered. "I know I do. I don't know how it would ever work with either of them again anyway. Not after what happened."

Josie and Marley shared a look.

"The right guy will come along," Marley said.

"You just have to be ready when he does."

I nodded. "I'm ready and waiting. I hope it doesn't get much worse than this."

PART III

PART III

35

HOUSTON
FEBRUARY 5, 2017

K risten bounced from foot to foot on the sidelines. "I can't believe we're at the Super Bowl. I can't believe we're at the Super Bowl. I can't *believe* we're at the Super Bowl!"

"You keep saying that."

But I had the same jittery energy. The Falcons hadn't been in the Super Bowl since 1998. This was only the second time in franchise history. And we were going to be on the field for it.

"How are you holding up?" Kristen's boyfriend, Hong Min, asked. He was an assistant offensive line coach. He'd played ball at Oregon in college and then a year for the Seahawks before moving into coaching.

"All nerves," she admitted.

"We've got this."

A small crowd formed around them on the sidelines. It wasn't unusual, but then I saw that there were people who weren't even normally on the sidelines here. Our friends in PR and scouting and marketing. My throat bobbed as I saw Cole among them. Our eyes met, and he winked. I quickly looked away.

What were they all doing here? What was Cole doing here?

One thing was certain: Kristen didn't seem to notice. Hong Min kept her occupied, so she didn't pay attention to anything else.

Then, he dropped to his knee in front of her.

She shrieked.

My hands flew to my mouth. "Oh my God!"

Hong Min produced a black box and opened it to reveal a giant diamond ring. "Kristen Ng, will you do the honor of marrying me?"

"Yes!" she gasped, tears forming in her eyes. "Of course, yes!"

Hong Min slid the ring on her finger and then picked her up, twirling her in place. Cameras were on them, filming the proposal for their networks. And everyone cheered and swooned over the Super Bowl engagement.

I stepped forward to congratulate them at the same time as Cole. I flinched backward. I'd seen him around work in the six weeks since we'd broken up, but luckily, we didn't have to run into each other if we didn't want to. I mostly stayed in the training room, and with the Super Bowl fast approaching, I'd been too busy to do anything but work.

It had been six weeks since we'd been this close together. The hardest and most grueling six weeks of my life.

This wasn't like the other times, where we had been too far apart to make this work. This was me actively avoiding him. Me saying that I couldn't do this. Me trying to move on for the first time in my entire life.

He'd begged me not to leave after what happened on Christmas Day. He stuck around Savannah, even after I paid for a flight home so I didn't have to drive with him. He didn't think I was serious until Marley and I cleared my stuff out of his house and took Sunny with me to live with her. Then, it had sank in that I was leaving. I was really walking away.

But seeing him made it worse. Made it painfully clear that I hadn't even come close to moving on.

I said my congratulations to Kristen and Hong Min and then retreated, but Cole followed me.

"Lila," he said, stopping me in my tracks.

"Did you help plan this?"

He nodded. "Yeah. Me and a few of the other guys."

"It was romantic. She's going to be a mess the whole game."

"Worth it."

I nodded. "I should probably get back to work."

"Hey." He grasped my arm. "I've missed you."

"I can't do this."

"It's only been six weeks. We can work this out. We've gone longer than that before and made it work."

I shook my head. "What we have is fundamentally broken."

He winced at my words. "How can you think that?"

"Because I watched you throw the first punch."

"I know, but ..."

"After I told you to let it go and not let him antagonize you."

"I didn't know you'd been together at Georgia–Flor-ida. It was a shock. I just reacted. I'm sorry."

"I know you are, but you apologize and you apologize, and it doesn't make a difference. It doesn't change your behavior."

We'd already had this conversation. We'd had it more times than I could count in those early days. I told him what had really happened at Frat Beach. Not that it justi-fied it, but we'd been broken up, and I'd been wasted and mad. It hadn't been what Ash painted it as, but it hardly mattered because it got the reaction he'd wanted from Cole. He hadn't even stopped to think. Even after all of our fights about it.

"Please, Lila," he said. "I still love you, and I know that you feel the same."

I closed my eyes and sighed. "I do care about you, Cole. That hasn't changed, but it doesn't fix the problem."

"I'll do anything."

"Now but not before."

"Give me one more chance."

My stomach knotted, and I felt sick again. One more chance was exactly what I wanted to give him. I wanted this to work. I wanted to look into his face and know that we could move on from this. But I didn't know that. The last eight years had proven that he had consistent behav-ior. He wasn't going to change. Not for me at least.

"I can't."

"Look, come celebrate with me after the game."

"Cole ..."

"We can leave it up to chance," he offered desperately.

"If the Falcons win, then you celebrate with me. And if we don't then ... then I'll back off."

I chewed the inside of my cheek. Celebration didn't mean a date. It was a risk, but I could see the hope in his face. And I hated dashing it, even after all this time.

"Okay. If we win, then we'll celebrate, but it doesn't mean dating."

A smile broke across his face. The one that I remembered from college. The real smile. And I wanted to believe that this would turn the tides. That we'd come out on top of this, but I didn't have that unshakable faith any longer.

I'd grown up and grown out of it.

THE GAME WENT INTO OVERTIME.

"You have got to be kidding me."

"I know," Kristen grumbled.

"Twenty-eight to three, and they came back with twenty-five unanswered points," I grumbled. "What the fuck is even happening?"

Kristen just shook her head.

Then we watched the Falcons lose the coin toss in overtime.

And lose the game.

The Patriots cheered victoriously to a game we should have had in the bag in the third quarter. I stood, stunned, on the sidelines as the players walked off the field.

It was over.

We'd lost the Super Bowl.

All of that energy and our best year since the '90s, and it had ended this poorly. I followed the rest of the training team off the field. I couldn't stomach watching the victory celebrations.

I'D CHANGED, and I was about to head back to the hotel when Cole found me.

"There you are."

"We lost," I told him.

He nodded. "I know. It was fucked."

"Yeah."

I felt defeated. I wanted to sleep for a week and not think about the crushing disappointment.

"That doesn't mean that we can't go out. We can get a drink to wash away the sorrow."

I shook my head. "No, I'm going to go back to the hotel. I just want to sleep."

"Lila, please ... I know I said we could leave it up to chance, but I thought ..." He ran a hand back through his hair. "I thought we could work this out."

"Cole, I can't. We left it up to chance ... and we lost. That's it. I need the time and space. I need to be alone. Just ... alone."

"I fucking hate this. I hate what happened and that we can't work it out."

"I hate it too."

And I did. So fucking much. I wanted to throw myself into his arms and say that none of it mattered. If it had been a one-time thing, that would have been different.

But this was the culmination of a long line of problems. I couldn't stay here and deal with that. I couldn't let it keep happening.

"Okay," he said with a sigh. "You've made your choice. As much as I don't like it, I do have to respect it. You want space. I can give you that. You want time. I can give you that too. But it's not the end for us, Lila. It's not the end."

Tears pricked at my eyes, and I hastily looked away. "I think it is the end."

"I told you once that I wouldn't wait forever for you. But I will."

I stepped back, hating what I was about to say. "You shouldn't wait. I'm not going to change my mind."

It might have been chance that the Falcons had lost today, but it felt like a nail in the coffin. We'd let fate spin us on the wheel, to pull us back together, and the universe had said *no*. That was enough for me.

36

SAVANNAH

JULY 22, 2017

"Remind me again why I agreed to this?" I asked Marley as we parked on a garage deck next to the riverfront property.

"Probably because you want to show Shelly Thomas how awesome you are."

"Yeah. Right. My vanity won out."

"Ego."

"Whatever," I said with a laugh.

We hopped out of the car and headed for the banquet hall overlooking the river.

"Plus, I made you suffer through my ten-year high school reunion. I should accompany you to yours."

"Yeah. I just ... we're probably going to see Ash."

"Oh, we definitely are," Marley said. "Didn't you even read the invitation?"

I pulled the invite out of my purse. "Uh, not really?"

"His family donated the space for the reunion. There's a thank-you to the Talmadge family in small print at the bottom."

I perused the invitation. And yep, there it was.

"Oh."

"But!" Marley said encouragingly. "It will be fine. We don't even have to talk to him. We can walk in, have a free drink, show those old mean girls what's up, and then find a real bar."

"This sounds like a supremely bad idea."

"You've had a shitty few months. What's the worst that could happen?"

I clapped my hand over her mouth. "Don't jinx us. The worst is always waiting around the corner."

She cackled. "Okay, fine. Chill. It's just an excuse to be in Savannah while Gran is sick. I don't know how much longer she has. I wanted you to be here, and I used this as an excuse."

"Mars," I said, pulling her into a hug. "I'm so sorry about Gran."

"Me too," she whispered. "I don't know what I'm going to do. I have teaching obligations, but ..."

"But if something happens to Gran, then take the time off that you need."

She nodded and looked away. "Yeah. I'll figure it out."

We took the elevator up to the top and stood just outside of the melee. St Catherine's and Holy Cross were having a joint reunion, like they'd had a joint prom. I hoped that it didn't go as poorly for me as prom had.

I took a deep breath and then walked up to the desk. Name tags were scattered across the table, and a chirpy girl from my class with the name tag *Val* checked me in. I grabbed stickers for me and Marley.

It was exactly what I'd expected the high school

reunion to look like. A little cheesy, a little Catholic. I was actually astonished they were serving alcohol. It must have been part of the deal of getting it off school property. I was thankful for whoever had made that call.

We beelined for the drink line and waited impatiently with what felt like the rest of my class.

"So," Marley said next to me as she eyed the crowd, "what are you going to say if you see Ash?"

"Nothing. I don't want to see or talk to him."

"Yes, you do."

"Shut up."

Marley laughed. "I mean, of course you want to talk to him, but I don't think that you should. Despite months of bad dates, you should probably take Josie's advice and be single. Find yourself or whatever."

"I know," I growled and then released a sigh. "I know."

"Let's forget about it. This isn't before. You're young, smart, and funny. You love your job. You have an amazing life in Atlanta. We're going to have a *Romy and Michele* type of night, complete with ridiculous dancing and a helicopter ride."

I snorted. "Did you invent Post-its?"

Marley rolled her eyes. "Obviously."

Once we reached the front of the line, we grabbed our drinks and then went to "mingle." And by mingle, I meant, mostly stand near the empty dance floor and wonder what I was doing here.

"I don't like any of these people," I whispered to Marley.

She snorted. "You were here for three years. You had to have liked someone."

"Yeah, Ash."

"Right." She picked at her nails. "Well, there's Shelly Thomas. Looks like she's coming over here."

I swallowed. It was the reason I'd come. I wanted to face my old nemesis. The person who had made my senior year living hell. Now that I was here, it felt childish. Like, what would I get out of this confrontation with Shelly? I didn't care about her. She couldn't hurt me anymore.

So, I took a deep breath, and let it out. "Let's just go."

"What? Really?" Marley asked.

"Yeah. Come on."

I took one step before I heard a voice behind us. "Marley Nelson."

I didn't know that anyone else even knew Marley here. But I did know Derek Ballentine. He'd been the star of Holy Cross's basketball team. He'd been good enough to play at UNC on scholarship. I had no idea how he knew Marley.

Marley's eyes widened in shock and then narrowed to pinpricks. "Derek."

"How are you doing? I haven't seen you since—"

"I remember," she snapped.

I glanced at Marley. She sounded ... angry. Like really angry. Who was this Marley who actually got irritated by some strange guy? A Holy Cross boy at that. Marley mostly didn't give any fucks about anyone.

"Hey, Derek," I said to defuse the tension.

He smiled at me. He'd always been handsome, but

the years had been good to him. He was no longer just tall and gangly. He filled out his sharp suit from years of basketball. Must have been doing well enough for that suit.

"Delilah, right?" he asked.

"That's right."

"You dated Ash Talmadge."

My cheeks heated. "I did."

"He's a cool guy."

I nodded. "Sure."

"Leave her alone, Derek. Can't you see you're making her uncomfortable?"

"Oh, calm down, minivan," he said with a laugh. "We're just reminiscing."

"Minivan?" I asked.

"We should go. Good-bye, Derek."

Marley grabbed my arm and pulled me away from Derek. But she did nothing to douse my curiosity.

"What was that?"

"What was what?" she asked.

"You freaked out on him."

"He's an asshole."

I pulled her to a stop. "Okay. But I've never seen you act like this."

She clenched her jaw. "He went to Harvard Law when I was there for my PhD. He's an ass."

"But he's hot."

Marley ground her teeth and looked away. "So?"

"Oh my God, are you into him?"

"No!" she gasped. "How could you even suggest that? I hate him!"

"Fine line."

"Maybe for you!"

"All right." I raised my arms in surrender. "If you say so."

I glanced back at Derek, wondering what exactly he'd *done* to Mars to elicit such a reaction. Marley wasn't like me or Josie. She wasn't one for dramatics. If she said she hated him, well then, he must have earned it. I found it surprising that it had never come up. Marley always divulged everything. Why would she hide this?

But when I looked over at Derek, I noticed the person who stood next to him. My heart clenched at the sight of Ash in a suit, holding a glass of whiskey.

Pulled by an unseen magnet, his eyes found mine. So impossibly blue in this light.

He smiled. An invitation.

I wanted to go to him. I wanted to dive deep into him. It would be so easy. I could see it in the curve of his lips and the arch of his eyebrow and the twitch in his jaw. If I gave in here, I'd never look back.

But I wasn't ready for that. I wasn't ready to give in and never look back. It was the first real time that I'd ever tried to move on from both Ash and Cole. I needed to be alone. I needed to see if there was someone else out there worth my time.

Just because I hadn't found anyone promising yet didn't mean I needed to run back to Ash. Even if my heart thudded at the prospect. At a piece finally going back into place. Not quite whole. Not without them both. But fuck, close enough.

"Lila," Marley whispered. Her eyes darted between us. "Are you going to talk to him?"

Ash raised his glass to me. And oh, how I wanted to go. It had been hard without him. Without Cole.

Ash was finishing his MBA. Cole had taken his dream job as a Falcons scout, putting him on the road most weeks out of the year.

I never saw either of them. Just like I'd wanted.

I'd wanted to move on.

And I still hadn't.

I took a step back, away from him.

"No," I whispered.

Marley shot me a sympathetic look. "Are you sure?"

"No," I repeated.

I tipped my head at him. We didn't have to speak. He knew my thoughts as if they were painted on my skin. He knew that I'd missed him and I wanted to talk to him. Knew that I'd already made my decision. That pushing me would get him nowhere with me.

Still, he took that step forward. The want, the ache, the need still there. For both of us.

"We should go," I told Marley.

I turned my back on Ash, just as I'd done to Cole. I needed more time. If I could survive without them.

And the jury was still out.

37

SAVANNAH
DECEMBER 24, 2017

"This is the last one," my mom said.

She dropped a box at my feet, and I stared at the half-dozen of them in dismay.

"How do I have this much stuff?"

"Beats me, but I want it out of my house."

"Just throw it all away. I clearly haven't missed it."

My mom gave me *the look*.

"Your cheerleading jacket? Your high school yearbooks? The dance trophies?"

"Fine," I grumbled. "I'll go through it all."

"Good. Now, are you sure about mass? We're not leaving until Steph shows. You still have time to change your mind."

I wrinkled my nose. The last thing that I wanted to do was go to Christmas Eve mass at the cathedral where Ash and Cole had fought on the church steps. No, thanks. I'd be shocked if I ever stepped foot inside that place again.

"I'm going to pass."

My mom sighed. "All right. Well, if you change your

mind, Steph and the kids are coming over in an hour. Elle and Gary are meeting us at the service."

"Sounds good, Mom."

Mom kissed the top of my head. "I'm glad you're here and in such a better place. When I saw you this summer, I was so worried."

"Don't worry about me."

"Can't help it. That's my job."

She smiled and then headed back down the hall. I hated that I made my mom worry. Though she'd had reason to worry. I'd been a *wreck* for months after what had happened. I'd thought that I'd never get over it. Never feel comfortable in my own skin again. Not to mention, dating had been a catastrophe. Though most of it had gotten better. I'd dated more duds than good guys, but it had shown me more of what I actually wanted from a relationship. I knew who I was again.

It was probably easier that I hadn't seen Cole or Ash pretty much all year. Cole's new job had taken him out of the department. No one saw him anymore, and our mutual friends knew better than to bring him up. And Ash had been absent as well, finishing his MBA.

Everyone said that time would help me move on, but I hadn't found that to be true. I'd gone longer time spans without them, and it hadn't ever changed anything. I didn't expect it to this time either. But at least, this time, it wasn't an acute pain, but more of a dull ache. So, I kept my head down and focused on getting my life together.

I'd even asked for Christmas Eve off from work, so I could come down here to be with Mom instead of in New Orleans with the team. I'd numbly watched the loss from my mom's TV. It was the first game I'd missed in years, and the loss made it worse.

Which was how I'd ended up cleaning out old boxes of my stuff. I felt bad about tossing the dance trophies and yearbooks. So, I made a pile to keep and a pile to discard. The discard pile growing rapidly. I didn't have much room in my studio apartment back in Atlanta.

My hand settled on a stack of pictures under the yearbooks. My heart clenched. It was the dozens of pictures my mom had taken of me and Ash at prom. I was in my silvery blue dress and he had the matching bow tie. We looked so *young*. So young and so happy. So in love. I'd had no idea what would happen that night. I flipped through a bunch before putting the whole lot in the keep pile. I couldn't look through them. It hurt too much.

I dumped out the next box onto my already-messy floor and began to sort. I swallowed as I moved from high school to college. And there, amid the chaos, was a group of photographs from my sunflower session with Cole. Our heads tilted together, love apparent on our faces. I squeezed my eyes shut. God, it all felt so long ago. Like a strange and distant past when there had been nothing between us.

The photos glared up at me, and I turned them face-down in the keep pile. Then my fingers closed over an old keychain, and I laughed through the pain. A Coke keychain. The one that Cole had given me that first birthday together.

Jesus, I hadn't gotten rid of anything. My hand tightened around it, my heart squeezing with the motion. I could imagine us together as I managed to get two Cokes out of the vending machine. Him dancing with me as we rejoiced in my superpower.

But Cole was gone.

Ash was gone.

I pushed myself away from the pile of memories. I couldn't keep doing this right now. I needed air.

I dropped the keychain down on the keep pile, grabbed my jacket, and headed for the front door.

"Where are you going?" my mom asked.

"Out."

"It's almost dark."

"Just going for a walk in the park to clear my head."

"Okay," she said in that disapproving mom voice. "Be safe."

"I will. Love you," I called as I jogged out the front door.

I didn't stop jogging until I reached Forsyth Park. It was farther than I normally would have walked, especially in the cold. But I wanted to get away, and the running at least helped clear my head.

I made it to the fountain and paused to catch my breath. The park was unsurprisingly deserted on Christmas Eve, and I walked around the fountain a few times before leaning back against the surrounding railing.

It was hard to believe that a year had gone by already. It simultaneously felt like no time at all had passed and it had been a lifetime ago. How had we gotten to that point?

I probably should have done something productive, like open up Tinder in Savannah and see if I matched with anyone else who hated Christmas this year, but I couldn't bring myself to do it. I didn't want to *date* anyone else. No matter what everyone had said, the last year of dating had shown me how good I'd had it with both Ash and Cole. Separate from the other, the relationship had been amazing, and I hadn't been able to duplicate that. I wasn't sure I ever would be able to.

With a sigh, I sank down to the cold ground, leaning my back against the fountain barrier. A family skipped past me. A high school couple held hands as they walked the perimeter of the fountain and then took a seat at a bench farther away.

Everything about that felt too familiar. How many days had Ash and I met up here? Too many to count. Back before everything had fallen apart. Back when it had been so easy.

"Hello, stranger."

I whipped my head up and found the source of my thoughts walking toward me in a black peacoat and dress pants. I blinked, sure that I was imagining Ash standing before me. But he wasn't from my imagination; he was real.

"Ash?" I asked, quickly climbing back to my feet.

"Hi, Lila. Merry Christmas."

"What are you doing here?"

"I came to find you."

I tilted my head. "How did you know that I was here?"

"Well, I didn't. I went to your house, and your mom told me where to find you."

"Traitor," I muttered under my breath.

He chuckled softly. "If it's any consolation, she threatened me with bodily harm if I hurt you."

"That doesn't sound like my mom."

"She said that you're doing a lot better and she never wants to see you hurt like you were last year. I assured her that I didn't want to hurt you, just to talk. She said that was fine, but if you came back with another broken heart, no one would ever find the body."

I didn't know why, but I couldn't stop from laughing at that. My mom, the good Christian woman, threatening Ash Talmadge. Hilarious.

"God, I love her."

"She's great. Raised one hell of a daughter."

"Four," I reminded him.

"Yeah, but her Amy bloomed."

I flushed at the *Little Women* reference. Oh, how we always came back to this moment. Where I was the youngest sister coming into my own and he was the boy I'd always loved from afar.

"What are you really doing here, Ash?" I asked, crossing my arms.

"I want to talk," he assured me.

"You never just want to talk."

"You're right," he agreed. He leaned back against the railing next to me. "I couldn't stand the thought of you being in Savannah and not seeing you."

"We've both lived in Atlanta for the last year and not seen each other."

"It's different. You know it is," he said, meeting my gaze. "This is home."

And he was my hometown boy.

I sighed, releasing the tension between us. What good did it do, carrying it around? I missed him. I'd just been thinking about how I wanted things to be different. I'd had a year to get my thoughts together, and they'd told me that while I could be alone if I wanted to, I'd had it good here. Just like this.

"It is," I agreed.

"What a year it's been," he mused.

I nodded. "Did you have fun at the reunion?"

"Without you? No."

"Oh."

"Did you?"

"I had more fun at Marley's."

"That makes sense. More of your friends went to public school anyway."

"I had this absurd thought that I'd show up at our reunion and show Shelly how amazing I am now."

"How'd that go over?"

"It didn't happen. I don't have to prove anything to her. It was just ... petty." I glanced up at him. "Even admitting that I still thought about what she had done would only prove that she won."

"Do you still think about it?"

"I think about you," I whispered. "I wonder where we'd be if it hadn't happened."

"I'll always find a way back to you, Lila. Hasn't the last decade proven that?"

I swallowed and nodded. It had. Ash was my one constant. He was never too far away.

Ash tentatively reached out, linking his pinkie around mine. A chill ran up my arm at the contact. This wasn't like high school, and somehow, it felt so similar. Like a new beginning. A new first.

"Another year gone," he said. "How many more years do we have to keep ending up here, alone?"

"I don't know, Ash."

"I'm still here, Lila. I still love you." He tugged me closer. "Come back to me. Let's start over again."

Our bodies were only an inch apart. I stared up into that all-too-familiar face. The sharp contours of his cheeks and the bright blue of his eyes and the tilt of his head and the perfect shape of his lips. It was all so easy. As easy as breathing.

I nodded. "Yes."

And then his mouth fitted to mine. The place it had always belonged. The moment etched in stone, here in our hometown.

38

SAVANNAH
DECEMBER 24, 2018

"Come on." Ash opened the passenger door and held his hand out to me.

I put my hand in his and dropped my heels down onto the pavement. "What's this? I thought you'd finally convinced me to go back to church."

"Detour."

"All of that needling, and you opt for a detour instead of Christmas Eve mass," I said as he helped me to my feet.

"It's tradition."

We'd started a year ago at Forsyth Park. It only made sense to spend Christmas Eve here again. So, I tucked my arm into his, warming my hand inside his peacoat pocket, and followed him into the park.

"Your parents are going to be mad if we're late," I teased.

"They'll get over it."

"My mom will understand at least."

He grinned. "She's just glad that I convinced you to come back to church."

"Well, sorry that I have a negative association with it now."

"That's why we're going to write new memories. No more church fights."

"God, no."

The last year had been a blur of good. If I'd thought that I'd made a hasty choice, our year together had proven to me exactly what I'd already known. Ash and I worked. I'd sublet my studio and moved in with him in Atlanta. When he wasn't busy with work or finishing his MBA, he spent weekends flying to football games with me. As soon as he'd graduated, he'd fully taken over the Atlanta branch of Talmadge Properties. He had both more freedom to do whatever he wanted and more work, but he was born for this job.

I'd also been promoted to a more senior position and found I loved the new responsibilities that came with the job. It was a relief to be seen as an asset in the training room.

Life was good.

Better than it had been in a long time.

Ash pulled me against him to steal a kiss. "I love you, Lila."

"I love you too."

He smiled wider and then linked our hands, drawing me toward the fountain. It was all lit up and empty. Just like it had been last year. A guy walking his dog passed us, and then we were completely alone.

"I like this. We'll have to do this every year."

He nodded. "I'd like that."

We talked like that more and more. About a future. When we'd been together last time, I'd avoided all talk of the future. I was desperate to get through PT school. I didn't know what I wanted, and I still hadn't completely forgiven him. It was hard to believe we'd ever hurt each other that much.

We reached the fountain, and I leaned forward against the railing. A year ago, I'd still been a wreck. Running away from the past and memories. And now, I was in such a better place. It felt surreal to be back here with Ash.

"Lila," Ash said softly.

I pulled my focus away from the fountain and found Ash holding a box in his hand.

I gasped as he sank to one knee.

"Delilah Grace Greer, will you do me the honor of being my wife?"

He opened the box to reveal a large princess cut diamond with a pair of matching diamonds on either side. It was stunning and glistened with brilliance.

Tears formed in my eyes. I'd never been the kind of girl who cared about weddings. I'd never pictured mine before. Never gotten to this moment in my mind. Not because I didn't want it, but because there were always two men and not just one. Two sets of baby blues. Two smiles. Two different men.

And now, I was here. It was one pair of eyes, one smile full of joy and hope and wishes, one man. Just Ash.

"Yes," I gasped. "Yes. Of course, yes! Oh my God!"

Ash stood swiftly, pressing his lips to mine. Then he

removed the diamond from the box and carefully slid it into place on my ring finger. I marveled at the diamond, the weight of it on my hand. It felt … perfect. Like it was always meant to be there.

"I love you," he told me fiercely.

"I love you too."

I threw myself into his arms, and he picked me up, swinging me around. I laughed, giddy, my heart full to bursting.

He beamed. "Plus, I have one more surprise, love."

"Another surprise?"

And then I heard my two best friends rushing across the expanse, straight to the fountain.

"Oh my God!" I shrieked as Marley and Josie barreled into me.

"Congratulations!" Marley crowed.

"We're so happy for you," Josie said.

We hugged and jumped up and down and made fools of ourselves there in that park. And I didn't care one bit. This was the best second surprise that Ash could have planned.

"How did you get here? Were you hiding? How did this happen?" I demanded.

"Ash called me," Marley started.

"For some reason, her and not me."

"Because you're thousands of miles away."

"He told me he was planning to propose on Christmas Eve and wanted both of us there. So, I got with Josie, and we planned it out."

"I fucking hid in the bushes for you, bitch," Josie said with her imperious Hollywood voice.

"Josephine Reynolds, hiding in the bushes. Coming to theaters, Fall 2019," I joked.

She swatted at me. "Let me see that goddamn ring."

I held my hand out so that Marley and Josie could admire it. They oohed and aahed appropriately.

"This is a good first-marriage ring," Josie said.

Ash cleared his throat. "Excuse me?"

Josie winked at him.

"What's your third-marriage ring going to look like?" Marley teased.

"Look, I like to keep my options open."

Marley and I exchanged a look. Josie's second marriage hadn't even lasted a year. I thought she needed to take her own advice and spend a year single. Not likely.

"Can we talk wedding dates now?" Josie asked. "I'm booked up for filming through May. So, my bridesmaid's duties will have to be June or after."

"This isn't about you," Marley said.

"Isn't it?" Josie asked.

I shook my head at her. "We just got engaged. I have *no* idea what date we'll get married."

"June sounds nice," Ash agreed.

"Perfect!" Josie said.

"June?" I said. "That's only six months away."

"We can't do fall or winter because of the Falcons season, and I don't want to wait until 2020. Who knows what could happen then?"

"June," I whispered. "Fuck, I better get started."

Josie laughed. "Get a wedding planner. It'll be a snap."

Marley touched my arm. "I'll help."

"Thanks," I said. "I'm getting married!"

And all three of us screamed and twirled around in a circle. Until Ash couldn't stop laughing at us.

"Do we still have to go to church?" I asked. "Or can we go celebrate?"

"Church was a ruse," he said with a smirk. "Our friends and family are waiting downtown to celebrate."

"What?" I gasped. "A third surprise?"

"Anything for you."

Then he kissed me. My *fiancé* kissed me.

I drowned in him.

Nothing could ruin this night. Nothing at all.

39

NASHVILLE

MAY 18, 2019

M y stomach was in knots as I waited at the back of the procession. Kristen was dressed in an exquisite empire wedding dress, prepared to walk down that aisle. I should have been thinking about the fact that my own wedding was only a month away. Comparing it to everything I was going to be doing in a month's time.

Instead, I was thinking about Cole.

Cole, who was going to be here today.

Kristen had told me that she'd received his RSVP. And since then, I'd spent the last two days in Nashville, stressed out and wondering what the hell I was going to do or say.

I hadn't seen him in so long. He was on the road all the time, scouting for the Falcons. Even when he was in the office, I never saw him. We were secluded enough to not cross paths unless we wanted to. And the last year, it had been easier not to.

Up until Kristen had let me know about his RSVP, I'd been certain that he'd be gone this weekend. That he wouldn't have time to fly to Nashville to see Kristen and Hong Min say their *I do*s. Either way, I would have been in attendance since I'd agreed to be a bridesmaid two years ago. It had taken a lot of time to coordinate bringing in Hong Min's family from Thailand and Kristen's extended family from Vietnam. And now, we were here and about to walk down the aisle, and I still had no idea what to say.

"Ready?" Kristen's mom asked everyone. She was a wedding planner by trade and had taken on the task of her daughter's wedding with glee.

"We're ready, Mom," Kristen said.

"Okay. And go."

I was at the end of the long line of Kristen's bridal party. Behind her two sisters, three friends, Hong Min's sister, and an aunt. The entire thing was quite an affair with eight bridesmaids, eight groomsmen, four flower girls, three ring bearers, and two dogs. But it was perfectly Kristen. Huge, elaborate, and far from traditional.

I held my breath as I took the first step down the aisle. My eyes scanned the room. It was a large, open-air chapel in the Tennessee mountains. Large enough to accommodate the two hundred and fifty people in attendance and not feel packed in like sardines.

But still, I could tell at a glance that Cole Davis wasn't in attendance.

My heart sank.

It shouldn't have.

I was getting married in a month.

But it still did.

Ash was away at his bachelor party this weekend. He'd wanted to come to the wedding, but this weekend was the only time that Tanner could plan the bachelor party. I waved him off and told him to have a good time. There was a look in his eyes when I left for Nashville, the day before he jetted off to Vegas. Worry. He knew Kristen was my and Cole's mutual friend. But he'd gone. He trusted me.

And here I was, disappointed that Cole wasn't here.

Fuck.

I shook off the lingering disappointment and focused on the ceremony. I actually couldn't see much of it, being at the end of the line, but it sounded beautiful. There was a whole section in both Thai and Vietnamese for their extended family. A proclamation that I couldn't understand but also somehow understood perfectly. They declared their love in their family's native tongues. A stunning display that brought tears to everyone's eyes.

The pastor returned to English for the end of the ceremony. "And I now pronounce you man and wife. You may kiss the bride."

Hong Min stepped forward, pulling Kristen into his arms, and kissed his new bride. Everyone cheered from the audience. I applauded from my spot as a bridesmaid, smiling so hard that my cheeks hurt.

Their exit music began, and they danced merrily down the aisle, all preceding me out of the room. I headed back down the aisle. Even though I knew Cole wasn't here, I couldn't stop looking. Hoping.

I hadn't wanted to have this conversation. It was the coward's way out to not even tell him that I was engaged.

But I didn't want him to know. I didn't know if I could survive hearing his fury. Or worse ... him convincing me otherwise.

I wasn't naive enough not to know that what worked so well between me and Ash this time around was my avoidance of the elephant in the room. It was better if Cole was out of sight, out of mind. So much easier if I didn't have to love him so acutely.

As I stepped out into the Tennessee summer heat, I inhaled sharply. Feeling like I could breathe for the first time. I didn't have to have this conversation. I didn't have to have the impending showdown. The anxiety had been a weight on my shoulders, and it had been lifted.

"Congratulations!" I said, hugging Kristen when it was my turn.

She pulled me close. "I love you. I'm so glad you're here."

"Me too."

"I wish Cole had made it."

I swallowed. "Me too."

"He texted me right before we got lined up and said he couldn't make it in. He was in Knoxville and thought he'd be done by now. I meant to tell you ..."

"It's okay. It's your wedding day. Don't even consider it! I'm just so happy for you."

"Thank you. It was even better than I ever could have imagined."

Kristen was whisked away by her groom and enormous family. I let her be. She hadn't even needed to tell me about Cole, but that was Kristen. Ever the matchmaker. She was still bummed that it hadn't ended up working out after she'd tried to get us back together in the first place.

I wandered back into the bridal suite while they took family pictures. I had a feeling that would take at least an hour, and I wanted a drink as I waited. I poured myself a glass of champagne, reaching for my phone.

I had the drink halfway to my lips when I saw that Kristen wasn't the only one who had gotten a text from Cole.

Sorry I couldn't make it today. I was looking forward to seeing you, sunflower. I'll be back in Atlanta next month. Can we get a drink?

My stomach tightened. Next month.

Next month, I was getting married.

I couldn't see him.

I wanted to see him.

But I knew that I couldn't.

I didn't plan on repeating my worst mistake. As much as I wanted to see him, I didn't trust myself around him. It wouldn't be fair to Ash.

So, I shut off my phone without answering, downed my glass of champagne, and went back out to the party.

KRISTEN AND HONG MIN made their grand exit, a horse-drawn carriage and all. Then I got into the first ride back to the hotel and was ready to crash. Even though a few of the guys kept insisting that I come with them to the hotel bar. I was definitely too drunk for that. I'd already scandalized some elderly family members with my dance moves, and I had an early flight. Probably best to just crash.

"No, no, I'm good," I told Michael. "Go have fun. I'm too drunk."

"Ah, you're no fun, Greer," he teased.

"I'm so lame, I swear." I giggled and backed into the elevator. "Have fun."

As the doors shut between us, I waved and then slumped back against the wall, relieved. Maybe I should have insisted that Ash come with me. Weddings were not as much fun, alone.

I stumbled into my hotel room, kicking off my heels on the way. My feet ached. I wanted to lie on my bed with my feet against the headboard to get circulation back into them, like I used to do with Channing in college, but the room was spinning, and lying down was starting to sound like a bad idea. I grabbed a bottle of water out of the fridge and guzzled the entire thing, swallowing it down with some Tylenol.

I collapsed back on the bed just as my phone rang. Those assholes were probably trying to convince me to come back down to the bar. If I felt this bad right now, I couldn't imagine how I'd feel if I went back out.

"Hello?" I said, answering the phone.

"Lila."

"Cole," I gasped as if I had been thrown into ice-cold water.

"Hey. You sound drunk."

"I am drunk."

"Good party?"

"Yes."

"I decided to say *fuck it* and drive into Nashville."

My jaw hung open, but I said nothing.

He continued in earnest, "Thought I could surprise everyone. I texted Kristen, and she and Hong Min are going to come down to party some more."

"Oh."

"I just pulled into the hotel."

My mouth went dry. "Oh."

"Say something, Lila."

"I'm already in bed."

"That's not a problem," he said softly.

"I have an early flight."

He sighed. "It's one drink."

I laughed softly. "I've heard that before."

"I want to talk to you. I've had an interesting year. Let me tell you all about it."

Oh, *he'd* had an interesting year, huh?

One drink. One drink to tell me all about his interesting year. How I wished it were that easy. But it never had been, had it? I'd known what could happen when I had that one drink with him in New Orleans all those years ago. I hadn't been able to pull away from him, and I'd ended up hurting everyone. That was my mistake. I couldn't regret where it had led us. I couldn't regret any time spent with Cole. But I didn't want to do it again.

And there were only two options for what would happen if I went downstairs:

1. We'd fight like cats and dogs. Scream at each

other. Hate each other for the ring on my finger.

2. Or we'd fuck.

That was it.

Neither option was preferable. The fighting would be terrible. I already knew what he'd say about me marrying Ash. I didn't have to hear him say it. I didn't have to second-guess my heart. I already knew how I felt about Ash. I already knew how I felt about Cole. I was in love with them. Both of them. If I saw Cole, he'd know. He'd know exactly how I felt.

But I'd made a choice.

I'd made a commitment.

Ash had gotten down on one knee and proposed. I'd agreed.

That was all there was to it.

So, if we went with option two, I'd ruin everything. Again.

"I can't," I finally said.

"Lila ..."

"I have to go actually."

"Wait ..."

But I didn't wait. I hung up and threw my phone across the bed. I watched it light up again and again. Cole calling. Trying to get me to talk to him. But I couldn't. I just ... couldn't.

I curled into a ball on my side and stared at the phone until it stopped lighting up. Then I cried.

I'd chosen.

But it didn't make it any easier.

40

REHEARSAL

JUNE 14, 2019

"Okay, you'll kiss," Courtney said. "Do you need to practice that?"

The wedding party laughed at the wedding planner's question. Ash and I joined in. He stepped forward and pressed a chaste kiss to my lips. His eyes saying he wouldn't be so gentle tomorrow. I smirked up at him.

"Excellent. Then Lila and Ash will walk back down the aisle to the music change. Each bridesmaid will partner up with a groomsman. Josie with Tanner. Marley with Derek. Once they pass you, the front row will follow them out. Mr. and Mrs. Talmadge will go first. Then, Ms. Greer will lead the rest of your family out. Any questions?"

This felt like the easiest part of everything. The whole ceremony wasn't going to be that long. Thankfully, I'd gotten it so that we didn't have to do a full mass. It was bad enough that I was getting married in this cathedral. Ash's mom, Cynthia, had insisted on it. And my conversion. Which had been a whole ordeal. We hadn't been sure I'd get it all done in six months so that we could get married in a Catholic ceremony. But we were here.

I was thankful that we'd hired Courtney so that she could deal with Cynthia through much of this. She did an excellent job at running interference.

"Great. Let's run that part. Ash and Lila, if you please."

I took back my fake bouquet that the girls had made at my bridal shower, looped arms with Ash, and walked down the aisle. It was surreal that, tomorrow, we'd be doing this for real. After more than twelve years, this was forever after.

"Delilah, dear," Cynthia said, reaching for me before we even stopped.

As much as I was ready for this, I was not ready for her to be my mother-in-law. She was more like a monster-in-law. She'd *never* liked me, and the fact that her son was in love with me and marrying me didn't seem to have changed her opinion. I hadn't done anything right since we'd started the process, and I doubted I ever would in her eyes.

"There's still some time for mass," she insisted. "Delilah is Catholic now. We could have a full mass."

I cringed. The last thing I wanted was a full mass at my wedding. I was technically Catholic, but that was too much of an affair for me. We'd been fighting about it for months.

"Mrs. Talmadge," Josie said with a wide Hollywood smile.

"Yes, Josephine?"

Despite Josie's mother's reputation, Cynthia was

smitten with Josie. She probably wished that Josie were standing in my place. Fat chance.

"Could I get your help with the florist? They were saying something about carnations for the rehearsal dinner."

"Carnations?" she gasped. "I didn't order carnations."

Josie winked at me and followed Cynthia out of the church.

"Sorry about her," Ash said with a sigh. "She's a handful."

That was putting it mildly. "It doesn't matter."

"I know she's been a stressor." He pressed another kiss into my hair. "I'm just ready for tomorrow."

"Me too."

"I know that we said no wedding gifts."

"You didn't!"

He grinned. "I couldn't help myself."

Courtney ushered everyone else out of the church and directed them to the rehearsal dinner. She smiled at us and gave us the minute alone that we both desperately needed.

Ash gestured for us to take a seat in a pew and then produced a box from the pew behind us. I hadn't even noticed that he'd brought it in or hidden it for this moment. Sneaky.

"I can't believe you did this."

"Can't you though?"

"Thank you," I said, touching the white-and-gold wrapped box.

I tugged on the shiny gold bow, letting the ribbon fall to my feet. I tore into the wedding wrapping paper and revealed a red rectangular box underneath it. I popped the top off and sifted through the mound of white tissue paper before I found what was tucked away.

My throat caught as I touched the leather binding of what I knew was a copy of *Little Women* before I pulled it out.

When I did, I nearly dropped it.

It wasn't just any copy of the book. It was the special-edition hardcover that Cole had given me. It had the same bright red leather binding. The same gold-embossed title. The gold-sprayed edges that were so soft and light that they were nearly biblical.

When I'd moved in with Ash, I hadn't been able to get rid of my copy. It was too perfect. I couldn't hurt books. I couldn't completely eliminate Cole either. So, I'd hidden it. Left it in a box that I'd never open and stuffed it in the closet, where things went to die.

For a fraction of a second, I thought he'd found the copy with the inscription in Cole's handwriting. That I'd been with Cole on the day in the note. But then I pulled the front page open, and Cole's inscription was missing. It said the same thing all the old copies of *Little Women* said.

Always your Laurie.
   —Ash

I released a held breath. Hoped that he hadn't noticed my terror or just interpreted it as something else.

"It's beautiful," I forced out.

"I'd never seen this copy before. I was scouring local

bookstores for something different for you. When I found this, I knew it was the one."

It was the one.

"I love it."

He kissed me and then stood to help me out of the pew. "Shall we go to our rehearsal dinner?"

I nodded and followed him out of the church. Josie and Marley were waiting for us. I widened my eyes when I saw them. They'd been my friends long enough to know an SOS when they saw one.

"Hey, Ash," Mars said. "Mind if we steal Lila for a minute?"

"Yeah, we'll be real quick. Girl business." Josie waggled her eyebrows.

"Sure," he said, kissing my cheek. "But bring her back in one piece."

"We'll try our best," Josie said.

We all watched as my groom disappeared down the street. Practically a skip in his step on the way to our rehearsal dinner. Meanwhile, I was standing in front of the church, trying not to have a panic attack.

"What happened?" Josie demanded as soon as he was out of earshot.

I threw the book into her hands. "That happened."

Marley raised her eyebrows. "Doesn't Ash always give you copies of *Little Women*?"

"Yes," I said. I shook my hands out and tried to keep my panic under control.

"*Always your Laurie,*" Josie read aloud. "Are you Jo or Amy? Doesn't he propose to one sister and marry the other? Isn't that fucked up?"

"Focus, Josie," Marley snapped.

"Cole gave me that book. That *exact* book. The same binding and gold letters and gold pages. He knew I loved the book but didn't know about my connection to it with Ash. So, Cole got me a special-edition copy." I pointed at it. "That copy."

"Shit," Josie muttered.

"Did Ash know?"

"No. I ... I hid it when we moved in together. It's in a box. But ... fuck." I walked away from them and paced back. "Is this a sign? It's the day before my wedding, and the universe is pointing at Cole."

"The universe isn't doing anything," Marley said calmly. "It's a coincidence."

"A big fucking coincidence."

"Do you still love Cole?" Josie asked.

Marley shot her an angry look.

I closed my eyes and clenched my fists. "Don't ask me that."

"This is just nerves," Marley insisted. "Tell her, Josie. Weren't you nervous before your weddings?"

Josie arched an eyebrow. "I'm not nervous before anything."

Marley huffed. "It's cold feet," Marley said. "It's normal."

"Unless it isn't," Josie said softly.

"Jesus, could you be helpful? She's having a panic attack."

"I am being helpful. I'm being realistic. You've loved both of these boys for years. It's not unusual that you might be having second thoughts right before the wedding. Especially with this," she said, holding up the book, "in your face. That doesn't mean you should act on them. It just means you should think about them. You can think about them with us. We won't judge you."

"I do still love Cole," I said softly, the words tumbling out. "I haven't seen him since I got engaged. I didn't want him to freak out."

"He would have," Marley said.

"I know."

"And now, you're marrying his mortal enemy tomorrow. How does that make you feel?"

I shrugged. "Ash isn't *my* enemy. I love him too. I want to marry him."

"Then that's your answer," Josie said, handing me back the book.

Was it that simple?

"I agree," Marley said. "It's been a rough path, but you're here. You're freaking yourself out because you still have feelings for Cole, and there's no closure. You don't need that closure to move on."

I nodded, hoping they were right. But I could already feel my stomach subsiding, my panic disappearing. I felt more like me again. I'd had a meltdown for no reason. It wasn't like Cole was going to show up tomorrow or anything. He didn't even know about the wedding.

"Okay. Let's go to the dinner."

"I do have to tell you," Josie said as the three of us linked arms, "your future mother-in-law is a total bitch."

We all laughed. At least we could agree on that.

41

WEDDING DAY

JUNE 15, 2019

E very girl dreamed about her perfect wedding.

But I hadn't dreamed of white dresses or bouquets or *I do*s. And when it came right down to it, I'd never imagined my future husband. What he'd look like or what he'd wear or how he'd smile when he saw me that first time.

Because for so long, there hadn't been just one face in my life ... but two.

Two faces. Two outfits. Two smiles.

Two men.

Cole and Ash.

Ash and Cole.

It felt surreal that today of all days, I was going to marry one and not the other. But it was here, and there was no looking back. I'd made my decision. In the end, we'd all made this decision. With our actions and our broken promises. We'd walked right up to today and let it happen.

I wasn't the typical blushing bride. There would

always be a part of me wondering if I'd done the right thing, chosen the right guy. If all the hell that we'd gone through together to get here had been worth it.

But I didn't have cold feet. I was ready for this.

Except now, my bridesmaids were missing.

I stuck my head out of the bridal suite. My three sisters sat at a table in varying shades of red. Two in floor-length gowns and one in a red suit jacket. They were all matrons of honor for this affair, but they wouldn't be standing at the altar with me. They'd be seated in the first row.

"Have you seen Josie and Marley?" I asked my sisters about my two best friends.

We'd known each other nearly our entire lives. Been through thick and thin. It wasn't like them to disappear on my big day.

"They said they had an errand," Eve said as she poured champagne into flutes.

Elle nodded. "They'll be right back."

Steph jumped from her spot and made me twirl in a circle. "You look gorgeous. I wasn't sure on the bust, but that dress is stunning."

I beamed at my sisters.

We'd all gone dress shopping multiple times. I'd thought I'd be one of those lucky ones who picked out the very first dress I tried on. But it hadn't been the case; it might as well have been the last dress I tried on. The thousandth dress I tried on. The dress was a full tulle skirt with a lacy balconette top and thin spaghetti straps.

Josie had told me it was likely bad luck that I was that

indecisive. Marley had rolled her eyes and insisted it meant nothing. Two sides of the same coin, those two.

I drank champagne with my sisters and stared down at the massive ring on my finger as I waited for my best friends to return.

"Don't drink too much," Eve warned. "You'll want to remember tonight."

Elle burst into laughter, and Steph joined her.

"Oh, I'll remember tonight," I assured them.

I couldn't imagine forgetting my wedding night even if I had one too many glasses of champagne. I checked my phone again. Seriously, where the hell were they?

"Maybe we should go look for them."

"You can't," Elle said. "You don't want Ash to see you before it's time."

Tradition.

It was pretty ridiculous, considering how long we'd been sleeping together. But it was ceremonial, and we'd agreed. It would make tonight even more special.

I was just about to send out a search party when Marley and Josie rushed back into the room, looking frazzled.

"Everything all right?"

Marley and Josie exchanged a look.

"What is it?"

"Nothing," they said together.

Josie continued, "Don't worry about it."

"Is it nothing, or should I not worry about it?"

"Both," Marley said.

I narrowed my eyes. That certainly didn't sound like nothing.

"It's this." Josie came to my side and pulled out a black case. "I know that I've always had my differences with my mom, but she'd want you to wear these today."

My hand went to my throat as I opened the black case to reveal the white pearls that I'd always coveted. "Josie! I can't wear these."

"Something borrowed," she insisted. "You've always wanted them."

"I have," I said softly.

Josie took them out of the box and strung them around my neck. They were dainty and just brushed my collarbone. They looked perfect with the white lace of my dress and my blonde hair pulled up in an intricate updo.

"Thank you," I told her, drawing her in for a hug.

"Okay, ladies, it's time!" the wedding planner, Courtney, said as she strode into the room.

She was the best of the best. She handled everything for the day of. I didn't know how I would have survived the last six months without her expertise.

Everyone moved into place. The string quartet began to play. My sisters went in first. Marley and Josie both pulled me in for a quick hug before stepping out into the chapel and proceeding down the aisle. I was last.

I touched the pearls Josie had given me for luck. Then I took a deep breath and walked into the chapel, alone.

The crowd had risen to their feet. But I only had eyes for one person in that room—my groom.

James Asheford Talmadge IV.

My stomach flipped at the sight of him in a tuxedo at the other end of the aisle. His perfectly tied bow tie at his neck. His smile was magnetic, and I couldn't help but return it. My mother wiped her eyes as I passed her in the front row with my sisters. Her last baby, finally getting hitched.

And then I was there. I took the final two steps up to the altar, passed my bouquet to Marley, and faced my groom.

"I've waited for this day our entire lives," Ash whispered.

"Me too."

A hush fell over the church as the service began. I heard little of it. The minutes passed in a blur. All I saw was the bright blue eyes looking back at me and the smile that said I was his world.

There was a pause in the ceremony. Just a moment. Barely a breath.

And everything collapsed.

The doors at the back of the church burst open. Everyone turned to as Cole Davis stepped into the sanctuary. The wedding planner trailed him. Whatever she was saying was lost in the drone of voices.

But I knew exactly why he was here.

I'd been a fool to think that he would let me go.

"I object!" Cole yelled into the church. "Lila, you can't marry him!"

And there I stood, on a precipice, ready to fall back onto that wheel that had always dragged us together. I couldn't have both.

So today, I had to choose: Ash or Cole.

SILENCE LINGERED in the space after Cole's objection.

I stood on the altar, paralyzed. There was buzzing in my ears, a sick feeling in my stomach, and suddenly, it felt as if everything were moving in slow motion.

Ash took a step forward. His mother's hand moved to her mouth in horror. His dad came to his feet. Courtney stepped in to intercede and stop Cole somehow.

But how exactly could she have possibly stopped Cole from getting inside? He was still as big as he'd ever been. Still the tall, built football player he'd been in college. There was no way anyone could stop him if he was determined.

One look into his blue eyes showed just how determined he was.

I should have known then what to do. The choice should have been easy, but it never had been. That was how we'd gotten here to begin with. The last time I'd been confronted with this choice, I'd decided on both and then walked away without either of them. I couldn't do that today.

Everyone stared at me.

Waiting for me to decide.

To tell Cole to leave and finish the ceremony.

"This isn't what you want," Cole insisted.

"Lila," Ash hissed.

He dragged my attention away from Cole. Away from the pleading look on his face for me not to make the mistake of a lifetime.

It was too much.

All of it too much.

Sensory overload.

In the space of a few seconds, I went from certain I was making the right choice to feeling like I couldn't breathe. My dress was too tight. Everything was too close. I couldn't get air in my lungs. I was panicking much worse than yesterday at the dress rehearsal.

It was then that I realized how much I'd been truly lying to myself. About everything. I'd said I was happy. I'd said that I was ready. Meanwhile, I'd been panicking at every turn that I was making the wrong decision. Freaking out for weeks on end that I'd run into Cole and have to explain myself.

Yet there was no explanation. No reason good enough for why I hadn't told him, except fear. The same fear I felt at this very moment with him standing in front of me. Ash beside me. My world in chaos.

I would have gone through with the wedding.

Stood at Ash's side.

Lived this life.

I could have done it.

And now, I couldn't see beyond this minute.

With a strangled gasp, I took a step back away from them both. I couldn't stand there with four hundred people staring at me. Three hundred and fifty more people than I'd wanted at this wedding. In a church I hadn't wanted to have the ceremony. With a priest I hadn't wanted. And all the compromises I'd made to satisfy the new family I was making, who had never even liked me anyway.

I wanted to say something, to apologize, but nothing came out.

And then I turned on my heel and fled.

42

WEDDING DAY
JUNE 15, 2019

The first step outside was like a cool dip on a hot summer day. I gasped in all the air that my lungs could hold. All the air that I couldn't breathe inside that stifling church.

I couldn't believe I'd done that.

After all that bullshit about making a choice, I'd still run from them. I had to decide. I *had* to. I'd thought I already *had*.

"Fuck," I yelled on the hallowed grounds. I couldn't bring myself to care.

I was just so angry.

So angry that I was even standing here.

What would people say about me fleeing my own wedding? Only minutes from saying our *I do*s. I knew exactly what Ash's parents would say. They'd criticize me, as they always had. They'd only put up with me because of Ash. And now?

Could I even blame them for thinking of me as some covetous bitch who had ruined their lives? The city of

Savannah would talk about this moment for years to come. I knew how they'd vilified Josie's mom. I'd seen the condemnation of other women. I would be just like them. And maybe I'd earned it.

My indecision had thrown us into this mess in the first place. If I could have put Cole behind me like I'd claimed I had. If I could have kept lying to myself that he didn't matter. That it would get easier with time. When I *knew* it had never gotten easier with time.

Ash was my first love.

But Cole was the one who had put me back together after Ash shattered my heart into a million little pieces.

It was impossible to separate them in my head anymore. We'd all hurt each other. Broken promises. Let loose our fury.

It was why I'd walked away in the first place.

Then I'd spent a year alone, thinking that it had taught me exactly what I wanted. That what Ash had said that day on Christmas Eve was true. That we'd always end back up right where we'd started.

But was that the truth?

Where we'd started was him lying to me about why he'd asked me out and then crushing me completely.

So, maybe we were there, but the places had been reversed. Because I'd definitely lied when I said I was ready and taking that first step out of that church had surely destroyed him.

"Lila!"

I squeezed my eyes shut. That wasn't the voice I'd expected to hear first out of that church.

"Lila," Cole repeated as he stopped behind me.

"Before you get mad, please listen to me."

"Before I get mad?" I demanded, whirling around to face him. "*Before* I get mad? You think I'm not already mad?"

"Yes, I know. I didn't want to do it this way."

I laughed humorlessly. "Doesn't change how it happened."

"It doesn't. But you can't marry him, Lila." He ran a hand back through his hair, which was just a little longer than he normally kept it. It curled at the edges, like it used to do in college under his baseball caps. My heart twinged at the memory. "You'll be miserable."

"Like I am right now?"

"You're not miserable. You're confused."

I stomped away, but he followed me.

"You're confused because you've never had to make this decision. You've never had to choose between us. You settled on the first person who threw himself at you. And that person was always Ash. It always was. He was lurking in the corners, like a spider waiting to drop down from his web to snatch you up."

"You don't know what you're talking about." I whipped around. "You weren't there. You weren't there to know any of this."

"And isn't that strange, considering I said that I would wait for you?" he said calmly. "I said that I'd wait, and I did. I waited, Lila. Because it was always you and me in the endgame. Always."

"You didn't wait," I insisted. "You were gone. You took a job to escape me!"

"You asked for space and time. I gave you space and

time. You can't exactly vilify me for doing exactly what you asked me to do."

I closed my eyes . They were exactly what I'd asked for. He'd done it. He'd given me the space to be alone. Ash had been the one to decide when I'd had enough time. When it was time for my isolation to be over.

Cole pushed forward, as if seeing that he was getting through to me. "Then, you went and got engaged while I was away."

"How did you even find out?"

"Josie called me yesterday."

"Oh God," I whispered, realizing exactly where my bridesmaids had been before the wedding. "Did she know you were going to object?"

"No. I tried to get back to see you before it started, but there was no time." He sighed. "But that's not the point. The point is that you went and got engaged and didn't even tell me!"

"That wasn't planned."

"If I'd known all I had to do was propose to get you to change your mind, I wouldn't have waited."

"What?" I squeaked.

"I'd planned to propose on New Year's." He withdrew a box out of his jacket pocket for emphasis. My jaw dropped at the sight of the ring in his hand. "I talked to your mom and everything on Christmas. She gave me her blessing. Then ... church."

My heart constricted, and I took a step back. "You never said anything."

"When would I have?" he demanded. He stuffed the box back away into his pocket. "You wouldn't see me! You sent me away, had your mom give me my suitcase back, and didn't talk to me for weeks. At that point, it would have been desperate to show you a ring you clearly didn't want. So, yeah, I left. I took the job I'd always wanted that put me on the road forty-plus weeks out of the year. Because I couldn't be in Atlanta without you or at work when I couldn't see you, and knowing I'd been a week away from making you my fiancée, only to royally fuck it all up, made me want to die."

I stilled. I hadn't known. My mom had never even hinted at it. But of course, he was right. I hadn't let him talk to me. I didn't want anything to do with either of them for a year. Not until I endured a year of the worst dates of my life. And by then, Cole had been gone.

"I didn't know," I whispered.

"It's not your fault. It's mine. Everything that happened here at this goddamn church was my fault. Ash might have instigated, but you told me to let it go, and I didn't. I leaned into it. But I'm not that guy anymore."

"What does that even mean?"

"I didn't just spend the year on the road, Lila. I spent the year trying to deal with all of my anger issues. I went to therapy and anger management. I figured out what the source of the issues were. It's not *gone* or anything, but I have much more control over it. I don't ever want to be the reason that you cry again. I want to be the man you always thought I was."

I was stunned into silence.

Cole had been at therapy? All this time, I'd thought he was avoiding me, trying to escape my ghost. But I'd been so wrong.

"This was what I wanted to talk to you about in Nashville. I tried to reach you."

"I couldn't," I said. "I couldn't talk to you."

"Because of him?"

I looked up at him, meeting those blue eyes. My heart on the line. "I'd made my choice."

Cole shook his head. "If it was a choice, then it implies there were two options, but I was gone. That's not making a choice. That's settling."

The words were like a bucket of water thrown over my head.

It wasn't a choice. I still hadn't made the choice between the two of them. I'd followed along down the easiest path available and never come up for air to question whether it was the right one. I hadn't wanted to consider it. But all of my panics and fears and worries made sense now. They all fit together like a puzzle I hadn't known was missing a few pieces before starting.

"That's a great theory," Ash said dryly.

I jumped at the sound of his voice.

I'd forgotten to anticipate him, forgotten that we were standing on the steps of my wedding. That I had a decision to make.

"This isn't about you," Cole snapped.

Ash glared at him. For a moment, it looked like he was going to say something in response. But then he turned away from him.

His gaze found mine. He held his hand out. "Come back inside with me. Let's finish this. This is how it was always supposed to end."

43

WEDDING DAY
JUNE 15, 2019

I stared down at his outstretched hand and saw my future laid out before me. I'd take his hand, leave Cole behind forever, apologize profusely about the interruption, and say *I do*. I'd deal with Ash's parents' fury for the rest of my life and live happily ever after as the girl who almost ran out of her wedding, effectively becoming the source of town gossip forever.

"Lila, please," Ash said, a note of desperation breaking into his voice.

"I just humiliated you and me and everyone else in that building. How can you want me to come back inside? How can you even look at me?"

"Because I love you, and I don't care about any of that other stuff. I don't care what anyone else says. I've loved you since I was seventeen, and I want you to be my wife."

Despair welled in my chest.

He really didn't care.

And he never had.

Not about how his parents felt about me or anyone

else's reactions to our relationship. He just wanted us to be together.

Even when it was entirely illogical, as it was in this moment, as it had been after Cole and I slept together in New Orleans. I'd never understood how he could compartmentalize his feelings.

"This is the wedding you've always wanted," Ash continued.

Cole snorted. "*That* wedding? With hundreds of people in a giant church? You think that's what she wants? Have you *met* her? Did you even ask her?"

I paled at the question.

How did Cole know me so well?

It wasn't the one that I'd hoped for. It was absolutely the wedding that Ash's mother had foisted on me. But I'd been happy to concede the points to marry Ash. I hadn't thought it sounded so terrible until it came out of Cole's mouth.

"Of course it is. She planned it," Ash snapped. "You wouldn't know anything about that because you've been miraculously gone since we started dating. Maybe go back to the hole you crawled out of and leave us alone."

"You still haven't asked her." Cole crossed his arms. "Lila, is that the wedding you want?"

I opened my mouth and closed it. Looked between them like a rabbit in a trap. There wasn't a right answer to that question. It wasn't that simple.

Ash shook his head. "It doesn't matter."

I jerked back at that comment. "What doesn't matter?"

"Anything that comes out of his mouth," Ash said,

gesturing to Cole. "He's here to break us up. Just like he always has. We decided long ago to keep him out of our lives." Ash looked at Cole. "That's why you're here, right? To fuck with her head? Make her think that she made the wrong choice? But we both know that she didn't. It's me. It's always been me. You were just in the way."

"If you want to tell yourself that," Cole said with a shrug. "You still haven't asked her."

"I'm not playing your games," Ash said. He held his hand out again. "Lila, let's go."

"I'm not playing games," Cole said. "Actually, I'm finally done playing your games. You'll say whatever you need to say to get her to walk back inside with you. And I already know one thing that you don't."

"What's that?" Ash snapped.

"She doesn't want to."

"Cole," I whispered softly.

"Tell him, Lila. Tell him the truth. It's clear you put up with all this shit to appease his parents."

"Please don't," I said.

And he did something I'd never seen him do before. He nodded and backed off. Just like that.

As if Ash weren't even standing there.

Like he'd really spent the last year working on himself and putting all of this aside. Of course, he'd probably never get over his anger about Ash, but that didn't mean he had to act on it. And he'd shown that he could control it when he needed to.

"I'm not here for him. I'm here for you. Just you, Lila." Cole turned his back on Ash completely. "You didn't tell me about all of this for a reason. You knew that I could change your mind."

Ash coughed. "Charming. The reason she didn't tell you is because, like adults, we discussed what to do about you. And we agreed *not* talking to you was for the better."

We had discussed it. I hadn't wanted to make the same mistakes. It didn't change the fact that avoiding Cole all this time had been monumentally difficult. And now, it was coming back to bite us all in the ass.

Cole didn't even hear him. "If I'm wrong, then take his hand, walk into that church. I'll never bother you again. If you don't love me, then I've already lost."

I stared into Cole's blue eyes. I heard the sincerity in his voice. The truth of what he'd said. That he'd worked on himself to be better for me. So that we could end up together. I'd never even imagined that he would actually do it. That he cared that much. When we'd last been together, he'd clung to his anger so strongly.

Now, we were back here on the church grounds with the last decision. The very last decision.

"Lila," Ash said, drawing my gaze back to him.

To the man who, minutes ago, I'd been willing to spend my life with.

The two men in my life ...

I'd always known that I couldn't have both. Even when I'd suggested it, I'd known it wasn't possible. Now, I had to choose one.

"If you don't want to walk back in the church, then let's go to the courthouse. I don't care how it happens," Ash said.

"Your parents do."

"What my parents think doesn't matter," Ash snapped. "I don't care about their opinion. It doesn't matter to me."

I blinked at those words. It was an interesting thing to say because it was such a lie.

"Then why was I forced to go along with everything they wanted for this wedding?"

Ash clenched his jaw. "You planned the wedding, Lila."

"I did within parameters. Do you not even see how much you capitulate to them?"

"I work for my dad," he said with a shrug. "I can't completely ignore their wishes."

I sighed. "Yeah, because if they had it their way, we wouldn't even be here right now."

"Don't you understand?" he said earnestly. "I don't care. If they bother you that much, then we'll do it all over without them. It doesn't matter. Only we do."

"I believe that you think that," I whispered.

I wanted so desperately to be as blind as I'd been to all of this pain. But my eyes were open. They were wide open.

Cole had known within moments of stepping into that wedding that this was all a disaster. That it couldn't possibly be what I wanted. And how come Ash hadn't seen me floundering through it? How hadn't I admitted it to myself?

More than twelve years ago, Ash had hidden me from his parents because he knew how they'd react. And that part of our relationship had never improved since then.

Why had I thought that it would all get better? That our married life would be better?

Now, we were here, arguing a moot point.

This wasn't possible.

There was no coming back from what I'd done.

There was no coming back from running out of my own wedding.

"Lila," he said, reaching for me.

I stepped back, and he stilled completely.

I squeezed my eyes shut for a second and then looked back at him. "I can't go back inside with you."

"Then let's go somewhere else."

"I can't," I said, my voice breaking. "I can't marry you."

Ash's arm fell to his side. His face was stricken. "You ... can't marry me?"

"I'm sorry, Ash. I'm so sorry." My hands covered my mouth. I breathed deeply. "I can't do it."

"Because of *him*?" he demanded, throwing his hand toward Cole. "Because of the bullshit he's throwing at you?"

"No. It's not Cole."

"Fuck," Ash said. "*Fuck.*"

"It's just ... he's not wrong."

"Are you kidding me?"

I bit my lip. "This isn't the wedding I wanted. It's the wedding your mother wanted. And I know I'm responsible because I didn't stand up for myself. But ... but you didn't stand up for me either." Ash's eyes widened at my words. "And you never have."

"I've *always* stood up for you against them."

"Then why are we here right now?" I asked as tears

came to my eyes. "I wanted fifty people in Forsyth Park. Somehow, I got *this*. And you didn't even *care*."

"Then let's do it over!"

I shook my head.

His Adam's apple bobbed. "So, you choose him?"

My gaze shifted to Cole. Steady and earnest and solid. He was right. He was right about all of it. I hadn't told him for so many reasons. Not to spare his feelings, as I'd tried to lie to myself. But because I had known that he'd change my mind. I had known that we'd been walking toward this path together before it crumbled on these church steps. And that I loved him too much to tell him. I still loved him too damn much.

"Yes," I whispered.

Cole broke into a smile at the same second Ash broke.

Ash kicked a loose rock, swore, and then stalked away from the pair of us.

"Ash, wait," I said, taking a step toward him.

But he didn't wait. He didn't slow down. He looked ready to put a fist through a wall. Not that I blamed him. Not after what just happened.

"Let him go," Cole said. "Let him walk it off."

"He's never going to forgive me. No one is ever going to forgive me."

"Do you need forgiveness?"

"I just ..." I sighed heavily and watched as Ash disappeared from view. "I wasn't lying to him when I agreed to marry him. I did want to do it. And then it all spiraled so far out of control. It wasn't what I'd agreed to by the end."

"That's all that matters, Lila," he said. "You don't have to justify yourself to anyone else. You did the right thing."

"You would say that."

"I would. But that doesn't mean I'm wrong. I was right about everything else, wasn't I? You do still love me." He took a step toward me.

I nodded with a sigh. "So much, Cole."

His smile reminded me of the first day I'd ever met him. When everything was shiny and new and he knew even then that he wanted me above anyone else.

"And you didn't talk to me because you still wanted to be with me." He took another step, bridging the gap.

"My feelings have never changed. In all the time and distance, they've remained steadfast."

"Same, Sunflower," he said, brushing back a loose curl. "Same."

"What do we do now?"

"Whatever you want."

"All of my stuff is still in the church. I can't go back in and get it."

"Leave it. Marley and Josie will handle it." He slowly slid his hand into mine. "Why don't we just go for a walk? Maybe grab milkshakes."

"Milkshakes?" I asked in disbelief. "In my wedding dress?"

He shrugged. "Why not? It's how we started."

"It is, isn't it?"

He squeezed my hand. "I love you, Delilah Greer. I love you with all of my heart."

I leaned forward against him, feeling his arms come tight around me. "I love you too."

He looked down at me. "And I'm not saying you have

to marry me right away." I laughed. "I'll give you a whole week."

"What if I never marry you?" I teased.

He tilted my chin up. "Then we'll just be blissfully happy for the rest of our lives."

"Is that a promise?"

"Yes."

His head dipped down, and he captured my lips with his. A promise sealed with a kiss.

Cole took my hand again, and we walked away from the church. Away from the biggest decision of my life. I was certain I'd made the right choice this time.

Though I'd have to deal with the aftermath, the moving out and moving on, I'd leave it all for another day.

Right now, I was here with Cole.

Where I was always meant to be.

And I wouldn't trade it for the world.

THE END

ACKNOWLEDGMENTS

This was a whirlwind journey of a book. It all started with a conversation with the inimitable Rebecca Shea posting on Facebook asking what was the craziest thing that happened at your wedding. I told her that after my wedding, I found out from my maid of honor that my ex had texted her that he was coming to object. She'd informed the wedding planner and security, given them his likeness with instructions to bar him from entering. Rebecca immediately messaged me and said I needed to write that book. So, I did. Sort of! It was the spark that lit the fuse inside of me to tell Lila, Cole, and Ash's story.

I also want to thank my alpha readers who suffered chapter by chapter while I was writing: Rebecca Kimmerling, Rebecca Gibson, and Anjee Sapp. And my beta readers who all cussed me out at the same part in the story: Lori Francis, Polly Matthews, Danielle Sanchez, Devin McCain, and Amy Vox Libris. Thanks Diana Peterfreund for listening to and encouraging my crazy ideas and helping me fix the early aughts high school romcom section.

Staci Hart for being the light in my perfectionist, enneagram 1 darkness. AND for designing the incredible cover for this book. I know it's always so fun spending hours on stock sites trying to find the perfect shot. Jovana Shirley for her incredible editing skills. Georgette Geras for proofing and sending me crying pictures while you read. Erin Mallon for fitting me into your busy schedule and narrating Lila's angsty journey. Danielle Sanchez for PR and marketing skills and also just loving this idea from the get go and helping me readjust my entire schedule to write it! Also, Devin my wonderful assistant who helps keep me sane and did the beautiful formatting and graphics for this book.

Also all of my author friends who helped me through this book and are the best support network: Nana Malone, Carrie Ann Ryan, Laurelin Paige, Monica Robinson, Kandi Steiner, Mia Asher, Corinne Michaels, Sierra Simone, Kayti McGee,

And as always, my husband Joel, who plots everything with and was #teamcole from the beginning.

ABOUT THE AUTHOR

K.A. Linde is the *USA Today* bestselling author of the more than thirty novels. She has a Masters degree in political science from the University of Georgia, was the head campaign worker for the 2012 presidential campaign at the University of North Carolina at Chapel Hill, and served as the head coach of the Duke University dance team.

She loves reading fantasy novels, binge-watching Supernatural, traveling to far off destinations, baking insane desserts, and dancing in her spare time. She currently lives in Lubbock, Texas, with her husband and two super-adorable puppies.

Visit her online: www.kalinde.com

Or Facebook, Instagram, Twitter, & Tiktok:
@authorkalinde

For exclusive content, free books, and giveaways every month. www.kalinde.com/subscribe

Lightning Source UK Ltd.
Milton Keynes UK
UKHW010717080222
398373UK00003B/242